D1191128

Jacqueline Susann's

Shadow

of the

Dolls

JACQUELINE SUSANN'S
SHADOW
OF THE
DOLLS

A Novel by

RAE LAWRENCE

BOOKSPAN LARGE PRINT EDITION

 CROWN PUBLISHERS, NEW YORK

This Large Print Edition, prepared especially for Bookspan, contains the complete, unabridged text of the original Publisher's Edition.

Published by Crown Publishers, New York, New York. Member of the Crown Publishing Group.

Random House, Inc. New York, Toronto, London, Sydney, Auckland
www.randomhouse.com

CROWN is a trademark and the Crown colophon is a registered trademark of Random House, Inc.

Printed in the United States of America

ISBN 0-7394-1838-6

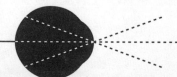

This Large Print Book carries the Seal of Approval of N.A.V.H.

FOR THE SHADOW GANG:
Madeleine R., Angelina P., Ian S.,
Lola B., and Spike R.

Valley of the Dolls was first published in 1966. Before her death in 1974, Jacqueline Susann wrote a treatment for a sequel.

This incomplete first draft was never published. Its pages were contemporary in setting and spirit. It was this material that provided the inspiration for *Shadow of the Dolls.*

The stories of Anne Welles and Neely O'Hara have been re-imagined and updated for a contemporary setting. This choice was made in order to keep the spirit of Susann's work. Fans of *Valley of the Dolls* will notice that liberties have been taken with the ages of Jacqueline Susann's characters and various other details of time and place.

The author is deeply grateful to Lisa Bishop, Jacqueline Susann's literary manager and "keeper of the Jackie Susann flame," for her encouragement and help in bringing Anne and Neely into contemporary times.

JACQUELINE SUSANN'S
SHADOW
OF THE
DOLLS

Prologue, 1987.

Whatever happened to Anne Welles? people used to ask.

It was a parlor game played at parties, after the dishes were cleared and the fresh bottle of vodka came out, after everyone had drunk too much but no one wanted to go home yet. Whatever happened to that sitcom star who got arrested for carrying the gun onto the airplane? Whatever happened to that rock-and-roll singer who married the swimsuit model? Whatever happened to that talk-show host, that child actress, that overweight comedian? And, Whatever happened to Anne Welles?

No one ever had to ask what happened to Neely O'Hara.

Everyone knew. She was still in the tabloids at least once a month.

The pictures were always the same: Neely caught off-guard, looking grim and puffy in her signature oversize dark blue sunglasses, wearing a thousand-dollar designer version of sweatshirt and track pants, her hair tucked up into a baseball cap, her hands covered with jewelry.

The headlines screamed from supermarket checkout stands: Neely O'Hara hires live-in psychic after third marriage fails! Neely and Liz make bizarre rehab pact! Neely O'Hara threatens suicide after record-company lawsuit! Neely O'Hara's Comeback Diet!

But whatever happened to Anne Welles?

Women recalled her Gillian Girl commercials almost word for word. They could recite the names of the products they had bought because of her. Candlelight Beige lipstick. Summersong perfume. Forever Roses nail polish.

What the men remembered was something else: a beautiful girl dancing across the television screen, her long dark hair streaming out behind her. Sometimes she wore an evening gown and swirled to an old Cole Porter tune. Sometimes she wore a little white bikini and kept the beat of a current disco hit. At the end of each commercial, she looked straight into the camera, looked straight into their eyes, and winked.

Where was she now?

She married some rich guy and moved to Europe, someone would say. Or: She went into rehab, my cousin's best friend is married to someone in Hollywood who saw the medical charts. Or: She invested in a chain of restaurants and lost almost all her money. No one really knew. To most of the country, it seemed that she had disappeared into thin air.

In New York, no one had to ask what happened to Anne Welles.

She still made the columns, she still went to parties, she still could be seen jogging around the Central Park Reservoir in the early mornings, her thick brown hair held back with red velvet ribbon. At thirty-four she was still beautiful, though the only photographs that appeared of her anymore were the grainy black-and-white pictures taken at charity events for the Sunday society pages.

She had married Lyon Burke and moved into a ten-room apartment on Fifth Avenue with a glorious view of the park. The Bellamy, Bellows and Burke Agency represented some of the highest-paid movie talent, so there was no need for her to work. Her only daughter, Jennifer, went to the most exclusive girls' school in the city. Anne filled her days the way so many other women did on the Upper East Side: exercising, shopping, getting facials and manicures, redecorating her apartment, entertaining her husband's business friends. Anne and Lyon were one of the most sought-after couples in the city, and every day's mail brought at least half a dozen invitations: to dinner parties, to museum galas, to weekends in the country, to charity events, to gallery and film openings.

Anne Welles Burke had gotten everything she dreamed of. She had married the man of her dreams, the first man she had fallen in love with. She had the child she always wanted, a sweet girl with Lyon's blue eyes and Anne's fine Yankee bone structure. She lived in the apartment she had always fantasized about, surrounded by the best furniture, the best carpets, the best paintings. She had come to New York with nothing, and now the city belonged to her.

New York! New York! In the early spring evenings, after Jenn had gone to her room to do her homework and before Lyon came home from the office, she took a glass of Chardonnay onto the balcony. She looked down into Central Park, full of pink and white blossoms. She looked west across Manhattan, where another spectacular sunset streaked the sky. She looked south at the skyline, still as breathtaking as when she had first arrived fifteen years before. And she said to herself: *Mine, mine, mine.*

Sometimes she poured a second glass of wine. Music wafted in from the open windows of a neighboring apartment, a strand of Joni Mitchell, or early Van Morrison, or an old Dionne Warwick hit she had forgotten the name of.

But she still remembered the words, and she still remembered the girl she had been when she sang them aloud to herself, dancing around her first New York apartment, a tiny studio in a West Fifties tenement building, with broken-down plumbing and linoleum floors. It came back to her now, how happy she had been in those days when she had nothing to speak of except a pretty face and a degree from a pretty college and all her pretty dreams. Everything was ahead of her then. She'd felt as though the whole city were whispering to her at night: *If, if, if.*

The second glass of wine never tasted as good as the first, but she always drank it faster. *Mine:* The perfect apartment filled with perfect things (who knew a throw pillow could cost three hundred dollars?), but no matter what the decorators bought it never felt finished or quite full enough.

Mine: The perfect husband, who had had so many affairs that she had stopped counting, stopped even caring. Lyon loved her as best he could; maybe it wasn't his fault that his love ran out a few yards short of fidelity. *Mine:* A perfect child, Jenn was everything to her, so why did she still feel half-empty inside?

And then she wondered: *Whatever happened to Anne Welles?*

1987.

Neely and her exercise instructor were in the sunroom, torturing each other.

"Kick! Kick! Kick!" cried Samantha. Neely was on all fours, her left leg stretched out behind her. The only thing she hated more than donkey kicks were stomach crunches, and stomach crunches were next.

"It hurts!" cried Neely. "I'm gonna throw out my back!" She rolled over and folded her hands across her chest. "That's it, I can't do any more today."

"We have another half hour to go," Samantha said. "Crunches, then cardio."

"No cardio. I'm beat."

"You won't lose any of that weight if you don't do cardio."

"Cardio, schmardio. Who has time." She grabbed her thighs. "I'm gonna go to Palm Springs and just have them suck it all out. Vvvhhhhzzz," she hummed, imitating a vacuum cleaner. "Vvvhhhzzzz! Vvvhhhzzz! All gone!"

After Samantha left, Neely treated herself to her traditional post-exercise snack: a tall glass of fresh-squeezed orange juice and two hazelnut truffles from Godiva.

She looked at herself in the mirror. Zaftig, but not fat. Maybe fifteen pounds over her ideal weight at most, and what was fifteen pounds? But the weight didn't go to the same places anymore, it all went a little lower. On stage they were able to hide everything, with custom-made undergarments that compressed and lifted and pushed every last extra ounce.

But here in the living room of her Las Vegas hotel suite, with the harsh desert sun streaming through the picture windows, wearing just a cotton tank top and leggings, here it was different. She turned to the side and examined her profile. Fifteen pounds would do it. The first ten she would have to do herself, and the last few pounds—the really hard ones—a little lipo would take care of those. She didn't look nearly so bad as those pictures they loved to print in the tabloids. She swore some of those photographers shot her from the least flattering angles on purpose, to make her look fatter than she really was.

Everyone knew the worse someone looked, the more the photographer got paid. Neely was careful not to eat in public anymore, ever since that one photograph of her sitting on a bench at Disney World holding a double-scoop ice-cream cone in each hand. She had been holding one of the cones for her manager's eight-year-old niece, but the photographer had cropped the child out of the picture.

Neely's manager arrived with the new outfit for her opening number.

"If I told you once, I told you a million times: no sequins on my ass!" Neely shrieked, throwing the costume across the room.

"Just try it on," he whispered. "Just try it, just to humor me. I promise you'll look fabulous in it."

"I'll look fat. Why are you trying to make

me look fat? I hate Las Vegas. I hate every damn person in this town. Gordon, did you see the audience last night? Fat, fat, fat! It's like a convention of fat people out there."

Gordon Stein picked up the dress and laid it gently across the top of the couch. Managing Neely O'Hara was surely one of the most difficult jobs on earth. He had been doing it for almost two years, and in that time he had developed high blood pressure, the beginnings of a stomach ulcer, and a skin condition that forced him to wear long sleeves even here in the desert, where the temperature most days went well into the nineties.

"Fat people with fat wallets," Gordon said. Neely's one-woman show was the most expensive ticket in Vegas, and her three-week run was entirely sold out. No matter what mistakes Neely made—bad marriages, bad television movies, even a bad exercise video that became a running joke on every late-night talk show for much of last year—she could still sell out Vegas, at top dollar, for as many weeks as Gordon could talk her into.

"Well, I can't take it anymore," Neely said. "You're working me to death. Meanwhile,

Barbra Streisand is getting pedicures and having tea with senators. How come I never get to have tea with a senator?"

"Neely, you don't know any senators."

"Well, I want to know one. Not one of these local guys, either. One of those handsome ones from back east who looks good on the tennis court. A Democrat, maybe. Don't you know any Democrats who need a girl to sing at their parties?"

"I'll ask around."

"I'm serious, Gordo," Neely said, her voice dropping to a kittenish whisper. "I got to hook up with one of these candidates. I got to get taken seriously again."

"Neely, you are well on your way to record earnings. You are entirely out of debt for the first time in five years. You are one of the most popular performers on the planet."

"I am, amn't I." Neely sighed. "I guess I should try on the dress, just to be nice."

Five minutes later she returned from the bedroom. The dress fit perfectly. The top was made of cherry-red satin, cut like a tuxedo, with swirls of beading all along the lapels. The bottom was sheer red chiffon covered in red sequins.

Gordon clapped his hands.

Neely ran her hands across her chest. "Not bad for thirty-three," she said.

"Not bad for *twenty*-three," Gordon said. "Neely, the hotel wants to book you for four weeks next Christmas."

"No way."

"I can get you a higher percentage. Do the arithmetic, Neely. We can't say no to money like this."

"Gordon, you're not listening to me. I'm doing Vegas instead of a classy theater in New York because I haven't had a hit song in over four years. I haven't had a hit song because the top writers don't send me their top material anymore. The top writers don't send me their top material because they want someone classy, like Barbra Streisand is classy.

"And it's not fair! I've got a better voice than her! And a better face! And I'm ten years younger than her! But she's the one with the movie-star boyfriends and all the political connections. I know way more about politics than she does!"

"Neely, you don't even read the newspaper. What do you know about politics?"

"I'm Irish, I could learn in ten minutes. I need a mentor. A senator would be perfect.

Or maybe one of those movie moguls. Preferably one of those faggot movie moguls."

Gordon raised his eyebrows.

"I'm thirty-three. On stage I might look twenty-three, but my knees feel more like fifty-three. So, you gonna make some phone calls for me or what?"

Gordon sighed.

"I'm thinking about next Christmas," Neely said. "I'm thinking it doesn't sound so bad. I'm thinking maybe I'll think about it a little more." Neely did the arithmetic. If she was getting a higher percentage, so was Gordon. He knew all kinds of people who knew all kinds of people. He was Jewish, and his brother was a fancy criminal lawyer in Los Angeles, so Neely figured he knew how to make this happen.

"And get me a subscription to one of the Washington papers."

"The *Post.*"

"Yeah, that one. Have it delivered to my dressing room, I can read it between sets," she said. "Man, I am beat. Gimme some ginseng, will ya?"

There were at least thirty dark brown bottles on Neely's dressing table. Vitamin C, vitamin E, vitamin A, six different B supplements, calcium supplements, iron supplements, a multivitamin for the morning, another one for the evening, lecithin, echinacea, vitamins to fight stress, herbs for energy, L-tryptophan for sleep, and at least a dozen things Gordon had never heard of.

Neely had hired a nutritionist she had read about in *Vogue,* and after a forty-minute consultation Neely had ordered up three thousand dollars' worth of pills and powders. The nutritionist had given Neely a chart of what she was supposed to take when, but Neely liked to improvise or, as she called it, "listen to what my body has to say."

This morning Neely's body was telling her she needed about a week's worth of a very special kind of herb that was grown only in Asia.

Gordon handed her the pills. She closed her eyes and washed them down with bottled water. It occurred to Gordon that the very act of taking the pill—hearing the reassuring shake of a half-full bottle, feeling the soft tickle as the capsules fell into her waiting palm, readying her throat with a preliminary sip of water, running the pills up from her palm to her fingers, dropping them into the crease of her tongue, swallowing, swallowing again, feeling them go down, opening her eyes and seeing she was still surrounded by bottles, that there were always more pills—was satisfying to Neely, that she loved pills, any kind of pills, the way other women loved chocolate or expensive Italian shoes.

"I killed them last night, didn't I," Neely said.

"You killed them."

The assistant to Neely's personal assistant came in, waving a copy of *People* magazine over his head.

"We're in it, we're in it!"

Neely's eyes widened. "Let me see that." She grabbed the magazine and flipped the pages in a rush, front to back, back to front. There she was, a tiny photograph no more than two inches high, on a page with at least ten other people.

"I'm supposed to be happy about this?" she asked. "Gordon, did you know about this?"

"I had no idea," Gordon lied. He had spent two hours that morning buying up every copy of *People* that Neely might run across, covering every gift shop and news-stand in their hotel and the next four hotels down the strip.

"Look at me! I look like a big joke! I can't believe they got a picture of me in that ridiculous headdress!"

It was a photograph from the Judy Garland medley that closed the first section of Neely's show. The number opened with "Somewhere Over the Rainbow," which showed off what great shape Neely's voice was in. It segued through a few bouncy show tunes, then through a few torch songs, and ended with the chorus line joining Neely for the last two songs. They reenacted the makeover scene from *The Wizard of Oz,* turning Neely from a cabaret singer wearing a simple black pantsuit into a Las Vegas showgirl in four-inch heels, black fishnet stockings, a gold lamé bathing suit, a vast glittering cape, and a towering head-dress piled with plastic fruit and peacock feathers.

It was the campiest number in the show, and every night the crowd went crazy. It was like a big wink at the audience—Okay, I'm in Vegas, you're in Vegas, but don't I look great and don't I sound great and aren't we having fun?—and some nights Neely even got a standing ovation right in the middle of the set.

She hated wearing the chorus-girl outfit; it was uncomfortable, and the boning in the bathing suit left big red marks across her stomach, and the headdress was so heavy that she felt as though her neck would break. But she couldn't argue with the applause. And she had to wear the headdress only for maybe ten seconds tops, right at the very end.

Who knew that would be the ten seconds that ended up in *People*?

"I mean, look at this, Gordo. You know the costume is a joke and I know the costume is a joke and everyone in the audience knows the costume is a joke, but the way they printed it here, it looks like Neely O'Hara has turned into a showgirl!"

"Neely, any publicity is good publicity."

"The show doesn't need any publicity, it's sold out, remember? I want them to print a retraction."

"There's no such thing as a retraction for photographs."

"Well, I want them to make it up to me. Why can't they just run a nice interview with me, like the ones they do with everyone else? You know, I could hang out in my kitchen and flip waffles or something."

"Pancakes. You flip pancakes, not waffles."

"*People* hasn't done me since I got out of rehab, what was that, more than five years ago."

"The publicist calls them once a month, Neely. There has to be some kind of story. They're happy to run a story about you, but first there has to *be* a story."

"Like what? Like the rest of the losers they're always writing about? Like I have to be drinking, or drugging, or getting arrested for shoplifting tampons, or what? I have to be banging some guy twenty years younger than me, or saving the whales, or be diagnosed with some horrible disease so everyone can feel sorry for me?"

When the show was over, Neely went home to Los Angeles and wrote two dozen checks, each for one thousand dollars, to twenty-four different political campaigns. Within two weeks the invitations started pouring in: to fund-raising lunches in Beverly Hills, to dinners in New York and Washington, to parties in Chicago and Miami.

She spent three days on Rodeo Drive getting made over. She bought four beige Armani suits with matching shoes. She got a new, sleek haircut and learned to use a lighter hand with her eye makeup. She kept the red lipstick and most of the jewelry, but the overall transformation was startling. She looked like the kind of woman who was married to a studio head, though when she opened her mouth, she was still pure Neely O'Hara.

She had a part to play. She wanted Madison Square Garden, not Las Vegas hotel theaters. She wanted her own hit songs, not covers of someone else's standards. She wanted a man who could take her to all the respectable A-list parties, not some gay set designer who cared only about the hottest new restaurant. She wanted the kind of guy who had real power. Who would make people sit up and notice: Look who's in love with Neely O'Hara now. Who had been to the best schools and knew all the best people. Who picked up the check.

The rules had changed. Broadway was over, movie musicals were over, one-night stands were over, even cocaine was almost over. Show business was full of lawyers and bankers and people with fancy business-school degrees. It was a different game now, but it was still a game.

And Neely would learn how to play it. She was going to get back on top again! She would show those fucking idiots at *People* just how classy she could be. They'd be begging to take her picture, to come to her house and take pictures of her bedroom, her garden, her newly redecorated formal living room with the French furniture and the Christmas tree in the corner. She would get what she wanted, because she always did. But first she had to find the right man.

Anne could feel herself beginning to shine. It was only seven blocks from her apartment on Fifth Avenue in the Seventies to the doctor's office on Park in the Eighties, but the day was unseasonably hot. It was the middle of May, just before eleven in the morning, and already the temperature hovered at eighty degrees.

Anne resisted the impulse to get out her compact and apply a thin layer of sheer powder. No makeup, the nurse had told her. No moisturizer, no powder, no eye cream, no sunscreen, and please go light on the salt and go light on the alcohol for at least forty-eight hours before the appointment. It had all been pretty easy, except for the alcohol. Last night Lyon had asked her to come along for a business dinner with a client who was in from Los Angeles.

"Booze-ness dinners" is what Lyon called them. He always ordered a few bottles of wine, and by the end of the dinner everyone was happy, and telling their best stories, and feeling like best friends, and pretty much agreeing to whatever plan Lyon had unveiled sometime between when the main course was cleared and the coffee arrived. Anne could never manage to get through these dinners without at least one glass of Scotch and two or three glasses of wine. Invariably, she was the lightweight at the table.

The doctor's office had a Park Avenue address, but its entrance was on a leafy side street, around the corner from the wide dark blue awning where residents came and went. There was a small brass nameplate and buzzer that turned like a large metal key.

Inside, the walls were covered with excellent copies of obscure paintings by famous Impressionists. Anne sat on a leather sofa and filled out the usual forms.

"My grandmother used to own that one," said the woman sitting next to her. Her ash-blond hair was pulled back into a chignon, and on her ears were enormous square sapphires.

Anne looked up. "The original? I love Monet."

"That *is* the original. Nonny had to sell it after the crash in 'twenty-nine."

Anne gasped. "That's a real Monet?"

"Everything here is real. With his kind of fees, the doctor can certainly afford it, don't you think? Everything here is real except *them*," the woman said, pointing to the two nurses standing at the reception desks.

The nurses were dressed in identical tight white shirtdresses, belted to reveal their tiny waists and narrow hips and opened an extra button or two to show a few inches of spectacular cleavage. Both had perfectly proportioned jawlines and elegant noses and flawless skin and the kind of wide cheekbones that made photographers swoon. Their legs, bare of stockings, were smooth and tanned and unmarked by age or experience.

The woman gave Anne a stage wink. "They get all the work they want, at no charge. Free advertising for the doctor, if you know what I mean. By the way, he did a gorgeous job on you. You don't look a day over thirty-six."

Anne folded her hands over her medical questionnaire, hiding her name, address, and age, which was thirty-four years and seven months. "Well, actually . . ."

The nurse called the woman's name and she stood up, tucking her hair behind her ears. "He's a genius, isn't he? Not a scar on you."

Anne sat alone, staring at the painting that was so perfect and so beautiful, she had just assumed it was a fake. All the scars are on the inside, she thought.

The nurse handed her a green cotton robe and insisted Anne strip down to her underpants, even though she was here only for a consultation about a little bit of face work.

"You never know," said the nurse, lifting her eyebrows.

I used to look ten times better than you

do, and the only plastic surgeon I had was named Mother Nature, thought Anne.

The doctor looked like a casting agent's idea of a kindhearted country doctor, except for his watch, which was French and worth at least three thousand dollars.

"So," he said, pushing gently at the skin on her neck. "How does your husband feel about all of this?"

"He doesn't know I'm here."

"Is he encouraging you to have a little work done?"

"We haven't ever talked about it. Why do you ask?"

"Oh, sometimes the husband puts pressure on the wife, makes comments about how her body is changing, that sort of thing, and even though the woman isn't crazy about surgery she might come to see me just to make him happy."

"My husband isn't like that. And I'm only thirty-four! Really, it's just these little lines coming in around my eyes and on my forehead that I wanted you to take a look at. I've been reading about all these new procedures, and, well, I don't know. I probably just should have gone to my dermatologist. My husband would probably laugh if I'd told him I was coming here. He thinks I'm perfect."

"Those are the ones who put the most pressure on their wives. Men think they're marrying a perfect physical specimen, they're really into this idea of their wives being the most beautiful woman in the room, and then when things start changing, as they inevitably do, sometimes the men can't make the transition."

"My husband isn't like that," Anne said. "This is for me."

"You used to model, didn't you?" the doctor asked.

"You have a good memory," Anne said. "That was a long time ago. I was the Gillian Girl. I did all their makeup and perfume ads for years. In the seventies? You might have seen me on television, in a little white bikini, dancing around to really bad disco music."

"No, that isn't it. People used to bring in your print ads. To show me what they wanted to look like. 'I want Anne Welles's nose' is what every third woman used to ask. Elegant, not too small, absolutely straight." He moved her chin to the side and inspected her profile. "I finally get to see the original."

"You said 'used to.' What nose do they ask for now?"

"Oh, same nose, pretty much, just some other model's name. Someone who's in all the magazines this year."

Someone a lot younger, Anne thought. Someone who still has everything ahead of her. Someone who still jumps out of bed in the morning looking forward to her day. Someone who doesn't know what it's like to bury a best friend. Someone who hasn't met her Lyon yet.

Anne decided against the injections recommended by the doctor and spent the summer covered in sunscreen, under a broad-brimmed hat, drinking gallons of water and eating huge salads and drinking only wine, only at night. It wasn't so hard to do. Jenn was away at camp, and Lyon was up in Maine, where two of his most important clients were starring opposite each other in a movie about an archaeologist who falls in love with a prostitute.

Here in Southampton everyone looked like Anne's mother, or one of Anne's aunts, or someone Anne's aunts would have approved of. The house was small, but the property was lovely and close to the ocean. Anne had bought it two years ago, right after Jenn's seventh birthday. Lyon had argued for East Hampton, but Anne said there were too many movie people buying houses in East Hampton, which was another way of saying East Hampton was a place she was likely to run into someone who had slept with Lyon, or wanted to sleep with Lyon, or was friends with someone who knew the woman Lyon was thinking of sleeping with next. On bad days, Anne felt as if all the women in the world fell into one of these three categories.

Today was a bad day. Lyon hadn't telephoned in nearly a week. She knew better than to try telephoning him in Maine. Ages ago, they had made an agreement never to call each other on a shoot. Anne hadn't worked in years, but she still held up her end of the bargain. If she called his hotel, the receptionist would tell her that everyone was on the set. If she called the set, they would tell her that Lyon was in a meeting.

It was a typical Southampton day. Jogging at seven, breakfast at eight, correspondence at nine. Lists at ten (a local girl came in for light cleaning and the grocery run), dance class at eleven, then lunch with friends, friends being the wives of men Lyon did business with, at a restaurant that served nothing but hamburgers and half a dozen salads chopped into pieces so fine that you could barely tell what was in them.

And then the afternoon, the long horrible August afternoon, the house too quiet, the telephone ringing every twenty minutes with an invitation to someplace she didn't want to go, the sun beating through the wide picture windows (the sun was her enemy now; what she would give to undo those two California summers of tanning and gin), the beautiful beach spread out before her, and absolutely nothing to do.

The hour between three and four was the hardest. It was too early to start getting ready for dinner. It was too late to start anything new. In the city this was the best hour of the day; it was when Jenn came home from school, friends in tow, giggling, telling dumb jokes, spilling cookie crumbs across the carpets. Anne curled up on the couch and tried to read a book, but she kept falling asleep after just a page or two.

She smelled him before she saw him.

Lime cologne, sandalwood soap, unfiltered cigarettes.

"Lyon," she said. She opened her eyes. He was holding a small red box tied with a silky white ribbon.

"Darling."

"What time is it?"

"Almost five. Happy to see me?"

"Oh darling, of course I'm happy to see you. I just—"

He sat on the edge of the couch and stroked her hair. "Kiss," he said, leaning over. He tasted of cinnamon mouthwash. "Ah. I see. You're angry with me."

"I'm not angry. Just give me a minute. I just need to adjust. I wasn't expecting— well, you haven't called in over a week."

"It's hell on the set. A total disaster. You know what it's like. We're all wrecks. I'm a wreck."

"Oh dear."

"Here. I brought you this."

It was a pair of enormous coral earrings, shaped like shells and swirled with gold.

"My God, Lyon, they're gorgeous. I love them. What they must have cost."

"You should read the business pages,

darling," he said. "We're having a spectacular summer."

"We are?"

"An unbelievably fantastically fabulous summer."

"Lucky us," said Anne. She had stopped following the stock market. They had long ago divided their labor. Lyon took care of the business and their stock portfolio and the taxes and all the insurance. Anne took care of Jenn's trust fund, the co-op, and the house in Southampton.

"We are rich," Lyon said.

Anne smiled. "We were rich before. We were rich in June."

"Well, now we're richer. Let's go someplace wonderful for dinner."

"Or let's stay in. I'll grill us some steaks."

"I haven't been to a decent restaurant all summer. Let's go out. I've made a killing in the market, and I want to take my beautiful wife out to dinner."

Anne changed into a white cotton piqué sundress and white high-heeled sandals. She twisted her hair into a knot at the nape of her neck and snapped the lever-back earrings into place. On each wrist, a wide gold bangle bracelet, and around her shoul-

ders, a pale yellow sweater that set off her
hair.

Lyon chose a restaurant in East Hampton
that was crowded and noisy and filled with
people they knew. They didn't have a reservation and they hadn't called ahead, but of
course there was a table, in a good corner,
with an excellent view of the room. The
food was fair. The service was slow. The
wine list was impeccable.

Every few minutes someone stopped by
the table to say hello to Lyon, to exchange
gossip, to ask how the movie was going, to
introduce a new girlfriend, to show off a
new wife.

"We haven't had ten uninterrupted minutes since we got here," Anne said when
the coffee arrived.

"I forgot what a scene this place can be."

"It's always a scene."

"We'll catch up when we get home," said
Lyon.

"Let's have a nice quiet weekend, just the
two of us."

"How I wish. I fly back the day after tomorrow."

"Oh Lyon, not really."

"No choice. I shouldn't even have come

down at all." He took her hand and kissed the inside of her wrist.

"Maybe I'll fly back with you."

"Darling, how I wish you could." He told her how miserable it was in Maine, how everyone was fighting, how the two stars weren't speaking to each other, how someone threatened to walk off the set at least once a day.

"She's a spoiled brat," said Anne.

"A spoiled brat getting paid two million dollars to grin and bear it."

"Why can't you ever manage any normal people?"

"They're all normal when I find them. Sweet and normal and cooperative and grateful for everything I do. Then I ruin them."

"You ruin them, or success ruins them?"

"Can't have one without the other. Listen. I go to London for a week in September. Come with me then. I'll get us a room at the Savoy."

After dinner they went to a birthday party for the wife of a producer Lyon occasionally worked with. There was a bar in the dining room, a bar by the swimming pool, and a third bar in the formal garden that led down to the beach.

The producer greeted them both with hugs. "Lyon, my man, I knew you'd make it. Anne. You look like a dream. As always."

Lyon led her out to the pool. Couples were dancing to old Burt Bacharach songs on a wooden deck that had been built on the lawn. People wandered over to say hello. It was a gift Lyon had always had, making the party come to him.

A woman Anne knew from the tennis club came over with a gin and tonic in each hand.

"Have you seen Arthur?" she asked. "I've lost Arthur."

"Haven't seen him, Stella," Lyon said.

"Well," Stella said. She took a big swallow from one of the drinks. "Well, well, well. Anne, your earrings are adorable."

Lyon excused himself to go make a telephone call.

"God, I love his accent," Stella said. "I was always such a sucker for an English accent. How long have you two been married?"

"Ten years."

"Me too! Lyon, what a catch. He always makes the party-game list."

"What party-game list?" asked Anne.

"Oh, you've never played with us? This is fun. We can play now. Okay, how many people are here, would you say?"

"One-fifty, maybe two hundred," said Anne.

"A lot of people. A lot of rich, beautiful, successful people."

"That's one way of looking at it."

"Now. Think of all the men here. Imagine someone waved a magic wand and Lyon didn't exist. Who else in the room would you want to be married to?"

"I can't imagine."

"Oh come on, Anne, don't be a stick-in-the-mud. I won't tell. Who? How about him?" Stella pointed to a lawyer who had just successfully sued a national tabloid for libel.

"Don't think so."

"Why not?"

"Just because," Anne said.

"Because even though he's rich and smart and funny and probably great in bed, he's also fat and short and probably has hair all up and down his back, right? You don't have to say it. He never makes the list. Okay. How about him?" Stella nodded at a real estate developer who had just gotten divorced from his third wife.

"No."

"You see, he'd be on my list. He's totally charming and he'd take me all over the world and then he'd dump me, dump me in some horrible way, dump me the way he's dumped all his other wives, but I'd get a great settlement, right? I could definitely stand to be married to him." Stella had finished her own drink and was now starting on Arthur's. She tilted her head at another lawyer, on the far end of the dance floor. "And also, to him."

"Are you and Arthur having trouble?" asked Anne.

"Trouble? No trouble. He's fucking my colorist, but this too shall pass."

"You're not serious."

"What's the point of being serious?" Stella said. "Anyway, she's not such a great lay. I know this for a fact."

"How do you know?"

"Because Arthur never feels like fooling around, I mean hardly ever, anymore. I can't remember the last time we did it. It's the great irony of life. Whenever Arthur is having a really hot affair, he turns into this absolute stallion. He just never stops. He's like a teenager. It wears me out. So, you know, the girl can't be much in bed."

"Oh Stella. I'm so sorry."

Stella shrugged. "But she's a genius with foils." She bowed her head and shook her long auburn hair across her shoulders. "She can fuck my husband all she wants, so long as she does this for me every six weeks."

Lyon was back. "I found Arthur. He's in the kitchen, they're all singing Gilbert and Sullivan. Anne, I'm bushed, shall we?"

They rode halfway home without talking. Lyon whistled along with the radio.

He turned to her at a stoplight. "Do they all flirt with you this way when I'm not around?"

"They're not flirting, they're just being polite."

"Oh, my dear, dear innocent girl. They are flirting. When a man looks at your knees, that is most definitely flirting." He grinned. "Promise me you will never wear that dress when I'm out of town."

"You're always out of town."

"You know, you flirt back. Just a little."

"I don't!"

"You do."

"I do not flirt."

"You flirt so well, you don't even realize you're flirting." They were home now. "You flirt like a princess. Unapproachable and come-hither all at once."

"Have you been flirting with princesses?"

"You see," Lyon said. "There you go."

She turned off the alarm while he got out the key. Inside, she bent over to take off her heels.

"Leave your shoes on," he said.

Upstairs it was dark and warm and smelled of the sea. She sat on the far side of their bed and waited for him to tell her what he wanted. He ran his thumb back and forth across her mouth. *I'm too tired for this,* she thought, holding him against her lazy tongue, hoping he would come quickly. His sounds were the sounds of a man slipping into a warm bath after a day of hard physical labor. When it was her turn, he started at her feet. He took his time, kissing the backs of her knees and the hollows of her hips, and she read a hint of rebuke in his ardor. Afterward, they undressed slowly and silently, hanging their expensive clothes on padded hangers.

"I miss you," she said.

"I miss you more," he said. "How are you, darling?"

"In general?"

"Right now."

"Right now I'm happily, deliriously satisfied, sir."

"New pajamas?" he asked.

"Old. Just haven't worn them in a while."

"Lovely."

She felt herself beginning to drift off. His fingers were pulling at her pajamas. She was as tired as he was eager. The combination seemed to excite him. In a few minutes it was over, and he was fast asleep, and she was wide awake.

She tried to remember the last time they had done it twice in one night. Had he kissed her? Had they said good night? She wondered, what would his mood be in the morning. She wondered, how old was the girl in Maine.

Neely found the man she was looking for at a fund-raising dinner for local Democratic candidates. The campaigns weren't terribly important, but the host ran one of the top-notch agencies and the guest list was guaranteed to be pure A-list.

Her daily horoscope had read, "Pay attention to those close to you." For a moment Neely thought this might refer to her twin sons, Bud and Judd, who lived with their father (Neely's second ex-husband) a few miles away. She hadn't seen them in a couple of weeks. It was hard to keep track of fourteen-year-olds. They rarely called her when they were staying with Ted. Judd spent most of his free time closed up in his room, playing on his computer. Bud (who recently insisted that everyone call him "Dylan") was usually off at clubs with his friends from high school.

Dave Feld was closer than that. He was seated next to her at dinner. Neely did a quick clockwise sweep of the table, starting with herself. Neely, Dave Feld, the hostess, one of the high-profile candidates, an actress with a current box-office hit, a big-name criminal lawyer, the wife of a studio chief, an actor who'd been active in the Democratic Party for years, a television producer, someone from some big consulting firm in Washington.

The second-best table. Pretty good for a crowd this big, but still. It made Neely crazy that you weren't supposed to ask where you'd be seated before you attended these things. It was unbelievable to her that someone could ask a big star like Neely O'Hara to show up and to write a check, and there was never any guarantee where she'd be seated. It seemed like something an agent would be able to negotiate, but Gordon had explained (first slowly, then with a bit of impatience in his voice) that when people entertained in private homes, questions about the seating chart were considered bad form.

Dave Feld had all the right credentials. He owned a big piece of a production company that currently had four prime-time hits on two different networks. He had grown up in Washington and moved to Los Angeles right after graduating from NYU. He had gotten divorced six months ago, just before his fiftieth birthday.

"I love your tie," Neely said. She swept her eyes down the length of his tie and slowly brought them back up, lingering on his mouth. He drove her home, and they made out in the front seat, just like teenagers. Neely knew better than to invite him in. Recently divorced men needed to be strung along a little. So she strung him along, and two months later he invited her to spend the summer with him in East Hampton.

Neely loved East Hampton. She loved Dave's big house, which he'd been able to keep after the divorce by giving his wife the house in Beverly Hills, the apartment in Greenwich Village, and the condo in Aspen. She loved all the party invitations, as many as a dozen a day on the summer weekends. She loved the humid weather, which did miracles for her skin. She loved that the place was full of gay men, most of whom still thought Broadway was the center of the universe. From behind her big blue sunglasses, she watched them recognize her and nudge each other when she walked through the little shopping district in search of tiny scented soaps and imported hair conditioner and whatever else there was to buy. That's right! Neely O'Hara is in town! She was a big, big deal in East Hampton.

And the fifteen pounds just melted away.

Dave wasn't a stud, but he knew how to use his hands. Like most divorced men, he liked to cuddle, but he was a sound sleeper and Neely could usually pry herself loose after the first annoying half hour.

The Burkes lived somewhere nearby, but she never saw them. Their names came up in conversation at parties or at the beach, but they seemed to move in a slightly different circle. Neely was relieved. She hadn't seen Anne in seven years, not since her affair with Lyon. What kind of person cared about who was fucking who seven years ago? But that was so like Anne: making a big deal about sex and never actually having any. Southampton was just the right place for her, with all the other no-talent country-club princesses.

In August they were invited to one of the most exclusive and talked-about parties of the season, a fund-raiser for an environmental organization at the home of a movie director who had a huge spread right on Georgica Pond. Here was a guy who wouldn't even say hello to her in a Hollywood restaurant, and now she was invited to his house! Neely was starting to get the hang of how these summer places worked.

People were much friendlier here than in New York or Los Angeles. If only someone had told her this fifteen years ago, when real estate cost a fraction of what it did now. Just think of all the connections she could have made.

Everyone at the party was dressed casually. It seemed to Neely that the more money someone had, the less they cared about their clothes. It was a form of showing off, really. Faded polo shirts, unpressed chinos, well-worn deck shoes: an arriving stranger might have guessed this was a group of suburban bankers or, even worse, college professors.

Neely spent the first hour with Dave, moving from group to group. Everyone loved Dave, and everyone loved his television shows, which had just enough sophisticated technical touches and narrative twists to keep the critics happy. Lawyers were always coming up to them and offering plot ideas for the show set in a law firm, and doctors were always suggesting situations for the show in a hospital.

That was another thing she had noticed about the Hamptons. People had opinions about everything under the sun: television, movies, books, politics, fashion, music, and most of all the stock market. For people who considered themselves artistic, Neely had never heard so much talk about the stock market.

When the conversation turned to the price per share of a major computer manufacturer, Neely drifted away, toward the bar.

"Will you sing a little, later?" the hostess asked. "We rolled the piano out by the pool."

"I never sing at private parties," Neely replied. In California, people would have known better than to ask.

"Just one song. Did you know my husband studied music in college? He can play anything, in any key. He'd be thrilled, he has all your records."

"I'll think about it," Neely said, which they both knew meant no. She regretted it instantly—what a great story it would make when she got back to California, that she had sung while the director George Dunbar played the piano for her, right in his own backyard.

The party rolled on as the sun set behind the house. The lawn was ringed with scented candles to keep away the mosquitoes. George Dunbar made a speech about the importance of protecting wildlife, someone gave a toast to endangered species, a woman from the environmental organization announced how much money the party had raised, people clapped.

"And," George announced, "I will write another check, in the amount of twenty thousand dollars, right here tonight, if Neely O'Hara will do us the immense honor of singing just one song for all of us."

What a bastard, Neely thought. Dave put his arm around her and squeezed with pride. Twenty thousand dollars for a bunch of birds! For a second she wondered whether there would be some way to split the money, fifty-fifty. Twenty thousand dollars, and she wouldn't see a penny of it.

The crowd began to clap in rhythm. "Song! Song! Song!"

Neely smiled. She pictured herself back in California, hanging out with the Dunbars, just her and Dave and George and Sandy on a Sunday night, George getting out some old sheet music, Neely seated beside him on the piano bench. Maybe they'd cook a little pasta together in the kitchen. Maybe they'd watch a video of one of George's

movies, just the four of them in their stock-
ing feet, sharing a big bowl of popcorn.
Once word got around that she was in
George Dunbar's inner circle, everything
would change.

And so she sang. It was one of her old
torch songs, in an easy key that wouldn't
give George any trouble. She gazed at Dave
for the first few bars and then worked the
crowd for the rest of the number. On the last
three notes, the breathtaking high notes
that she could still hit with confidence, she
stared right into George Dunbar's eyes.

Then she made a star's exit, not waiting
for the applause to end, not waiting for the
hugs and the handshakes. She walked
slowly back to the house and found a small
bathroom off the kitchen where she could
reapply her makeup and give them all time
to talk about how amazing she had been,
how she still had it. She wondered whether
there was any chance George Dunbar
would offer her the opening song in his next
movie. He owed her, he owed her big-time.
But why talk of owing, when now they were
such good friends? It wouldn't even be like
asking him for a favor. He'd have a demo
cassette at the house, and he'd play it for

her and Dave some evening, and she would start singing along, she would show him just how the phrasing should go, and he would beg her to do it. *Of course, George,* she would say. *Anything for you.*

She heard murmuring in the kitchen. She pressed her ear against the door.

"It's almost nine and no one is leaving."

"It's a wonderful party, Mrs. Dunbar," came the voice of the Polish housekeeper.

"Too wonderful. I have to get them out of here."

"Do you want me to put out the candles?"

"They're all so drunk, they won't even notice."

"They'll notice the bugs."

"Brilliant! Have the guys put out the candles. I want everyone out of here by nine-thirty. Our dinner reservation is at ten and they'll never hold it for us on a Saturday night."

"For you, they will hold the table. Of course they will hold Mr. Dunbar's table."

"No way anyone is going to hold three tables of eight on a Saturday night, not even for George Dunbar. Tell the bar to cut off the booze."

Neely gasped. There was another party after this one; this wasn't even the real party! This was what the East Coast was like, a social onion, you peeled layer after layer, you thought you'd arrived, and then you discovered there was something else to want, something even more exclusive, even harder to get.

And Dave Feld hadn't been invited. Maybe he wasn't so important after all. There were still three good weeks left to the summer season; maybe it was time to start thinking about trading up.

"Call the restaurant and ask them to start seating even if we're a little late. The Burkes will probably get there ahead of us."

So it was Anne who would get to go to the Dunbars' special little dinner party. Without having to sit through this long, boring cocktail party, without having to write a check like everyone else. It isn't fair, Neely said to herself. It's never been fair.

She stayed in the bathroom another fifteen minutes. Let Dave worry about her; she was sick of his midlife crisis, his neediness, his endless talk about life being short and making every day count. Next week Judd and Dylan were coming for a week's visit, and she was looking forward to the distraction.

Her sons would have everything. Ted was a great father, she had to admit that much, and he had done it nearly all on his own. But now that they were almost grown up, it was time for Neely to get involved. What did Ted know about the best schools, the best people?

Neely pictured them sitting in Dave's backyard, having a talk about buckling down and getting good grades. Judd would go to Harvard, and Dylan would go to Yale. They'd make friends with kids from nice families. They'd all go out to dinner, the boys and their girlfriends and their girlfriends' parents. She tried to remember the names and ages of all those Kennedy cousins.

Who needed East Hampton? It was a good place to start, but everyone knew the real power summered on Cape Cod and Martha's Vineyard. She would peel another layer, and another layer after that, and she would leave these people behind, because she always had, because life wasn't about looking back, it was all about looking forward. With her voice and her guts, what could stop her? Maybe she didn't have Anne's pretty face, her pretty breeding, and her pretty Radcliffe degree. Maybe she had something better.

No one gave a better party than Anne and Lyon. On the first Thursday in October, when everyone had come back from the Hamptons, they took a yellow legal pad and two matching fountain pens to a small Italian restaurant with wallpaper in a pattern of zebras, and they began to plan the guest list for their annual New Year's Eve celebration.

Over red wine and stuffed mushrooms, they went through last year's guest list, gossiping about everyone's behavior. There were good guests (people who arrived early and stayed late, people who danced, people who sent thank-you notes) and bad guests (people who hid in the library all night long, people who dropped ashes on the carpets, people who got sloppy when drunk).

"She was the one who spilled her salad on the wing chair?" Lyon asked.

"And never offered to pay for the cleaning," Anne said. "It cost me four hundred dollars to have that cushion reupholstered." She raised her eyebrows, and Lyon crossed the name off the list.

When the main course came, they moved on to the additions: new clients, new friends, new spouses, the parents of Jenn's new friends. A new neighbor in Southampton, a writer whose third book had been a surprise bestseller, the model who had been tapped to represent Gillian's new line of anti-aging products (only in her late twenties and already retired from the runway), a schoolmate of Lyon's who had just moved from London to New York.

"Do you think we'll still be giving this party thirty years from now?" asked Anne.

"As long as I've got the strength to open a champagne bottle," said Lyon. "I picture you exactly the same, with a pack of grand-children."

"How many grandchildren?"

"Three," Lyon said. "Two girls and one boy."

Anne gave him a sad smile. "Only three?"

"Darling," Lyon said, "not tonight, we're having such a lovely time." Anne wanted another child, and another after that. Lyon wanted no more children.

When the second bottle of wine arrived, the cuts began. A couple who had argued publicly for three years in a row. A man who had taken out a vial of cocaine right in front of the building's grandfatherly elevator operator. Various ex-wives and ex-husbands. Anne and Lyon had a two-year rule about divorces: they never took sides publicly, and they continued to invite both halves of the couple for two years following a messy divorce.

At the end of two years, a decision was made. Which one had they managed to stay friends with? Which one had invited them to a party or a weekend in the country? Which one still did business with Lyon? Which one still did charity work with Anne?

Almost always, it was the man who stayed on the list. The women just seemed to drift away. They moved up to Woodstock and fell in love with carpenters. They went to Europe and found younger men. They resettled in California and discovered yoga. They moved back to their hometowns and got jobs with the local newspapers. A few stayed in New York. They got new haircuts and redecorated their bedrooms. Anne saw them for lunch, but rarely in the evenings.

They were finished by the time the coffee arrived.

"I was thinking, maybe we could scale back a bit this year," Lyon said. "On the little things that no one really notices."

"Such as?"

"We don't necessarily have to serve top-shelf liquor all night long."

"Lyon, liquor is the one thing everybody does notice."

"Well, I'm sure you'll think of something. This party has gotten so expensive."

"I thought we were having a good year," Anne said.

"We are, we are, a fabulous year. But we've got a huge tax bill coming in, and don't forget the balloon payment on the mortgage."

"I thought we set that money aside in August," Anne said. She remembered Lyon calling their stockbroker from Southampton. A stock he had bought the year before had tripled in value. Lyon had given the broker orders to sell and then put the money aside to cover the balloon payment. They had gone out to dinner to celebrate, and taken along four friends, and ordered several bottles of expensive wine. Anne could still picture Lyon laying eight crisp new hundred-dollar bills on the black-and-white-checked tablecloth.

"We did, but then something else came up. An incredible opportunity, this little electronics firm I heard about. We just have to sit tight for a few months."

Anne wanted to know more but was afraid to ask. Years ago she had almost lost him over money. Whenever the subject of money came up, his mouth tightened, and Anne changed the subject.

When she was younger, she believed that love conquered all and that marriages failed only when the love ran out. But their love for each other had run out long ago, and still their marriage hummed along comfortably in second gear.

She couldn't point to anything in particular. It had happened gradually over the years, with every affair Lyon had, with every long absence. She stopped waiting up for him to come home from the airport. He stopped showing up with flowers.

Sometimes she wondered whether people still whispered about it. It had happened so many years ago, but in New York no one ever forgot where your money came from.

Originally the money had all been Anne's. She had invested her Gillian earnings in the stock market and had a brilliant run of luck. Lyon was making a decent living as a writer, enough to be comfortable, but not nearly enough to take on a wife and family. Anne desperately wanted to marry him, but she knew he would be too proud to live on his wife's earnings.

So she had arranged to loan him money in secret. She loaned a large sum of money to a friend, who in turned loaned it to Lyon, and it was with this money that Lyon bought his share in the agency and made himself rich. The angriest she had ever seen Lyon was the day he discovered that his seed money had come from her. By then they were already married and Anne was pregnant with Jenn.

Lyon paid her back, but their marriage was never the same. On some level she had bought him, bought herself a husband the way other women buy a new face or a new car. After he wrote her the last check, they never really talked about money again. Lyon took care of the finances, and once a year she signed their joint tax return. She had credit cards, and a modest savings account that covered the mortgage for the South-ampton house, and a checking account into which Lyon deposited three thousand dol-lars a month.

It wasn't love that made a marriage go. It was money. Sometimes when they were watching a movie together and the couple on screen declared passionate love for each other, they both had to turn away. Anne would reach for an emery board, Lyon would reach for his drink.

The waiter brought over the check. Lyon folded the guest list into his coat pocket.

"We don't have to give this party," Anne said. "We can go to London instead. Or even just to Southampton if you like. A quiet family Christmas would be just fine with me."

"Nonsense," Lyon said. "It isn't anything like that." He reached for her hand and kissed her on the cheek. "Nothing you need to worry about. Don't frown, it will give you lines."

She smiled, though of course that gave you lines, too.

She looked around the restaurant.

Friends waved from a far table. Wherever Anne and Lyon went, people knew them, people noticed them. They were a fabulous New York couple. They had a fabulous New York apartment where they gave fabulous New York parties. Maybe there were couples with happier marriages, couples who still loved each other the way they had on their wedding day.

But Anne thought of everyone she knew, she thought of every one of the two hundred people on the piece of paper in Lyon's pocket, and she couldn't name a single one.

And then came the telephone call that turned everything upside down.

Anne was lingering in the bathtub, even though the water was cooling. Lyon had just left for the office, and the maid was clearing the breakfast dishes. The caterers would arrive at ten, the florist at eleven. At noon two people from the salon would come by to do her hair and nails. It was a perk from her Gillian Girl days that she had come to rely on, even though it cost a fortune; she loved private service, especially on a busy day like this.

New Year's Eve! In twelve hours the apartment would be packed and noisy. Anne practiced the deep breathing she had learned in yoga class and tried to ignore the ringing telephone.

The maid knocked on the bathroom door. Anne's lawyer was calling, and he said it was urgent.

The lawyer sounded nervous. Had Anne signed the papers yet? The documents needed to be signed and notarized before the end of the year in order to avoid a big tax payment. Was she planning to come by the office and drop them off? Had Lyon explained everything to her? Did she have any questions?

"Howard, forgive me," Anne said. "I have no idea what you're talking about."

There was a long pause where neither of them spoke. Anne stood in her bedroom, shivering against the cold. She counted her wet footprints in the thick green carpeting: two, four, six, eight. She listened to Howard inhaling at the other end of the line.

"Perhaps I had better come by. I can be there in an hour."

"Just tell me," Anne said. "It's bad news, isn't it?"

The money was gone. Lyon had taken too many risks in the stock market, and they had taken a tremendous loss in the October crash. There was a huge mortgage payment due in January on the Fifth Avenue apartment, and the only way to cover it was to dip into Jenn's trust fund.

"I don't understand. I thought we were having a great year," Anne said. She remembered their trip to the Hamptons over the long Thanksgiving weekend. The signs of the stock market crash were everywhere. Abandoned construction sites where people had run out of the money needed to finish their houses. "For Sale" signs on land that had been bought with confidence just a few months earlier. Properties with untended lawns and ragged landscaping where the owners could no longer afford a gardening service. Why hadn't Lyon said anything?

Anne hung up and spent the next hour poring through files in Lyon's study. There it was, in brokerage and bank statements going back to the beginning of the year. Lyon had methodically sold off their blue-chip holdings and invested in riskier stocks. In the first half of the year they had seen enormous gains, and with each month Lyon grew more daring, dipping into their savings accounts and buying more stock on margin. Then, in October, it all fell apart.

Anne looked at their November statements. She scanned their portfolio for the sturdy, conservative stocks she had brought into the marriage. All that remained of the stocks she had bought with her Gillian Girl earnings was less than five thousand dollars of AT&T.

She took out a calculator and did the arithmetic. There was her inheritance from her mother and her aunt Amy, which had been put into a trust fund for Jenn. There was the house in Southampton, which in four months they would own free and clear. There was the apartment on Fifth Avenue, which still carried a big mortgage. There was Lyon's share of the agency, which could be converted to cash only if he sold out his interest to his partners. Paintings, jewelry, a couple of fur coats, the nice Persian carpets, some very good furniture: even at market prices, these wouldn't fetch enough to keep them going.

Anne thought back to the nights Lyon had been tense at the dinner table, to the hushed telephone conversations he held behind closed doors. She had assumed he had a new girlfriend, and she had never asked him whether anything was wrong.

But everything was wrong. They were broke. They were ruined. And in less than ten hours, everyone they knew would be coming over to wish them a happy New Year.

It was a marvelous party. Not even midnight, and already people were dancing. In the dining room, furniture had been pushed back against the walls, and an old Junior Walker song was playing. Lyon was holding court in the living room, telling stories from his early days on Broadway. In the kitchen, the caterers were packing up the remains of dinner and laying out dozens of rented champagne flutes on silver-toned serving platters.

By the time Lyon had come home, the party staff had arrived and Anne was busy checking on details. They hadn't had a moment alone all night, which was just fine with her. She hadn't decided what she wanted to say or do. She hadn't signed the papers. She supposed Lyon would want to sell the house in Southampton, her beautiful house, and she couldn't bear the thought of losing it.

Anne wandered from room to room, chatting with guests. The party was more crowded than usual; who were all these people she didn't know? She felt her problems following behind her, like a little shadow she didn't have to look at or even really think about. Ah, Valium. Drug of valor. She had tucked four yellow tablets into the cuff of her glittery silver sweater before the first guest arrived, just before the maid had gone around to all the medicine cabinets, packing the pharmaceuticals into a shoebox that was now hidden under the bed.

In the study, four women with European accents were discussing the difference between Americans and the French.

"But American mothers tell their daughters nothing about marriage," someone was saying. "American girls think marriage is all about orgasms!"

"American girls are not very practical,

which is why they are always so disappointed."

"American girls are practical, but about
other things."

"Such as?"

"Shoes and underwear. You see them
wearing running shoes right on Madison
Avenue! And then the cotton underwear,
the white cotton underwear!" Everyone
laughed.

"But I'm serious. My American niece, she
has no idea how to choose a husband.
They sent her to Princeton, where there are
plenty of nice rich boys from good families.
Did she find a husband? No, of course not.
And did my sister-in-law ever encourage
her? No, of course not. So now the girl is
thirty, and she lives in a little apartment on
Third Avenue with three cats. Hopeless!"

Anne went into the bathroom and un-
folded the cuff of her sweater. Fabulous,
how small pills were now, how much easier
they were to hide. The pills had little
V-shaped holes in the middle, and the first
time Anne had seen one she had mistaken
the hole for a heart. Just like me, she
thought now, something small with its heart
cut out.

In the guest bedroom, Stella was comforting a woman who looked as if she had just finished having a good cry. Stella patted the bed beside her and offered Anne a cigarette.

"He's a shit," said Stella. "It's really that simple. You could go into therapy for ten years if you wanted, but I'm telling you in the end that's all it is. It's not your fault. You married an asshole."

"I'm forty-five!" Marianne said. She turned to Anne. "I hope you never turn forty-five. You have no idea what it's like. No one warns you."

"You don't look forty-five," Anne said. "Really, not at all."

"Well, I am. Do you know any forty-five-year-old single women? Do you have any idea what it's like? I'll be dating grandfathers with bad breath and potbellies. You know what I am? I'm some old geezer's third-wife material."

Stella shook her head. "You're getting all worked up. You told me years ago you wanted a divorce."

"That was years ago, when everything was different! And I should have left him years ago. I knew someday he'd have a fucking midlife crisis and dump me, I don't know why I waited. I could have left him when I was still in my early thirties. I'd be re-married by now, I'd have found some nice guy and had a couple of children and started over."

"Men," Stella said.

"Men," Marianne said.

"Men," said Anne.

"They think life is nothing but a big game," Stella said.

"And they make the rules," Marianne said.

And then they go and break them all, Anne thought.

In the hallway, a handsome man with brown hair and a gray mustache grabbed her by the elbow. "You still owe me a dance from last year," he said. "I haven't forgot-ten."

Anne smiled, trying to remember which woman he had arrived with. Keith ran the news division at one of the networks and had a house in Sag Harbor. Every year he brought a different date to the party, and every year he flirted with Anne.

"Yes," she said. "But first I have to peek in on my daughter." Jenn was sleeping calmly through the noise, one hand tucked under her pillow.

One more pill. There were all sorts of new things out now, but she still preferred Valium. It was the Grace Kelly of sedatives: both modern and classic at once.

It was three A.M. before the party really thinned out. Unless one lived within walking distance or had a private car, getting home would be a chore; there were never enough taxis on New Year's Eve. At four there were still six guests left. Arthur and Stella, collapsed against the sofa cushions. A young couple they knew from Southampton, two lawyers who could not stop talking about their new apartment on Riverside Drive. A woman named Pamela, whom Lyon had been flirting with all night—at one point they had gone out together to buy cigarettes and not come back for half an hour—but Anne was too tired to care. And someone named Gregory, who seemed to be Pamela's date and was annoyingly peppy, considering the hour.

Anne brought out coffee. They gossiped about the party . . . who had danced, who hadn't, who had gotten too drunk, who was wearing clothes just a little too sexy . . . and picked at leftover cookies. Arthur dozed off and began to snore lightly.

"Well," Stella said. "This was the best party ever, and now it's time to go home."

Everyone stood up. Stella and Arthur had a car waiting downstairs; did anyone need a ride? They discussed the geography of who lived where. Stella and Arthur were headed to the San Remo in the West Seventies, yes, they'd be happy to give a ride to the couple on Riverside in the Eighties. Pamela's date also lived on the Upper West Side, and yes, there was room for him, but of course he had to see Pamela home to her apartment off Gramercy Park, in the opposite direction.

Anne cleared the coffee cups, and when she returned to the living room a plan had been made, and people were pulling on their coats. Lyon had a coat on, too: the five West Siders would pack themselves into one limousine, and Lyon would see Pamela into a taxi.

Goodbye! Goodbye! Happy New Year! Happy New Year! Anne was in her pajamas within minutes. She sat on her bed and smoked a cigarette. It was delicious to be alone, and she suddenly wasn't one bit tired.

She reached under the bed for the shoe-boxes full of things the maid had hidden there, because you never really knew about guests, even your friends: the pills, the better jewelry, the zippered leather case with their passports and credit cards.

She laid the jewelry across her pillow. Most of the pieces represented something she and Lyon had celebrated together: a Tony Award, a movie deal, a stock split, a big client signed. All of Lyon's biggest triumphs were recorded here, in gold and platinum and precious stones.

Some of it, she knew, was what Stella called "guilt baubles"—those seemingly spontaneous "no special occasion" gifts that had perhaps marked the end of a complicated affair. Anne had always wondered whether husbands regretted these later: how much harder it was for a man to forget a mistress when his wife wore a glittery reminder around her wrist.

There was only one gift here that celebrated something they had done together: the strand of pearls Lyon had given her when she brought Jenn home from the hospital. Anne fastened the pearls behind her neck.

Much of the rest of it would be sold. She went to the window and looked out across Central Park. The sky was beginning to lighten to a misty gray.

She tried to imagine everything ahead of them. Would they start over? They could find a way to build it all back, however long it took. Five years, ten years, fifteen years. She would be nearly fifty years old.

And what would happen to Jenn? The whispers would follow her everywhere. *They lived on Fifth Avenue until. . . . Her father used to, but then. . . .* Anne had seen what happened to the daughters of scandal. She pictured Jenn at eighteen, going off to college, and someone lifting an eyebrow from across a campus lawn. *Yes, those Burkes. You don't remember? Let me tell you.*

Or would they start over and do something different? They could move to a little cottage in the English countryside. Lyon would write books and Anne would garden and Jenn would have a great big sheepdog to play with.

Eventually he would leave her. She had

felt it for years. At the dinner table, at the beach. At the doctor's office, as she jogged around the reservoir. Every time she went alone to a parent-teacher conference at Jenn's school, every time she comforted another friend going through a tough divorce. She was no different from all the other women she knew. Eventually it would be her turn.

She was just this, only this: the first Mrs. Lyon Burke. Stella would take her out (for lunch, not dinner), and Anne would tell amusing stories about going on bad first dates. She would spend a weekend in Woodstock, she would start taking yoga classes. It wasn't a question of *if.* It was just a matter of *when.* Now or later? Thirty-four or fifty?

She closed the curtains and sat on the bed. *I'll be Anne Welles again,* she thought. And then: *I'm still Anne Welles. I can still be Anne Welles. It isn't too late.* She might not have the energy to do it for herself. But she thought of her daughter and felt herself grow strong and awake.

Behind the boxes under the bed were the two big suitcases they used for trips to Europe. She called the garage to have them bring the car around. It took her less than twenty minutes to pack. The doorman was too polite to ask questions.

Buckled into the backseat with her favorite pillow and stuffed elephant, Jenn slept all the way to Southampton. Anne sang along with the radio, an oldies station that was playing songs from her first years in New York.

I will survive! The gas station attendant didn't even blink at the sight of a woman in pajamas and a full-length mink coat. The roads were empty, and they made every light. The sun was rising over the ocean.

Anne tucked Jenn into bed and turned on the heat. No telephone messages, no surprise. What was there to say? She hadn't left a note. It was possible Lyon hadn't even come home yet.

She got under the covers, pulling the mink across her shoulders for extra warmth, and at long last fell into a deep, dreamless sleep.

1988.

Anne sat in the waiting room of the TBK Agency, examining her manicure. Not bad, considering that she had done it herself. She hadn't had a professional manicure since she'd left Lyon three months ago—it was a luxury no longer within her budget. Her cuticles needed trimming, and there were a few little bumps on her right pinkie, but it wasn't the kind of thing a man would notice.

She had been waiting for fifteen minutes. She knew what that meant, to be the kind of client who was kept waiting in an outer office. But what choice did she have? She hadn't worked in years. She was starting all over again, back at the bottom. After one expensive lunch at the Russian Tea Room back in January, the head of TBK had farmed her out to a younger agent who had been in the business for less than five years.

"Trip Gregory can take better care of you than I can," she was told. "He doesn't travel so much, so he'll have lots of time for you. He's young and hungry, which is what you need. And he has great contacts in advertising—you'll see. He'll get you a commercial in no time."

And now it was early April, and Trip Gregory was keeping her waiting. Well, what did she expect. She had gone on more than a dozen auditions, and so far nothing had panned out. The shampoo company had decided they wanted someone younger. The pain-reliever company chose someone older. The pet-food people thought she was a little too glamorous, and the perfume people found her not quite glamorous enough.

At last the receptionist waved her into Trip's office.

"Sorry to keep you waiting," he said. "But I have some great news." A chain of luxury hotels was looking for a spokesperson to appear in all their television and print ads. Auditions were scheduled for June, and shooting would begin in September.

"You would be perfect," Trip said. The intercom buzzed. He held up two fingers and picked up the phone.

Anne knew what that meant, too: being the kind of client you don't hold calls for. He was talking to another client—from his tone of voice, Anne guessed it was an attractive woman—and after a couple of minutes she tuned him out. She looked at her watch, thinking of her train schedule, trying to guess when their appointment would be over. If she was lucky, she'd have time to walk to Penn Station and would get to save five dollars in cabfare.

It was unbelievable, how tight the money was now. She had made a budget when she left Lyon, figured out how they had just enough to squeak by, but there were always expenses she hadn't counted on. When she was rich, she had never paid attention to how much the little things cost. Now it was all she thought about. When she woke up in the morning, she tried to figure out if she had enough cash to get through the day. When the telephone rang, she hesitated before picking it up, wondering if it were a credit-card company calling about a late payment.

It was as if she were divorcing Lyon only to marry this other person, this constant presence, this financial anxiety that now colored everything she did.

Trip hung up and folded his hands. "Like I said, someone like you would be perfect."

"Someone *like* me? Or me?" Anne asked.

"You know what I mean. They want to target the business executive with a big-time expense account, the kind of guy who is on his way to the top but not quite there yet. They're looking for someone with a lot of class, but not too sexy. Class, because the guy has to feel like he's staying at the best place in town, the kind of hotel that says he's at the top of his game. And not too sexy, because he's sitting at home watching this commercial with his wife, and if he's spending a lot of time out of town, she's probably wondering about whether there's any hanky-panky on the road."

Anne smiled. "Attractive, but not threatening."

"Exactly," Trip said.

She laughed.

"What's so funny?"

"I'm sorry. You wouldn't have any way of knowing this, but that's almost word for word what they told me when they hired me to be the Gillian Girl. Anyway, it sounds wonderful."

"There'd be quite a bit of travel in September and October. Sure you can handle it?"

Jenn would just be starting at a new school. Anne didn't even have a baby-sitter out in Southampton, let alone someone who could be trusted to stay overnight with Jenn. "I'll think of something. September is a long way off."

"Okay, then," Trip said. "I'll get something scheduled." He stood up, her cue that their appointment was over. "You look great, by the way. Let's talk next week."

"But . . . what about between now and then? I mean, September is months away. There must be some other work I can do in the meantime."

Trip sighed and sat back down. "It's dead right now. There's nothing out there. It's practically summer, and you know how it is in the summer. You'll probably see more advertising people out there in the Hamptons than here in Manhattan. So relax for a few months."

Anne leaned forward. "I can't relax. Trip, it's been months, and I haven't seen a single check."

"Be patient."

"I've got bills to pay."

"That's what alimony is for."

"I won't get alimony."

"Are you kidding me? What kind of divorce lawyer do you have?"

"A very good one, believe me. It's a long story." Somehow her lawyer was managing to get her out of her marriage without any debt and with a custody arrangement that would limit Jenn's visits with Lyon to four weeks a year.

"I just assumed Lyon was footing the bills."

"There's child support, but it won't cover my expenses." She didn't want to tell him that she had taken the train in from Long Island—her car couldn't be trusted for long trips, it needed transmission work that she couldn't afford. "Do I have to spell it out for you? I'm *broke.*"

Trip rolled his eyes. "Love that word, *broke.* No one is poor anymore, just broke. Oh, honey, don't get teary on me. Please, anything but that." He handed her a tissue.

"Well, if it makes you feel any better, you aren't alone."

"Really."

"You'd be surprised. With the crash last October, a lot of people have it hard. Why do you think some of these jobs are so tough to get? People are taking work they would have raised their noses at just a year ago. You know who took that pet-food job?" He mock whispered the name of an actress who had starred on a prime-time soap opera in the late seventies. "So that's the competition that's out there now. If it makes you feel any better."

Anne smiled. "Well, it does make me feel better, but it doesn't change the fact that I'm totally broke."

Trip shook his head. "A woman walks into my office wearing three thousand dollars on her ears and tells me she's broke."

Anne fingered the small round diamonds that Lyon had given her on their fifth wedding anniversary. "These aren't worth three thousand dollars."

"My family is in the jewelry business. I know what I'm looking at."

"Well, I can't exactly sell them."

"Why not?"

"Because . . . I don't know, I just can't."

"Sentimental value?"

"Hardly."

"Have you ever heard the expression 'estate jewelry'?"

"Of course."

"And what do you think it means?"

"When someone dies, it's the jewelry that's left as part of their estate."

"And why do you think it ends up for sale?"

"Lots of reasons," Anne said. "Maybe to pay estate taxes. Or maybe it's out of fashion. Or maybe the jewelry has been left to a charitable organization, and they get to sell it and use the proceeds."

"Let me tell you, there's no such thing as estate jewelry. Just ask your neighbors on Fifth Avenue."

"Ex-neighbors."

"It's divorce jewelry. It's Chapter Eleven jewelry. It's my-husband-is-a-compulsive-gambler-and-he-just-spent-the-month-at-Saratoga jewelry. Women like you sell their jewelry all the time. We just call it estate jewelry so the customer doesn't have to think about someone else's bad luck when he's writing a check equal to two months'

salary. If you want to hold on to your ice because it reminds you of some wonderful
evening when you were Mrs. Lyon Burke
and the world was your oyster, fair enough,
but please don't complain to me that you're
broke."

"Now you're being cruel."

Trip leaned back and crossed his hands
behind his head. "I'm just being realistic.
You want it both ways, Anne."

"What does that mean."

"You want to start all over again—let's
call it what it is, we've talked about it before, the whole Gillian Girl thing was, like,
five centuries ago—you want to start all
over and make a career for yourself. And at
the same time, you want to hold on to this
'I'm a lady and we came over on the
Mayflower' bit. Well, you can't do both."

"Some choice."

"At least you have a choice. You think
you're the first thirty-something divorcée to
walk through the door looking for work? We
see them all the time. For every hundred
that come see us, we agree to represent
maybe one or two."

"I'm honored."

"You should be."

"So why did I make the grade?"

"You know, when they first passed you on to me, they basically told me it was a favor. Professional courtesy to Lyon and all that. We figured you'd go on two or three auditions and call it quits. Find a rich boyfriend, start the hunt for a second husband, maybe get a job at a gallery or a real estate company like most of the Upper East Side types do. But then . . . well, I'm not sure how to say it. You *surprised* me."

"Really."

He laughed. "You aren't like the rest of them. Underneath it all, you've got guts."

She laughed with him. "Guts and about two hundred dollars in my checking account."

He wrote a name and a West 47th Street address on the back of his business card. "Here. He's my cousin, he won't rip you off. Those earrings will take care of you all summer."

It was turning out to be a lucky day. First there was the news of a good audition and the check from the jewelers'. Then she made her train with five minutes to spare.

And best of all, when she got back to Southampton, her car started.

Anne stopped at the supermarket to pick up a few things for a celebration dinner with Jenn. After weeks and weeks of living on a shoestring budget, she splurged on a pint of name-brand ice cream and some colored felt-tip markers for Jenn.

"Special occasion?" asked the cashier at the checkout line. Gretchen was a local girl who always had a joke or story ready for Jenn. Even when the line for Gretchen's register was the longest one at the market, Jenn always insisted they wait to check out with Gretchen.

"I had some good news today," Anne replied. "My goodness, what happened to you?"

Gretchen had a black eye, and her left arm was in a sling. "Oh, it looks way worse than it is. I fell down the stairs night before last, tripped over a pair of shoes. My own fault for leaving them there. I am such a slob!"

"Your arm—is it broken?"

"Yeah, but it isn't serious." Gretchen smiled. "I'm just a big klutz."

At the end of the counter, another girl was

bagging Anne's groceries and shaking her head. "Yeah, and I can think of someone who is an even bigger klutz."

"Shut up, you," Gretchen said. She turned to Anne with a wide smile. "Coupons?"

Anne unsnapped her Kelly bag and laid out a half-dozen coupons. "There you go. And who do I see about posting something on the bulletin board?" she asked. She took out a pale pink 3-by-5 index card. "Does the manager approve them first?"

"You're looking for an au pair?" Gretchen asked.

"Not exactly," Anne said. An au pair was exactly what she needed, but it was hardly within her budget. "I'm looking for someone who would want to take one of the extra bedrooms in exchange for a very low rent and a couple of nights of baby-sitting a week."

Gretchen looked at the card. "Wow, this is low," she said.

"It's a very small room," said Anne.

Gretchen slipped the card into her apron pocket. "I'll give it to him when my shift is over," she said.

Out in the parking lot, the bagger helped

load Anne's groceries into the backseat. Anne fished in her bag for a loose single.

"Nice pocketbook," the girl said.

"I've had it for ages," Anne said.

"You don't get it, do you. About Gretchen."

"Get what?"

"The broken arm. The black eye."

"What do you mean?"

"Like she fell down the stairs! What a lame excuse. I mean, how many times a year can a girl fall down the same stairs? It's her husband who did it to her."

"Gretchen is married? She can't be more than nineteen!"

"She's married, and he's a real asshole. He has two hobbies, drinking beer and beating up on Gretchen."

"Why doesn't she leave him?"

"Don't ask me, I never figured out why she got married in the first place."

Anne turned the ignition, but the car refused to start. She waited a few minutes and tried again, but still the engine wouldn't turn over. There was a knock on the window.

"Need a lift?" Gretchen asked.

Anne shook her head and rolled down the window. "It'll start, eventually."

Gretchen pulled the card out of her pocket. "Listen, are you serious about this? Because I was sort of thinking about moving, and this sounds perfect."

"Why don't you come over tomorrow and look at the room?"

"I'm sure the room is fine," Getchen said. "I'm kind of in a rush."

Anne recognized the look in Gretchen's eyes: the kind of bravery that wouldn't last long. "You can move in tomorrow if you like."

"I don't have much stuff," Gretchen said. They made the arrangements quickly, each woman slightly nervous that, given a few more minutes, the other would change her mind.

"And Saturday night," Anne said, "some friends invited me to dinner in East Hampton and I was planning on bringing Jenn along, but it's going to be awfully boring for her. If you're free from seven to around eleven, that would be wonderful."

"I'm free," Gretchen said. "Free as the wind."

"Perfect," said Anne.

*   *   *

Dinner on Saturday was with a gay couple who had moved to the Hamptons in the early sixties. Jerry was an architect, and Curtis ran a party-planning and catering company. Their favorite activity was making fun of all the new people who were moving out to the Hamptons—the same people, Lyon used to point out, who were making them unbelievably rich.

"Fifty thousand dollars' worth of land-scaping!" Jerry said, finishing a story about a house he had designed for a banker and his wife. "The most gorgeous house I've done in years, all simple lines and glass, and then they go junk it up with this dreary English shrubbery. The most high-main-tenance plantings you can imagine. They'll need two full-time gardeners."

"Which may be exactly the point," Curtis said, winking. "A gardener for him, and a gardener for her."

Jerry rolled his eyes. "Curtis, don't be evil. So, Annie, do you have any gossip for us? Bring back any juicy tidbits from Man-hattan?"

"Nothing much," Anne said. "I had lunch with Stella, that's about it. Heard about all the parties I'm not invited to anymore. I'm sort of dreading the summer."

"Not me, I can't wait," Curtis said. "I have seventeen weddings to do, and every one of them is pull-out-the-stops. Ka-ching, ka-ching! It was so slow this winter, I nearly lost my mind."

"I'm the one who lost my mind," Jerry said. "Having you around the house all the time."

The phone rang, and Curtis went to get it. Jerry poured another inch of cognac into Anne's glass. "And how is the dating scene?"

"What dating scene? Anyway, it's too soon."

"Bitch!" Curtis cried from the kitchen. "You total bitch!" When he came back in, his face was bright red. "Can you believe it? I'm meeting with Mrs. Lightman on Monday about her daughter's wedding, and Oona was supposed to have all the sketches ready, and she just called to say she's gotten a job offer in Los Angeles and she's quitting on me."

"That's what you get for hiring someone with a name like Oona," Jerry said.

"Don't joke. I'm sunk. This is a five-

hundred-thousand-dollar wedding, and I
don't have a single thing ready to show. I'm
sunk, utterly sunk."

"You can tap-dance with the best of
them, darling."

"It's a *theme* wedding. South of France.
And now I have thirty-six hours to pull it together."

"Hey, I have an idea," Jerry said. "Annie
has given some pretty spectacular parties
over the years. Maybe she can help out."

Curtis turned to Anne. "Oh my God," he
said. "How do you say 'perfect' in French?"

"Parfait," said Anne.

"So, imagine this is your party, what
would you do?" he asked.

"We never gave theme parties. We always thought, I mean, Lyon thought . . . you
know. They're so . . ."

"Vulgar?" Curtis said. "You can say it, I
won't be offended. Okay, then: your party, if
you had a zillion dollars to spend and you
wanted to make sure every penny of it
showed."

"Let's see. Jenn's old music teacher in
the city is from Paris—she and a few of her
friends play parties on the weekends. It's a
delightful little group with an accordion and

a singer who sounds just like Edith Piaf. For the right amount of money I bet they'd love to come out and play."

"*Sacré bleu!* Now keep going," said Curtis.

"No fair," said Anne. "You invited me here for a nice dinner and now you're trying to put me to work."

"Annie, darling, I'm in a jam and I need you to help. How can you say no?"

"*Non,*" she said in her flawless accent.

"You have no choice, you have to help. That's what friends do." He got out a notebook and a fresh bottle of wine. They spent the next two hours making plans.

The meeting with Mrs. Lightman and her daughter was a success. They loved Curtis's sketches, and they loved all of Anne's last-minute ideas: decorating the altar with lavender-scented candles, getting seat cushions in eight different mix-and-match fabrics from Pierre Deux, buying antique toy sailboats to float in the swimming pool.

"You're a genius," Curtis whispered to her in the car on the way home. "Come work for me this summer. They adored you. All my clients are going to adore you."

"Some of those clients used to be my friends. Wouldn't it be awkward?"

"Awkward for who? Not for me."

"Okay, awkward for them."

"Maybe twenty years ago, but these days divorced women are expected to work. They buy their houses from divorced women. They buy their art from divorced women. It's no different from being an interior decorator, really."

"Okay, then. Awkward for me."

"Don't be so old-fashioned. And by the way, these parties are a wonderful way to meet eligible straight men. There's always an uncle or a business partner lurking around. I'm promising you dozens of rich, eligible, good-looking heterosexuals. How can you turn me down? Even if you get this advertising job, it doesn't start until September. I can pay you in cash. These clients of mine, it's almost all about new money, they're dreadfully insecure and when they get a load of you, well, it will be just like today. You put them at ease in a way that I can't. They trust you."

"There's a lot I don't know."

"I agree. But you've got style, and you've got those glorious cheekbones, and you have just the right pedigree. Everything else can be taught. Please. As a favor to me."

They had pulled up in front of Anne's house. The shutters needed repainting, and the hot-water heater was on its last legs. At Southampton prices, the money from the sale of the earrings would go only so far.

"All right," Anne said. "Promise me it will be fun."

"It will be fun, and crazy, and sometimes impossibly busy. You've never really seen me when I'm cranky."

"Curtis, you're cranky all the time."

"And that's just one of the many reasons you love me," he said.

She kissed him on the cheek. "Love you to bits," she said.

In May, the town began to hum in anticipation of the summer season. All around Main Street, trucks delivered heavy cardboard cartons filled with additional inventory for summer visitors. Restaurants extended their hours. Window boxes began to bloom.

Anne felt like a young girl watching her older sister get ready for a party, a party Anne wasn't invited to. She was starting to see what the summer would be like. Curtis had hung four panels of blackboard on one wall of his office and chalked out a calendar that was five feet high and twenty feet long. The parties and weddings he had been hired to plan were written in thick yellow chalk. Work that had been contracted to someone else was written in green chalk. Work that was still up for grabs was in pink. And in white chalk: every social event he had heard about—family barbecues, golf tournaments, cocktail parties, fund-raisers— anything that might generate a last-minute telephone call for a bartender or a few platters of canapés.

It was ten o'clock on a Thursday morning, and Anne was alone in the office, staring at the blackboard. She had been invited to only one party, the annual clambake that Stella and Arthur gave in early August. She had gotten a few invitations to fund-raisers; the envelopes had all been addressed to "Mr. and Mrs. Lyon Burke," with labels spat out by a computer that hadn't been updated in years. Anne had learned to throw these away as soon as they arrived. The days of writing a five-hundred-dollar check for a cocktail party in support of endangered species were over.

The hotel commercials had fallen through. Anne had had a terrific audition, only to find out two days later that the entire campaign was being canceled. Each time she was rejected, it was a little harder to rebound. She was beginning to feel like an endangered species herself.

It wasn't just the money. She had been sleeping alone for almost five months now. At first it had felt delicious: the clean sheets, the mound of pillows all her own, waking up at dawn to utter quiet, the long private cup of coffee after Jenn left for school. For the first time in her life, she read the entire newspaper every day, every section in order, every word of every section. She was fascinated by exactly the kinds of articles she used to skim over—war stories from Eastern Europe, news of economic collapse in Latin America, debates over tax initiatives in Washington. But there was no one her age to talk about any of it with. At night, after Jenn went to bed, she felt herself turning into the lonely college girl she had been at nineteen, the girl who spent all evening in the library, all day in classes. The girl who loaded up her dinner tray with the same dinner every evening (a slice of bread, three slices of cheese, a bowl of salad, and a piece of fruit) and sat at the same cafeteria table with the same three girls, night after night.

Curtis and Jerry kept telling her it was time to get out there and date, and she kept replying that she wasn't ready yet, but of course that wasn't the truth of it. No one had asked her out. No one even flirted with her. Everything her single friends had complained to her about was turning out to be true.

Not that she had ever really dated to begin with. In high school, everyone went around in groups. One chilly night in tenth grade she had found herself sitting next to a boy at a football game, and he had taken her hand and squeezed, and she had squeezed back, and suddenly they were a couple. He was from a fine Yankee family (bankers and lawyers and four generations at Dartmouth), and she was from a finer Yankee family (the money mostly gone, but the breeding flawless all the way back to the 1600s), and everyone just assumed they would marry and settle down in one of the big clapboard houses in town. Willie liked to kiss a lot, and sometimes after a beer or two he would slide his hand up under her sweater.

He never formally proposed. They came home for Thanksgiving weekend freshman year (Willie from Dartmouth, Anne from Radcliffe), and on Saturday night, after an evening at the movies with friends, he drove her down a wide side street and pointed to a large Victorian house with a wraparound porch. It belonged to one of his uncles, a man whose children had all settled elsewhere, in Boston and Providence and beyond.

"I want us to live in a house like that," Willie said, coasting to a stop. Anne could still remember the sounds of leaves being crushed beneath the tires, of the car's engine disengaging, of a dog barking in the distance.

"That's always been one of my favorite houses," Anne said. He nodded and pulled out a ring, a not-quite-engagement ring. It had belonged to his grandmother, a small perfect opal surrounded by tiny diamonds.

She had worn the ring all through college. Four years without dates. Not that any of her friends ever went out on anything that remotely resembled an old-fashioned date.

They went to parties and danced in a big group and went home with the boys who danced the closest. They stayed in the library till closing and walked home with the boys who played footsie under the table. They went to bars and drank in a group and went to bed with the boys who walked them home.

Willie's uncle died just before Christmas break of their senior year. They parked in front of the house, and he turned off the headlights. "It's mine now," he said. "It's ours."

"I want to go to New York," she said. It just flew out of her mouth. She had never even been to New York, she didn't even know anyone who lived there—at school, the New York girls were like a group of glamorous aliens, they wore eye makeup and suede boots and smoked cigarettes and lived in apartments off-campus—but as soon as she said it she knew it was true.

Willie cut the engine. His uncle's house looked so big, and the ring felt so small. They both cried. Willie cried from heartbreak. Anne cried from excitement, from fear. New York was something she had read about in novels, something she had seen in the movies. She would be just like Audrey Hepburn, she would wear elegant little dresses and have romantic adventures with glamorous older men. Or she would be just like Katharine Hepburn, she would wear perfectly cut trousers and stride into a room with authority and grace.

As it turned out, she was just a secretary in a talent agency. People came and went, barely noticing the girls who brought them coffee. And then one day Allen Cooper came in and swept her off to dinner.

"Hungry?" Allen had asked. She'd nodded and hadn't realized till afterward that he'd been talking about food. He was the sort of man who said "Pick you up at seven" without asking if she were free or telling her exactly where they were going. Anne was pretty sure men like that didn't exist anymore.

And then there was Lyon. Had they ever gone on a real first date? He was just there, another agent in the office, the good-looking one with the British accent, the man who flirted with everyone. One afternoon she was sitting at her desk, typing a letter, and he came around and stood behind her. He was saying something—telling a story, repeating a joke, she couldn't remember—and she felt as though all the cells of her body were rearranging themselves in his presence. It was like a science experiment from the third grade: spread the metal filings out across a piece of cardboard, hold the magnet underneath the cardboard, watch the metal rearrange itself in the shape of the magnet.

She couldn't see him, but she could feel his breath on her neck. *He is going to seduce me,* she thought, and then a minute later, *I am going to let him seduce me.* It happened in a hotel room, and afterward, shy and beaming, she wrapped herself in a rented sheet.

And then there was Kevin Gillian. Lyon was in England, he had left the agency and was writing a novel; it seemed he might never come back. Kevin took her to a party and flirted with her gently—he was older, courtly, almost paternal—and she never for a moment considered that it was anything other than a little harmless business socializing. At the end of the party he held her coat for her, and as she slid into it, she felt him lift her hair from underneath her collar and smooth it across her shoulders. When he kissed her, he held her throat with the tips of his fingers.

Beautiful women were his work. He ran a cosmetics empire—makeup, perfume, hair care, a dozen different product lines—and installed Anne as his princess. She traveled with him, she modeled for him, she entertained for him. Their sex was not passionate, but it was enthusiastic and varied. He liked to keep the lights on and watch her move. He would not rest until she had come twice. *It is what it is,* Anne thought. He made her very rich, and he cared for her as much as she cared for him: just enough to keep it going, just enough to keep both of them from looking elsewhere.

And then Lyon came back. Now that it was over, now that it was years later and she could barely remember the heat of their first years together, Anne tallied it up on one hand. Four men. She had only ever kissed four men, had slept with only two, had never been on one real date.

I am totally unequipped, she thought now, looking at Curtis's wide blackboard. She sat at her desk and let her head drop onto her folded arms, and her eyes filled with tears. The years when men sought her

out, the years of being pursued and seduced, the years of letting the world come
to her, they were all over now. She was single, and she was lonely, and she had no
idea how to make things different.

Curtis came in, carrying a bag of crois-
sants and fresh coffee.

"Annie!" he cried. "I have just done the
most awful, wonderful thing. You are going
to kill me, but you have to kiss me first."

She lifted her head and smiled. "I'm
afraid to ask."

"I've fixed you up on a date! A blind date!
With the most delicious man. He's a banker,
he used to be married to my cousin Camille,
you know, horrible Camille with the fake
teeth. He lives in Connecticut, and he does
something terribly important for one of
those terribly famous investment firms.
Long story short: He's in New York for a few
days and he called to see if I wanted to
have dinner, and I told him that unfortu-
nately I was way too busy but could I send
a stand-in."

"Curtis, you didn't."

"Oh Annie, I did. Listen, this one is a
catch. And he's totally available. So call

Miss Gretchen because you've got a big date tomorrow night."

"Tomorrow?"

"He's only in town for three days. Oh, this is so exciting. You must promise me that you won't move to Connecticut until the summer is over. I need you at least through Labor Day."

"Curtis, I haven't even met him yet. And, I don't know. A blind date. I've never been on a blind date."

"Annie darling, there are countries, entire continents, where people get blind *married.* So I think you can handle one blind date. Think of it as practice."

"Tell me more about him."

"What do you need to know? Isn't it enough that I approve of him? His name is Bill Carter, and he has a good job and a full head of hair and about four hundred women chasing after him. You're not supposed to be giving me a hard time. You're supposed to be down on your knees, saying, 'Thank you, Curtis, I'm so grateful to you, Curtis.' "

"I'm so grateful to you, Curtis."

"Promise me you'll wear that little blue suit with the gold buttons."

"I promise." She smiled. "A date. I hope I can remember what to do."

"It's like riding a bicycle, except you get to wear lipstick. Oh, this has put me in such a good mood."

"It's sort of scary to watch. I think you're even more excited about this than I am."

"I'm delirious with glee! I can't wait!"

"Oh Curtis. It's just a blind date. It may not work out. Don't get your hopes up."

"Honey, this is going to be even more fun for me than it is for you. You get to go on a date, but I get to do something better." He lifted a croissant and slowly twisted it apart, smiling like an old-time movie villain. "I get to tell Camille. I get to call her up tomorrow night and tell her that her ex-husband is dating Anne Welles, the former Gillian Girl!"

Neely sat in front of the vanity, flossing her back teeth. She hated flossing. It was unbelievable to her that here in the most expensive hotel in New York City, a place where you could call someone to do practically anything and everything, she still had to floss her own teeth. You paid someone to wash your hair, you paid someone to tweeze your eyebrows, you paid someone to bring your meals and walk your dogs, but flossing was something you still had to do yourself.

She could hear Dave gargling in the bathroom. Good old Dave. They had been seeing each other for nearly a year, and it had gotten boring months ago, but he was too good for her career to let go of just yet. He took her to all the right parties, and her picture was in the papers all the time now. She had recorded the theme song for the new James Bond movie that was scheduled for release in a couple of weeks, which guaranteed she'd be back on the radio all summer long.

And she would probably get an Emmy nomination for a guest role on a courtroom drama he owned a piece of. Originally Dave hadn't thought her right for the part (the wife of a record-company executive murdered by a teenage fan), but she'd finally talked him into it. Not that talking had anything to do with it. It hadn't taken Neely long to figure out when was the best time to ask Dave for favors: he might be a killer negotiator at the office, but in the bedroom she knew just what buttons to push.

Tonight she had a big favor to ask. She was wearing a black lace nightgown over a black satin bra that fastened in the front. She cupped her breasts, lifted them two inches, released them, lifted them, and dropped them again. She wished she hadn't let Dave talk her out of a breast lift. In six weeks they'd be back in the Hamptons, which meant string bikinis and the whole world staring at her boobs. Why did she have to listen to him, anyway, it was her body. Six weeks: plenty of time for a lift and maybe some little implants, too.

Dave came up behind her and stroked her hair. He was wearing the pair of gray-striped silk pajamas she had ordered from London. He caught her eye in the mirror and smiled.

"You look gorgeous tonight. I couldn't wait to get you home."

She leaned her head against him and closed her eyes. "It was a fun party." She rubbed her head back and forth.

"Mmm. That feels nice."

"Honey, why don't you give me a party this summer. My birthday's coming up."

"Sure, baby. There's that new restaurant

that opened over the winter, we can rent the whole place."

"I meant a real party. At the house. You have that great big house with all that land out back, and you never give any parties."

"Too much work."

Neely could feel him starting to get hard. She leaned forward. "Too much money, you mean."

"It's not about the money. Don't stop, that feels nice. You know it isn't about money."

"Then what is it about? What's the point of having that kind of house if you never throw parties?"

"A big party like that takes over your whole life. My ex-wife used to give one every summer, and it nearly gave her a nervous breakdown. What's the matter with going to a restaurant? What's the difference?"

"It's different, that's all. Everyone knows it's different." Neely knew exactly the kind of party she wanted and what kind of people would be on the guest list. "You don't have to do any work, you can hire these people who do everything for you."

"It's too late anyway, all the weekend nights are pretty much booked."

Neely leaned back again. "There might be a Saturday night in August that's still open."

"Mmmm. Okay, I'll think about it."

"Promise?"

"Promise."

She turned around and loosened the drawstring of his pajamas. "Are you thinking about it right now?"

"I'm thinking about it right now."

"You keep on thinking about it, then. Don't stop thinking about it."

She took the tip of him in her mouth and swirled her tongue around him three times. She began to work the length of him, her tongue flicking from side to side, her fingers circling the base of him.

He was all the way hard now. She took him out of her mouth and gave him a squeeze.

"Don't stop now," he said.

"Oh baby," she said, teasing him with her fingers. "Don't I always give you everything you want?" She began again, sucking harder, waiting for the low moans that meant he was about to come. Her tongue was everywhere, her fingers, too; it had been months since she'd blown him this way, since she'd let him come in her mouth.

He was moments away from it. She stopped again and held him against her cheek.

"Not yet," she said. "Not just yet."

"You're killing me."

"How bad do you want it?"

"As bad as it gets."

"And what would you do for it?"

"Anything you want. Anything."

She began again, first slowly, then quicker, then slowly again, and when his moaning started she pressed two fingers hard into him, all the way in the back, and she did not stop, and he realized now that she would not stop, that she was all his, that everything was his. He watched himself come, her lipstick all smeared, watched her inhale, exhale, swallow, inhale again.

Afterward, in bed, he pulled at the edge of her nightgown.

"You don't have to," she said. "Just hold me."

In a few minutes he was out. When he began to snore, she lifted his sleep-heavy arm from around her waist and went to the sitting room to make a cup of tea. She wasn't tired at all. She got out the hotel stationery and began to make lists. A list of

Dave's friends, a list of her friends, a list of the people they owed invitations to, a list of the people who could help get her work.

"Come Celebrate Neely O'Hara's 34th Birthday!" she wrote across the top of one page.

That didn't look right at all.

"Neely O'Hara Turns 34!" she tried again, but that looked even worse. Maybe the party consultant could help her with the wording. She could visualize the invitations, purple ink on heavy pink stock.

She gave it one more try. "NEELY O'HARA HITS THE BIG THREE-OH!"

Perfect.

The next night, they went downtown for dinner with some of Dave's friends. It was the kind of restaurant Neely hated: the crowd was full of television people and models, and the food was bistro French, which made it nearly impossible to stick to the high-protein, no-carbs diet she had been on for the last five weeks. But Dave loved any place that was hard to get into, and right now this was the hardest table in New York City.

The conversation was all about deals and numbers and network gossip. Dave's friends both worked in television, the husband in news, the wife in sports. There wasn't anything either of them would ever be able to do for Neely, so she let her mind wander and checked out what the models were wearing.

There, just two tables away, sat Anne Burke and a man she didn't recognize. Neely watched them talking or, rather, watched the man talk while Anne smiled.

"Oh, my God, she's on a date!" Neely cried.

"What?" said the wife.

"Someone I used to know. Long story."

The wife turned and looked. "Oh, I know him."

"Oh yeah, who is he?" Neely asked.

She lowered her voice and nodded slightly toward her husband. "You first."

"Okay. Anne Burke, but I guess she's back to being Anne Welles now. Up until a few months ago she was Mrs. Lyon Burke. Know him at all?"

"A little, from parties. I've heard the stories, of course."

"Yeah, well, they're all true. Guy couldn't

keep his pants zipped if you paid him a million dollars." The men continued their separate conversation. Neely leaned over and whispered, "And she never knew about any of it."

"You mean she never wanted to know."

"Whatever. Little Miss Priss. Butter wouldn't melt in her mouth, or anywhere else, for that matter. We used to be friends, but once they moved to Fifth Avenue, if you weren't on the social register, you were off the list."

"I think they say *in* the social register."

"Oh yeah? On it, in it, whatever. She dropped all her old friends like that." Neely snapped her fingers. "They are definitely on a date."

"How can you tell?"

"Body language. Look how they're both using their hands when they talk."

"So, did you . . . ever?"

"Ever what?"

"You know. Lyon Burke."

"Now that's a personal question."

The wife shrugged. "Okay, my turn, I'll go first." She named two football players, three tennis stars, the owner of a baseball team, and a basketball coach who had just written a best-selling book on personal motivation.

"Wow."

"Before I was married, of course."

"Good thing your husband can't hear us."

"Are you kidding? He loves it. And he loves that people know it. He'd find a way to tell them himself if it wasn't in such bad taste. Makes him feel like a stud. Why do you think he went out with me in the first place? Sometimes I think everything our mothers told us was wrong. If you fuck a lot of guys no one has heard of, you're a slut. But if you fuck a lot of famous guys, you're a prize. Okay. Your turn."

Neely thought a moment. Lyon Burke, but so what? A bunch of Hollywood people, some actors, some directors, some producers, but so what? What she really wanted to be able to say was, "I fucked the king of England," or, "I fucked the president of the United States." But there was no king of England. And there hadn't been a fuckable president since Marilyn Monroe was alive. All these newspaper columnists whining about why nobody cared about politics anymore, when to Neely the answer was obvious: Put a good-looking man in the

White House, and people would start caring again.

She threw a few names across the table to even things up. "So, who's the guy?" she asked.

"His name is Bill Carter, and everyone at the network worships him because he got all his big clients out of the market before the crash. He used to be married to my friend Camille, but about five years ago he came home early and found her IFD with another woman. Nasty divorce."

"IFD?"

"In flagrante delicto."

"He was married to a lesbian?"

"Oh, Camille isn't a lesbian. Camille isn't really anything. She was just bored, you know, stuck up there in Connecticut all day, drinking margaritas by the tennis court, one thing leads to another, you know how it goes." The woman lifted an eyebrow. Neely wondered whether this was a kind of pass. "I just had the wickedest idea."

"Oh yeah?" Neely said.

"Let's send them a bottle of wine."

Neely laughed. "You are wicked."

"A bottle of really expensive wine."

"A bottle of really expensive wine and half a dozen oysters!" Neely signaled the waiter.

"Who shall I say it's from?" the waiter asked.

"Old friends," Neely said.

"Don't turn around," Bill said to Anne when the wine and oysters arrived. "Just keep smiling and keep looking at me."

"Who is it from?" Anne asked.

"A friend of my ex-wife's. I'm so sorry about this. It was one of those divorces where everyone had to take sides."

"Is there any other kind? At least it's a very nice wine."

"I'm going to send it back."

"Don't give her the satisfaction. You know that whatever you do, she's just going to run home and tell your ex about it."

"In that case, let's pour the wine and have a toast. And you have to promise me you'll look into my eyes longingly the whole time. If we're going to give her a story, let's give her a really good story."

They fake-flirted throughout dinner, touching each other as they talked. Bill told her about growing up in Greenwich, about his three children, all in college now, and his work at the bank. Anne talked about Jenn and life in Southampton. Though Bill was ten years older, and had gone to Yale, they knew a few people in common. A partner of Bill's who lived in Anne's old building. Bill's younger brother, an architect who lived in Bridgehampton. A friend of Anne's from college, who had married and moved to Greenwich. *Suitable* was the word Anne kept thinking of, *entirely suitable.* He was exactly the kind of man she had been bred to marry: loyal, responsible, conservative, good-looking in a sturdy sort of way, and not the least bit exciting.

They both drank more than they had planned to. Bill called for the check. "How are you getting home?" he asked. "It's too late to drive back."

"I do it all the time," Anne lied. Her car was parked in a cheap outdoor lot on the far side of the West Side Highway. She prayed the engine would start.

"That's crazy. I've got a car coming. The driver can drop me off at my hotel, and then he can take you out to Southampton."

Anne tried to calculate what this would cost.

"It's a company car, I've got to pay him for the whole night whether he takes you home or not. Please."

She was about to say yes when she saw Neely approach. *Thin again,* thought Anne. The clothes were a surprise: in a scoop-neck black T-shirt, well-cut black trousers, and black boots, Neely looked nearly elegant. There was still a little too much jewelry (bracelets on both wrists, and complicated earrings that did not quite work with her loose shoulder-length hair), and there was still that soft line of dark blue eye-pencil smudged into her lower lashes. But the Neely who stood before her was so different from the Neely she carried around in her memory that Anne found herself wondering whether it was really possible, how much could one person change? *She's an actress,* thought Anne, *and on the inside, surely the same.*

How long had it been? Years? Anne could not recall the last time they had talked.

"Like the wine?" Neely said. She extended her hand to Bill. "Neely O'Hara. Old friend of Anne's."

Bill stood up. "Bill Carter. New friend of Anne's."

"You sent the wine?" Anne asked.

"Whodja think?" Neely said.

"It was lovely," Anne said.

Bill excused himself to call for the car.

"Don't mind if I do," Neely said, taking his seat. "So. You're looking good."

"You too," Anne said. "You look . . . you look happy and rested."

Neely laughed. "Yeah, I took a big long rest on the Isle of Collagen. Listen. I have a favor to ask."

"Do you."

"Come on. I know all about your divorce. Let's let bygones be bygones."

"That's easier said than done, Neely."

"Fine. You got something you want to say to me, spit it out."

"I don't have anything to say to you."

"Really?"

"I just wish you would go away."

"Well, I'm not going away. In fact, we're both going to be in the Hamptons this summer, and we know plenty of the same people, so let's find a way to bury the hatchet already."

"It's not so easy."

"Why not? Who cares about Lyon anymore, anyway? You look like you're doing all right with Bill What's-his-name."

"I barely know him. We just met." Anne was sorry as soon as she said it.

"Oh yeah? Whaddaya know. You looked awfully cozy over those oysters. I would have guessed—" She watched Anne pull back. "Oh, never mind. I just thought, you know, why give Lyon the satisfaction? Why still act like we're fighting over him? I mean, I can barely remember anything about him. It was so long ago, and I was wrecked the whole time. He turned out to be a big loser. He didn't deserve you, Anne, he never did."

"Let's change the subject, Neely."

"Okay. Never mind."

"So. What's the favor."

"Dave's giving me this big party in August. For my thirtieth birthday."

"A little late for your thirtieth birthday, don't you think?"

"That's the favor. If you could just, you know, let it slide about my age."

"Why should I?"

"I can help you, Anne."

"Help me what?"

"Come on. You think I don't know the

score? This is a small town, I hear all the gossip, Dave has a lot of friends and boy, do they love to gossip. I know this much: You're broke, and you can't get any work."

"You can stop now, I get the point."

"Like I said, I can help you. I can help you big-time. And all you need to do is sort of forget the year I was born in. How hard is that?"

"We're not friends anymore, Neely. I don't want to be friends with you ever again."

"Sometimes we don't have a choice."

"Meaning what, exactly."

"It's just how life works. We don't get to choose our families. And we don't get to choose the people we love, either. Think about it. Did you really choose to fall in love with Lyon? Or did it just happen?"

Anne swirled what was left of her wine. "It just happened."

"And friends are the same way. Think about who your friends are. We can choose the people we hang around with, but we can't really choose our friends."

Bill was back, shaking his head. "So sorry, there was a line for the phone. The car will be around in just a few minutes."

Neely stood up. "Well, anyway, Anne. You

think about it. And see ya in the Hamptons." She turned to Bill. "Very nice to meet you. You don't look like a banker."

"What does that mean?"

"Oh, it's definitely a compliment. Gotta go."

The car was an enormous dark blue Lincoln. Inside, jazz was playing. Bill took her hand. She felt woozy from all the wine, from the oysters and the too rich sauces.

"I want to kiss you," Bill said. "But I'm not sure you want to kiss me."

"I . . . I don't know what I want."

"Surely you don't want to be alone."

"No one wants to be alone. But I haven't been with anyone since the divorce, and, I don't know. I'm a little bit at sea."

"Close your eyes."

He kissed her. It was a perfect kiss, but she felt nothing. Perfect evening, perfect man, perfect kiss, and inside she felt absolutely nothing.

"I see," he said. "Well. Look, this is the part where I say I'm going to call you, but I think I'd rather wait for you to call me." He handed her his business card. "Whenever you're ready."

They pulled up in front of his hotel. Anne

had a sudden urge to follow him up to his room, to get wildly drunk and let him pull off her clothes and have the kind of messy, wild sex that she should have had in college, would have had if she hadn't married Lyon so young. She wanted to act as if there were no consequences, act as if nothing mattered, act on impulse—in short, she wanted to act as if she were someone else entirely.

"Thank you for a lovely evening," she said. "Dinner was wonderful."

"So Neely O'Hara is an old friend of yours?" Bill asked.

Anne smiled. "Not really a friend," she said. "And not really so old."

Anne kept Bill's card in her handbag for the rest of May. The first weekend in June, she and Gretchen spent two days in a whirlwind of housework, washing the curtains, rearranging the silverware drawers, reorganizing the closets, and the card ended up in a pile of bills that didn't need to be paid quite yet.

"Where do you want these?" Gretchen asked, pointing to three shoeboxes filled with old snapshots from Anne's first years in New York.

"Oh God, I can barely bring myself to think about those anymore," said Anne.

"Can I peek?"

"I guess," Anne said.

The photograph of Anne with Neely and Jennifer North was on top.

"Wow, you were a total babe!" Gretchen cried. "Oh, I'm sorry, I mean you're still a babe. But this picture. You were a babe-and-a-half!"

It was a photograph Jennifer had taken with a self-timing camera set up on a dresser top. The three of them were in a hotel room, getting ready to go to a party in Beverly Hills.

"Man oh man, look at your hair," Gretchen said.

"I don't miss hot rollers," Anne said with a laugh.

"Who is she?" Gretchen asked, pointing.

"Jennifer North."

"She's . . . she's beautiful. She's more than beautiful. She's perfect. You guys were friends?"

"Best friends." Anne told her the story, how Jennifer had been discovered, the movies she had made, the men she had slept with. "It was a real Hollywood story, the kind that doesn't happen anymore. I haven't heard the phrase 'sex symbol' in ages, but that's really what she was. People looked at her and all they could think about was sex. But there was so much more to her. She was the nicest, sweetest person I ever met. All she wanted was to find some nice man and settle down and have babies."

"So what happened?"

"She finally found the man of her dreams, and then she got breast cancer. And she couldn't bear to tell anybody. Jennifer was a lot of wonderful things, but she wasn't strong. She freaked out when they told her exactly what the surgery would do, and took some sedatives to get through the night. Too many, as it turned out."

"She overdosed?"

"Accidental," Anne lied. "You know, from the minute I found out I was pregnant I just knew it was going to be a girl, and I knew I would name her after Jennifer." She took the photograph from Gretchen and put it back in the box. "Let's put these away before I get all weepy. We still have the whole downstairs to do."

In July, Anne spent a day catching up on bills. She tossed Bill's card in the cut-glass bowl where she saved paperwork to be filed—receipts that might be needed for income taxes, address changes that would be copied over into her Rolodex when Christmas-card time rolled around again.

August was cooler than expected, and sometimes Anne awoke in the morning wrapped up like a mummy in her summer quilts. It was amazing what could happen to the bedclothes when you slept alone. One morning she woke up to find she had completely reversed herself—her head pressed against the foot of the bed—with the three extra pillows piled on top of her back.

It was the day of Neely's party. Curtis had been preparing for it all week. Anne had taken a few days off to spend time with Jenn, who was in a deep sulk after finding out that her trip to visit Lyon in London was being canceled at the last minute. *Too much work, trouble on the set,* Lyon had told them. *Too much fun, a new girlfriend on the set,* Anne suspected.

Today they were baking berry pies. Gretchen had bought several pints of blueberries at one of the farm stands outside of town. Jenn was watching her roll the cool dough across a floured wooden board.

"I bet we have enough to make four pies," Jenn said.

"At least," Gretchen said.

Just when the last pie was coming out of the oven, Curtis telephoned in a panic.

"I have tragic news. I need you to come over right away."

Anne thought of Jerry—his smoking, his weight. "Oh, my God, what's happened?" she cried.

"It's terrible. Three people called in sick on me this morning. Three of my best people."

"Three? How could three people get sick all at once?"

"Annie, sweetheart, someday when I have the time, when I'm not in total crisis mode, when I don't have one of the biggest parties of the year in four hours and half my staff unconscious in bed with the flu, remind me to explain to you about these little things called germs. Meanwhile, I need you. I desperately need you."

"Anything you need."

"I need you to come over and help with Neely O'Hara's birthday party."

"Except that."

"Please. Pretty please. Pretty please with Robert Redford on top."

"I can't. You know I can't."

"I wouldn't ask if it wasn't an emergency. No one even has to know you're there. You can help with setup and then hide in the kitchen the whole time. But I cannot do this by myself."

"Oh, Curtis. I don't know what to say."

"You don't have a choice. You have to say yes."

"Can I think about it?"

"And Gretchen, I need Gretchen, too. Can she wait tables? Tell her I'll pay her eighty dollars for the night, in cash."

"Someone has to look after Jenn."

"I need both of you. You can bring Jenn, maybe we'll even let her help."

"Curtis, I don't think this is going to work. Anyway, Neely won't want me there."

"What Neely O'Hara wants is a dinner where it doesn't take an hour to serve all the guests. I'll take care of Miss O'Hara."

"Look. I just . . . I just can't."

"You're my friend. I need you."

"It's more complicated than that," Anne said.

"It's never more complicated than that.

Friends help friends. If this party doesn't go well, every potential client between Quogue and Montauk will know about it within twenty-four hours."

"Give me five minutes to think about it."

"Absolutely not. I'll pick you up in an hour. What's Gretchen wearing?"

"Black jeans and a tank top."

"Fine. I'll bring a white shirt for her. Please do something with her hair so it doesn't look so . . . so *mall.* And Annie?"

"Yes, Curtis."

"Remember. I love you a lot."

"I love you, too."

"I love you truly and deeply, the way only an aging queen with a weight problem can love the most beautiful ex-supermodel in the universe."

Anne hung up and turned to Jenn and Gretchen. "Guess what?" she said. "We're going to a party."

"Whose party?" Jenn asked. "Is it going to be fun?"

"It's not that kind of party," Anne said.

Anne was in the kitchen, watching the pastry chef dust two hundred pieces of flourless chocolate cake with powdered sugar in the shape of a comet. Gretchen was outside, clearing dinner dishes and trying not to stare too hard at all the celebrities. Jenn was upstairs with Neely's son Judd, losing at Monopoly. Dylan was locked in his room with the headphones on, listening to the Beastie Boys.

Neely was outside, under the stars, waltzing across the midnight-blue dance floor that had been built next to the tennis court and stenciled with various constellations: Orion, the Big Dipper, Sagittarius. Originally Neely had wanted a circus-themed party, striped tenting and jugglers and rented animals. Curtis had talked her into an astronomy theme by saying three magic words: "It seems classier." They were the same words he had used to talk her out of the belly dancer, the see-through dress, the individual strawberry-cheesecake desserts.

There was a new moon and a clear sky. At the far corners of the lawn, large rented telescopes were set up, manned by astronomy students brought out from the city. Guests lined up to look at the rings of Saturn and the tail of a minor comet.

Neely swirled around the floor with George Dunbar's wife's cousin, a senator from the Midwest visiting on vacation. Candlelight reflected off the folds of her dress, a simple silvery knit, cut straight with slits at the side for dancing and a deep V-neck that showed off the new cleavage she had bought in Palm Springs.

"I'm having a wonderful time," he said, looking down at her chest.

"Me too. Dave is such a doll. I didn't even want this party, but he insisted, he practically had to twist my arm, and I'm so glad he did." Where was Dave? He had left the table just as the main course was cleared to go get the cigars, but that was at least ten minutes ago. She looked over the senator's shoulder and saw Dave leaning over a telescope with a young redhead in a tight green dress. Probably someone's date. The woman had long legs, impossibly long legs, the kind of legs that Dave couldn't help but check out when he and Neely went to the beach together.

Each time Neely circled back around with the senator, she found Dave and the girl, still stargazing together. It was probably harmless flirting—Dave was a producer, maybe the girl was an actress, so it went—

but it seemed to be going on a little too long. And those legs. There were so many parts of the body to nip, to tuck, to lift, to augment or reduce, to peel and inject. But so far there was nothing anyone could do about Neely's not-quite-long-enough legs.

The photographer appeared with a fresh roll of film just as the band segued into a Latin number.

"Oh, I gotta go fix my face," Neely said. "You made me work up a sweat!"

"I apologize."

She winked. "I kinda like it." Everyone said he had the happiest marriage in the Senate, but you never knew. She didn't want to let go of Dave until she had a better prospect all lined up.

"You should come visit us in Washington sometime."

"I'd love to. I love Washington. And of course I'd love to meet your wife."

"My wife travels a lot," the senator said.

"If I were married to a man like you, I wouldn't leave you alone for a minute."

"And if I were married to a woman like you, I wouldn't leave you alone, either." They walked together toward the bar. "But that's the sad thing about life, isn't it? People like me don't get to marry people like you."

"What exactly does that mean?" Neely asked.

"I meant it as a compliment. You know. A beautiful woman with a past." He signaled to the bartender. "But you must come visit us sometime."

"Yeah, sure," Neely said. She watched him order a very expensive glass of Cognac. She walked back to the house, her face burning. What was worse? That men like him would never think her good enough? Or that they thought it so obvious, they didn't mind saying it?

There was Anne at the kitchen table, making checkmarks on a pink index card.

"Everything going okay?" Neely asked.

"Just peachy."

"You're a peach for helping out. Hey, who is that waitress with the pink lipstick?"

"I'm not sure who you mean."

"You know. Bad dye job, black jeans a little too tight, some pretty nasty acne scars."

"Oh. You mean Gretchen. She's my baby-sitter, actually. She's pinch-hitting as a favor to Curtis."

"Yeah, well, can you assign her to another table?"

"Has she done something wrong?"

"Nope, I just want her at another table. Put her at table ten," Neely said. That's where she had placed all the obligation guests: her accountant and his wife, Dave's cousins, and various unglamorous neighbors. Gretchen was not especially attractive—bad skin, large nose, and a terrible overbite that there had never been money to fix—but from the neck down she was gorgeous, and Dave had noticed, and Neely had noticed Dave noticing.

"No trouble," Anne said. "I'll send over one of the guys. Whatever you like." *Whatever, whatever, whatever,* she thought. Earlier in the evening, nervous about whom she might run into, Anne had taken some Xanax. The pill had kicked in just as the first guest was arriving. It was the loveliest feeling, like falling back into a soft, deep featherbed. She had brought another, just in case, but so far no one had come into the kitchen except Neely and Dave.

Upstairs, Neely applied more powder and another coat of lipstick. One of her sandals felt a little wobbly; she saw that the heel was beginning to separate from the sole. She went to the big walk-in closet at the far end of the master bedroom to find another pair of sandals. What went with silver? White? Black patent leather? She switched on the closet light and heard the pop of the light bulb giving out. She sat on the floor of the closet, feeling her way along the rows of shoes, trying to figure out, from the curve of a heel or the width of a strap, which pair was which.

Someone came into the bedroom.

"I just love seeing these big old East Hampton houses," a woman was saying. "You have the most fabulous artwork."

"My ex picked out most of it," Dave said.

Neely caught her breath. The voice sounded young, not like anyone she could identify.

"How ex?" the woman asked.

"Very ex."

"How long have you been with Neely O'Hara?"

"A little over a year."

"I love her records. My mother was a huge fan. I can't wait to tell her I got a tour of Neely O'Hara's house."

"It's my house. Her house is in Los Angeles."

I should get up right now, Neely thought, but she stayed cross-legged on the floor of the closet, leaning forward a little so she could see them both through the open door.

"Well," the girl said. "She's a very lucky woman. I bet they were falling all over you, after you split with your wife."

"Not really."

"Oh, come on. An attractive guy like you? I bet you had to fight them off."

"Not really."

Neely watched the woman push the bedroom door closed and twist the lock.

"Hey," Dave said.

"Hey yourself," she said. "You know I'm really attracted to you. You have a really . . . a really powerful presence."

"I can't do this."

"I know you feel it, too. I can tell when you look at me."

"We should go back down."

"All right." She leaned against the wall and began hiking up the green dress, over her knees, up past her waist. "I just want you to see what you're missing."

"Come on, this isn't the time."

"I can make you come in two minutes."

She slipped a hand into her lace bikini. "I'm already wet just thinking about you."

"Hey, come on. I think you've had a little too much to drink."

"And it was such lovely champagne. . . . mmm. You can just watch if you want." She closed her eyes and began breathing through her mouth. Dave moved toward her, undoing his trousers. She wrapped a leg around his waist and clasped her hands behind his neck.

It didn't even take two minutes. She pulled down her dress and smoothed the back of her hair.

"I can't believe we did that," Dave said.

"I knew I was going to fuck you the minute I saw you."

"I have to get back to the party."

"Right, the party. Hey, how well do you know Jamie Walters?"

"Well enough. We've worked together on a couple of things."

"I'm auditioning for him next week. A cable show, women's lifestyle stuff? Gardening, cooking, decorating, like that. Maybe you could put in a word?"

"I thought you lived in Phoenix."

"I'm thinking of moving back here. If I got

this job. We could be neighbors. You could come by and borrow a cup of sugar any old time."

"Let me think about it," Dave said, unlocking the door. "You wait a minute here, I don't want anyone seeing us together."

The woman went to Neely's dressing table and fluffed up her bangs. She picked up a few perfume bottles, examined their labels, and then dabbed some Chanel No. 22 behind her knees. Neely lay down on the floor of the closet. It wasn't fair; it was her party and everything was turning out wrong. All the vitamins in the world couldn't make this feeling go away.

Downstairs, Anne had snuck into the back bathroom behind the kitchen to pop another half tab of Xanax. She ran the tap water with the lights off, drinking from her cupped hands.

Through the open window she could see the couples dancing, hear the old Cole Porter tune that Lyon used to hum in her ear. She watched Stella and Arthur taking a dip in the corner of the floor. She watched people who had called once or twice, inviting her to a lunch or afternoon at the ballet. She watched people who had invited her daughter over for a play date, sharing a quick and awkward cup of coffee with her when she came to pick up Jenn. She watched people who had never called at all.

Not that she had found any of these parties so thrilling when she was invited to them. But now, leaning against the cold porcelain in a small, dark bathroom, she felt the bright red rage of a woman who has been overlooked. She was Cinderella without glass slippers, without a Prince Charming to carry her away. She was stuck, and no one seemed to notice.

When the pill kicked in, she turned on the light and looked in the mirror. Back to work. The check would help cover her real estate taxes, and maybe even a facial. She sure needed one.

Neely came down to find Anne counting out soup spoons, humming along with the band.

"There you are," Anne said. "Dave was looking for you."

"I bet. Get me a glass of champagne, will ya?"

Anne lifted an eyebrow.

"It's just champagne. Oh, all right, never mind, I'll get it myself." Neely poured herself a glass and sat down at the table. "So, how's the auditioning going?" No matter how bad things were for Neely, they were worse for Anne. This little chat would be just the thing to cheer Neely up.

"Could be better. I almost had a great commercial, but then they canceled the campaign."

"You're kidding."

"I wish."

"Well, something else will come along. Hey, I have an idea. I know about this great job."

"Neely, you don't have to. A deal's a deal." Anne noticed how quickly Neely went through the champagne. "Happy thirtieth birthday, kiddo."

"Yeah, right. Listen. I know a guy in cable, he's auditioning for someone to host a women's lifestyle show. Cooking, gardening, decorating, like that. Want me to put in a word?"

"That's okay."

"What, an old friend can't do you a favor?"

"I don't need your help."

"Fine, whatever," Neely said. "You know, make a point if you want to, but you know who you're really hurting? That ten-year-old kid upstairs. Anyway. Never keep the photographers waiting," she said, chugging the last of her champagne.

Fifteen minutes later a fat man with thick gray hair came in, holding a freshly lit cigar.

"Are you Anne Welles? What am I saying. Of course you are. You haven't changed a bit." He held out his hand. "Jamie Walters."

"Hello. I'm sorry, I can't quite place you."

"Neely sent me in here to meet you. She said you might be interested in a little cable project I'm working on." He gave her his business card. "Can you call me on Monday? What am I saying. Of course you can call me on Monday." He left without waiting for her answer.

After the plates were cleared, after the band went home, after the final cup of coffee was served and the last few guests wandered down the long driveway, after Gretchen carried a dozing Jenn piggyback to her car, after Neely and Dave went upstairs and the staff packed up, Anne went outside to find Curtis smoking a cigarette and looking through one of the telescopes.

"What a beautiful night," he said. "Have a peek."

Anne took a look. "I don't know what anything is," she said.

"It doesn't matter."

Anne walked to her car through the damp grass. It was a half-hour ride home. Trees arched over the road like a canopy. Van Morrison was on the radio, a song she had heard a hundred times without really listening to it. She turned up the volume and it felt as though he were singing directly to her, in a wise, clear voice full of sadness and hope and magic.

She had been down this road a hundred times, too, more than a hundred times, but it looked different to her now, as if every little thing—the street lamps twinkling between the trees, a white balloon caught on a traffic signal, a bouquet of roses abandoned on the hood of a parked car—had a special message for her. *I never noticed anything when I was with Lyon,* she thought, *and here it all is, here it all is.*

She was home by three. Jenn and Gretchen were eating blueberry pie straight from the tin.

"We can't sleep, Mom," Jenn said. "So we're going to stay up all night."

"I tried," Gretchen said.

"That's okay. Give me a fork," Anne said.

Gretchen could not stop talking about all the famous people she had seen, what they had worn and said and how much they had drunk. A rock-and-roll singer had given her his autograph on the back of a menu card . . . a soap opera actress had told her she had pretty eyes . . . had Anne noticed that the radio talk-show host was wearing a toupee? . . .

"I would have worked for free," Gretchen said.

"Don't tell Curtis that."

"And I got a tip!" she said, taking a hundred-dollar bill out of her pocket.

Jenn was all sugared up and giggling. She described everything in Judd's room: his computer, his collection of CDs, his science-fiction posters. "And he gave me this shirt!"

It was an old plaid-flannel shirt, coming apart at the elbows.

"I guess he must have liked you," Anne said.

"It's called Black Watch," Jenn said.

"He's almost sixteen, but I still beat him at Monopoly two times."

The sky was beginning to brighten. They had nearly finished a second pie.

"When does the sun come up, Mom?"

"Soon, sweetie." When was the last time she had seen the sun come up? She thought back: months ago, the night she left Lyon. A beautiful thing happened every day, a million beautiful things; you only had to go looking for them.

"Let's get the sleeping bags and go outside to watch," Anne said. They made cocoa and dragged the deck chairs out onto the lawn.

"We have to whisper," Jenn said. "Everyone is sleeping."

"But we're wide awake," Gretchen said.

Anne pulled her sleeping bag just up to her eyes. Underneath the soft down, she was smiling. *So: this is my life. So: this is my family.* It wasn't very much, but right now it seemed like more than enough. Right now it seemed perfect.

1989.

Neely closed the script and tossed it on the floor. There was no point in finishing it—it was like all the other movie scripts she was getting these days, junk that everyone else had already turned down. Mothers, mob wives, and hookers. Like she was going to play the mother of some twenty-three-year-old brat with two pictures under his belt!

She stretched her legs under the covers and took another sip of herbal tea. It was already eleven in the morning, but she still hadn't gotten dressed or checked her telephone messages. What was the point? There was nothing to do in Los Angeles during the day except have lunch and shop. She didn't want to eat with anyone; the Oscars were in three weeks and she really needed to lose five pounds. And she didn't feel like shopping—not until she was back down to her target weight.

She had turned off the ringer on the telephone, but she could hear the little click of someone leaving a message. Probably just Gordon, good old Gordon. He had booked her for three weeks in Las Vegas at the end of May, and it was the best contract she had ever gotten.

At least someone was out there working for her. Her new film agency wasn't doing anything except sending her lousy scripts, as far as she could tell. Neely didn't like these new guys, even if everyone said they were the best. Their office gave her the creeps—it was all pale colors and polished surfaces and Abstract art on the walls. It was like visiting a law firm. She missed the good old days, the autographed pictures and the men in bad toupees who offered you hugs and dirty jokes. The new guys wore thousand-dollar suits and two-hundred-dollar sunglasses, and behind the glasses their eyes were cold and expressionless. They were like the FBI, but with better haircuts.

And it was costing her a fortune, even if she didn't shoot a single frame. Dave had made her set up her own production company—that was the way it worked, everyone did it, you had to get a piece of the pie. So now she paid some girl three minutes out of film school a ridiculously high salary to sit in an office all day and do God knew what. It seemed to Neely that she was basically paying someone to sit around reading magazines. Liza wore little black eyeglasses and size 38 Armani jackets. When Neely visited the office, all she could think about was how much those jackets cost and where the money had come from. Plus the secretary, plus the expense account, plus the fresh flowers, plus the rent. It drove her crazy, so now she went by only once or twice a month. It was just a very expensive place to go for a pee if you were driving around and needed a place to stop.

She felt as though she were stalled in bad traffic on a hot summer day: angry and impatient, with nowhere to go.

"Take it easy," Dave had told her. "You have plenty of work and plenty of money and two great kids. And me. Life is to be enjoyed."

"Maybe you're exactly where you want to be, but I want more," she told him. "There'll be plenty of time to stop and smell the roses when I'm old and fat and my voice is gone. I remember what it used to be like. I want to make movies again. I want another Oscar."

"Be patient. It'll happen."

"Not if I don't make it happen. Cher got a fucking Oscar. Cher! That part shoulda been mine."

"Come on, Neely."

"Someone should have sent me that script."

"Neely, the movie took place in Little Italy. Not Little Ireland."

"Well, Cher isn't Italian. She's Albanian."

"Armenian."

"Stop correcting me, you're always correcting me. Pardon me if I didn't go to college, I was too busy making two hit records and winning an Oscar and, oh yeah, having a couple of babies."

"I didn't mean it that way."

"Yes, you did. You never let me forget it. You and your fancy friends. Looking down your noses at me because maybe I had to work my way up to get where I am, it wasn't just handed to me on a silver platter."

"Neely, come on. Everyone loves you just the way you are."

What amazed her was this: Dave actually seemed to mean it. No matter how crazy she got, Dave would just ride it out until her temper tantrum passed. He seemed to be able to laugh off her moods without ever making her feel that he was laughing at her.

Neely had always been attracted to men who were older than she, who took care of her and gave her advice and looked after her every need. After a while, the more they did for her, the less respect she had for them. She stopped looking up to them. And one thing she knew: guys like that would always be able to find another woman—someone who didn't know them as well as the woman they were with—to look up to them. Neely never actually had to dump a guy. What she did instead was drive them away. That's what her shrink told her. Dr. Mitchell called it passive-aggressive behavior.

So Dave had the occasional little fling; that was just how men were. So he was fifty-two, and more than a little overweight, and no superstar in the kip. He was appealing in a sort of big Jewish teddy-bear kind of way, and he looked after her, and he was wonderful with the twins, and no matter what she did he kept on loving her. He was also the first man whose success was entirely independent of her own—he had never tried to make a single nickel off her talent.

Neely realized that there was always going to be a better man out there . . . someone more attractive . . . someone richer . . . someone more powerful . . . she would always be able to talk herself into waiting until the perfect man came along. She didn't want to end up like Helen Lawson, dying alone in her suite at the Pierre with nothing but a shelf of awards and four Persian cats to keep her company.

Neely wanted to get married; Dave didn't.

"Why ruin a good thing?" he said. "Marriage changes everything."

But Neely was sick of the magazine captions that described Dave as her "steady"— it was so undignified! She hated all the little phrases they had to use when they traveled together ("my friend" . . . "my guest" . . .

"the lady will have") because they couldn't say "my husband," "my wife." Most of all, she was tired of going out with friends and being the only woman at the table who wasn't wearing a ring. She swore she would find a way to get Dave to propose to her. Maybe in June. He was taking her to Greece, a little vacation on a romantic island that Neely kept forgetting the name of. It would be fun to get engaged before the summer, to show off her diamond at all those parties in the Hamptons. And then a Thanksgiving wedding: perfect.

Neely turned on the television and flipped around. There was Anne, arranging flowers and talking about the history of Holland's obsession with the tulip. The set for *A Woman's Touch* was a huge kitchen with a wide pine table in the center. Guests sat on high stools and drank coffee out of enormous mugs and talked to Anne about cooking and gardening and how to construct fabulous window treatments out of department-store bedsheets. As if Anne had ever had to lift a finger herself. Still, Neely had to admit that Anne looked pretty good on camera.

She went downstairs to make a fresh cup

of tea; two more cups of tea and she'd be able to get through the morning without eating. A stack of newspapers and mail was piled up on the counter. Invitations to parties . . . another manila envelope from Liza . . . some magazines that Dave had picked out for her. . . . She grabbed the New York dailies and got back into bed, turning past the news to the gossip columns.

Vanity Fair's profile of actress **Helen Lawson**, scheduled to hit newsstands next week, has made its way into the hands of several film producers. Lawson died last November at age 62, just two days after taking the final curtain call for her wildly successful revival of *Hit the Sky.* If you ask us, there's enough material in this great lady's life for six movies; they don't make dames like Helen anymore. . . .

A movie based on the life of Helen Lawson! As if anyone still cared about that dried-out has-been bitch. At the end, her voice had been a mere quivering ghost of its former self, full of vibrato and whispery high notes. Much of the score of *Hit the Sky* had been reorchestrated because Helen's vocal range was about half of what it once was. In two of her big numbers, she had even been reduced to talk-singing her way through the more difficult verses. Still, she had performed to a sold-out house every night.

The fags always did love Helen, Neely thought, and then, *I wonder if there will be a character based on me?* Neely had gotten her first big break in one of Helen Lawson's shows, back when she was a pudgy teenager fresh off the summer-stock circuit. Neely tried to imagine who could possibly play her. They would have to get an un-known, a young girl who would steal the movie, like Judy Garland singing "Dear Mr. Gable" in *Broadway Melody of 1938.* Even in death, Helen would be upstaged!

The microwave buzzed; her hot water was ready. *Poor Helen,* she thought, smiling a little, *poor old Helen.*

June came and went without a ring. Neely was spending the summer in New York, working on songs for a new album. On Thursday afternoons, Dave picked her up and they drove out to East Hampton, with a cooler full of cheese on the backseat. Dave had stopped smoking cigars and was now into various kinds of imported cheese that could be gotten only in the city. After dinner he would bring out the cheese and discuss each one with their guests. Neely was on a new diet that didn't allow her to eat any dairy, so she would just sit and smile and nibble at a plate of grapes. Some nights the cheese smelled even worse than the cigars.

Tonight they were going over to George and Sandy Dunbar's house for a small informal dinner party. Just eight people! Neely was wearing a V-neck purple T-shirt, blue jeans, and a pair of black leather sandals with thin straps that buckled around her ankle. She wrapped a navy-blue sweatshirt around her shoulders for when it got cooler. A pair of large gold hoops was her only jewelry, a little bit of mascara and a soft mauve lipstick her only makeup.

She wished the whole world could see her, going over to the Dunbars wearing nothing special, because she had learned, over the last two years, that was the way to do it: the less effort you put into your clothing, the more it showed how close you were to your hosts. But that was the problem with these small get-togethers: no one ever saw you—no press, no photographers, no one to make jealous. It would be just like one of those interviews in *People,* the ones where someone famous, someone with all the money in the world, keeps telling the reporter that what they really like to do is stay home with a few close friends. And now, because of Dave, Neely was one of those friends.

And Sandy would even be cooking! Though Neely had learned what that meant, too. It meant she would be expected to help carry things and possibly even chop a vegetable. Well, that was how these people did it. The ones with the most money were the ones who were allowed to act as if they didn't have any money at all.

They were the first to arrive. George thanked them for the two bottles of Merlot and the wheel of Roquefort that Dave had picked out for after dinner. Sandy hugged Dave and offered her right cheek to Neely for the briefest hello kiss.

"Come into the kitchen," Sandy said after the first glasses of wine were poured. "You can help me with the salad." The kitchen smelled of onions and garlic. Dinner was some sort of Spanish dish that Neely had never heard of. Fish stew was what it looked like. Stew! That was the other thing she had noticed about these rich women: they loved to make stew. And out on the deck, covered with plastic, was an enormous gas grill, top of the line, perfect for steaks.

"So, how's everything?" Sandy asked.

"Well, my boys are coming next week, so we're getting the house ready for them."

"How old are they now? Seventeen?"

"Sixteen," Neely said. "Beverly Hills sixteen, if you know what I mean. Ted gives them everything they ask for." Ted was doing production design now and often worked late into the night. As far as Neely could tell, the boys were pretty much raising themselves.

"Time to start thinking about college," Sandy said.

"Judd's already taking college courses. He's this total computer genius, and he's been in this special program since ninth grade. I don't know where he gets it from, Ted and I are both lousy with numbers. And he's just the sweetest kid."

"And—I'm sorry, I'm so bad with names."

"Dylan."

"Dylan. Of course. That's a beautiful name."

"Well, actually his name is Theodore, after Ted, and we always used to call him Buddy, but when he turned twelve he started insisting everyone call him Dylan. Dylan Casablanca, can you imagine? The girls just eat him up. He's my wild one."

"Well, that's what sixteen is all about. Ashley is fourteen, and I keep telling George, Watch out, you have no idea what's about to happen." Like other second wives Neely had met, Sandy had bred quickly and often to secure her position. She and George had five children, each less than two years apart.

"Yeah, well, if you ask me, Ted gets a little kick out of Dylan's bad-boy behavior. Not that he would ever admit it."

"They never do," Sandy said. "Here, help me with this pepper."

Neely stared at the bell pepper, unsure of what to do. Wash it? Carve out the stem? She sliced it around the middle and stared at the seeds, what looked like hundreds and hundreds of seeds. She began picking them out with her fingers.

"Oh, here, it's faster if you just rinse it," Sandy said, taking the pepper pieces back. "Could you grab a stick of butter from the refrigerator?"

There appeared to be two refrigerators. Neely chose the closest one and was relieved to find a box of butter sitting on the second shelf. On the top shelf were large bowls of various kinds of fish cut up into pieces, and shellfish cleaned and ready to go. There was also a bowl of chopped garlic and a bowl of diced onions. Everything that might have left a smell on Sandy's freshly manicured fingers had been taken care of earlier in the day by the cook.

Dinner was the usual mix of industry gossip and political disagreements, though Neely never understood what they were arguing about, since they were all Democrats and always supported the same candidates. All the men wore rumpled chinos: George, Dave, Terry, and Brian. Terry was a character actor who had made his mark in the New York theater before moving out to California. Brian was a partner at the agency that represented Neely. Their three wives looked so alike, they might have been sisters. Same shoulder-length blond hair, streaked with foils, with bangs and layers in front cut to look as if they were growing out. Same pinkish-brown lipstick. Same noses. Neely guessed none of them had been born with that nose. The only woman she had ever met who had that nose naturally was Anne Welles.

After dinner they put on another layer and went out to the deck for coffee, dessert, and Dave's fabulous cheese. The moon was up, and Ella Fitzgerald was playing.

"Neely, let's go for a walk down by the pond," George said when the coffee refills came around.

Neely looked at Dave, who leaned back and nodded. "Sure, okay," she said.

They walked down to the dock. George was telling her about his new movie. They were going to be shooting in Australia starting in October.

"So, how's your movie business going?" he asked.

"Well, I'm sure you already know. It's not going. At first I thought I was just getting all the lousy scripts. Now I'm beginning to think there's nothing out there *but* lousy scripts."

"You turned down the Helen Lawson story."

"You bet I did. I'm not going to take a bad part just for the sake of taking a part. I haven't made a movie in, in how many years?—it feels like a million years. So everyone is watching, you know? They ought to just call it *Helen Dearest.* I knew her, and she was the meanest woman alive."

"You know we bought the rights a couple of weeks ago."

"You're gonna direct it?" Neely asked. "Really?"

George chuckled. "No, we'll get someone else to direct it. My production company bought it. I think there could be a great film there."

"Really?"

"The early material is fantastic. Some of the best dialogue for women I've read in a long time."

"Well, they must have made it all up, because half of everything Helen ever said was a lie, and the other half was nothing but four-letter words."

"You really hate her."

"She hated me first!"

George laughed.

"No, I mean it!" Neely said. "First she tried to ruin my career, then she tried to take credit for discovering me. She was the worst backstabbing cunt I ever met."

"Well, that's not how we're making the picture. Helen is incredibly sympathetic. She gives up everything to make it on Broadway, only to learn that she's trusted the wrong people all along the way. Think *All About Eve,* with musical numbers."

"But that's bullshit! That isn't how it was at all."

"It's the movies, Neely. How it was is whatever we decide to show the audience. Ten years from now, do you think anyone will remember the real Helen Lawson? All they'll remember is this movie. And this movie has a great part for you in it. You could win an Oscar for this role."

"Come on."

"It could be your *Coal Miner's Daughter.* Your *The Rose.* The sound track alone could make you a fortune."

"Geez, George. You're quite the salesman. But I'd rather wait for a good dramatic part."

"I think that might be an awfully long wait."

"And what does that mean?" she asked.

"You know how many thirty-plus actresses are out there competing for the same parts? This is going to sound harsh, but I'm saying it as your friend. Actresses with better credentials than you have. Do you think you'll get anything half a dozen of them haven't already turned down?"

"Well, thanks a lot."

"Be realistic, Neely. You're an expensive risk."

"I'm not so expensive! I have my own production company now. I don't need to get a ton of dough up front."

"The insurance companies don't see it that way. Your last three pictures came in wildly over budget because of shooting delays, and in every case you were the reason for those delays."

"I've been clean for four years. Maybe I have a glass of wine now and then, but alcohol was never my problem."

"You know how much cast insurance costs now? Last year I shot an eighty-million-dollar picture, and four million went straight to the insurance company. No one can afford to bet on you, even if you do think you are a safe bet."

"Geez, if this is supposed to be a pep talk, you aren't doing a very nice job of it."

"We're willing to take a risk on you, because you're a friend, and, to be absolutely honest, because I think you're the only person with the voice to carry the picture. But with insurance costing what it does now, producers aren't lining up to make another Neely O'Hara movie. I'm just telling you like it is. You can ask Brian, he'll say the same thing."

"Oh, yeah, the agents, the agents. All they care about is their damn packages. They're looking out for the director, they're looking out for the screenwriter, they're looking out for themselves, meanwhile who's looking out for me?"

"Neely, you have to think about this part. At least take a look at some of the script. Everyone is going to love Helen Lawson when this movie comes out. Every woman who has ever been betrayed by a friend, every woman who ever lost a man to another woman, every woman who ever dreamed of a glamorous life, every woman over the age of thirty who wonders whether she's made the right choices, they're all going to watch this movie and say, That's me! Those are my mistakes! Those are my dreams!"

"Enough already. I'll think about it."

"We really want you to do this."

"We?"

"Me and Dave. We've talked about it."

"You talk about me with Dave behind my back?" Neely said, her voice growing louder.

"Dave and I are old friends. I talk about Sandy, he talks about you, what do you think we talk about?"

"You're ganging up on me. I can't believe you're ganging up on me! It isn't fair!"

"We just want what's best for you."

"And what's best for your production company."

"Maybe it's the same thing."

"Man oh man. I can't believe Dave is doing this to me."

"Neely, sit down." They sat facing each other on the long wooden bench that lined the dock. "I'm only going to say this once. Promise me you'll listen without interrupting. Promise me you'll listen with an open mind."

"Okay, okay."

"You have one of the great voices of the century. You have an amazing talent, a gift from God, really, a talent that you've nearly destroyed more than once. But you're still here. You can still sing, and you're still beautiful."

He took her hand and continued. "In some ways, you and Helen are very much alike. Don't make that face, just listen. Because deep down, Helen knew she was alone, and she knew the only thing she could really trust in life was her own talent. And deep down, I think you're the same way."

Neely could feel the tears welling up. "I do feel alone a lot of the time," she whispered.

"You've had a hard life, Neely." He handed her his handkerchief.

"I've tried, George. I'm still trying. I'm just not like other people."

"You're special, Neely. You'll never be like other people. Forget Helen Lawson. This movie is your chance to show everyone who *you* are."

They sat together in silence, listening to the waves lap against the rowboats.

"All right," Neely said. "All right, then."

George patted her knee and gave her a quick kiss on the forehead. "I'm going back up now. You sit here a little bit, I know you have a lot to think about. Everyone loves you, Neely, just remember everyone loves you."

He walked back up to the house, turning and waving to her just before the path curved and she fell out of sight.

He was exhausted. He wondered how Dave did it, day after day, he wondered what it was like to love a monster like Neely. Whoever ended up directing the picture would age five years in five months. Some days he wished there were a way to make movies without actors. They were all children: needy, vain, insecure, willful little monsters.

But oh, that voice. George Dunbar knew they needed that voice. When he got back up to the deck, he gave Brian a wink, and Brian slipped away to make a telephone call. The first draft of the papers would be drawn up by the time the West Coast offices opened on Monday morning. Neely would not have time to change her mind. They would make the picture, and if Neely didn't fall apart, she might even get an Oscar nomination. And once she was back on top, Dave would be history. George knew that much about actresses: Women with hit pictures always traded up. He would make sure the set was full of attractive men who liked to flirt.

Everyone would win. Neely would get her movie. Dunbar's production company would get the profits. Dave would get his life back, and Sandy (who couldn't stand Neely, who had told George more than once that East Hampton wasn't as much fun now that Neely was around) would start fixing Dave up with some of her divorced friends.

When Neely came back, Sandy brought out a bottle of their good Cognac and began to pour. A wind had come up from the water, and it was almost too chilly to sit outside.

"To friendship," George said, sounding a little weary, lifting his glass to toast.

"And to the director," Brian added, clinking his glass to George's.

"To the director," said Dave.

"To the director," murmured the other guests.

"To the director," Neely said, last of all, her clear voice not the least bit tired.

"You have to come over," Neely was saying to Anne on the telephone. "Summer is almost over and I haven't seen you in a year! Except on television, of course."

"Let me call you back in ten minutes," Anne said. Gretchen and Jenn were out on the porch, flipping through fashion magazines. It was eleven in the morning, and already hot, and no one had the energy to go to the beach.

"Don't play so hard to get," Neely said. "I did get you that job, after all."

So Anne packed up their swimsuits and now here she was, sitting with Neely on the deck, picking at her lobster salad. In the pool below, Jenn and Gretchen were practicing their dives. Judd sat at the edge of the pool, reading a science-fiction novel. Dylan was stretched out on a chaise, listening to music through headphones, his eyes hidden behind mirrored sunglasses.

Neely could not stop talking about Helen Lawson. She had brought out a stack of

photocopied clippings and nightclub photographs.

"You know what I can't get over?" Neely
said. "She seemed so old when I first met
her, all used up. But you know what? She
was only in her forties. Pretty much the
same age as Barbra Streisand is now.
Hardly ancient. But enough about her.
What's going on with you?"

"Starting in September they're going to
tape the show in New York, so we're moving back to the city," Anne said. She had
found them a place to live for well below
market prices—a friend of Jerry's had a loft
in Tribeca filled with expensive paintings
and was looking for someone to half sublet,
half housesit while he spent the year in Italy.
It was a huge space, with room for
Gretchen, who planned to get a job bar-
tending "so I can see movie stars all year
round." Jenn's old school had agreed to
take her back on scholarship.

"You're going to rent out the house?"
Neely asked.

"No, we'll come up on weekends. I don't
want Jenn to lose contact with her
Southampton friends, in case this show
doesn't work out." With the move coming

up, Anne had tried to talk Gretchen into fil-
ing for divorce, but Gretchen was too afraid
of what her husband would do. Three times
in the last few months he had come banging on Anne's door in the middle of the
night, drunk and cursing, threatening to set
the house on fire if Gretchen didn't come
home with him. Anne had called the police
each time.

"That Gretchen has quite the body,"
Neely said. Judd usually spent all day working on his computer, and Dylan practically
lived at the beach, but today they were
glued to the pool. Gretchen was wearing a
shiny turquoise string bikini. It slipped a little with every dive. Through the clear water,
the boys could watch her pull her suit back
into place. "She should do something about
that nose, though. And those teeth."

"She can't even afford to go to the dentist," Anne said.

"Yeah, I guess I've forgotten what it's like
to have no money."

Anne sighed. "I haven't."

"Come on, Lyon's taking care of things,
isn't he?"

"He takes care of Jenn. I'm on my own,
pretty much."

"But you have your own show!"

"It's cable, Neely."

"You should ask Lyon for more money."

"I'm not asking him for anything."

"You know, he's doing really well now. He's making a ton of dough since he joined that new agency. Los Angeles agrees with him."

Anne didn't want to ask Neely about Lyon. They hardly ever spoke anymore; now it was all just about flight arrangements for Jenn and an occasional phone call when his check was late.

"Don't pretend you aren't curious," Neely said.

"I'm a little curious, I admit it. Do you— do you ever see him?"

"Nah, Dave and I have run into him in restaurants a couple of times, but that's it. He's with a different woman every time. But I guess I'll start seeing more of him."

"Really," said Anne.

"He's buying a house in my neighborhood. Can you believe it? It's a tiny house, but he gets the swanky address. So, you know, it wouldn't kill him if you hit him up for a little more cash."

"I don't want his money."

"All right, all right. Enough about Lyon. Look over there."

Jenn was sitting at Dylan's feet, wearing his headphones, bopping her head along to the music.

Neely giggled. "I think she has a little crush on him."

"She's only eleven," Anne said.

"Maybe you forgot what it's like to be eleven. You know, I'm in my thirties and I still get crushes. It's ridiculous! You know who I have a crush on right now?"

"I give up."

"Harrison Ford! Is that crazy or what? I've never even met him. But that doesn't stop me from thinking about him. Sometimes, in the kip with Dave, if things are slow getting started, I just close my eyes and pretend I'm in bed with Harrison Ford. I gotta tell you, wow, it really works for me."

Anne laughed. "I don't think I want to hear this!"

"Who do you think about?" Neely asked.

"I don't think about anyone," Anne said.

"I didn't think so," Neely said. "You know what you need? You need to get laid. You're turning into a big grouch. Women are just like men that way. How long has it been?"

"Let's change the subject."

"You know what they say. What's good for the goose is good for the gander."

"It would have to be the other way around," Anne said. "We're the geese, the men are the ganders."

"Whatever. The point is, you need a little gander action. Don't you ever feel a little frisky? I know I'm feeling a little frisky."

"But you have Dave."

Neely stood up and slapped her stomach. "Look at this. Totally flat. I'm in the best shape I've ever been in since I was a teenager. It doesn't have anything to do with Dave. I'm just in the mood for a little fun, that's all."

"Do you . . . do you have . . . an arrangement?"

"We're not married," Neely said.

"But still."

She wiggled her left ring finger. "If he wants me to act like a wife, he's gonna have to cough up the paperwork. Anyway, Dave's in California for another five days. I'm going to a party tonight, why don't you come?"

"I can't."

"You mean you don't want to."

"Okay, I don't want to."

"You didn't even ask me what kind of party it was."

"It doesn't matter, I don't feel like going out," Anne said.

But Neely went on. She had not forgotten how to talk Anne into things, and anyway, wasn't this in Anne's best interests? It wasn't natural, the way Anne kept herself cooped up, still licking her wounds after the divorce. And it was only her first divorce!

Anne took another sip of her gin and tonic and watched her eleven-year-old daughter attempt to flirt with a sixteen-year-old boy. *He's stoned,* she thought, *he is so obviously stoned.* She watched Neely's sons toss a beach ball back and forth over Gretchen's head; she watched Gretchen jump up, laughing, her wet breasts bobbing in the thin blue suit; she watched Dylan throw the ball at Jenn, hitting her on the back; she watched Jenn shriek with delight and strike a pose of fake anger, one hand on a nonexistent hip.

"You won't have to dress up, it's not that kind of party," Neely was saying. "The car will come at eight."

*　　*　　*

Anne sat in the back of the dark blue town car, rubbing a bug bite on her left ankle. She was wearing the clothes that Jenn and Gretchen had picked out for her: a well-worn pair of Levi's 501s, a white ribbed tank top, a red cotton cardigan cut like a sweatshirt, red espadrilles. The jeans were beginning to fray at the knees, and when she lifted her arms her bra straps peeked out from beneath the tank top, but Jenn had insisted this was proper party attire. Gretchen had fluffed up Anne's hair with a blow dryer and lent her a pair of big silver hoop earrings.

"You look wonderful!" Neely cried when she got into the car at East Hampton. Neely was wearing black jeans and a low-cut yellow T-shirt. Her eyes were rimmed with navy-blue liner. "We are such babes!"

She leaned forward and gave the driver the address. "Love Shack" was playing on the radio. "And turn up the music!" she said.

"Here," she said, handing Anne a businesss card for the car service. "In case we get separated. Dave's account number is on the back, just give them a call. And also, just in case, take these." She took out two condoms.

"I don't think so!" Anne said. "You carry condoms?"

"Oh, baby, what planet are you living on. And I don't carry them. I stole them from Dylan's stash." She giggled. "And he has quite the collection. My little heartbreaker. Just take them, you can always throw them out later."

The party was in a sprawling modern house set back in the woods. It was noisy and crowded with hundreds of people Anne didn't know, which made her first nervous, then relieved. The first vodka tonic went down quickly. Neely was dancing with a man in baggy surfer shorts. Anne sat on a window ledge, trying to make the final inch of her second drink last as long as possible.

A man came up holding two clear drinks with limes in them.

"Don't I know you from the city?" he asked. He had curly black hair cropped close and a gold stud in his left ear. "Vodka or gin?" he asked, holding out both drinks.

"I don't think so," Anne said. "Vodka. Thank you."

"Yeah, sure, I know I've seen you around.

Maybe we work in the same neighborhood?" He named a large ad agency in the
East Forties.

"No, I live out here year-round," Anne
said.

"No kidding. Well, you look like someone
I know. Or maybe you look like someone I
should know." He smiled and sat down next
to her. They made small talk for a few minutes, the man flirting, Anne resisting, until
he finally gave up and left. Another man
came over ("Haven't we met somewhere?
You're a friend of Jeanine's, right?"), and in
five minutes he was gone, too.

Finally Neely returned, her brow damp
with sweat.

"Don't tell me," she said. "You're having a
terrible time."

"No, this is nice. It's fun just to watch."

"Liar. I saw you giving guys the brush-off.
Who were they?"

"Just guys."

"Guys trying to pick you up?"

"I guess." Anne sighed. "I'm sorry. This
just isn't my style."

"Annie, there are at least fifty good-
looking, totally respectable single guys at
this party, guys who make good money,

have good jobs, guys who, if we were in the city, women would be lined up to meet. What's the problem?"

"It just isn't—it just isn't something I do."

"You mean it just isn't something you know how to do."

"Maybe."

"Listen to me. You don't have to do anything. I was watching you. A guy gets a little aggressive, sits too close or whatever, and you pull away. You gotta flirt a little. Stare at his hands. Look at his mouth. Send him a signal. It's the easiest thing in the world. Guys like this, they'll do all the work. They're on the hunt. You just gotta relax and let them take care of everything." An old Rolling Stones song came over the sound system. "Oh man, come on, come dance with me." She pulled Anne onto the dance floor.

They were surrounded by women dancing with each other. Anne couldn't remember the last time she had danced at a party. The third drink had gone to her head. She felt herself loosening with the music, shaking her hips, moving her arms higher and higher. After the first couple of times, she didn't bother to pull her tank top back over her bra straps.

"One more!" Neely mouthed when the music segued into an old disco hit. Anne was smiling now, tossing her hair back and forth. Men were coming onto the dance floor in pairs, joining the women. She could see them watching her, looking her up and down, and it felt wonderful. *I still have it,* she thought. *Yes, oh yes, I still have it.* She danced with one man, then another, eight songs in a row, and she felt as if she could dance all night. She looked around for Neely . . . where had she gone? A slow song came on, and a man reached out for her with two hands . . . people were coupling off . . . but she smiled and turned away. All she wanted was to shake and shake and shake to loud, fast music, to keep shaking until she could shake loose this little knot inside her, the knot that had been there ever since Lyon had gone.

She got another drink and went outside for fresh air. She lifted up her hair and let the wind blow cool against her damp neck.

"You're a marvelous dancer," someone said. He was tall, in a pressed chambray workshirt and baggy chinos. He looked to be somewhere in his early forties, with thick gray hair brushed straight back from a strong face.

"Thank you," she said.

He offered her his right hand. "Patrick Weston. Friend of the host," he said.

She shook his hand. "Anne Welles. I don't think I've even met the host, but he throws a fabulous party."

"We're partners at the agency. Are you in advertising?"

"No, thank God." She laughed. "Oh, I'm sorry, that came out wrong."

He laughed along with her. "No, that's okay, it's a rotten business. I have to ask you, did you study dance?"

She shook her head.

"You move like a dancer. I could have watched you dance all night." He moved closer.

"I didn't see you out there."

"No, I don't dance, I just like to watch. I just like to watch beautiful women, actually." She recognized his accent: prep school, money, the confidence that comes with years of getting what you want. "You don't look like the kind of woman who usually comes to these parties," he said.

"What do I look like?"

"Different."

"Different how?"

"Just different. Have we met some-where?"

"No, I don't think so."

"I'm sure I know you from somewhere."

"No, I really don't think so." She shivered.

"Chilly?"

"I left my sweater inside."

"Let me go get it for you."

"You don't have to."

"I'm going in anyway to get a drink. And then, you know what I'd like to do?" he asked. "I'd like to sit somewhere quiet and have a civilized conversation with a beauti-ful woman. What do you think?"

"I'm not really thinking about anything right now."

He smiled. "Promise me you'll wait right here."

She described her sweater, found an empty bench, and sat in the cool dark. The music had gotten fast again, but all she could hear was the pounding bass. He came back, carrying her sweater and his jacket over one arm.

"Tell me about yourself," he said.

"There's nothing much to tell."

"Okay, then I'll tell you about myself." He was from Vermont and had come to New York by way of Dartmouth and Wharton. He was divorced and lived in the East Nineties with a golden retriever, several good pieces of Stickley, and a collection of Civil War memorabilia that had been left to him by his grandfather. He touched her as he talked, on the arm, on the knee. She looked at his mouth: square jaw, narrow lips, a small scar across his chin.

They went for a walk. At the end of the street there was a little Cape Cod house painted gray with blue shutters.

"My place," he said. "Nightcap?"

She felt the little knot seize up inside her. "Oh," Anne said. "I don't know."

"No one ever knows," Patrick said. "Close your eyes." He took her face in his hands and kissed her softly, lips closed. "Nice," he said. "I promise you, I'm the perfect gentleman."

Inside there were old Persian carpets and paintings of sailboats. They sat together on the sofa, listening to a Louis Armstrong album.

"I'm going to kiss you again," he said. "If you want me to."

She stared at his hands, watched him lift them into her hair. Her mouth fell open, and the kiss, the long, delicious kiss, sent something jumping inside her.

"Are you nervous?" he asked.

"It's been . . . it's been a really long time."

"Ah. I see. Well, you've come to the right place. It's been a long time for me, too. I don't meet that many women who . . . who move me. We can take it slow. Tell me what you want."

"What I want is . . ." she said. But she couldn't figure out how to finish the sentence. She wanted him to take her in his arms and make the little knot go away. Because she knew what it was now: it was fear. "I have no idea what I want. I feel like, I feel like I don't remember anything at all. About this."

"Let me remind you," he said. They kissed again. She leaned back into the sofa, felt his lips on her neck, his hand on her breast.

"What you want is to be seduced," he said.

His bed was soft, the sheets white with

blue scallops. She kept her eyes closed the whole time: as he lifted her shirt over her head, as he pulled open her jeans, as he warmed her up with his mouth, as he opened a drawer and got out a condom, as he kissed her on the ear and whispered, "Relax, relax, easy, easy does it." When she came, she didn't make a sound.

Afterward he lent her a T-shirt and made her chamomile tea. "Would you like to stay over?" he asked.

"What time is it?"

"Just after four. I'm hell in the morning. And I'm going to have a killer hangover." He shook some aspirin out of a large bottle and offered her three. "But I do make a very good cup of coffee."

"Thank you, but I should go," Anne said. She didn't want Jenn to wake up and find her gone. She called the car service and got dressed. In a cup at the edge of his bathroom sink, there were two well-used toothbrushes and two different brands of toothpaste. On the top shelf of his medicine chest, there were an eyelash curler, a tube of mascara, three lipsticks, a half-empty box of tampons, and a sample-size bottle of Shalimar.

In the doorway he kissed her, a friendly, sexless kiss, and tousled her hair. "You're amazing," he said. "I'll call you."

She smiled and waved goodbye. She knew he would never call. She would probably never see him again. Or she might run into him in the city; he'd be walking his dog and she'd be taking Jenn to school, and they would nod to each other, perhaps even wink. Or she'd see him at a party, let friends introduce them as if they were strangers, Anne-Welles-pleased-to-meet-you, he'd be with a woman who wore Shalimar— girlfriend? wife?—who looked a little tense around the eyes.

The way I used to look, Anne thought as the car pulled into her driveway. She knew she ought to feel guilty, but all she felt was happy, deliriously, deliciously happy, as if somehow her life were about to start all over again. For the first time in years, she fell asleep without even thinking of taking a pill. The little knot was gone. In her dreams she was dancing, to a song without words, to a song that never stopped.

1990.

Anne sat at her rented steel desk and watched the sun set over the Hudson. There weren't many things to like about this suite of offices on the far side of Eleventh Avenue in the Fifties. The neighborhood was so dirty that each day when she arrived at work, she headed straight to the ladies' room to brush flecks of soot from her face and clothes. It was dangerous after dark, and at the end of the day the women paired up to walk over to the subway stop on Eighth Avenue. There wasn't anywhere decent to grab lunch. From the outside, the building still looked like what it had once been: an industrial ware-

house used to store manufacturing equipment and automobile parts. Inside, the ele-
vators were slow and creaky, the carpets
mottled with mysterious stains.

But the sunsets were spectacular. A pink
glow fell over Anne's notes for the next
day's show. There were three guests on tomorrow's schedule: a travel expert demon-
strating how to pack for a two-week vacation using only one carry-on suitcase, a
dermatologist explaining how to give yourself a facial using inexpensive products
from the local supermarket, and a singer
who had recently announced she was a vic-
tim of child abuse and had just published a
ghostwritten memoir titled *All There Is.*

Jamie Walters came by, waving a sheaf of
faxes.

"We did it!" he said. "The ratings are in,
and we're up by five points. Get your coat,
let's go out and celebrate."

He took her to the Lancer Bar and ordered martinis for both of them.

"Five points. You know how many advertising dollars that translates to?" he asked.

"Does this mean I'm getting a raise?"
Anne asked. Her current contract would be
up for renewal in six months.

"It gets even better than a raise. You wouldn't believe who called up today." The local affiliate of one of the major networks had expressed interest in picking up the show. Jamie had set up a meeting for the next Friday. "They're giving us exactly ten minutes to make our pitch. We're talking real money, Anne. We'd be in every major market. And you know what kinds of guests you could get?" He snapped his fingers. "Anyone you want. They'd be lining up to get on. This is the big time."

"But they already have perfectly good shows at both nine and ten A.M.," Anne said.

"Annie, baby, what planet are you living on." Jamie laid it out for her. The ratings of the nine A.M. show had been slipping for months, and the two co-hosts couldn't bear to speak to each other off camera. The host of the ten A.M. show was going through a messy divorce and had gained so much weight, her producers had had to rebuild the set in an attempt to hide the bottom half of her body as much as possible.

"And you're perfectly comfortable capitalizing on other people's misfortunes," Anne said.

"Listen, Annie. Good luck is just another name for someone else's bad luck. This is television. They're vulnerable, so I'm making my move. If it were the other way around, these people wouldn't hesitate to make a move on me. Didn't you learn anything at that agency?"

"That was a long time ago."

"Show business doesn't change. The only time you move up is when the other guy is on the way down." He opened his wallet and handed her four new hundred-dollar bills.

"I want you to go to Saks and get yourself something nice for next week's meeting."

"I can wear my navy suit, it will work just fine."

"Yeah, I know, but you need a new coat and some new shoes. These network guys are always checking out your shoes. When's the last time you bought yourself a nice pair of shoes?"

"Shoes don't show on camera," Anne said.

"Well, get yourself a pair that looks expensive. We only have one shot."

On Saturday Anne went to Saks and picked out a pair of black patent-leather

Ferragamo pumps with little gold buckles and a wool-lined trench coat on markdown. With the leftover money, she picked up a red sweater and some clear lip gloss for Jenn. By Tuesday everyone in the office was buzzing about their meeting.

"How did you hear?" Anne asked one of the cameramen.

"Jamie's so excited, he can't stop talking about it. And a friend of mine at the station told me they all know about it over there, the tension's so thick you could cut it with a knife."

"Well, wish me luck."

"You don't need luck, you just gotta walk in and smile and let Jamie do the talking. And you better take me with you when you hit the big time!"

Anne told Jenn over dinner that night.

"I hope this means we can move out of this dump into a real apartment," Jenn said.

"This is hardly a dump."

"I don't want to live in a loft anymore! I want a real bedroom, with real walls, not just dividers. And my own telephone. And I'd like to live someplace that wasn't four million miles from my friends."

"Even if I get this job, I'm not sure we'll be

able to afford the Upper East Side again," Anne said.

"But it isn't fair!" Jenn cried, pouting. "No one wants to come all the way down here. If we stay here much longer, my life is going to be ruined."

"I hardly think so."

"Mom, you don't get it! You don't remember what it's like to be thirteen!"

"It's only November, you won't be thirteen for another six weeks."

"Well, I feel thirteen. All my friends are thirteen and some of them are even fourteen."

Fourteen going on twenty-one, Anne thought. She was still shocked by the girls at Jenn's school, what they wore, how they spoke, what their parents let them do. They wore sexy clothes and too much makeup, and some of them even snuck out to bars at night. Jenn had rolled her eyes when Anne gave her the lip gloss and the red cardigan, and she'd immediately taken the subway up to Saks to exchange them for light purple lipstick and a tight black turtleneck.

"Some of your friends are growing up a little too fast, if you ask me."

"Mom, you act like this is still the fifties."

"Thank you very much, but I'm not that old."

"No, you just act like it!"

"And what does that mean."

"You don't let me . . . I don't get to . . . I never get to . . ." Jenn was starting to cry now. "I don't get to have any fun. You never let me do anything!"

"Jenn, name one thing I haven't allowed you to do."

"You didn't let me stay over at Alice's last month."

"Her parents weren't home. This is New York. You can't stay over at someone's house if her parents aren't home."

"And you didn't let me go to Christopher's birthday party."

"Christopher is sixteen, and you told me the party didn't start until ten o'clock."

"Well, there are plenty of other things, but maybe you don't know about them because I don't even bother to ask you because I know you'll say no."

"Such as."

"Never mind, what's the point."

"Try me."

"Why should I bother."

"You aren't even giving me a chance," Anne said.

"Okay. Okay. Alice's cousin is a photographer, and he came over and took all these pictures of us, and mine came out really good. He said I could even be a model."

Anne felt a catch in her throat. "What kind of pictures?"

"See what I mean!" Jenn screamed. "Just pictures! Just regular pictures!" She got out her knapsack and pulled out a manila envelope. "Take a look if you want." She ran to her bed and pulled the divider shut. That was one of the nice things about a loft, Anne thought: there weren't any doors to slam.

Anne spread out the photographs across the table. They were eight-by-tens, four of them, two in color, two in black and white. Jenn was wearing full makeup—foundation, contouring, powder, and glossy lipstick. Her eyes were rimmed with kohl, and her brows had been filled in and brushed upward. Her long, light brown hair was teased up at the crown and lit from above to emphasize the dark blond streaks that came in every summer.

In the first black-and-white photograph,

she was shot in profile from the shoulders up, her eyes closed, her hair blown back by an unseen fan. Around her long neck was a strand of borrowed pearls. She looked elegant and mysterious, a debutante with a naughty secret.

In the next black-and-white picture, she was wearing what Anne guessed was one of Alice's mother's ball gowns. The dark velvet dress was cut tight on top and full below. Jenn was barefoot, laughing, her head tilted slightly back, a pair of four-inch heels in her left hand. She looked like a woman who had stayed up all night and was still ready for fun.

In the third photograph, Jenn was wearing a blue-and-green flannel shirt unbuttoned all the way down to her jeans, and nothing underneath. She had her hands on her hips, and her feet were planted a foot apart. She looked strong and defiant, like a woman who knew how to get exactly what she wanted and whom she wanted to get it from.

It was the final photograph that unnerved Anne most of all. It was a close-up of Jenn, from her bare shoulders up. She was wearing just a hint of pink lipstick, and a few freckles showed through her makeup. Her mouth was slightly open, and she stared straight into the camera. There was no story behind this photograph, no character being played. She was just a beautiful woman, full of sex.

Anne poured herself another glass of wine. There was Anne's pretty nose, her fine jaw. There were Lyon's hungry eyes, his full mouth. Anne could not bring herself to make the connection between twelve-year-old Jenn and the creature in the photographs. How could her sweet little girl look so knowing? How did her pretty little princess manage to look so full of mischief? How could a girl who had never been kissed, who didn't even need a bra, come across as a beautiful temptress?

She found Jenn in bed, the covers pulled all the way up to her neck.

"They're beautiful pictures, darling," Anne said. "You're beautiful. But you're too young."

"Lots of girls my age do modeling. And it's good money."

"Oh, honey. You're just not old enough yet."

"When will I be old enough?"

"I don't know."

"Next year?"

"I don't know. Maybe."

Anne took a Valium and got into bed. Soon it would be Jenn's turn. She should be thrilled for her daughter, but she was only depressed . . . because maybe that meant her own turn was over . . . because it made her feel all of her thirty-seven years.

Just as she was falling asleep, the downstairs buzzer rang.

It was Gretchen. Her left eye was swollen, and there were bruises on her hands.

"I'm sorry," she said, fighting back a sob. "My right hand's all fucked up and I had trouble finding my key."

"My God, what happened," Anne said.

"He waited for me to get off my shift," Gretchen sobbed. "I've never seen him so angry . . . I thought he was going to kill me. One of the waiters came out just in time and scared him off." There were red marks on her neck, and the back of her shirt was torn.

Anne made them a pot of tea.

"I don't know what to do," Gretchen said.

"We can worry about it tomorrow," said Anne. "I know you're sick of me saying it, but you need to find a lawyer and get out of this marriage." She gave Gretchen a Xanax and sent her to bed. She sat in a rocking chair, reading magazines; when she was sure Gretchen had fallen asleep, she took another Valium and got back under the covers.

"Mom? Are you awake?"

"Jenn? Sweetie, it's almost three in the morning. You have school tomorrow."

"I'm scared."

"Oh sweetie, it's safe here. Nothing bad is going to happen, I promise."

"Can I stay with you tonight?"

"Of course, darling. Go get your pillow." Anne moved to the side of the bed and pulled back the covers for Jenn. She listened to her daughter breathe in the dark.

"Mom? I'm sorry about before. I didn't mean to fight."

"I'm sorry, too. Come over here and let me give you a hug." Anne opened her arms, and they curled up like spoons.

"I can't sleep. Can I have a pill, too?"

"You're too young, sweetie."

"Can I have a half? Alice's mother lets her have a half."

"You can fall asleep without a pill. Let's close our eyes now."

On Friday Anne wore her new shoes and her new trench coat and got to the office at nine sharp. Her secretary handed her a stack of pink message slips. The meeting with the network had been canceled at the last minute.

"Did they say why it was canceled?" Anne asked.

"Nope, just that they were sorry and they would call back next week."

Anne dialed Jamie, but he wasn't in. She read the newspaper, returned some phone calls, looked at next week's guest list, but she couldn't concentrate.

Finally, he came storming into her office. His face was red, and his voice was shaking.

"Where the fuck were you!" he shouted. "Where the fuck were you!"

"What do you mean? I was right here."

"We had a fucking meeting! You knew we had a meeting!"

"But I thought they canceled it," said Anne, handing him the message slip.

"Why would they cancel?"

"I don't know, I tried to call you, you weren't here."

"Because I was there!" Jamie shouted. "Jesus Christ."

"You could have called."

"By the time we figured out you were missing-in-action it was too fucking late. Better I tell them you were run over by a bus than that you were sitting at your desk doing who knows what. You know how hard it is to get ten minutes with these guys?" He looked at the message slip. "Who took this message?"

"Reception."

"And did anyone call back to confirm the cancellation?"

"To confirm the cancellation? She calls back to confirm appointments, but who calls back to confirm a cancellation?"

"Oh, Anne, what am I going to do with you? Do you realize what's happened here? Do you see there's no telephone number on this message slip? Anyone could have called and left this message. Anyone who didn't want you to show up. You blew it."

"How was I supposed to know?" Anne said.

"Everyone knows this stuff, this is basic stuff. This is television, for Christ's sake. You can pretty much assume at any given time there are twelve people waiting to stick a knife in your back. Only twelve, if you're lucky."

"But who?"

"But who, but who," he mimicked. "Gee, I don't know. How about someone who doesn't want their show to be canceled. Or someone who wants this job as badly as you do, and is willing to do whatever it takes to get it. You need a list? You want me to make you a list?"

"No thanks, I get your point."

He sat down, rested his elbows on her desk, and rubbed his forehead. "It was humiliating, waiting there."

"I can call them. I'll find a way to explain it. I'll call them next week."

"By next week they'll have signed someone else. You think I want to work in cable my whole life? You want to work in cable your whole life? Maybe this is enough for you, but it isn't enough for me. This rinky-dink show on a rinky-dink channel."

"Thanks a lot." She sighed. "I don't know what to say."

"There isn't anything to say. This is a fucking mess is what it is. I'm watching my whole life go down the tubes here."

"Jamie. Come on. The ratings are great. You're looking at ad revenue—"

"I'm looking at *bupkis!* Nada! Zilch! Oh, excuse me, I forgot to tell you. They're selling the channel, to some company out in fucking Wyoming. They were just waiting for the ratings to come in so they could jack up the price. You know what that means? New management. New budgets. New everything."

"You knew about this," Anne said. "And you didn't tell me."

"I didn't think I'd have to tell you! I thought we could get out before the deal went through."

Anne went home early and called her agency.

"So that's the whole story," she said. She could hear Trip Gregory lighting a cigarette on the other end of the line. "What should I do?"

"Let me make a few calls," Trip said. "Maybe I can set something up for next week."

"Great, I'll tell Jamie."

"Please don't."

"But it's his show."

"Anne, you're the one they're interested

in, not Jamie. You wouldn't be in this mess if he had kept his mouth shut. Jamie Walters may be a nice guy, but he's a loser, and he'll always be a loser. You want to work in cable your whole life?"

"That's the second time today someone has said that to me."

"Give me one week. Promise me you'll sit tight for one week. And don't say a word about this to anyone."

Four days later, Trip and Anne went to lunch with the producer of the nine A.M. show and the head of programming at the International Broadcasting Corporation affiliate.

"*Morning Talk* may have ratings trouble, but rumors of its early death are greatly exaggerated," the producer said. "We just have a little personnel problem. Which is where you come in."

"We love Charlie, everyone loves Charlie, he's not the problem," said the man from IBC. Charles Brady had come up through the news ranks—first radio, then nightly news—and at age sixty was practically an American institution. "Women love him, men trust him. We want to keep Charlie in this time slot. But the chemistry . . ." He lifted an eyebrow. "I take it you've watched the show? What do you think?"

"I haven't really noticed anything wrong," Anne said, leaning back.

"Sometimes he looks uncomfortable," Trip said, leaning forward. He tapped Anne's knee under the table. "Not terribly uncomfortable, just a little . . . I'm not sure of the right word. Impatient?"

Both men smiled. "Well, he's on camera for an hour every day with a woman who . . . well, I'm not sure how to say this."

"She isn't really up to Charlie's level," said the first producer.

"She isn't really that smart," said the second.

"She's a little too show-biz for nine A.M."

"I don't even think she reads the paper on a daily basis."

"The audience can see Charlie wince when she mispronounces words."

"And that giggle."

"And the hairdos."

"She can be a little abrasive. She's wonderful, we're not saying she isn't wonderful."

"She just isn't wonderful in the right way."

Trip tapped Anne's knee again. "And Anne . . ."

"We think she might be wonderful in just the right way." He turned to Anne. "Charlie wants to meet you. It wouldn't really be an audition, it would be more like a conversation."

"In front of a camera, of course."

"Just our secret, of course."

"Assuming you're interested, of course."

"Of course she's interested," Trip said.

"And this Jamie Walters business, you understand that there really isn't any room for him at the network, of course."

"That's obvious," Trip said. "It's all perfectly obvious. What do you think, Annie?"

She looked at her twenty-dollar omelet and laid down her fork. "Well. Charles Brady. I remember watching him on the IBC news during the Kennedy assassination. He's practically an American institution."

The men laughed. "We'll get it set up, then."

Trip walked her to the subway station at 51st Street. "This is it, Anne, this is your big chance."

"But what about Jamie? I thought they wanted to pick up the show."

"This is even better. Charles Brady!"

"But what do I tell Jamie?"

"You don't tell him anything. I'll take care of Jamie."

"It doesn't feel right, after everything he's done for me."

"Listen, Anne, Jamie hasn't done anything for you. You did it all yourself. He was just the lucky bastard who was able to pick you up for cheap when your chips were down, and he had a nice ride, but it's time for you to move on. This is the way it works."

"But they called Jamie about picking up the whole show. That's how this all started."

"Are you sure?"

"Of course I'm sure."

"Because that's what Jamie told you?"

"Yes."

"How do you know? How do you really know?"

"I trust Jamie."

"Anne, you have to get over this trust business. How do you know they weren't interested in you, and just you, from the beginning? Why trust Jamie? Do you think he tells you everything? Did he tell you the channel was about to be sold?"

"That's different."

"Jamie Walters is like all the rest of them.

He's out for Jamie Walters, and everyone else comes second, including you. If things were reversed, he wouldn't think twice about showing you the door. This is your chance. Repeat after me: This is my chance."

"This is my chance," Anne said softly.

"Again, please, with feeling."

"This is my chance," she said, and then louder: "This is my chance."

"There you go."

"Ugh, it hurts my brain to think this way," said Anne.

"Which is why you have me. You leave everything to me."

She felt a rush of warm air come up from the subway and heard the rumble of a train entering the station. She hurried down the stairs, feeling for her token as she went. She made it through just before the doors started to close.

There was one seat left, and she took it. At Grand Central Station, the conductor announced that the train would be making only express stops for the rest of the trip downtown. When they left the station, the lights went out, and Anne held her purse tight against her lap.

From the dark train, through dirty windows, she watched the tunnel walls speed by, a blur of concrete and metal and faded graffiti. The rhythm of the old tracks beat a measure of four. *This is my chance, this is my chance, this is my chance.* The train raced downtown, and sooner than expected, here she was, almost home again.

By the second week of January, the deal was done. The show had been renamed *Morning Talk with Charles Brady,* and Anne was scheduled to start in early March. The station sent over boxes of videotapes for her to watch, and lined up eight two-hour sessions with a performance coach. "You're perfect," they told her, "but this is live television, so you're going to have to learn some tricks of the trade."

Jenn was going out to visit Lyon during her week-long school break, so Anne would have plenty of time to get up to speed. She made appointments with a hairdresser, a manicurist, a facialist, and a real estate agent. With her new salary, a real apartment was at last within reach. Jenn and Gretchen had already begun circling ads in the newspaper, mostly on the far side of Second Avenue, a neighborhood that was close to Jenn's school but not too expensive.

Lyon telephoned two days before Jenn was scheduled to fly out to Los Angeles.

"Bad news," he said. "Things are a mess on the set." He was representing an actress who was starring in a film about a truck-driver's wife who wins the lottery. Her guitar-playing boyfriend had just dumped her for the model who had starred in one of his band's videos. The actress had taken to showing up late and picking fights with the director.

"I'm there from dawn to dusk," Lyon said. "I don't see how I can take Jenn right now."

"Lyon, you *can't*," Anne said. "You can't do this."

"Easter will be here soon enough, she can come at Easter."

"You haven't seen Jenn since August. She's thirteen now, Lyon, do you have any idea what an angry thirteen-year-old is like?"

"Anne, I don't get home some nights until after eight. What is she going to do all day?"

"That's your problem."

"What do you want me to do?"

"Did you know her friend Alice's parents are taking a group of girls to Aspen for the week, and I told Jenn she couldn't go because of this California trip? Do you know what's going to happen if I tell her the trip is off?"

"Maybe it isn't too late for her to go to Aspen."

"Oh, *please.*" Anne looked up to find Jenn standing in the doorway. She was wearing a pair of sunglasses that Lyon had sent at Christmas and was trying on a blue-and-white-striped sundress she had bought just for the trip.

"I just can't, Anne. I just can't right now."

"You can and you will. Jenn is right here, I'm going to put her on the line."

"Anne, wait—"

"Daddy? Hi, Daddy. I'm wearing my new sunglasses. They are so cool."

"Hi, gorgeous. I bet you look fabulous in them."

"Can you take me to Santa Monica this time? Alice says I have to go to Santa Monica."

Anne watched Jenn's shoulders fall.

"Oh," Jenn was saying. "That sounds not

so great. But I could bring books and stuff, they give us tons of homework, and you could rent me videos. . . . I wouldn't be bored. . . . But, Daddy . . . it isn't fair, it isn't fair." She handed the phone to Anne. "He doesn't want me to come visit," she said. "He doesn't want me around."

Anne took the phone back. "It sounds like you handled that very well."

"Do you have to be such a bitch," he said.

"It's a good thing Jenn is standing right here, because otherwise I'd be able to say exactly what I'm thinking."

"You don't have to say it, I can guess. Look, there must be some way around this."

"I'm hanging up now, Lyon. You have two hours to figure this out. Two hours."

But it was Gretchen who figured it out. She came home from an early shift to find Jenn crying in the bathroom and Anne lying on the couch, rubbing her temples.

"What if I went to California, too?" she said. "We could do girl stuff during the day, and then at night you and your father could hang out."

"Could we go to Santa Monica?"

"Sure. And can we go to Disneyland?" Gretchen asked.

"Sure! Mom, what do you think?"

"Mom is thinking that it would be very nice to have the house to herself for a week," Anne said. She was also thinking of how much the last-minute plane fare and the rental car would cost and how much she would enjoy asking Lyon to pay for it. "Mom is thinking this is one wonderful plan."

"We both have to order dessert," Neely was saying. "And not sorbet or fruit tarts, either. Real desserts. A zillion calories. With whipped cream. This is a special occasion."

It was the night after Jenn and Gretchen had flown out to California, and they were celebrating their good news: Anne's new job, and the shooting of the Helen Lawson picture, which would at long last start next month.

"Why not," Anne said. "I can't remember the last time I had dessert."

"And let's get some more wine. This bottle is almost empty," Neely said. It was eight o'clock in the theater district, and the restaurant had cleared out. "What the hell, let's get some champagne. You come here much?" she asked.

"I don't really go anywhere much," Anne said. She still wasn't dating. Every three or four months, Patrick Weston called her. They would meet at a bar near his apartment, have a few drinks, and fall into bed.

"Each time I think, That was nice, but that's it, I'll never see him again, and then a few months later he calls, and I think, Why not? There isn't anything else going on in my life." Anne took a sip of the champagne. "I can't believe I'm telling you this."

"You don't talk about this stuff with Stella?"

"My God, Stella is the last person I'd want to know about this."

"So who do you talk to, then?"

"No one, really," Anne said. "Curtis is thumbs-down on this kind of thing."

"I'm honored, then," Neely said. "I guess you figure you can tell me because whatever you do, I've done a thousand times worse." She smiled. "That's what I never got about the Catholics. Who would want to confess to a priest? Now if you put a hooker behind that grate, I'd be in there every week and I wouldn't hold anything back."

Anne laughed. "There's an idea."

"So," Neely said. "Does this guy have potential? Maybe you should try going out on a real date or something."

"I don't think so. The first hour, before the alcohol kicks in, we hardly know what to say to each other. We really don't have a single thing in common."

"Except in the kip."

"Except in the kip. I can't believe I said that!" said Anne.

"Don't worry, your tongue won't fall out. So, it is what it is. Everyone could use a fuck buddy. Man, you know what I really want right now? I want a cigarette. I haven't had a cigarette in years and years. You want one? I'm gonna get some smokes from the waiter."

"What about your voice?"

"One cigarette. I'm feeling naughty."

"Okay, one cigarette," Anne said. It was so easy, talking to Neely. Anne felt that she could say anything in the world, and Neely would never disapprove.

They inhaled their Marlboro Lights, Neely blowing perfect smoke rings.

"Listen, when you talk to Jenn, tell her they can use my pool. Lyon's pool is about as big as a bathtub. I'll call the boys and let them know."

"I can't believe they're already eighteen." Judd would be hearing from colleges soon; Neely was confident he would get in everywhere he applied—Stanford, Princeton, MIT. Dylan had lousy test scores and was taking the year off before applying again.

"He doesn't know what he wants to do," Neely said. "And when I was eighteen, I already had a career and a husband." She turned to the side. "So, you haven't noticed anything different about me?"

"Your hair is different?" Anne offered. Neely had grown her hair down to her shoulders and colored it strawberry blond.

"My hair is always different. You don't notice anything else?"

"Like what?"

"I had a little work done a couple of months ago." She stroked her jawline. "They kinda pulled all this up."

"But you're only thirty-six!"

"It's my genes, what can I do. You should have seen my mother. You can't really tell, can you. My plastic surgeon is a genius. If you're ever looking."

"Oh, I could never," Anne said.

"Everyone does it, Anne."

"I didn't mean it that way. I just can't imagine it for myself, that's all."

"Yeah, well, with your genes, you're lucky, you probably won't need anything done for another ten years."

"In ten years I'll only be forty-seven. Did it—did it hurt very much?"

"It hurts like you wouldn't believe. They give you tons of Percocet, but all that does is take the edge off. Heroin, they should give you heroin! And you can't imagine how disgusting it is, afterward. The oozing! I hired a nurse and checked into a hotel for three weeks. Having a kid is nothing compared to getting your face done."

The waiter arrived with the check.

"Listen, Anne, I want to ask you a serious question, and I want an honest answer. Are we friends again?"

"Of course we're friends again."

"No, I know, we get together a few times a year, talk about men, talk about our kids, blah blah blah, have some laughs. But I'd like us to really be friends again. I miss you.

Everyone else, they see me as"—she made little quotation marks with her fingers— " 'Neely O'Hara.' But with you I'm just Neely."

Anne wished she had another cigarette. "So much has happened to us, Neely. Not all of it good."

"Well, we're older and wiser, right?"

"I'm older, but I don't really feel any wiser," said Anne. She was thinking about Lyon, about Neely and Lyon. She had not forgotten what it was like, to be sitting alone at midnight, knowing your husband was in bed with your best friend. She knew Neely was thinking about it, too.

"That was so long ago, Anne."

"I don't want to talk about this." She was thinking about her job, her fabulous new job, which never would have happened without Neely, and she knew Neely was thinking about that, too.

Neely laid down her plastic. "We're even now, okay? Are we even?"

"We're even," said Anne.

"And anyway, we're always gonna be friends, whether you like it or not. Because the only people who ever really know you are the people who knew you when you were on the way up. You're always gonna know me better than anyone else, and vice versa, whether we like it or not."

"To 'whether we like it or not,' " said Anne, lifting her half-empty glass of champagne.

"To 'whether we like it or not.' " And now when Neely smiled, Anne could see the difference, she could guess at where the scars were, she knew what the knife had taken and what it had left behind.

Jenn sat by the side of Neely's pool, smoking a cigarette. Gretchen was lying on a chaise longue, reading a fashion magazine. Dylan was taking photographs with the new thousand-dollar camera his father had bought for him. Ted had insisted that he do something constructive on his year off, so Dylan had signed up for photography classes.

"If my mother ever sees a photograph of me smoking, I'll have to kill you," Jenn said.

"She won't see these. Stop smiling. It's sexier if you don't smile."

Jenn lifted her chin and looked off to the side.

"Hey, that's pretty good," Dylan said.

"I'm practicing to be a model. Here, I'll show you." She arched her back over the side of the chair and let her long hair fall to the ground.

"This is going to be so cool," Dylan said.

"At home I practice in the mirror," Jenn said. She spent hours at it, after school and before Anne came home, flipping through magazines and copying the models' poses.

"You have the body for it," said Dylan.

She hoped she wasn't blushing. "I do?"

"Yeah. Long legs, long neck, no tits."

Just wait, I'm only thirteen, she wanted to say. It made her crazy that Dylan still treated her like a little girl. Five years wasn't such a big age difference, or at least it wouldn't be such a big difference when they were both a little older. Lyon was almost ten years older than Anne, and no one thought anything of it. *Someday, someday.*

Jenn had it all worked out. She rehearsed the scenarios at night, before she fell asleep. She would become a famous model, and Dylan would become a famous fashion photographer, and they would meet in Paris during the spring shows (Jenn at eighteen, Dylan at twenty-three) and fall in love, right in front of the Eiffel Tower. Or maybe they'd be in Miami, shooting on the beach while salsa music played in the background. Or in New York, they would run into each other at some hip nightclub. Jenn had never been to a nightclub, but Alice had snuck into a few with her older sister and described them in detail to Jenn, right down to the mirrors in the bathrooms and the color of the tiles over the bar. Jenn and Gretchen had spent the last three days hanging out with Dylan and Judd at Neely's house, and Jenn didn't want to go home ever again.

"Your turn," Dylan said to Gretchen.

She lifted the magazine over her face. "No way! I hate having my picture taken!" She hated her crooked grin, her nose that photographed even wider than it already was, the little acne scars that looked even bigger in photographs.

But Dylan kept clicking away. "Sit up straight," he said. "Cross your legs at the ankle."

She kept her face hidden behind the magazine and followed his instructions, moving her legs to the left and then the right, arching her back, twisting her torso into profile. She could tell where he was from the clicks of the camera.

"Hey," she said, realizing he had just taken half a dozen close-ups of her cleavage, "hey, that's enough of that, mister."

"You have a great body," he said. "You should show it off more."

"Yeah, right," Gretchen said. "You're an evil thing."

"I'm getting some more iced tea. Does anyone want iced tea?" Jenn called over.

"No thanks," Gretchen and Dylan said in unison.

Jenn could hear them laughing from the kitchen. She wished Gretchen would go away, far away, or at least to Disneyland. When she got back to the pool, Dylan was taking pictures of Gretchen's feet.

"What are you guys doing tonight?" he asked.

"Going out to dinner with my father," Jenn said.

"Nothing," Gretchen said.

"Wanna come out with me and my friends? We're checking out a new club."

"I don't know," Gretchen said. "Maybe."

"Can I come, too?" Jenn asked.

"I thought you were going out to dinner," Dylan said. "Anyway, you're too young, you won't get in, you have to be twenty-one."

"But you're not twenty-one!"

"Yeah, well, they know me."

"I can pass for twenty-one. My friend Alice and I go to clubs all the time in New York. We get dressed up and put on makeup and no one ever asks us for ID."

"And what does your mother say about that," he asked.

"I wait till she goes to sleep, and then I sneak out," Jenn said. Alice lived in a large apartment on Park Avenue, a series of rooms strung along a hallway, so it was easy for her to fool her parents. "It's easy," Jenn said.

"I'll think about it," Dylan said.

Lyon took Jenn to a restaurant in Brentwood, and when they got back from dinner Gretchen was gone.

"Don't you think it's weird, Gretchen going out with a bunch of kids?" Jenn asked her father.

"What's the age difference—four years? That really isn't so much," Lyon said.

"Dylan isn't even old enough to drink," Jenn said. "If they got in trouble, Gretchen could be arrested."

"I hadn't thought of that."

"You shouldn't let them go out," Jenn said.

"She's an adult, she can take care of herself," Lyon said. "I'm certainly not going to spend my time worrying about Neely's children. Any more than Neely worries herself." He wished Jenn weren't spending so much time at Neely's house. At first he hadn't minded—they had a lovely pool, and he didn't have to be anxious about Jenn and Gretchen driving around a strange city with plenty of dangerous neighborhoods. But Jenn just came home grouchier every day. It was painful to watch her moon after Dylan, who Lyon guessed was encouraging this little crush. And once he thought he smelled pot on Gretchen's clothes. Who knew what went on in that house, two unsupervised eighteen-year-old boys with too much money and too much time on their hands. Lyon remembered what he had been like at eighteen: the last person anyone would want one's thirteen-year-old daughter to spend time around.

Jenn got into her pajamas and they watched a Steve Martin video until midnight. Lyon dozed off and began to snore.

"Daaaad," she said, poking him. "Time to go to bed."

She got into bed and waited half an hour, until she was sure he would be fast asleep. Gretchen still wasn't home. The rental car was in the driveway, so Jenn guessed they had taken Dylan's car.

She put on a pair of jeans and running shoes and pulled a sweatshirt over her pajama top. She made a pile of pillows under the covers, just the way Alice had described to her, and tiptoed down the stairs.

On the way to Neely's house she passed a woman walking a poodle, but other than that the streets were empty. The driveway was full of cars, and the lights were on in Judd's room. The rest of the house was dark.

There were at least a dozen people around the pool, drinking beer and smoking cigarettes. She didn't recognize anyone.

"Hey, who are you?" someone asked.

"Jennifer Burke."

"Are you a friend of Judd's or Dylan's?" someone else said.

"Both, I guess."

"Really," said a girl in a very short knit dress. "Well, that's a new one. Have a beer."

Jenn didn't like the taste of beer, but she took one anyway. They were playing reggae on a boom box and gossiping about people she didn't know. No one seemed to expect her to talk. When they passed the pot around, she shook her head.

"No, thank you."

"Don't like dope?" the girl asked.

Jenn had never smoked dope. "Actually, I'm allergic."

"Oh really? I never heard of that."

"Yes, it's very rare. But I am allergic. If I had even one puff, I'd stop breathing and you'd have to take me to the hospital. I'll have another beer, though." The second beer tasted better.

"Let's go swimming," one of the girls said. She pulled off her clothes and jumped into the pool. Her breasts were enormous, and white against her tan body.

"You're staring at her tits," one of the boys said to Jenn.

"I am not!" Jenn said.

"You are too. So is everyone. Don't worry, she loves it. She's always the first one to take her clothes off." He started to unzip his jeans.

"I have to go pee now," Jenn said. She

went to the bathroom off the kitchen, but the door was locked.

"Nobody's home!" came a voice from behind the bathroom door.

"We don't want any!" came another voice.

"Goddamn those Jehovah's Witnesses!"

Jenn went upstairs. Judd was wearing headphones and playing a computer game.

"Hey Jenn, didn't know you were here. Wanna play?" he asked.

"I'll just watch," she said.

"You weren't hanging out with those cretins downstairs, I hope."

"Sort of."

"Ugh," Judd said. "I can't wait to go to college. This town sucks. Is that a beer in your hand?"

"I just took a sip," she said.

Jenn still couldn't figure out what made one identical twin so attractive and the other one so . . . so just plain normal. They had the same face, the same thick, dark eyebrows, the same gray eyes. Judd was paler and wore his hair short; Dylan was tan, and his hair reached the top of his collar. But other than that, they looked exactly the same. Except they were completely different.

Judd had been in her fantasies, too. Sometimes he was the best man at their wedding, a yellow rose tucked into the lapel of his fine gray suit. Sometimes he was sitting with Jenn by the side of a hospital bed, waiting for Dylan to come out of a coma after his plane crashed, the plane he had chartered so he could get home in time to accompany Jenn to the Academy Awards. Sometimes Judd was dying from some rare incurable disease, and Jenn was comforting Dylan, holding him in her arms, now she was all he had left in the world.

"You have a computer at home?" Judd asked.

"Sure, everyone has a computer," Jenn said.

"Here, let me show you something cool." He pressed a few keys, and fireworks exploded across the screen.

"I have to find a bathroom."

"Use ours," he said, pointing to a door. "And you shouldn't drink beer, you're too young for beer."

Jenn ran the water while she peed. Dylan's bathroom! Dylan's razor, Dylan's shampoo, Dylan's deodorant! She pressed one of the towels to her face, but it just smelled like a towel with a little bit of hair conditioner on it.

There were two doors to the bathroom. Loud music was coming from the one that led to Dylan's room, a metal band she couldn't identify. She pushed the door open a little.

"Hello?" she whispered. "Anyone home?"

Two bodies were stretched horizontally across the bed. They didn't hear her as she stepped into the room. They were doing . . . what were they doing? Dylan was on his back . . . Gretchen was facedown on top of him . . . but they weren't kissing, their heads were in the wrong place, it was all turned around. Gretchen's mouth was moving up and down . . . Dylan had one hand on Gretchen's backside . . . his other hand was squeezing her breast . . . Gretchen was moaning with pleasure. . . .

The bottle of beer crashed to the floor. Dylan turned his head.

"You. Get out of here."

She ran through the bathroom, past Judd, down the stairs, around the pool, now filled with naked people, she ran all the way home. She willed herself to forget what she had seen, but she could not forget, and she could not fall asleep. Was that what people did? Was that what men wanted? She could never . . . she would never . . . but Gretchen had liked it; it was a gross thing, and Gretchen liked it. Jenn wondered what they had done after she left. They had probably laughed about it, laughed at her.

An hour later there was a knock at the door.

"Jenn? Can I come in? I know you aren't asleep. . . . Jenn? I know you're mad at me. I'm coming in now."

"I never want to see you again."

"Jenn, let me explain. It isn't what you think. I'm coming in."

Jenn pulled the covers over her head. Gretchen sat on the edge of her bed.

"It wasn't anything serious, Jenn. We were just having some fun. We were kind of drunk, and we were both feeling horny. I was just having fun."

"I know! I saw! You were having a great time!"

"I didn't mean for you to find out. I know how you feel about Dylan, I'm sorry."

"You knew? You knew and you did it anyway? I wouldn't kiss a boy if I thought you liked him. You're a slut. You're a filthy slut."

"Hey, no fair. I haven't been with anyone in months. It just happened, Jenn. It just . . . I don't know . . . I've felt so shitty about my-self for such a long time, and then Dylan started taking pictures, and telling me I was so beautiful . . ."

"He told you that? I don't remember that."

"Oh, Jenn. Come on. I promise it won't happen again."

"It's too late," Jenn said. "I never want to see you again."

"Come on, look at me. Yell at me if you want to, but at least look at me."

"No. Go away."

"Okay, fine. We can talk tomorrow."

"No, I mean go all the way away. This is my father's house. You don't belong here. I want you to leave."

"And where exactly do you want me to go."

"I don't care. That's your problem. We're not friends anymore, I don't care what you do."

"Fine. Whatever."

"And I'm going to tell my mother. Just wait till she finds out."

"You know, you may not understand this, but what Dylan and I do, what Dylan and I did, it isn't really wrong. It isn't anything your mother doesn't know all about."

Jenn pulled the covers back. "You're disgusting."

"She won't be shocked. Dylan and I are both old enough."

"He's just using you, he doesn't really love you," Jenn said.

"Whatever."

"You better be out of here in the morning, or else."

"Or else what?"

"Or else, or else . . ." Jenn tried to think. "You know what I'm going to tell my mother? I'm going to tell her I walked in on you doing it with my father. Then she'll be shocked. You'll see what happens when I tell her that."

"That's crazy. You wouldn't."

"Oh yes, I would. I'll say I got up in the middle of the night to get a glass of water, and I was feeling sick, so I went to get my father, and when I opened the door there

you were. In his bed. Doing it. Doing it, doing it, doing it."

"She won't believe you."

"Oh yeah? I'm her daughter. Who are
you? You're no one. You're just some
townie trash. Wait and see. She'll believe
me."

"Until she talks to your father, and then
she'll find out you're lying."

"Oh man," Jenn said. She'd stopped crying now. "You are so dumb. You're even
dumber than you look. I'll tell her you've
been flirting with my father all week, and
parading around in that stupid little bikini,
and I walked in on you . . . you . . . sucking
each other. She'll believe it. He's done way
worse. She hates my father. She'll want to
believe it."

"You wouldn't do that to your own
mother."

"Sucking," Jenn whispered, "sucking,
sucking."

"You're an evil little brat. I can't believe
this."

"If you're here in the morning, that's exactly what I'm going to do. Now get out, or
I'll pick up the phone and call her tonight."

Gretchen stood up. "You know what? You

don't deserve Anne. If she knew what a bitch you really are, it would break her heart."

"The only thing that's gonna break her heart is when she finds out you've been fucking Lyon Burke all week."

"That's an ugly word. And I don't care what you look like, you're an ugly little girl."

Gretchen went to her room and packed her bag. She counted her cash: sixty-three dollars and twenty cents. In the kitchen, there was an emergency stash of two hundred dollars rolled up in a cookie tin, and she took that, too. The gas tank in the rental car was nearly full—they hadn't gone to Santa Monica, they hadn't gone to Disneyland, they hadn't gone anywhere they had planned. She backed out of the driveway without turning on the headlights and drove toward a city where she didn't know a single soul. To the bottom of the hill, without braking, the lights turning green all the way down.

1991.

"This wig is killing me," Neely said. "I can't take the itching anymore, someone get this fucking thing off me."

"One more take," the director said. "And then we can all go home. Jerry, she needs a little more powder."

They weren't even a third of the way through shooting *Stage Center,* and Neely's nerves were already beginning to fray. She was constantly arguing with the director, who kept telling Neely to "go warmer" with her character. And he had never even met Helen Lawson! But he insisted they had to show the audience more of Helen's sympathetic side.

At least the makeup people had gotten it right. They had redrawn her lips and her eyebrows and used false eyelashes and heavy black eyeliner to make Neely over into a glamorous 1950s screen vixen. It was the scene where Helen learns the love of her life has been shot down while flying over Korea. Neely was pretty sure this guy had never existed or, if he had, was just another one of Helen's flings, another pretty boy to keep her busy between shows. But the director was adamant that Neely play it like true love.

"Helen Lawson never loved anyone except herself," Neely had told him.

"We're not looking to win the Pulitzer Prize for biography," the director replied. "We want to sell tickets. The audience has to love Helen."

When the shot was over, Neely pulled off the wig without waiting for the hairdresser and stomped back to her trailer.

"Out! Out!" she yelled at the assistants. "I need some time alone. Geez, can't a girl pee in peace?" She lay down on the sofa, exhausted. It would take them at least an hour to reassemble her—to take the pins out of her hair, to lift the wig tape from her neck and behind her ears, to remove the individual false lashes, to clean her face, arms, and chest of makeup, to put on the herbal mask that kept her from breaking out, to wash her hair and blow it out so that she'd look decent at dinner, to reapply her everyday makeup . . . The clock was running, but let them wait. What was the point of being a star if you didn't get to make people wait?

There was a knock at the door.

"I said not yet!" she screamed. "I'll let you know when I'm ready. Until then, hold your fucking horses."

"Still in character, are we?" came a British accent.

Neely opened the door. "Lyon. What are you doing here?"

"Just popping in for a look." He represented the actor who was playing Helen's manager. "You were extraordinary in that last scene."

"Extraordinary good or extraordinary bad?" Neely asked. "Extraordinary" was like "special"—a word people used when they didn't want to say what they thought.

"Extraordinary good, extraordinary marvelous. You've really captured her."

"Yeah, I have, haven't I."

"You *are* Helen Lawson."

"I am, amn't I," Neely said.

"Except better."

"And better looking!" Neely said. "You want some tea or something?"

They sat on two chintz-covered armchairs, facing each other. "What is this?" Lyon asked, sipping his tea. "It tastes like vegetable broth."

"It's disgusting, I know, but it's really good for you." She waved her long red nails at the kitchenette. "No booze in here, if that's what you're asking."

They chatted for a few minutes, exchanging gossip.

"Well. It was lovely to see you again," Lyon said.

"You're leaving?" Neely said. She had nowhere to go—Dave was in New York, the boys were at Ted's house, and she had stopped socializing with the rest of the cast after the first week of shooting. She didn't like to be alone at night; thinking about Helen all day left her emotionally drained and in need of distraction. But you could never really make plans to see people during a film. You never knew how late the shooting would go and what kind of shape you'd be in when the day was over. Lyon wasn't her friend, but it wouldn't kill him to take her to dinner. "I thought maybe we could grab a bite."

"I'd love to, but I already have plans."

"It's just that I'm working on this scene, it's the late sixties and Helen is realizing she might never have children, and I don't know. It just isn't working for me. Something is missing. I thought maybe you could help me out. You know, tell me some of the old stories, help fill me in. But who wants to go down memory lane, right? I guess that wasn't such a happy time for you." She dipped a cotton puff in face cream and massaged it up and down her neck.

Lyon thought back to the sixties. He was in his late twenties, just arrived in New York from London to work at Henry's agency, and the city was one nonstop party, a party where there were no rules except one: Everyone had to have a good time. Those were his glory years.

"I loved the sixties," he said.

"Well, what would I know. I was just a kid watching it all on television."

"We could do an early dinner in Santa Monica," he said.

"Great, I'll be outta here in twenty minutes. Pick me up at the gate." She watched him leave the set. *Still not an extra ounce on him,* she thought; he still walked like a young man.

"So where is everyone!" she yelled. "Get your asses over here, get this shit off my face!" The makeup people came scurrying over. "And get out the hot rollers," she said. "I have a date."

Lyon took her to a restaurant where they specialized in single-serving pizzas with unusual toppings. He told her stories of his early days in New York—the clubs, the music, the clothing, the haircuts. He didn't talk about the women, but Neely knew there had been plenty of them.

"What is it with all the goat cheese on menus these days?" Neely said. "And where did all these goats come from, all of a sudden?" She stared at her pizza: goat cheese, apples, and fresh rosemary. "I think it probably tastes better if you don't think about what's in it."

When the waiter came around and asked if they would like another glass of wine, Neely nodded.

"I'm allowed," she said. "Alcohol was never really my problem."

Lyon smiled. "Believe me, I'm not monitoring your behavior."

"It's just the hard stuff, no booze, but it's nice to have wine with dinner a couple of nights a week," she said. "I get so wound up on the set. I think I forgot what a grind it all can be." She looked around the room; everyone was dressed casually, in jeans and T-shirts, but it was an A-list crowd, mostly movie people with a few television actors thrown in. Lyon always knew the hot places. They had gotten one of the best tables without a reservation. And unlike Dave, Lyon didn't act chummy with the captain or call the waiters by name. Lyon was pure class.

She had to give him credit: he had almost lost everything, but he had managed to fight his way back to the top in just a few short years. He had kept several of his biggest clients and added some young actors who were starting to make names for themselves in smaller independent films.

Neely believed that anyone with determination and nerve could make it in Hollywood—the test was whether you could pick yourself up and do it all over again after that first time you got knocked flat on your back. She had done it herself more than once. And now Lyon had done it, too.

Maybe Anne had been a little too hard on him. So he fooled around; what man didn't? A man who didn't fool around a little on the side probably didn't have a very strong sex drive. And what did Anne have now? Nothing: no boyfriend, no prospects, just some overgrown preppie who called her up for a desperation fuck three times a year. Anne had made a mistake, the same one most women made: she took sex too seriously.

"I bet you were a real stud back then," Neely said, circling the rim of her wineglass with her pinkie. "I can just picture you with long hair and a Nehru jacket."

"And a beard!" Lyon said. "Though that didn't last long."

"I bet you looked great in a beard."

"Every man should grow one once," Lyon said.

"Sometimes I think I was born too late," Neely said. "I missed all the fun stuff." She did the math. How old was Lyon now? Forty-eight? Forty-nine? It wasn't fair, how some men just got better looking with age, while women just fell apart.

"How old are you now?" Lyon said. "If I'm allowed to ask."

"Officially?" Neely said. She knew that in this light she could easily pass for a woman in her late twenties.

"Ah," Lyon said. "I see. Hollywood arithmetic. Well, you look extraordinary. Extraordinary good."

The wine was making her feel warm everywhere. *Oh, what the hell,* she thought, *who really cares?* Anyone who would care was thousands of miles away. She rested her elbows on the table and cupped her face in her hands. A bit of red lace peeked out from the deep V-neck of her black T-shirt.

"And I feel extraordinary good," she said. Lyon had deep lines in his face, but he still seemed far from fifty. That was another thing Neely knew: A man felt only as old as the woman sitting across from him. She looked at his hands, then slowly raised her eyes, to his shoulders, to his mouth, and she met his gaze and held it, neither one of them blinking for the longest time.

"You really haven't changed one bit," he said.

"Neither have you," she said.

They drove home, listening to an old Miles Davis record. She sat with her legs crossed, her flowered skirt falling loosely around her knees.

"Come in for a drink?" she said when they pulled into her driveway.

"It's late," he said. "Maybe another time." He offered his right hand.

She lifted his hand to her mouth and laid his fingers on her lips.

"Neely," he said. An old ballad began to play, the soft bass carrying the melody.

"Shhhh, don't talk." She took the tips of his fingers between her lips and held them, softly, just the beginning of a kiss.

"Neely," he said, his voice lower.

She closed her eyes and arched her head back. He pressed his thumb against her lips and she opened her mouth, just a little, just enough, and he ran his thumb along her top teeth, across her tongue, and she rolled her tongue around his thumb. It all came back to her, the feel of his kisses, the smell of sandalwood and limes, the way he reached under her shirt and unfastened her bra— Lyon always liked it with some clothes left on, Lyon always liked it a little dirty—and she heard the soft purr of his seat moving back, and he pulled her on top of him, pulled her skirt up, the music had stopped, and there was nothing but the sound of their own breath and bare skin against smooth leather.

"I'll take that drink now," he said. The lights in the house had come on automatically with sunset; she turned them off one by one as they went upstairs.

"Penny for your thoughts," Lyon said. They were lying in bed, facing each other, only their toes touching.

"My mind is a complete blank," she said. *I deserve this,* she thought, *I deserve to have what I want.*

"Mine too," he said. "An utterly happy blank." *We deserve each other,* he thought. All the years had slipped away. He had forgotten what it was like to be with a woman who knew the worst in you and wanted you anyway.

He took a sip of the vodka, took a chunk

of ice and crushed it between his back teeth.

"That doesn't hurt?" she asked.

"I like the cold," he said, stretching his arms in a yawn, rolling away from her. "Sweet dreams."

It was the first week of November, and Anne was watching an all-news station, knitting fisherman's caps for the people who worked on her show. It took two nights to knit each cap; by the second week of December she'd have made enough to cover Christmas presents for everyone on her list. The gray merino felt soft between her fingers. Knitting soothed her, especially this pattern, simple ribbed rounds on five wooden needles that she had been given by her aunt Amy for her eleventh birthday. Jenn was already in bed, reading Jane Austen.

The phone rang; it was Patrick Weston. It was only seven o'clock, but Anne was already in sweatpants and home for the night.

"So how have you been," he said.

"Busy. I can't believe Christmas is less than two months away."

"I read about you in the papers. Congratulations, it sounds like everything is going great."

"And you?" Anne asked.

"Same old same old. Listen, I have an enormous favor to ask."

"Really."

"An insanely enormous favor."

"Uh-oh, this doesn't sound good."

"I have a wedding to go to this Saturday, in Bedford, and I need a date. What do I have to say to talk you into it."

"You want me to go to a wedding with you?" Anne said. She had never met any of his friends, couldn't even name one. "You're kidding."

"I'm desperate. God, I'm sorry, that came out wrong. I mean . . . what I meant was . . ."

"I know what you meant. Patrick, I don't think this is such a good idea."

"Come on, why not. I'm good company. I'll have you home by twelve. It's my cousin Nicole, it's this huge family wedding, and I can't go alone."

"And you just realized this tonight."

"Long story, let's just say the girlfriend is now an ex-girlfriend."

"People go to weddings all the time without dates."

"Not in my family. And anyway, if I call them now, Nicole will have a fit, she's already had ten nervous breakdowns about seating arrangements. I'm begging you. I'll do anything."

"Anything?"

"Name it."

Anne couldn't think of a single thing she wanted from Patrick Weston. "I'm drawing a blank. Wait a minute, I just thought of something. What are you doing on December first?"

"Whatever you say." His voice grew flirtatious.

"Don't get too excited. I'm moving, I could use someone to help." She had hired professional movers, but in New York City you always needed extra people to watch the truck and help carry valuables.

"Deal," he said. "Black tie, I'll pick you up at three-thirty."

"What kind of black tie?" she asked.

"It's Bedford," he said. "Think headbands and pearls."

"I've got just the thing."

She knitted for another hour, falling

asleep in front of the television set. When she woke up the loft was dark.

"Jenn?" she said. "You sleeping?"

"I *was* sleeping."

"It's only nine, I wasn't sure."

"I have to get up early tomorrow," Jenn said. "We have a quiz in history."

Anne got into bed and fell asleep again, only to wake up a few hours later. She could no longer sleep through the night without help, but she hadn't made it to the pharmacy before closing, and her prescription bottles were empty. She fell asleep for a little while, a shallow sleep filled with odd dreams, and then woke up again, the cycle repeating itself in half-hour intervals. The harder she tried to sleep, the worse it got. The blankets were twisted around her legs; the pillows felt too soft; there was a smell of fried grease coming in from the restaurant downstairs. She stared at the ceiling, full of anxious thoughts. She remembered a phone call she had forgotten to return, a credit card bill she had neglected to mail, a thank-you note it was now too late to send.

She thought about Gretchen, how Gretchen had disappeared seemingly into thin air. Lyon had called Anne to ask what he should do; they decided they would both talk to the Los Angeles police, who didn't seem particularly interested in Gretchen's story. Gretchen's husband told the police that she had a history of running away—hadn't she run off to New York without telling him?—and she'd show up sooner or later. Jenn said Gretchen had mentioned some cousins in Northern California she wanted to visit. Lyon pointed out the missing two hundred dollars.

But it didn't feel right to Anne, the way Gretchen had simply dropped the car off at Los Angeles International Airport and vanished without a trace. *But she was practically family,* Anne had told Lyon, *and always so responsible.*

It set something off in Lyon, to hear Anne say *responsible;* it was the word she always used when she didn't feel he was holding up his end. *You were always too trusting,* he said.

Now she thought of every horrible thing that might have happened to Gretchen. She knew it was just a chemical thing, her brain begging for the pills she was out of, but she could not make the anxious thoughts stop. By three in the morning she was a wreck.

The loft was freezing; she couldn't wait to move to a building where the landlord kept the heat on. She got two down comforters out of the closet and knocked on the divider to Jenn's room.

"Sweetie? Are you cold?" There was no answer. Anne tiptoed in. Jenn had pulled the covers up over her head against the cold. Anne covered her with one of the comforters. She stroked Jenn's shoulder, remembering what it was like to be young and sleep through the night without a care in the world.

But it wasn't her shoulder. Anne pulled the blankets back. There was nothing but a pile of pillows, stretched out the length of Jenn's body. At the bottom of the bed was a folded note.

Dear Mom,
     If you're reading this I guess that means I'm busted. Please don't worry, I'm safe and I'm with friends and I'll be home before breakfast. I promise I would never do anything to make you worry. I have thirty dollars so don't worry I'll take a cab.

Love, Jenn

Anne felt her heart drop in her chest. She dialed Alice's house.

"Rachel? It's Anne Burke. Is Jenn there?"

"Anne? What time is it?"

"It's just after three."

"Is Jenn supposed to be here?"

"No, of course not. She's supposed to be *here.* But it looks like she snuck out. I'm sorry to wake you, but I'm out of my mind with worry, and I just thought—"

"Don't give it a thought. Hold on, I'll check Alice's room."

Anne sat and waited, wishing she still smoked.

"She's not here," Rachel said. "And actually, Alice isn't here either."

"My God, where do you think they are?"

"At a friend's house?" Rachel said. "I have no idea."

"I'll make some phone calls."

"Anne, it's the middle of the night. Who are you going to call? Anyway, they probably snuck into some club." Rachel sighed. "It's that age. How much trouble can they get into?"

"Are you joking?" Anne said.

"Jenn's a good girl, they're both good girls. This is just some harmless fun."

"Alice has done this before?"

"Well, yes. Jenn hasn't?"

"Not that I know of."

"Oh, it's your first time. Oh dear. You sound awfully calm. My first time I got completely hysterical." There was the sound of a cigarette being lit.

"Well, I'm not calm."

"They all do it, you know. And they come home safe and sound every time. It's pretty innocent, really. They just like to dress up and put on makeup and pretend they're grown-ups. Maybe they have one drink, maybe a few cigarettes. You know, at this point I just count my blessings. At least we're in New York and they aren't being driven around by teenage boys. It could be worse."

"I don't see how it could be worse."

"At least they're popular, and that's what their crowd does," Rachel said. "I'd rather have a few sleepless nights than some bookwormy daughter who never has any fun."

"I was a bookworm," said Anne.

"Look, Anne, I'm going back to sleep. Let's talk in the morning."

"How can you sleep when the girls are

out who knows where, doing God knows what? How can you possibly sleep?"

"I'm going to take some Tuinal and sleep like an angel. Good night, Anne."

Anne tried television, knitting, reading a bad novel, but nothing worked. At four o'clock she telephoned Lyon.

"Hello?" came a woman's voice at the other end.

Anne had never seen Lyon's new house, but she pictured him in a king-size bed, wearing black silk pajamas, lying next to a twenty-four-year-old blonde in impossibly small underwear.

"Please get Lyon," she said. "This is his ex-wife calling from New York, and we have a family emergency here."

"Anne?"

"Neely?"

"Yeah. What kind of emergency?"

"Is Lyon there."

"Of course he's here. If I wanted to sleep alone, I have a perfectly good house of my own. Hold on a minute, he's in the bathroom, he'll be right back."

Anne heard the click of a cigarette lighter.

"You're pissed off, aren't you," Neely said.

"I don't want to have this conversation right now."

"Look, Anne, I know you don't give a flying fuck who Lyon sleeps with, and I know you don't give a flying fuck who I sleep with, so why do you care if we're in the feathers together? What do you care about your leftovers? If you were really over him, you wouldn't give a shit."

"I don't care."

"Good, that makes it easier."

Lyon came on the line. "Anne. What is it."

"Jenn's missing. Well, maybe not really missing." Anne described what had happened and her conversation with Alice's mother. "She's only thirteen," Anne said. "I can't believe this is happening."

But there was nothing they could do. They agreed to talk again when Jenn came home.

"And Anne," Lyon said. "I'm sorry if . . . this is awkward. Are you angry."

Fuck off, she thought. *You deserve each other.* And then she thought of Aunt Amy, rolling a ball of gray yarn from a skein draped over Anne's fingers, talking about knitting, how easy it was if you followed the rules, life was all about rules. Count your stitches after every decrease. Never change yarn in the middle of a row. A lady never lets anyone see her cry. A lady never lets an angry word pass her lips.

"Good night, Lyon," Anne said. She got back into bed and waited. By the time Jenn got home, she was too exhausted to fight.

"Oh, you were right about the headbands," Anne said to Patrick. It was a beautiful church. Sprays of lilies were tied to the ends of the pews with fat pink ribbons. The bride wore a white satin gown, and there were eight bridesmaids in pink moiré dresses of a precise length that was flattering on no one.

Dinner was at a country club nestled in a grove of pine trees.

"We used to sneak onto the golf course at night and make out," Patrick whispered after the salad course was cleared.

"Don't even think of it," Anne said. "You promised I'd be home by midnight, and I'm holding you to it." They were seated at a table of five cousins and their dates. Everyone looked so much alike, it was hard for Anne to remember which ones were family.

It was the usual small talk: who had bought a new boat, who was going to which football game on the big weekend, who was moving up from the city and who was moving back.

"I knew you'd fit in," Patrick said.

It was just like Anne's hometown, only a little richer and a little shinier. She was wearing a midnight-blue velvet skirt and a white satin shirt with ruffles down the front, a pair of pearl earrings, and a single gold bangle bracelet. It was the exact same outfit she might have worn in college, only instead of white opaque tights and patent-leather flats, she had graduated to sheer black stockings and pumps with conservative two-inch heels.

"You have no idea."

The band segued from Dixieland to an old Cole Porter tune.

"Let's dance," Patrick said.

"Oh, I don't know. This is just a pretend date."

"Then let's just pretend dance."

He was a decent dancer, stiff from the waist down but careful about his footwork. She couldn't remember the last time she had danced. She wondered why Patrick seemed like much more fun as soon as she decided she definitely wasn't going to sleep with him ever again.

They went out onto the glass-enclosed patio to get some air, joining a group of people Patrick knew from summers in Maine. He held Anne's waist lightly as he made introductions.

"Nice to see you again," said Bill Carter. "I hear good things are happening for you at IBC. Charles Brady, he's practically an American institution."

"I'm learning so much from him," said Anne.

"Such as?"

"He makes me read six newspapers a day. Six! And he quizzes me, so there's no way I can slack off. And he gives me notes after every show. No matter how much I prepare for an interview, he always thinks of something I should have asked."

"It sounds rather intimidating."

"It is, but in the best sense. It's like being in school. It turns out I like being pushed a little."

A waiter came by with a tray of champagne and cigars.

"I hate cigars," Bill said.

"Really? I never met a banker who hated cigars."

"Genetic mutation," he said. "Can I talk you into going back inside and having a dance?"

It was a fast song. They shuffled together, with an occasional twirl.

"Tell me you aren't really dating Patrick Weston," said Bill.

"Why shouldn't I really be dating Patrick Weston?"

"No reason. I just don't think you are."

"And why is that?"

"He's being way too nice to you. I've seen him around his girlfriends, he's an absolute heel."

Anne laughed. "And I thought we were fooling everyone."

"I'm sure you are. But remember, I make my living by not being fooled by people like my good friend Patrick." The band struck up a waltz. "Ah, much better." He pulled her closer. "This I know how to do." He spun her around the floor. He had a strong lead; she guessed he had been sent to dancing lessons as a child. The next song was a tango.

"Well, perhaps not," he said. "Let's get

some fresh air." They sat at a wrought-iron table overlooking the lawn.

"I missed all the leaves this year," Anne said.

"Stuck in the city?"

"There's an unbelievable amount of work."

"There's always an unbelievable amount of work," he said. "And there's always time to get out and look at the leaves, if you want there to be."

"I guess. But I'm still proving myself."

"To Charles Brady?"

"A little." It was easy to talk to him, and she found herself saying things she hadn't even told Curtis, things she didn't even know she felt until she heard herself say them.

"Charlie says I have to learn how to make things happen for myself. He says I'm too used to having men look after me. And it's true. First at the agency. And then Kevin Gillian." She told him how Charlie lectured her about being tougher in her interviews, about learning to ask uncomfortable questions. "But I'm just a big softy," she said. "I have the questions all written down, and then at the last minute I decide not to ask them."

"But it's your job to ask them," Bill said. "It isn't personal, it's just business."

"How can you separate them?"

"If I told you some of the things I had to do at the bank, you'd be appalled." He told her about a deal he had made, a loan withheld and a family business bankrupted. "But it was the right thing to do. Everyone has to play his part. You learn to leave it behind at the office."

There was something about him that was so different from the other men she knew, but she couldn't put a word to it. It felt so comfortable, sitting with him at a country club, chatting about work. He had all the old-fashioned values she had been raised with and then rebelled against. *And if I'd never left Massachusetts,* she thought, *if I'd stayed and married and done everything I was supposed to do* ... It no longer seemed such a terrible fate. Everyone she had met tonight seemed perfectly nice and perfectly smart and perfectly happy. She wondered whether she had traveled in a big circle and was just now arriving at the point where she'd first started.

A new waltz was beginning.

"Let's," he said.

"Let's." This time she relaxed into his arms and leaned back into his turns. It felt more like floating than dancing. The band followed with another tango.

"Oh well," said Anne.

"You don't tango?"

"Not in years. You?"

"Not in front of my aunt Mary," he said. He took her hand and led her back outside. The music was faint, but they followed along, a proper waspy tango, shy footwork and not much eye contact. When the song ended, they were in a dark corner filled with balloons.

"I want to kiss you, and I'm pretty sure you want to kiss me," said Bill.

She closed her eyes. It was a nice kiss. Everything was so romantic—the music, the scent of freshly raked leaves, the balloons floating at her feet, the stars twinkling through the glass ceiling, in New York you never saw the stars—she wanted it to go on forever. She felt no passion; what she felt was something else, the feeling of being protected, and it felt even more precious to her, even more desirable.

"You never called me," he said.

"I'm sorry. It was such a crazy time."

"May I call you, then?"

On the way back in, they ran into Patrick.

"Pumpkin time," he said. "The car's out front."

They sped back to the city, listening to an oldies station and talking about music.

"You hit it off with Bill?" Patrick asked.

"I never met a banker who knew how to tango."

"Oh, we all learned how to tango," Patrick said. "Or at least whatever cleaned-up version of the tango was considered suitable at dancing school. Bill's just the only one who remembers everything he was ever taught."

"I like him," Anne said. "If you don't mind. I like him a lot." They pulled past the toll-booth, onto the bridge, back into Manhattan.

"He's a great guy," Patrick said. "He's so, he's so something."

"What is the word."

"What is the word?" he asked.

"I have it," she said. "He's so grown-up."

* * *

Neely was pregnant. She told Lyon the day she got back from New York, where she'd spent Thanksgiving weekend with Dave and his friends.

"Congratulations," Lyon said. "Dave must be thrilled." They were having dinner at Neely's house, grilling steaks on the deck.

"Oh, I haven't told him yet," Neely said. "I wanted to tell you first."

"Well, we've had a great ride," Lyon said. "I hope we can stay friends."

"I got plenty of friends, I don't need any more friends," Neely said. "You don't get it, do you?" She broke into a big smile.

Lyon just stared at her. "Neely, you can't be serious. I thought . . . but you said . . . it can't be possible."

"I guess I forgot to tell you that Dave had a vasectomy years ago. So it's definitely your kid, if that's what you were about to ask." She rubbed her stomach. "I'm six weeks along. And this isn't going to be like last time. I'm not going to work, I'm just going to lie around looking at my big fat belly. And it better not be twins again!"

Lyon poured himself a fresh glass of bourbon. "I'm in shock."

"Yeah, well, don't worry. I won't show for

another month or so." Shooting was over, and the publicity work was swinging into high gear. Interviews had already been lined up with the glossy magazines that had the longest lead times to press. In another week, Neely would go back into the studio to start recording the songs. If everything worked out right, she'd have her baby right around the time the picture was released. She couldn't wait to tell her publicist about the pregnancy; she'd get everything— everyone loved a pregnant celebrity—all the talk shows would be fighting over her, and she'd get some fabulous new clothes to show off her big belly. And then, when the baby came, she'd finally get the cover of *People*!

"Neely, I can't do this. I'm too old. I can't do this. We can't do this." It was the oldest trick, the simplest trick there was, and he couldn't believe he had let it happen to him.

"Baby, I got news for you, we've already done it. I thought you'd be happy."

"Why would I be happy? You told me you were using something."

"Don't give me that look. I wasn't lying, if that's what you think. People get pregnant using diaphragms all the time. Maybe I got a little careless once or twice. . . ."

"Careless doesn't begin to describe it."

She had never seen him so angry. She had thought he would sweep her into his arms, and ask her how she was feeling, and lay his head against her stomach, and tell her he loved her. She had been waiting for him to say it, waiting for weeks, and now everything was going wrong. She burst into tears and ran inside.

"Neely!" he shouted, running after her. "Neely, let's talk about this, we can work something out."

She raced to her bedroom and slammed the door, locking it behind her. "Forget about it! Just forget about it! There's nothing to work out. I can have this baby by myself, I have plenty of money, you can just wash your hands of the whole thing if that's what you want."

"That's not what I want. Let me in."

"Why should I?"

"We have to talk."

"I'm not getting an abortion. Don't think you can talk me into one, that is definitely not happening."

"Let me in."

"I mean it, Lyon. Don't even bring it up."

"I won't, I promise. Now let me in."

She unlocked the door and lay down on the bed. "Say what you have to say, and then I want you to leave."

"I just need some time to get used to this," he said. He sat on the edge of the bed and stroked her hair. "Neely, I care for you, I care for you deeply." He was past the point of being able to fall in love—he couldn't even say that he had ever really loved a woman, not all the way, not the way they wanted to be loved, not the way Anne had once loved him. "I just never saw us this way."

"What way is that?"

"As . . . as a couple. The way you and Dave are a couple."

Dave, Schmave, she wanted to say. Her publicist had insisted she stop being photographed with Dave so much. "He just looks like some old Jewish guy. It ages you to be photographed next to him," Neely was told. They had set up her escorts for the last couple of parties she had attended. In the last few weeks, she had been photographed at movie openings with the star of last summer's big action-adventure movie (his homosexuality a well-protected secret) and a television actor who had just quit a hit series in the hopes of getting established in film. Photographs from both evenings had been picked up and printed widely. Each time she was in the same pose: a half step ahead of her date, their left hands clasped, his right hand around her waist, both of them looking at a spot a few inches to the left of the camera.

"Right, me and Dave, the perfect couple. You want to know about me and Dave?" She went to her dresser and opened the top drawer, taking out a large leather jewelry box. "Here's what Dave gave me for my last birthday," she said, throwing a long strand of baroque pearls onto the bed.

"And the birthday before that," she said, tossing a Cartier tank watch on top of the pearls.

"And the birthday before that, and last Christmas, and the Christmas before that." A pair of emerald earrings, a heavy gold rope bracelet, an amethyst necklace with a diamond clasp in front. "And to celebrate my album, and our second anniversary, and oh yeah, Valentine's Day year before last." A Rolex, two more pairs of earrings.

She reached into the pile of jewelry and held half of it up in her fist. "How much do you think this cost?"

"I have no idea," Lyon said. "A lot. Quite a lot of money."

"Guess," she said, lifting the jewelry higher.

"I can't guess," he said. He hadn't bought jewelry for a woman in years, not since Anne. He had gotten Jenn a pair of pearl stud earrings from Tiffany's for her thirteenth birthday, and that had been it since the divorce.

"Okay, I'll tell you, it's no secret, the whole mess is insured. Two hundred and forty-seven thousand dollars! Almost a quarter of a million dollars in jewelry! And you know what?"

"What."

"No fucking ring!" she screamed. She threw the jewelry onto the floor. Lyon watched it hit the wood, the smaller pieces rolling under furniture. "All I want is a little three-hundred-dollar gold ring." She fell on the bed, covered her head with a pillow, and began to sob. "No one loves me," she said. "No one loves me *enough.*"

Lyon curled himself around her, rubbing

her shoulder. "I love you," he said. It was a thin love, and it was all he had, and he knew it was all Neely had, too.

She turned to him. "Oh Lyon, I love you, too. Don't I make you happy? Aren't we good together?" She took his hand and placed it on her belly. "That's our baby. A little boy, or a little girl, a baby we made together."

Six weeks . . . he tried to figure out the night, which night . . . Images came to him, images of Neely in bed, the things she did to him, the things they did to each other . . . and now she had her hand on his chest, she was unbuttoning his shirt, and he felt his body responding, his body betraying him again . . . and there was nothing tender in it, he didn't kiss her, this time it was all about power, she was wild and angry, she pulled at his hair and bit him on the chest . . . pieces of jewelry were still in the bed, he felt them cut into his skin . . . in the end, he pinned her arms over her head and took her hard, not thinking about anything except his own pleasure.

Afterward he lit a cigarette, flicking the ashes in the last of his bourbon.

"Marry me," he said.

"I know I can make you happy, I know we can make each other so happy," Neely said.

"No one can make me happy. And I doubt any man can make you happy. Marry me anyway."

In the morning, he woke up hungover, the taste of liquor still in his mouth. He took a long shower, the hot water scalding his scalp. Down his back were little red welts from the pieces Dave had given her, the marks that the gold had left behind.

1992.

Lyon and Neely were married in a private ceremony two days before New Year's Eve. The only witnesses were a partner of Lyon's from the agency and Gordon Stein. Lyon wore a navy-blue suit and a red Ferragamo tie printed in a pattern of little champagne glasses. Neely wore a red silk suit and no jewelry except the pair of cushion-cut sapphire earrings Lyon had bought her for Christmas. She hired a photographer, who was asked to sign a confidentiality agreement and to photograph Neely only from certain angles. She had already gained fifteen pounds. They had told no one about the pregnancy.

Neely had broken off with Dave in a ten-minute telephone call. She had all the jewelry he had given her reappraised, reinsured, and delivered to the safety-deposit box where she kept her birth certificate, various legal documents, and her first two wedding rings.

Lyon told Anne in a slightly longer phone call, the day before Christmas Eve. Neely had poured him a tall glass of bourbon, then snuck downstairs to listen in on an extension. Anne fought against the gathering tears, her voice trembling, the telephone held slightly away as she sniffled into a tissue. No matter what, she would not cry. They argued over who would tell Jenn, Anne insisting she could do a better job of it, Lyon insisting it was best left to him, both of them hoping in the end it would fall to the other.

Anne finally agreed to call Jenn to the phone. Anne sat at the edge of the bed and watched her daughter crumple. *This is what divorced fathers do,* Anne thought. *They ruin Christmas for their children.*

"It's your fault," Jenn said to Anne afterward. "Everything is your fault." It seemed impossible that Jenn could still be hoping that her parents would get back together. But there it was. Jenn sulked her way through Christmas, unpleased by her presents, even the buttery leather jacket Lyon had shipped out by overnight courier. Jenn had hinted and begged for months, ripping photographs of black leather jackets out of fashion magazines and mailing them to Lyon; but now the expensive gift, so clearly purchased to soften the blow, was tossed back into the large cardboard box and left under the tree.

Anne and Jenn spent Christmas break tiptoeing around each other's moods. It was too cold to take walks, and everyone they knew had gone away for the holidays. They spent entire days without getting dressed, eating take-out Chinese food at odd hours. They watched old black-and-white movies on their new VCR. Anne knit a sweater; Jenn changed her nail polish daily, from one dark violet to another, piling the smeared cotton balls in an ashtray on the floor. At night Anne broke a Valium in two and gave half to Jenn, leaving the other half in a tis-

sue on top of the television set. In the morning the tissue and pill would be gone.

On New Year's Eve, Anne slept late, waking up to find Jenn in the kitchen, two
tabloid newspapers spread open on the
table. Both papers carried the same photograph: Neely smiling into the camera, holding a small bouquet of roses, Lyon behind
her with his hands on her shoulders, his
eyes closed, kissing her just above the ear.

"We should get them a present," Jenn
said. They bundled up and fought their way
through crowds of tourists on Fifth Avenue.
Inside Tiffany's, they kept their sunglasses
on. The floor was filled with couples looking
at china patterns. Jenn pointed out a large
crystal punch bowl with matching glasses,
a design of leaves engraved around the
rims.

"No one serves punch anymore," Anne
said.

"It's ugly, isn't it," Jenn said. She smiled
for the first time in days. "Let's," she said.
Anne got out her credit card; Jenn gave the
clerk Neely's address. In the elevator on the
way down, Jenn took Anne's hand.

They went to Bergdorf's and spent hundreds of dollars on makeup, working their

way from counter to counter, each little purple bag being put into a larger purple bag. Then they walked over to Madison Avenue and kept on spending, a red cashmere sweater for Jenn, a striped silk scarf for Anne, black boots for both of them. The spending made them giddy and hungry.

When they reached the Seventies they stopped for a late lunch. Jenn took out all of the lipsticks and lined them up on the table. They tried on each one, passing Anne's mirrored compact back and forth between them, blotting and wiping on pale blue tissues.

Jenn held a lipstick under Anne's nose. "What is this supposed to smell like?" she asked.

"I don't know," Anne said. "It's just lipstick smell. You know, I can only remember my mother having one tube of lipstick, this pinky-coral color that you hardly ever see anymore. She only wore it for special occasions, I think that one tube must have lasted for thirty years. She put it on with a little gold brush. I don't think the tube itself ever touched her lips. Brush, blot, brush, blot. And it smelled exactly the same way."

"You hardly ever talk about her," Jenn

said. "I don't really know very much about any of my grandparents. What was she like?"

"Very strict. Very Yankee. Very old-fashioned. She wore her gray hair pulled back into the same little bun every day of her life. After she died, I found this photograph, she would have been just out of high school, she was wearing this amazing chiffon dress with beading around the neck. I barely recognized her. She looked so beautiful and so happy, like a movie star, almost. But I never knew her that way. I guess it all ended when she married."

Anne lit a cigarette. "She hated New York. She was so angry that I left Lawrenceville."

"Why?"

"She thought nothing good would come of it." Anne realized her mother may have been right. "She wanted a different kind of life for me."

"A different husband," Jenn said. "Not Daddy."

"Oh, sweetie, don't even think it. Then I wouldn't have you."

"Are you going to get married again?" Jenn asked, the tears coming back into her voice. "Are you going to marry Bill?"

"Bill? We've only been out on two dates. It's a little early to be thinking of marriage."

"Alice's mom says all women are looking for the same thing: Prince Charming."

There is no Prince Charming, Anne wanted to say. *Only Prince Charming-Enough.*

Jenn outlined her mouth in hot pink. "I'm never going to get married. I'm just going to fall in love a million times and have lots of romantic adventures." She held the lipstick up to her nose and closed her eyes.

My beautiful daughter, Anne thought, *the most beautiful girl in the world.* "And what does it make you think of?" she said.

Jenn inhaled. "Kissing. Getting ready for a party. Being grown-up." She opened her eyes and smiled. "You."

The punch bowl arrived a week later. Neely opened the enormous box and inspected the punch glasses one by one, looking for cracks.

"I didn't know people still served punch at parties," she said to Gordon.

"Me neither," he said. They were sitting in Neely's big bedroom, opening wedding presents. She had told only a few people that she was pregnant—Gordon, her film agent, her dermatologist—and hadn't left the house since the wedding. Gordon came to visit her each morning, bringing gossip and glossy magazines. Liza came in the late afternoons, bringing different gossip and news about the Helen Lawson picture, which was getting terrific advance press. Judd was at Harvard, and Dylan was up in San Francisco, taking photography classes and living in a rambling apartment with three friends from high school. Lyon left for work early each morning, returning in the evenings to find Neely asleep in front of the television set.

"Maybe punch is making a comeback," Gordon said. "The pattern is gorgeous."

"Well, Anne would know," Neely said.

"I have some great old punch recipes from this New Orleans cookbook. Heavy on the rum."

"I wonder how much this cost."

"A lot," Gordon said. The small pile of things that Neely would keep was to his left. The larger stack, of what would be returned, sat to his right. On his lap was a pad of paper with a list of who had given what. It had fallen to Gordon to write all the thank-you notes. He had perfected an imitation of Neely's rounded, girlish scrawl years ago.

Neely calculated what the gift had cost and what it could be exchanged for: jewelry, of which there was never enough. She sighed. "I guess I gotta keep it. What with the kid visiting, and all."

"And how are things with Little Miss Jail-bait."

"What a daddy's girl. But I'm gonna make her like me if it kills us both. Not sure how I'm going to do it, but I'll figure something out."

"You always do."

"And she's spoiled rotten. You should see what Lyon gave her for Christmas! Fourteen years old, and she's wearing an eight-hundred-dollar black leather jacket! And she's never had to wash a dish in her life. When I was fourteen, I was already practically supporting myself."

"Well, Lyon probably still feels guilty about the divorce," Gordon said, knowing instantly that he had gone too far, wishing he could take it back.

Neely lifted an eyebrow. "Don't forget, buster. *She* left *him.* Snuck out in the middle of the night like a call girl stealing a wristwatch."

Gordon giggled.

"What's in that box?" Neely asked.

It was a case of expensive champagne from a hotel in Atlantic City where Neely performed every few years. "Now *this* is a classy gift," Neely said. "Get us some ice cubes and let's open a bottle."

"You're not supposed to put ice cubes in champagne."

"What are we, in France? It doesn't change the taste." Neely didn't want to wait for the bottle to chill. She had been cheating nearly every day since Thanksgiving: a secret glass of wine when she was alone in the house, a Percocet from the last of her postsurgery stash, some codeine-laced Tylenol she had found in Lyon's medicine cabinet.

They drank the champagne from coffee mugs. "Gordo, I gotta start working again. I'm losing my mind just sitting around like this."

"Doctor's orders."

"What does he know! With the twins, I was out rehearsing six hours a day right up to the last two weeks."

"You were twenty years younger then."

"Thanks for reminding me."

"Miranda Claiborne is younger than you, and her doctor is making her spend her entire pregnancy flat on her back."

"Miranda Claiborne is pregnant?" Neely asked. "I thought she was making that Vermont movie with Perry Hayes."

"She was, and then the first week of shooting she announces she's pregnant. Turns out she's been trying for years. They thought they'd be able to shoot around it, but then her doctor ordered her straight to bed. Here, I've got a picture somewhere." He pulled out a magazine. "See how jowly she looks?"

"I thought that was just for the part. I read they made her gain twenty pounds to look more like a farm wife."

"That's what everyone thought. The insurance company had a fit. They shot all the exteriors to get the snow, and now everything is suspended until April."

Neely read the article. Every major actress in Hollywood had fought for this plum role, a housewife in rural Vermont who falls in love with a famous artist who has come home to settle his grandmother's estate.

The film was based on a novel that had sold millions of copies. Neely had listened to it on tape, fast-forwarding through the sections about how maple syrup was made, replaying the famous sex scene, set in the attic where the grandmother's quilts are stored.

"It says here they're looking for an unknown," she said.

"Who else can they get on such short notice? And anyway, with Perry Hayes in the lead, they could put Margie Parks in that role and still sell tickets."

"That'll be one ugly kid," Neely said. "I don't know what would be worse—looking like Miranda Claiborne's husband, or looking like Miranda Claiborne before she had her face fixed. Hey, it says here she's due the same week as me!"

"Lovely, you can get adjoining rooms at Cedars-Sinai."

"The bitch!" Neely cried. She imagined the publicity now: she would have to share the spotlight with Miranda Claiborne and who knew who else. *People* would run one of those "everyone is doing it" photo montages on its cover. Or even worse, Miranda Claiborne would get all the press and Neely would be relegated to a sidebar and one small photograph. What mother would want her baby to have that kind of start: up-staged at birth.

"We certainly are cranky today, aren't we," said Gordon.

"You'd be cranky too if you were shut up like an invalid, a prisoner in your own home."

"Listen, I have a great idea." Gordon stood up and put out one hand like a traffic cop. "Promise me you won't say a word un-til I've finished."

"Refill my mug and you have a deal."

"Okay. Here goes. Five nights in Las Ve-gas this October. An evening of standards. No dancing, no backup singers, just Neely O'Hara solo with a five-piece band. Stand-up bass, a real old-fashioned jazz-club feel. No sets, no costume changes. The Judy-Garland-in-a-tuxedo-jacket-and-tights look. You can start rehearsing right away, I'll bring in a piano player. Throw in a holiday song, we'll get a live single out in time for Christ-mas." He watched her face. "Well?"

"Maybe," she said. "Maybe. Let me think about it."

"If we want October dates, I have to start making calls pronto."

"I need to make another movie, Gordo. I'm going to lose all my momentum if I don't." She knew he didn't want to hear it: Gordon made his money from her singing and her recordings but received nothing from her filmwork. "Don't make a face. I'm not saying no. I just, I just thought things were going to work out differently."

If only she didn't feel so tired. If only she weren't getting so fat. If only the baby had come a year later. If only, if only, if only.

"Who sent us that atrocious punch bowl?" Lyon asked when he got home that evening.

"It's from Jenn and her mother," Neely said. They were lying in bed, watching a detective show, trying to guess who the murderer was.

"The mistress," said Lyon.

"The wife," said Neely. "The mistress is too mean to have done it. It's a setup. That's what you're supposed to think. It's definitely the wife."

"Interesting casting," Lyon said. "The wife

is prettier than the mistress, don't you think?"

"And stupider." She didn't recognize the actress. "Who is she? She reminds me of someone."

"Looks a little like Jennifer North, don't you think?"

"She does!" Neely cried. "It's spooky, almost. So, Gordon told me Miranda Claiborne is due the same week as me."

"What an ugly little baby that will be."

"I guess it's time to tell people I'm pregnant."

"Whenever you're ready, darling."

She patted her stomach. "I'm definitely starting to show. I can't even fit into any of my shoes anymore."

"Foot rub?" he asked. She nodded. It continued to surprise her how utterly wonderful Lyon was being about the pregnancy. The massages, the errands for strange food at odd hours, the way he put up with her foulest moods, who would have guessed? He didn't even go out at night anymore, he rushed home straight from the office, often with a huge bouquet of flowers under his arm.

"I gotta tell you," Neely said, "you really are Mr. Wonderful."

"That I am. Don't let it get around."

"I mean it. You're, like, the perfect husband."

He kissed her knees and rested his head just under her belly. An old song ran through his head, *so easy to love,* and he reached for her hand. It was easy to love Neely, to give her everything she wanted, because what she wanted was so easy to give. With Anne it had never been enough. Anne had wanted a hero, a soulmate, a knight in shining armor. Anne had wanted the kind of man he could never be.

With Neely it was different. He and Neely were alike: neither one would ever be able to care about another person as much as they cared about themselves. How nice it is, Lyon thought, to come home to a woman who isn't constantly disappointed. He began humming. He turned his mouth into the crease of her thin nightgown and hummed right into her.

"Oh," Neely said. "Wow. What are you doing? Oh my."

He lifted his head. "Name that tune."

She felt his tongue through the fabric. Ted

hadn't touched her during her first pregnancy, but Lyon was after her all the time. Afterward they turned the television back on and watched the final five minutes of the show.

"I told you it was the wife," she said.

"You know everything."

"Lyon, I have to ask you a question. And you have to promise me an honest answer."

"Uh-oh."

"Really. What if—what if I hadn't been pregnant? Do you think we still would have gotten married? I mean, I know we probably wouldn't have so soon, but maybe, I don't know, what do you think? What do you think would have happened?"

"I hate 'what if' questions."

"I need to know. Because it's so good between us. And not just here," she said, patting the bed.

"We belong together," he said.

"And if there hadn't been a baby."

"Neely, these last few weeks . . . I've never been happier. I can't explain it, but our life—our life together—it feels right to me."

He was the first to fall alseep. She watched him breathe. The house was so quiet, she could hear freshly made ice falling in the kitchen. Their life seemed almost too perfect.

What would happen when the baby came? When there was crying in the middle of the night. When there were diapers to be changed.

She thought back to the day Anne gave birth to Jenn. Where had Lyon been then? Thousands of miles away, in Los Angeles on business. That whole first year of Jenn's life, where had Lyon been? Most nights he had been with Neely, in a series of forgotten hotel rooms, in too many cities to name. Neely remembered it well. He hadn't felt that guilty. At the time, she had figured that Lyon just didn't care for babies that much. Lots of men didn't. Neely didn't care what the experts said: men were men, they were made differently from women, it wasn't natural for a man to feel the same way about a baby as most women did.

What had she done? Lyon would have married her anyway. They would have had a wonderful marriage. Who needed more children? In two years she would be forty and Lyon would be fifty-one, what was she thinking? The house would smell of diapers.

She would never get her body back. How long would it take for Lyon to find someone else?

Hormones, she told herself. *Go to sleep, it's just hormones.* She rolled over toward her husband, felt the wet spot beneath her, and then rolled back away.

Liza came over the next afternoon, looking skinnier than ever. They sat in the dining room, a plate of crisp ginger cookies between them. Only Neely was eating.

"So," Neely said after they'd gone through the list of scripts that had come in. "Give me the scoop on Miranda Claiborne."

"Well," said Liza. "The official story is that it was an unplanned pregnancy. They'd been trying so long with no luck, blah blah blah, when she missed her first period she just thought it was stress. She gave Perry Hayes this whole long sob story, and you know he's such a big family man, the wife back in Texas and eight kids running around, he just gave her a big hug and said he was happy for her. He's the one who told the studio, she was too chicken to do it, he said they better not kick up a fuss, blah

blah blah." Liza's best friend from college worked for Perry Hayes.

"But a friend of mine's cousin saw her at the ob-gyn last fall," Liza continued, "and she says Miranda Claiborne had been taking fertility drugs for months. The rumor is that the insurance company thinks she had artificial insemination, in which case they don't owe the studio one penny. So the lawyers are going at it. Meanwhile the studio is having a fit trying to hold on to people for another two months. Now they're saying Miranda Claiborne was never right for the part, they never wanted a movie star, Perry Hayes can carry the box office on his own, blah blah blah. That's just bullshit. The fact is, if the insurance company doesn't pay up, they can't afford a big name."

Neely nibbled at a cookie. "It's a great part," she said.

"Totally great," Liza said. "Everyone who's seen the script says it's even better than the novel. They're trolling for a stage actress they can get on the cheap. Perry Hayes is in New York, he saw four plays last week."

"Listen," Neely said. "I want you to set up

a lunch with Perry Hayes right away. I have to fly to New York next week anyway."

"A lunch?"

"Yeah, you know. The meal in the middle of the day, the one that comes after breakfast and before dinner."

"Oh. I don't know if I can do that."

"Of course you can do that. Call your little friend."

"You're not thinking . . . but Neely, we already tried, they said, they said they wanted . . ."

"I know what they said. That was then. This is now. And right now they're up shit's creek without an actress."

"Neely, please don't shoot the messenger, but I think they're looking for someone more, more . . ."

"More what? What is it? They don't think I'm right for this role? Look at me." Neely stood up and turned on the overhead light. "Do I look glamorous to you?" Her hair, unwashed for three days, was pulled back in a low ponytail. She wore no makeup, and her face had filled out with the extra weight.

"The thing is," Liza said, "they're looking for someone younger."

"How much younger?"

"*Young* younger. Oh God, don't look at me that way."

"How old is Perry Hayes?"

"He'll be sixty in November."

"Let me get this straight, he'll be sixty in November, and I'm too old to play this part? That's pretty fucked up, don't you think? How old are you, Liza?"

"Twenty-eight."

"Twenty-eight," Neely said. "So, have you dated any sixty-year-old guys lately?"

"Neely, it's the movies."

"You know what a sixty-year-old is like in the kip? Let me tell you. It takes them about an hour to get it up. And their bodies, you definitely want to turn out the lights. And the hair, let me tell you about the hair!"

"Neely, stop, I get the point."

"Perry Hayes is a *grandfather.* So don't tell me I'm too old for this part. Are you gonna set up this lunch or what?"

"I'll, I'll make a call. I'll try."

"Good girl," Neely said. "Have a cookie."

"I'm not hungry."

"Have a cookie anyway."

Liza took a tiny bite.

"Delicious, aren't they? By the way, I love your jacket. Is it new?"

Liza nodded.

"You look good in blue. You shouldn't wear so much gray. It washes you out. Blue is much better. Men like to see a little color on a woman." She looked at Liza's pale, ringless hands. "You use sunscreen? What SPF?"

"Ten."

"You should get at least fifteen. And on your hands? The hands are just as important as the face. Don't forget to put sunscreen on your hands. I wish I had been more careful in my twenties. You know what they say about the sun. Most of the damage is already done by the time you graduate from high school. Twenty-eight. You'll notice it first around the eyes. That's where it starts. You want to call your friend from here? You can use the phone in the kitchen."

For her lunch with Perry Hayes, Neely wore a vintage flowered rayon dress that fell loosely around her waist and no jewelry except for her wedding band and a pair of pearl stud earrings. He talked about his ranch in Texas; she talked about her grandparents' farm in Maryland, what it was like to walk to the outhouse in the middle of the winter, how she had milked cows every day before breakfast.

"You know I want this part," she said.

"It's not up to me," he said.

She knew he was lying. The next afternoon they sat with the director, the scripts open on their laps. Neely had listened to a dialogue tape on the plane flight out, practicing a Vermont accent, dropping her R's and swallowing her T's.

"We'll call you in a few weeks," the director said.

After the audition, she went back to her hotel and telephoned Lyon.

"It sounds like it went terrifically well," he said.

"I'd take this role for nothing," Neely said. "Listen, I think I'm going to stay back here a few days. I'm not feeling so hot, I don't want to get back on a plane right away."

"Darling, shall I come out and fetch you?"

"No, that's okay, it's nothing serious. I just don't want to fly right now."

In the late afternoon it began to snow. The streets were icy, and all the flights to California were canceled. *A wasted lie,*

Neely thought, watching the storm from her window. She fell asleep early, waking at dawn to the sound of shovels scraping against the sidewalk. Her appointment wasn't for another five hours. She tried to read, but she couldn't concentrate. She turned on the television and flipped around. At nine she telephoned the doctor's office.

"Neither rain nor snow," the receptionist said. "Bundle up, the wind is fierce."

She paid for the abortion with cash. Afterward there was cramping, and pills that made her feel as though she were floating on a cloud. She had rented a suite in a little hotel in the East Eighties that specialized in guests recovering from plastic surgery. There was a big bedroom for Neely and a smaller bedroom for the nurse. A private elevator at the end of the hall took special guests down, one at a time, to a side entrance where they could come and go without having to walk through the main lobby.

She took an extra pill before she called Lyon. "Sometimes a miscarriage means there was something wrong with the baby," she said. She talked him out of flying to New York, the airports were still a mess, and promised him she would hire a nurse to accompany her on the flight back to Los Angeles.

He met her flight two days later. She stayed in bed until there was just one pill left. On the sixth day, she booked five hours at a day spa: facial, manicure, pedicure, haircut. She had already lost five pounds. She put on a tight black dress and took Lyon to a small Italian restaurant that served veal eight different ways.

"We can try again," she said. "If you want."

He shook his head. "All I want is you." He was on his third glass of wine. She knew the signs.

They got into bed and turned on the television. Neely had taken her last pill just after brushing her teeth.

"The accountant did it," Lyon guessed.

"No, it's the sister," Neely said. She kissed him on the ear, pulled at him with her teeth. "You be still," she said. "I have plans for you." She took him in her mouth, teased him to the brink, then stopped, then started again.

"Wait," he said, grabbing her under the shoulders, pulling her back up. "Not like that, not tonight."

"I can't," she said. "Not yet."

"Sssh," he said. "I'll be careful." His hand was between her legs. "Come on, come on."

"Don't," she said.

He took her hair in his fist and twisted her head back. His mouth looked mean. "Everything your way," he said. "Everything your way, all the time."

"Ow," she said, twisting her head away. "You're hurting me. Stop it."

"Tonight it's going to be my way," he said. "Turn over."

He pulled her down to the edge of the bed and stood behind her. He had never taken her this way before. He started slowly; she had forgotten how much it hurt.

"Do you want some more," he said. "Does Neely want some more."

She knew she had no choice. "Yes," she whispered. "I want some more." It felt as if he would never stop.

He leaned over, grunting into her ear. "Do you want some more," he said again.

"Yes, I want some more."

His sweat fell onto her bare back. He covered her mouth with his hand, then one last shove, and he came.

"You okay?" he said later, after he had brought up two glasses of ice water, after she had washed her face and put on a fresh nightgown.

She nodded yes.

He kissed her on the forehead. "My wife," he said.

They had been married for almost a month. Just as she realized it was the first time he had said it, he said it again.

"My wife."

He was asleep in minutes. Neely watched the end of the show alone. Lyon had been right: the sister was innocent, the accountant was the murderer. In the morning he would ask her how it had turned out, and in the morning she would lie.

1993.

Neely didn't get the part. It went to a twenty-four-year-old actress named Casey Alexander who had done a little television work and not much else. She was married to someone even older than Perry Hayes, a real estate developer who had escaped the Nazis just before the war. The newspapers called Casey "a natural," which was another way of saying she had no training whatso-ever.

Lyon recognized Casey's picture in *Entertainment Weekly:* She was the actress who looked so much like Jennifer North. He hid the magazine before Neely could see it, but soon more photographs appeared. Lyon knew a full-court publicity press when he saw one. Casey was getting a five-star buildup, including a full-page portrait in *Vanity Fair.*

"Casey Alexander, what kind of name is that?" Neely said to Lyon. "It sounds like someone who should be singing with the Muppets." She sulked for several weeks, throwing temper tantrums when the littlest things didn't go her way. Lyon knew the only cure was either to get Neely back to work or to spend a great deal of money on her.

He made some calls, and Neely took a role in a Mafia film set in New York. She wasn't in that many scenes, but the cast was pure A-list, and her agent assured her the part had "Best Supporting" written all over it. The Helen Lawson movie opened to spectacular reviews and stayed near the top of the box-office charts for much of the summer. Everyone was saying that a Best Actress nomination was a sure thing. On the last day of 1992, Neely and Lyon closed on a beach house in Malibu.

"Happy anniversary," Neely said, pushing the mortgage papers his way. They had been married exactly one year and two days.

"Happy anniversary," said Lyon. The loan was enormous. He had not wanted to take on such a large debt, but Neely was insistent. Wasn't the house worth far more than five million? Weren't they both making insane amounts of money? And wouldn't weekends in the Colony be good for their careers? Everyone knew that some of the best deals started right on the beach.

They drove out to catch the sunset, a cooler of white wine and sandwiches on the backseat.

"Spectacular," Lyon said. "Worth every penny. Now let's just hope the damn thing doesn't slide into the ocean."

"Oh, pooh," said Neely. She lifted her glass. "To 1993!"

Anne spent New Year's Eve weekend at Bill's house in Connecticut. They went to a party at the country club and then to a brunch given by a couple who lived one town over. The talk was all about dogs and horses and a fishing trip the men had taken the previous summer.

After coffee, the women decided to go for a walk.

"You won't be warm enough," the hostess told Anne. "I'll lend you a sweater."

The women walked through the woods, two by two. Up ahead were Cynthia, their hostess, and Mary, who was married to Cynthia's cousin Jim. Anne walked behind with Diana, whose husband was a partner at Bill's firm.

"Do you like living in the city?" Diana asked. "I could never. It's too noisy. I don't know how you manage to sleep at night."

"You get used to it," Anne said. They chatted about movies (Diana thought they were too violent) and music (Diana's son listened to rap, but it just sounded like noise to her) and the new president (Diana had gone to college with his wife, remembered her as being pushy and not very attractive).

"I guess all this must seem very boring and provincial compared to life in Manhattan."

"I was just thinking the opposite," Anne said, "how lovely it all is. You know, I grew up in Lawrenceville, it wasn't that different."

"*Those* Welleses!" Diana cried, clapping her mittened hands. "Of course! I had no idea. I thought maybe it was, you know, a sort of stage name." She gave Anne a wide smile.

Anne recognized the look: *You're one of us,* it said.

"So, I suppose it's getting serious," Diana said as they turned for home. "Will we be hearing wedding bells any time soon?"

"Who knows. We haven't really talked about it."

"How long has it been—a year?"

"A little more, actually." But in some ways it seemed to Anne like less. They had slept together only a dozen or so times—on a summer weekend to Maine, a few times at her apartment when Jenn was staying over with friends, a few times at Bill's house— and Bill didn't seem to be in any rush for more. It had taken her awhile to realize that he was waiting for her, waiting for her to decide what she wanted. She thought there might be other women in his life, perhaps someone at his office in New York or a divorcée up here in Connecticut. Women who weren't marriage material, women who could take care of his needs with no strings attached. But she was too shy to ask. She knew thinking about it should make her feel jealous, but she didn't really care. It was as if some part of her had been boxed up and put away, like a pair of outgrown shoes.

"Well, don't wait too long," Diana said. "Bill is a catch. And at our age they're few and far between, right?"

They were back at the house. Anne stomped the snow off her boots.

"How was the girl talk?" Cynthia's husband asked.

"Anne is from Lawrenceville," Diana announced. "I had no idea."

"*Those* Welleses?" her husband asked. He turned to Bill. "You didn't tell us."

"Didn't I?" Bill said. He looked at the three men and shrugged. "I just assumed."

The men turned to Anne with expert eyes. They knew how to size things up: a hunting dog by the slant of its head, a racehorse by the curve of its back, a man by how he behaved on the tennis court. Anne knew her minor television celebrity carried no weight with them, the kind of talent she possessed meant as much to them as the ability to do a handstand or speak fluent Italian; it was something you learned, as opposed to something you were born with.

"Bill, you devil," one of them said.

Bill winked at Anne. He had done it on purpose. She realized they were all standing in a circle, with Anne in the middle. Of course they would get married. Of course she would move up here, they would redecorate Bill's house (starting with the master bedroom), and soon these women would be her best friends. They would play tennis together on the weekends, she would learn bridge again. It was the most natural thing in the world.

That night Bill proposed. They were sitting in front of the fire, drinking a fine old brandy.

He got down on one knee. In a dark blue velvet box was his grandmother's ring: an enormous star sapphire buttressed by six diamond baguettes.

"Say you will," he said.

"I don't know what to say. I want to be married, I want to be married to you. But I don't feel ready." She felt foolish saying it, like a schoolgirl, instead of what she was: a few months shy of forty.

"Just try it on, then," he said, slipping the ring on her finger. The platinum band was slightly loose. He sat down, putting his arm around her.

"It's beautiful. I just . . . I just don't feel completely sure."

"I can be sure for both of us," Bill said. "You know, I've been sure from the beginning. I knew right away."

"I mean . . . what I mean is," she began, "I'm sure of you. That isn't it. It's *me* I'm not sure of."

He refilled her glass. "Maybe what you're waiting for, a sign, whatever it is, maybe it's never going to happen. You know, it isn't the same, at our age. We know too much."

"I don't understand."

"We know how much our mistakes cost. How much we can be hurt. Anne, I promise you, I will never do anything to hurt you. Ever. I love you, and I want to take care of you. Of you and Jenn. Forever."

She took off the ring. "I can't. Not yet."

"When, then."

"I don't know. I know I can't ask you to wait. I just wish, I just . . . I'm not sure how to say this."

"Just say it. I won't break."

She shook her head.

"The first time you got married," Bill said, "were you sure then?"

"That was different."

"But you were sure, weren't you."

"Yes."

"And you were wrong, weren't you."

"I suppose."

"This is real life, Anne. What we have together, it's as good as it gets. The other way—that doesn't last. You believe in it when you're young, but then you realize it doesn't last. If you're waiting for that again, my God. Are you waiting for that again?"

"I don't know," she whispered.

"If you are, it doesn't exist." He took her face in his hands. "I love you, Anne. This is love. This is what real love looks like." He kissed her. "This is what real love feels like."

They kissed for a while. She felt no passion; it was the same as always, nothing stirred in her until his hands were on her body, and then she began to feel herself heat up, slowly, so slowly, his large hands moving her along. She had seen him touch animals this way, watched him calm a nervous dog or a frightened horse with a few sure strokes. He carried her upstairs. They made love quietly, slowly. She could feel him about to finish, and then his hand was on her and they finished together.

"I love you," she said.

"I know," he said. "I think I know it better than you do."

"I just need time."

"I won't rush you," he said. "There's no rush."

"You," she said, kissing him again. "You're the best man in the world." Was it love, she wondered, or just an enormous feeling of relief? She imagined life as Mrs. William Carter. Perfect man, perfect house, perfect life. Wasn't this just what she needed? And just what Jenn needed—a stable home, another kind of man to look up to, a place where values still mattered.

Bill was right: she was waiting for something that would never happen. She was too old to find that kind of passion again. And even if she did, would she trust it? Did passion ever last? And that kind of man— how long would someone like Anne keep him satisfied? Maybe that kind of man needed another kind of woman, a woman whose blood ran hotter, a woman who was wild all the way through. Anne knew what she was, and she wasn't that. She was, at heart, a nice girl from Lawrenceville. A Welles. Her mother's daughter. Breeding meant more than inherited silver. It was who you were. How you were made. And who you were made for.

After Bill fell asleep, she snuck downstairs and put the ring back on. He would see it in the morning, and he would know.

Anne watched the Academy Awards alone, on the tiny television set she kept in the kitchen.

"Good for you," she said to the empty room when Neely went up to accept the award. Neely wore an elegant low-cut green velvet dress and a complicated diamond necklace that was surely borrowed. Anne counted the thank-yous: seventeen.

"And thank you, Helen Lawson, for being such a great old broad!" Neely said in closing. Her eyes were dry. Anne missed the old days, when actresses wept, and went on too long, and picked out their own clothes. Now everyone was tasteful and assured. There was a small army of people—stylists, jewelers, publicists—to protect Neely from making a mistake.

Anne didn't go to the movies anymore. There wasn't any time. There was work all day, and at night there was prep reading or

one of the parties the IBC publicity department told her to go to. On the weekends,
she drove up to Connecticut to see Bill or
out to Southampton with Jenn.

Morning Talk led their time slot in the May
sweeps. Charles Brady sent her a dozen
yellow roses, Bill a dozen red ones. Anne
was sitting at her desk, talking to one of the
producers about a series on automobile
safety, when her phone buzzed.

"I'm sorry, I asked her to hold all calls,"
Anne said. "This will just take a second."
She picked up the phone. "Yes?"

"I know you told me not to interrupt, but
it's Keith Enright," her secretary said.

"On the phone?" Anne said. Keith Enright
was the head of IBC network news. "For
me?"

"Yup. Well, his secretary. You're going to
take it, right?"

Anne looked at her producer apologeti-
cally. "Can I swing by in a minute?" she
asked him. Keith Enright was famous for
five things, and one of them was never returning phone calls. The producer nodded
and left. "Okay, I'm alone," she told her
secretary.

"Okay, here goes."

"Hello? Miss Welles?" It was Keith Enright's secretary. "Hold, please."

Anne waited for what seemed like two minutes. Why would Keith Enright be calling her? He had lunch with Charles Brady every couple of months, but other than that, he couldn't be bothered with anyone at the local affiliate.

"Anne," he said when he came on the line. "Anne Welles. How are you."

"Just fine, thank you. And you."

"Nice going last week. Very nice going."

"Thank you."

"Listen. Can you come up. There's something I want to ask you," he said.

"Well, sure. When would be—"

"Great, great. Hold on, we'll get it set up." There was a click, and then his secretary was back on the line.

"Miss Welles? How is two-forty this afternoon?" she asked.

"Just fine. I'll see you then." That was the second thing Enright was famous for: even the busiest executives at IBC scheduled their calendars at fifteen-minute intervals, but Enright divided his hours into six ten-minute slots.

The third thing everyone said about Enright was that he refused to talk to anyone on the elevator. There were four elevator banks in the IBC building, each one going to a separate set of floors. The first elevator bank went to the lowest floors, where there were offices for the local affiliate, for payroll and office services, and for IT. The mail-room was on three, *Morning Talk* on four. The second elevator bank went higher: to sports, legal, and finance. The third elevator bank went to the entertainment division, and the last elevator bank went to the high-est floors: the news division and the execu-tive offices in the penthouse.

Everyone joked that you could often tell which elevator bank people would use by what they looked like. Anyone who was ca-sually or unfashionably dressed was bound to be headed for the lower floors. Men in navy blazers and gray flannel trousers worked in sports. Men with fashionably col-ored ties and women in expensive suits— short, straight skirts and long, tailored jack-ets—worked in entertainment. The last ele-vator bank was the province of men who wore traditional white shirts and suits in a gray so dark that it was almost black.

At 2:25 Anne applied a fresh coat of lipstick, went downstairs to the lobby, and crossed over to the last elevator bank. She was still wearing her on-camera outfit: a peach silk suit, a white silk T-shirt, pale stockings, and camel-colored pumps with three-inch heels. There were five men on the elevator, and none of them spoke during the long ride up. They were dressed almost identically, except for their ties, which were slightly different shades of red.

She waited in Keith Enright's outer office for twenty minutes. The secretary offered her a beverage, then seemed surprised when Anne asked for a glass of water. The water arrived on a tray: a plastic bottle of French spring water and a glass a quarter full of ice.

The secretary twisted off the bottlecap.

"Thank you," Anne said, "I can take it from here."

"That's okay," the secretary said, sounding at once utterly polite and just a touch condescending. "We wouldn't want to spill anything on that gorgeous suit of yours."

At 2:41 Anne was ushered inside. The secretary followed behind with a fresh bottle of water and a cup of coffee for Keith

Enright. He was on the phone, his back to the room.

"I know, I know," he was saying. "But numbers are numbers. We can't wait till November." He swirled around and waved to Anne. "I know you can," he said into the phone, "we have full faith." He hung up without saying goodbye.

"So," he said to Anne. "How are things down on three?"

"Just great. It's four, actually."

"Of course, of course," he said. "Been awhile. I've been meaning to say hello." He stroked his mustache. That was another thing he was famous for: long after mustaches had become unfashionable, long after every other man had gone clean-shaven, losing the beard and the youthful sideburns, Keith had kept his mustache. It was steel gray and neatly trimmed, arching over a thin mouth and perfect white teeth that were the envy of the newscasters who worked for him. Anne guessed that Keith was somewhere in his early fifties. His thick salt-and-pepper hair fell forward onto his face. He looked more like an aging rock-and-roll star than what he was: one of the most powerful men in American television.

They hadn't spoken in years. Keith used to come to Anne and Lyon's parties, always with a beautiful woman on his arm, always someone different. He was one of those people who just disappeared from her life after the divorce: no more Christmas cards, no more invitations. Anne hadn't held it against him. At the time it felt as though pretty much everyone had disappeared, or rather, it was Anne who had disappeared: without the right kind of man, without money, without the right kind of job, she had simply ceased to exist for people like Keith Enright.

"I think we might have something interesting for you," he said. "I assume you've been following our little situation with the evening news."

Anne nodded. The month before, another network had gone after one of the weekend anchors. That had set a domino effect in motion, a flurry of telephone calls from agents, and secret lunches that nonetheless made it into the gossip columns, and speculation about who would end up where. In the most radical scenario, a dozen jobs were in play: on the evening news, the prime-time magazines, and the network morning shows that preceded *Morning Talk.*

"We may have a spot at one of the prime-time magazine shows," he said, his face blank.

Anne's expression did not change. She breathed in slowly through her nose, trying hard not to blink. It was something Charles Brady had taught her, and she heard his voice going through her head: *Don't smile so much, Anne, look them in the eyes and don't move a muscle.*

"May have," she said.

"There are stronger candidates," he said. "You don't really have the background for it. No news experience. No reporting in the field. It would be a pretty broad jump."

"I can do it," she said.

"I think you can, too. You have a touch, in the interviews, and now that we're doing all these celebrity pieces, all these Hollywood people . . ." He shrugged. "We have more than enough guys fighting over the other stuff." He picked up a pen and balanced it in the crook of his index finger. "They won't make it easy for you, you know. Don't expect a warm welcome."

"*May* have," she repeated.

"There are some others in the running. This isn't really the obvious next step for you. What would you say is the obvious place for you to go next?"

She watched the pen seesaw back and forth over his finger and didn't say a word.

He continued. "The morning show, right? Move you from the affiliate to the network? That's where the smart money is right now."

She lifted an eyebrow.

"I want you to think about this. We're going to be making a decision very quickly. It's a very tough game up here, I'm not going to kid you. You'll have my full support, but it's different rules up here." He waved toward the bank of offices on his right. "Competitive doesn't begin to describe it. So you need to think about whether you want to do it, whether you have the, the . . ." He paused, put down the pen.

"The *cojones,*" she said.

He laughed, and a second later she laughed, too. "And I don't want to get jerked around. I don't want a whisper of this in the press." He stood up and began to walk her out.

"Lovely ring," he said.

She lifted her left hand into the light. "A

gift, from a friend." She remembered the last thing Keith Enright was famous for, she remembered him brushing against her in the hallway of her old apartment, asking for a dance. "From my fiancé," she said.

"You know, the first year of a job like this takes everything you have. The job will have to come first. Your family, your friends—you won't have much left over for them."

"I'm ready," she said. Jenn was in high school. Bill had said he could wait.

They shook hands at the door. "Charlie was right about you," Keith said.

"Charlie has taught me a lot."

"Uncle Charlie taught me everything I know," he said. "Well, almost everything."

She was back in her office by three. She marched into Charles Brady's office and closed the door behind her.

"I have to talk to you. Now."

He grinned. "Been somewhere interesting?"

"You know where I was!"

"Oh, tell me. I want to hear you say it. I want to hear everything."

"Don't tease me."

He began to hum.

"What song is that?"

"You don't recognize it?" he said. He hummed another bar. "Up to the highest height. It's from *Mary Poppins.* Don't you watch *Mary Poppins* with that lovely daughter of yours?"

"Jenn is fifteen, Charlie."

"Sweet fifteen."

"You have to tell me what's going on."

"What's going on with what?"

"Come on. I know you know every little thing that happens up there."

"Sit down, dear. Get yourself a glass of water. Collect yourself." He waited. "That's better. What's happening is that you're being offered a remarkable opportunity. A once-in-a-lifetime opportunity."

"And?"

"And what?"

"It's got to be more complicated than that."

"Dear, it's always more complicated than that. You have a big brain. You figure it out." He leaned back and clasped his hands behind his head. "Tell me."

"Well," Anne said, "for starters, if they wanted me for this job, they didn't have to call me up there. And certainly Keith Enright didn't have to see me personally. I mean, all

they needed to do is have one of the producers call Trip."

"Good start," he said.

"I mean, everyone knows how the recep-
tionists gossip. It's going to be all over the
building by five P.M."

"Too true."

"So, what does that mean?"

"You tell me, dear."

"He's sending a message to someone.
To, I don't know, to whom? Wait, I'll figure
this out. . . . Oh. I see."

"Spell it out for me, dear."

She laid out her theory, outlining who was
jockeying for what at IBC's morning show,
how Keith was sending a signal that certain
people could easily be replaced.

"Very good," he said. "And?"

"He waved to someone at the end of the
hall, but I couldn't tell who it was."

"Well, what's at the end of the hall?"

"I don't know. I've never been up there.
You tell me."

He shook his head.

"Damn you," she said. She reached for
his telephone directory and flipped through
the pages, lining up names with their office
numbers, figuring out who had the corner at

the far end from Keith and working her way down from there. "Oh. I get it. So, so . . ."

"Continue."

"He's sending a message to the staff at the magazine show, too. About how he wants to fill the empty slot, assuming there is one. That he'll fill it with someone like me, instead of . . . instead of someone like them, some guy in a trench coat who can't stop talking about how he was shot at in Vietnam."

"And why would he do that?"

"So . . . so . . . help me out here."

"Oh no, it's much more fun this way."

"To reassure them?" she asked. "So a certain reporter doesn't jump networks. Oh. Wow, it's so obvious now. He was just using me!"

"Everyone is always just using everyone else. That's the gasoline that department runs on."

"I don't know how you stood it for all those years."

"Au contraire, they were the best years of my life."

"Ugh, it hurts my head to have to think this way."

"If you take this job, you'll have to think

this way twenty-four hours a day. Talent is only the tip of the iceberg. All the rest of it, the seven-eighths below water, is pure politicking. And that's just the people who are on your own team. Imagine all the fun and games when you add three other networks to the mix, everyone gunning for the same big interviews. You realize who you'll be up against. Those are women who came up the hard way. They'll stick a knife in you on Monday, send you flowers on Tuesday, twist the knife on Wednesday, take you to lunch on Thursday. Lesson number two: The more vicious they are, the more charming you must be. Keep going."

"If they bring me in . . ."

Charles Brady shook his head.

"When they bring me in . . ."

He nodded.

"When they bring me in," said Anne, "it will look like I was handpicked by Keith Enright. And I'm so much not the obvious candidate. So if it works, he looks like a genius. And if it doesn't work, then, then . . . that's the part I can't figure out. How long will I have to prove myself?"

"Through November. If it doesn't work, you're a movable piece again. He can leverage you in some other way. Keith Enright always needs a movable piece. Lesson number three: Have a long-term strategy. Would you like some advice? Tell Trip to take it easy in the contract negotiations. You can play hardball next year if things go well. Right now you're low man on the totem pole. It's not a bad idea to go in letting the big boys think they can push you around a little bit. Let them feel safe around you. Talk to them about their children, their precious children, every one of which is, of course, beautiful, brilliant, destined for greatness. Lesson number four: There is no such thing as too much flattery. Even the most cynical reporter is a fool for the right kind of flattery. I'm going to miss you, dear. Don't forget to come down and visit every once in a while."

"And you," Anne said. "They'll replace me with . . . who?"

He shrugged.

"You already have someone picked out, don't you."

"You'll be a hard act to follow. But the show must go on. Don't worry about me." He opened a desk drawer and got out a bottle of single-malt Scotch. "Let's celebrate." He laid two sterling-silver shot glasses on his blotter.

They spent the next hour getting tipsy on warm whiskey. "I'm proud of you," he said as they put on their coats. "Proud as can be." They said their good-nights.

"Hey," Anne said. "I forgot to ask. What's lesson number one?"

"Lesson number one. But you already know it. Watch your back."

June was a flurry of phone calls, everyone's summer rearranged at the last minute. Most weeks Anne would be stuck in the city Mondays through Fridays, her planned vacation weeks eaten up getting ready for the new show. Neely and Lyon were ripping out the kitchen and all the bathrooms of the Malibu house and had rented a place in East Hampton for the duration of the construction work. It was agreed that Jenn would stay with Neely and Lyon for all of July and commute back and forth with Anne in August.

Jenn arrived just before the holiday weekend. Judd picked her up at the Jitney.

"That's all you brought?" he asked. "Just the one duffel bag?"

She shrugged. "I'll shop."

Neely took her into town the next week. They bought sandals, and beaded silver jewelry, and long patterned skirts, and a dozen T-shirts in different shades of purple and blue.

"I can't believe all this hippie stuff is back," Neely said. "And I can't believe your mother let you put all those holes in your ear."

"I didn't ask her," Jenn said. She felt for the little silver hoops. "Can we stop at the drugstore? I want to buy some hair stuff."

"We have plenty at the house," Neely said.

"I need to put in some streaks," Jenn said. "It's already July, and I haven't been in the sun at all."

"You're going to do it yourself?" Neely said. "Why would you do it yourself?"

"I always do it myself."

"And it comes out all right?"

"It looks just like the sun did it. I've been doing it forever. You're not going to tell my mother, are you? She thinks it's natural."

"I don't tell Anne anything," Neely said.

This stepmother business was turning out to be fun. "Hey, why don't we go to the salon and get you some foils? My treat."

"Really? You mean it?"

"Sure. I'll get a pedicure and a manicure while we're there." It was high season, and they didn't have appointments, but Neely knew they would find a way to squeeze her in. East Hampton was becoming just like Beverly Hills. They spent several hours at the salon, Neely nodding yes to every service the staff offered. They emerged waxed, buffed, and polished.

"I love it!" Jenn said. "Thank you."

"You look better as a blonde," Neely said. "You'll come to my guy in Santa Monica the next time you're out."

Their last stop was to a store that sold beachwear. Jenn tried on a white string bikini.

"Wow," Neely said. "You're so skinny. Who knew what was under those baggy T-shirts."

"I'm just trying it on for fun. I can't. My mother would kill me."

"So don't tell her," Neely said. "You can be twenty-eight as many times as you want, but you're only fifteen once." They picked up six bikinis and two conservative tank suits for Southampton.

When they got home, Lyon was on the phone to the coast. With the time difference, there were still several hours of work to be done. Judd was up in his room with his computer. Dylan was still at the beach.

"Looks like it's girls' night out," Neely said.

They drove on back roads to an old laundry that had been converted into a restaurant. Neely ordered a bottle of Cabernet. "And two glasses," she said.

"Of course," the waiter said.

"Do you go out to eat much? In New York?" Neely asked.

"Not really. Mostly we order in. Or have salad bar." The wine made it easy to talk, and Jenn found herself talking about all sorts of things she never told her mother: about her friends, about school, about boys.

"And there was this one party," she said. "Oh my God. You aren't going to tell my father about this, are you?"

Neely lifted her right hand. "I swear. Are you kidding? Us girls have to stick together."

Jenn went on. Neely pretended to be shocked in all the right places.

Anne would die, Neely thought. "So, I gotta say this. You and your friends—you use condoms, right?" Even in the candle-light, she could see Jenn was blushing. "Dylan has a little stash in the second drawer of the table next to his bed. And a bigger one in an old guitar case in his closet. Don't say I told you. But take what-ever you want. He won't notice."

"It isn't like that," Jenn said.

"It isn't? You mean. Oh."

"It isn't like *that,* either. I'm just waiting for the right guy. Is that too old-fashioned? We do, we do other things. You know. I can't believe I'm telling you this. I feel so dorky!"

"I think it's sweet."

"I'm the only one, of all my friends." She was waiting for Dylan. But he still treated her like such a kid. He had taken her to a party a few nights before, then made her go home with one of his friends when it got late and the drugs came out. "Little sister," he called her, after the Elvis Presley song. But still, to be around him for an entire month, to see him every day: *Glorious,* she thought. That was her new favorite word.

"You want to hear something really shocking?" Neely said. She was on her third glass of wine. "I was a virgin when I married Mel. Can you imagine? Me? So believe me when I tell you there's plenty of time. Don't let men push you around. 'Cause they always will, if you let them. Men always want to be on top, even when they're on the bottom, if you know what I mean."

"Not really," said Jenn.

"You will. Okay, enough sex talk. You started thinking about college yet?"

"I'm only a sophomore."

"I bet you can get in anywhere you want from that fancy school of yours."

"I don't want to go to college."

"You're kidding me!"

"I can't believe I said that. I've never told anyone. But I don't want to go. I'm playing along, I went to all the meetings at school and everything. If you tell my parents, they'll kill me."

"You bet they would. I bet your mother has some place all picked out for you already."

"She wants me to go to Harvard, like she did."

"La-di-da. And your father?"

"Whatever my mother wants, you know?"

"Yeah, I know. So what do you want to do instead?"

"I want to be a model. I know it sounds crazy, I know everyone says it, but I can do it. I've had these pictures taken, by a professional photographer, he said they were good enough to show to a magazine. But then my mother found out and she had a fit and I had to tell him no. People are always stopping me in the street, asking me if I'm a model, and I don't just mean guys trying to pick me up, but people who really know. When I go shopping with my friend Alice, her family is loaded, you wouldn't believe how much money she spends on clothes, and the sales clerks are always asking me. And they know, they really know. But my mother says I have to wait. And we went to this party downtown, all these models were there, and they didn't look any better than me. And it's so unfair. Some of them are even younger than me, you know, but my mother is just so, just such a . . ."

A bitch, Neely thought. "So old-fashioned."

"Exactly! She just doesn't get it. What

does she think, I'm going to go to college and start modeling when I'm twenty-one? Twenty-one is too late. Twenty-one is old. Seventeen is pretty old, too, to be getting started, but my mother says I have to wait till I graduate. Some of these girls, they're my age, and you wouldn't believe how much money they make."

"Money is nice."

"It isn't just the money. It's my dream. I think about it all the time. I could be . . . glorious."

"Well then, what's stopping you?"

"I told you. I'm not allowed."

"Oh, please," Neely said. "You're waiting for permission? Let me tell you something. No one ever gives you permission. If you want something bad enough, you'll just do it. You can't worry about what other people think."

"You don't know what my mother is like."

"Darling, I know exactly what your mother is like. I know her better than you do. You think she asked her mother for permission when she left Lawrenceville and came to New York? Her mother forbade it. Her mother practically disowned her. But she did it anyway, she got on that train and came to New York with no friends, almost no money, not a fucking clue. You know why? It was her dream, and no one was going to stop her. And you think I asked anyone for permission when I dropped out of high school? I forged my father's signature on the papers and got on that bus before anyone found out. Because that was my dream. Because I knew. I knew what I wanted."

"I know what I want," Jenn said.

"Well, what are you waiting for? Why let all these other girls get the jump on you?"

"It's more complicated than that."

"You're just afraid, that's all. Afraid of doing something your parents don't approve of. Because nice girls want everyone to approve of them all the time, and you're a nice girl. Your mother's daughter."

"I'm not so nice."

"Really."

"I don't know."

"It's okay. Nice girls have nice lives. They have nice marriages to nice men and go to nice jobs, come home to nice apartments to take care of their nice children. They just don't get very far, that's all."

"My mother was a model, she was a big

model, and she wasn't even all that young, and—"

"I'm sure she told you a pretty story. But I was there. Some dried-up geezer wanted to get into her pants, and he happened to own Gillian Cosmetics, you can connect the dots from there. That's how the world works."

"I'm only fifteen."

"Darling, when I was fifteen I knew exactly what I wanted and exactly what I had to do to get it. And here I am. I'm the best actress in the world, and that's official." The Oscars were sitting on their rented mantelpiece. Lyon had tried to talk her out of bringing them to East Hampton ("It just isn't done," he'd pleaded), but Neely had insisted. What was the point of winning if you couldn't show it off?

"Maybe my mother would let me do a little catalog work. Or something like *Seventeen*."

"*Seventeen* is for kids. That's your big dream, to be in *Seventeen*?"

Jenn shrugged.

"You think I went to New York thinking, Hey, maybe I can get a job singing jingles, maybe I can get into a chorus line, wouldn't it be fun to be someone's understudy? No, ma'am. I went there thinking, I'm gonna be the biggest star Broadway has ever seen, I'm gonna do whatever it takes to get to the top. So I had to take a bunch of shitty jobs on the way up, but when I got home at night and turned off the lights, you know what I was thinking of? That little gold statue. You know how many times I rehearsed it in my head? What I would wear, what I would say. Only about eight zillion times. That's what it takes."

"I think about it too," Jenn said. Her fantasy was the cover of *Vogue,* and she had imagined it down to the smallest details: her makeup (smoky eyeshadow, sheer plum lipstick), her clothing (just the straps of a satin evening gown peeking up from the bottom of the photograph), even the color of the type (red, a rich classic red).

"The only thing stopping you is you," Neely said.

"First I have to get an agent," said Jenn.

"I can help you," said Neely. "If it's really what you want."

"You would help me?"

"Of course. What are stepmothers for?"

1994.

It was a piece of amateur videotape that people would remember forever, it had run so often: Neely O'Hara fleeing the house in Santa Monica, the flames just a few feet behind her, her red hair falling in disarray, her right cheek smudged with ash, her green satin dressing gown flying open in the hot wind, the handsome fireman reaching out for her elbow, an Oscar clutched in each sooty fist.

Anne was in the editing room, working on a piece about insurance fraud and natural disasters. It was an unseasonably warm Saturday in February, the kind of day that fools you into thinking spring is just around the corner, and the rest of the city had taken to the streets and the parks, giddy in the thin sunlight.

"Just another half hour and we'll have it," the film editor said. "Promised I'd be home by four." He ran the tape again. "They never get sick of seeing this one. Must drive Neely O'Hara crazy."

"Oh, but she loves it," Anne said. "She looks great, and that's all she cares about."

"But she's covered in schmutz!" the editor said.

"It's sexy schmutz," said Anne. Neely thought she looked glamorously tragic, like a young Italian actress in a film about war-torn Italy. The tight sash of her robe showed off her slender waist. When the robe fell slightly open, an inch of her best cleavage-boosting bra was revealed. Her legs were trim, and the glow of the flames had cast perfect lighting on her lifted profile. "It's her best angle," Anne said. "That's all she cares about."

They finished up twenty minutes later. Anne left her heavy winter coat behind and headed out in leggings, a thick off-white fisherman's sweater, and a pink cashmere muffler. She ducked into Saks to check out the shoes on sale. She was making good money now, excellent money, but it was mostly going into savings, and she rarely bought clothing at full price. Who knew how long this job would last? She bought two pairs of Italian loafers, then headed to the men's department to pick up a tie for Bill. He had offered to come down for the weekend, but she'd told him she'd be too busy working. Now she felt slightly guilty—it was going to be a gorgeous weekend, and with Jenn in Miami on a shoot, she had it all to herself.

The ties were fanned out on a mahogany table: pale yellow, olive green, soft pink, a hundred different blues. She held up one with a pattern of gold buckles on a red background. Very Connecticut. Very banker. Very Bill.

"Why can't a man find a decent paisley tie anymore," came the English accent to her left.

"Lyon," she said. "Hello. I didn't know you were in the city."

"On my way back from London. I'm staying at the Stanhope for a couple of days." He looked at the red tie. "He'll love it."

"I'm not sure," she said, putting it back. She ran a hand through her hair. "Beautiful weather."

"Beautiful weather."

"Glorious. As Jenn would say. Well, I'm off."

"Let me walk you."

They passed St. Patrick's Cathedral. A crowd had gathered to watch wedding pictures being taken on the wide steps. The bride had lifted her full silk skirt to reveal red stockings underneath.

"What would the cardinal say," Lyon said.

"Times sure have changed." She couldn't remember the last time they had had a conversation that went on for more than a few sentences that wasn't about money, or Jenn, or airline schedules. He looked thinner than she remembered, with more gray at his temples. There were new leather buttons on his green loden coat, the same coat he'd worn when they'd brought Jenn home from the hospital.

"Let me buy you a drink," he said. "We can talk about, I don't know, what can we talk about."

She laughed. "There must be something."

"Your fabulous career. Your impending nuptials."

"Why not," she said. Bill had pointed out how tense she got when she was on the telephone with Lyon. He had made peace with Camille, thought it proved that they had both gotten past the bad marriage, and wondered why Anne couldn't do the same. It was just five o'clock: one drink and she'd be home by a respectably early seven. She could call Bill and maybe he'd even still find a way to get down to the city. "Someplace close by," she said.

He took her to the Lancer Bar, one of the few places in midtown that wasn't filled with tourists.

"They're everywhere," Lyon said. He and Anne were seated at a banquette in the back. "They're taking over."

"It's great for the economy," Anne said.

"I feel like the New York I fell in love with is disappearing. The city is turning into something else, and I don't like it very much."

"Oh, New York is still here. You just have to look a little harder," said Anne.

They spent the first half hour talking about Jenn. The modeling was going well;

Gloss magazine was running a small picture next month, and the photographers enjoyed working with her. They had worked out a tutoring arrangement for the missed days of school. The other students often traveled—many of them were the daughters of diplomats or people in government—and Anne was assured that if Jenn kept up with her assignments, she would be graduated with the rest of her class.

"I still don't understand why she can't just be Jennifer Burke," Lyon said. "It's a perfectly good name." Lyon liked to make one or two disapproving comments about Jenn's modeling work. He was determined that Anne never find out about Neely's help.

"I guess there are too many Jennifers," Anne said. "Anyway, you should be flattered." Jenn had taken the name of Lyon's Spanish grandmother: Consuelo. It was exotic and elegant, with a whiff of old money.

"So it's going well, with Bill."

"It is," said Anne. Her sapphire flashed in the light.

"Set a date?"

"Not yet," Anne said. "I'm working like a dog, there isn't a moment to think about a wedding. And Bill wants the whole nine yards: the parties, the church, the reception. Maybe next summer." Anne and Lyon had gotten married at City Hall, with just two witnesses.

"I should meet him," Lyon said.

"At some point."

"He's a good man."

"He is."

"And you're happy."

"I am."

The waiter brought another round of drinks.

"It's so different, this time," she said. "I know what I want."

"Well, we should all get together. You and Bill and Neely and me. For a nice civilized dinner."

"Sure," she said, hoping it would never happen.

"You're not serious," he said. "I can't imagine a more frightening evening."

She laughed. "Me either. This," she said, waving a hand across the table, "this is about all I can handle."

"I keep hearing about these people who get divorced and then become friends."

"We can't ever be friends, Lyon."

"Thank God. Let's toast. To never being friends."

"Never," she said, smiling. "So, and how is it with Neely? Never mind, I can't believe I asked."

"No, it's all right. I mean, it's all right to ask. And it's all right with Neely, too. It's a, it's the right kind of marriage for me."

"Oooh, what does that mean?"

"It's taken me a long time to realize this, and I hope it doesn't come out wrong. But sometimes it's simpler to be married to someone who expects less of you."

"That doesn't sound like Neely."

"Oh, believe me, there are days when I think she's the most demanding person on earth, and she is that, but the things she wants—she knows exactly what she wants, and the things she wants are luckily the things I know how to give."

"I can't believe you're saying that! It sounds like therapy talk."

"Dreadful, isn't it. Well, I've been in California enough years, I'm picking up their lingo."

"I didn't mean to make fun. I understand," she said.

"I know what I am. Far from perfect. Neely takes me as I am."

Anne realized the waiter had at some point brought Lyon his third Scotch and that Lyon was already halfway finished with it. She felt their conversation was slightly disloyal, but what she couldn't figure out was, disloyal to whom? To Bill, who liked to tease Anne by referring to Lyon as "the third Mr. Neely O'Hara"? To Neely, who wouldn't be amused by the thought of Anne and Lyon having a quiet drink in this dark old bar? But Anne didn't owe Neely anything anymore. Anne was living by some code—a code of how women were supposed to treat each other, not because they were friends, but just because they were women and those were the rules—and it was a code that Neely herself had never observed.

Anne leaned back. "So, are you being a good boy?"

"What does that mean?"

"You know what it means."

"As good as I can be," he said.

She laughed. "And I know what *that* means."

"I have little slips," he said. "Nothing that

matters, nothing that really means anything, nothing that ever goes beyond a night or two."

"And she knows?"

"On some level she must. But it doesn't come up. Don't ask, don't tell. I'm thoroughly discreet. As is she. Don't make a face. I have to guess that Neely has her little adventures, too."

"And it doesn't bother you?"

"We're people, Anne. It's human. Monogamy is relative. If Neely's on the set for three weeks . . . well, we both know what that's like. I'm not going to sit around worrying about her. If she has a little fling, it's just that, a little fling. Our marriage is working, that's what counts."

Anne was shocked but also pleased: satisfied to discover that what she had been unable to do—keep Lyon faithful—was possibly something that no woman on earth was capable of.

"Everyone is made differently, I guess," she said. "I'm sure of Bill."

"Good, that's good," Lyon said. "You deserve a man like that."

Outside, it had just grown dark. They walked up Lexington, past the crush of shoppers outside Bloomingdale's. Anne felt the whiskey now. Her legs felt loose as they pushed through the crowd. The scent of roasted chestnuts seemed like pure happiness. New York when slightly drunk: there was nothing finer.

"Ah, Gino's," Lyon said as they passed their old haunt.

"It never changes," Anne said. "The zebras are still there."

They turned right on a side street. "I always wanted to live in one of these brownstones," Lyon said.

"I remember."

"I love the idea of a house that's only twelve feet wide. Look," he said. They stopped in front of a house with a red wood door. No one was home. "It's perfect."

"New York is full of beautiful houses," Anne said.

"And beautiful women," Lyon said. He took her by the elbow.

He was going to kiss her. It seemed like the most natural thing in the world. She lifted her chin and closed her eyes, waiting, curious. His hands in her hair, on the small of her back; the familiar press of his mouth; the scent of his cologne; the smooth wool of his old coat: her husband. How many times had they stood on a street just like this one, kissing. Anne remembered Lyon once saying the great cities of the world were the ones where people kissed on the streets.

She kissed him back, waiting for the feeling, the old feeling of her insides flipping over, like bedclothes tossing in the drum of a hot dryer. But nothing. Everything was exactly the same: his tongue, his teeth, his hands. But nothing.

She pulled away. "I have to go."

He started to speak, and she laid a gloved hand across his mouth. "I'm fine from here, it's just a few blocks." She turned away and began the walk home, her first few steps almost a run. She wondered, if she turned back, would he still be standing there, looking at her, waiting for her to return? Or would he already have gone?

"Goodbye, goodbye," she whispered as she crossed Third Avenue. The answering-machine light was blinking, but she didn't check her messages. She put on an old Joni Mitchell tape and lay on the sofa with the lights turned off. *Smooching,* she thought, *there's a word no one uses any-more.*

She knew, at last, all the way down in her bones, that she was finally over him. It was the most deliriously happy feeling in the world. She took off her boots and danced around the living room, waving her arms to the swooping melody.

But what if it wasn't Lyon, what if it was her? What if no man could ever make her feel that way again? What if that part of her life was over? She looked out the window. In front of the corner fruit stand, a couple was kissing. They kissed and kissed and then made a run for the crosstown bus. *Passion,* Anne thought. *What if I never feel passion again.* The light turned green and the bus pulled away. The next song was slower, and in a minor key, filled with high notes that the singer hadn't been able to hit for years. *How awful it must be,* Anne thought, *to have once had a voice like that, to hear your young self constantly on the ra-dio, and know you would never be able to sing that way again.*

Anne had read that the singer didn't care. She smoked cigarettes and painted and did other things. Anne rewound the tape and listened again from the beginning. *Better to forget,* she thought, twisting her ring, *better to forget.*

"Con-sway-low," Caitlin said, her midwestern accent flattening the vowels. "What kind of name is that?"

"Should we call you Connie?" said Megan. "I have an aunt named Connie. She collects cookie jars."

"Consuelo," Jenn said. "It was my great-grandmother's name. She was from Spain."

The three girls were in Miami Beach for a week-long catalog shoot. They had each brought a suitcase filled with almost identical items: a stack of white T-shirts, well-worn 501s, Great Lash in pink tubes, M.A.C. lipstick in Twig and Mocha. Their two-bedroom apartment was just four blocks from the ocean, but except for shoots they almost never went to the beach. There were three twin beds in the larger bedroom: one for Jenn, one for Caitlin, and one for Megan.

"Consuelo," Caitlin said again, her pronunciation improving. "I think it's pretty." She took out a framed photograph and set it on her narrow Formica-topped dresser. "My soon-to-be-ex-boyfriend. Isn't he a hottie?"

"Why ex?" Jenn asked.

"Because I'm never going back!" she replied. Caitlin was seventeen, fresh from Ohio, where she had been discovered in a shopping-mall modeling contest. "Do you have a boyfriend in New York?"

"Not really," Jenn said.

"What does that mean?"

"I guess it means no."

"I have, like, two boyfriends," Megan said. "My official boyfriend and my secret boyfriend."

Caitlin bounced on her bed. "Tell, tell, tell."

"The official boyfriend is the one my parents know about. He goes to my high school and is very . . . I don't know, like . . ."

"Appropriate," Jenn offered.

"Exactly," Megan said. "And my secret boyfriend is a senior in college, and if my parents ever found out about him, they'd kill me. Well, my father would probably kill him first, but I'd be next. He is soooo hot." She stretched out her arm and jangled a heavy silver cuff. "He got me this in Mexico."

"Whatever, you'll end up dumping both of them," Caitlin said. "That's what happens when you move to New York."

Megan rubbed the bracelet. "Well, I'm not giving this back." She was sixteen like Jenn, from a small town in Minnesota. She had been discovered at an airport, where she had gone with her parents to pick up visiting relatives. The arriving flight was delayed by two hours; her parents went to the bar and gave Megan ten dollars to go shopping with. Ten dollars was not much money by airport prices. At the gift shop, she approached an interesting-looking man (older, long hair, cool leather coat) and asked him if he would buy her a pack of cigarettes since she wasn't old enough to do it herself. The man turned out to be a fashion photographer flying home from rehab. He bought her a pack of Marlboros and took her to the parking lot, where telephone numbers and various promises were exchanged. In the version of this story later released by Megan's modeling agency, much was altered. There were no cigarettes and no rehab.

The girls unpacked, eyeing each other's clothes, comparing notes about hair conditioners and lip balms and emergency cures for the rare overnight blemish. They gossiped about Karen, their theoretical chaperone from the agency, who lived in the smaller bedroom. The girls had a nine P.M. curfew: after that, no visitors, no telephone calls. On the first night they figured out what the curfew really meant. Karen checked on them at nine P.M. sharp and then headed out to a club. Even their parents were not allowed to call them after curfew.

At nine-fifteen they sprang out of bed, pulled on their clothes, made up their faces, and snuck downstairs.

"Where should we go?" Caitlin asked.

"I heard about this restaurant," Jenn said. "But I can't remember the name." They walked over to Ocean Drive. The sidewalk was brightly lit and filled with people. Men called to them from slowly moving convertibles.

"It's just like on television!" said Megan. They spent two hours walking down ten short blocks and another hour and a half walking back up. "And we have six more nights."

When they weren't at a shoot, the girls

were supposed to be doing homework: they were all still in high school, and assurances had been made to their parents. But mostly what they did was play the sound track from *Reality Bites* over and over again. Megan had made a tape with "Baby I Love Your Way" inserted after every three songs.

Caitlin and Megan knew things that Jenn didn't. They had older sisters and vast high school sexual experiences. They knew how to befriend the older models in a "let me be your mascot" sort of way. They understood how to finagle a seat at the best table, how to get a ride home with the coolest boys, how to get people to pick up the check. They were ambitious in a way that Jenn wasn't: modeling was their ticket out and up. Their pretty faces were their get-out-of-jail-free cards, jail being the lives of their older sisters: community college, nursing school, a job at the cosmetics counter of the local department store.

Jenn knew things that they didn't. She knew how to pronounce menu French and how to talk to sales help in Spanish. She knew famous people and dropped their names when she was feeling insecure. She knew, from her mother, that the modeling didn't last forever, and she knew that there was a whole world waiting for her if the modeling didn't pan out: college, California, New York. None of this endeared her to the other girls. It didn't seem quite fair to them that Jenn was already somebody, that her safety net was so much more glamorous than theirs.

And Jenn had a secret, a terrible secret: She was a virgin. It seemed a ridiculous thing, to still be a virgin at sixteen. All the other girls she knew had already slept with at least one boy when they were fourteen. Sixteen was almost too late. Jenn knew boys expected things from a sixteen-year-old, a certain level of skill, various techniques, many of which she had read about in books. *This year,* she had promised herself on New Year's Eve. But it wasn't so easy to find the right boy, especially since there were no boys whatsoever at school. Alice had offered a cousin from Boston, but he had narrow shoulders and a wide butt. Jenn wasn't quite that desperate yet. Whoever it was, he had to look good in jeans.

Another thing Caitlin and Megan knew that Jenn didn't: how to flirt. Jenn thought she was supposed to be sexy. The other girls understood that it was all about making the boy feel sexy. Jenn thought she was supposed to be funny. The other girls knew it was more important to let the boy feel funny. When a boy said something clever, Caitlin and Megan opened their mouths and tilted back their heads and laughed. Jenn tried to think of something clever to say back.

And so it was that on the fourth night of their week-long stay, the other girls had already had a few little adventures. Megan had made out with a twenty-four-year-old Swedish model on the Lincoln Road mall and given a blow-job to an actor who claimed to be friends with Johnny Depp. Caitlin had hooked up with an actor who was in town shooting a music video. She told him she was nineteen. When she got back to the apartment, she showed Megan and Jenn the little toiletries she had taken from his hotel. It was the place everyone said Madonna liked to stay. The girls opened the tiny bottles, sniffing the shampoo and pouring the body lotion on the backs of their hands.

On the fifth night, they went to a party

celebrating the first issue of a new fashion magazine. Jenn wore a silver miniskirt that wrapped around and fastened with a red leather button. She borrowed a pair of silver hoop earrings from Megan and lined her eyes with black kohl.

They squeezed into a large back booth with a few older models and the various men the older models called over. The older models were doing the kind of work the girls dreamed of: magazine layouts, with clothing by famous designers, shot by photographers whose names the girls had memorized from years of reading fashion magazines. The women talked; the men paid for the drinks. One of the men was teaching Caitlin how to tie a knot in a maraschino-cherry stem using her tongue and her teeth. Megan got drunk and danced on a table.

"You're very quiet," one of the men said to Jenn. His name was Gunther. He was a German photographer who she guessed was in his early forties. She had seen his name in *Vogue* many times. He offered her a cigarette.

"Thanks, I don't smoke," Jenn said.

"Good girl," he said. "You're a good girl?"

"Sometimes," she said. "Sometimes not."

Gunther studied her face. "You should wear your hair back," he said. "Like this." He dipped the tips of his fingers in a plate of olive oil, rubbed it around in his palms, and then pushed her hair up and back from her perfect center part. He fluffed the hair at her crown, then twisted a few strands, pulling them across her shoulders.

"Better," he said. "And your lips, too matte." He swirled two fingers in the oil. "Open a little."

She opened her mouth.

"Relax. Make your lips soft." He smeared the oil across her lips and under her brow bones. "Much better. Are you having fun here?"

"Sure," Jenn said.

"I am very bored. This is not what I was expecting."

"Oh."

"I'm going to meet some friends for a drink. Would you like to join me?"

"Maybe."

"We can walk there." He named a good hotel.

"Okay," she said. "Just give me a minute." She went into the bathroom and checked her reflection, her wild hair. She took out her lipstick and smudged some color onto her cheeks. On the way out, she waved goodbye to Megan.

His friends were sitting in a smoky bar, chatting about new restaurants in London. Gunther held her hand and ordered Cognac for both of them. She was not expected to talk.

"I am very bored," he whispered into her ear. "Come upstairs for a drink."

This is it, she thought. His hands had been gentle. She knew he would not hurt her.

His room was expensively decorated and extremely small. Cameras were piled on the single chair. There was no place to sit except the bed. He put on the radio: Cuban music.

"I'll get us some water," he said. He returned from the bathroom with two glasses of water and some large dark green pills. "This will relax you," he said.

"What is it?" she asked.

"It's nothing, it's safe," he said. He took one first to show her.

"Okay," she said, opening her hand.

"Do you like to dance?"

"Everyone likes to dance."

"Dance for me," he said.

He turned up the music. She got up and began to dance, snapping her fingers to the beat. He was smiling, nodding, snapping along.

"Consuelo, you dance like a Gypsy!" he said.

She had been watching the other girls dance all week, and she copied their moves: running her fingers through her hair, spreading her open hands across her hips, leaning her head back as she shook her shoulders back and forth.

"Come here," Gunther said. She straddled his lap. "So beautiful," he said. "The most beautiful." He kissed her breasts through her T-shirt, licking the fabric over her nipples until it was almost transparent. "How old are you."

"Nineteen."

"Really. Nineteen. I don't think so."

"Almost nineteen. Eighteen," she said.

He pulled off her shirt and tossed it onto the floor. "Tomorrow I will take your picture," he said.

"I have to work tomorrow."

"Afterward," he said. "You know who I am?"

"Yes, of course." She thought how jealous everyone would be.

He ran a finger around her shoulder, over her collarbone, back and forth across her breasts, down to her belly. "This comes off," he said.

She unbuttoned her skirt and sat back down. Her black cotton underwear was cut high at the hips. He slipped his hand inside from underneath. She closed her eyes and let her head fall forward onto his shoulder. The pill was starting to kick in. Her body felt loose, she felt it would take all the energy in the world to remain standing, but at the same time she was fully alert: to the music, which was beautiful; to his breathing, which was heavier now; to the warmth that spread out from his touch. He had his thumb in front and two fingers inside her. She did not know what would come next. She had imagined it differently. She thought there would be kissing.

"Have you been with someone like me," he asked. "Someone older."

She shook her head.

"Ah," Gunther said. "You will learn. It

takes us longer." He lifted her off his lap and unbuttoned his trousers, then pushed them to the floor. "A little help, please," he said. She took him in her hand. He wasn't hard at all.

"With your mouth," he said. "There. Nice, very nice."

This was the part she had read about in books. She wet her lips and began. In a minute he was hard. He took off her underwear. He lifted her back up with one hand, spread her apart with the other.

"Oh, you have to make yourself wet again," he said. He took her fingers in his mouth, covering them with his spit.

Now she was confused. "I've never done this before," she said.

"Don't be shy. It makes me excited to watch."

"I mean," she said, "I've never been with anyone."

He leaned back on the bed. She slid to the floor. "Christ," he said. "A virgin."

"I'm sorry."

"I need a cigarette," he said. He lit one for her as well. It made her a little dizzy. "Come here, get off the floor."

She lay down next to him on her back. He

turned onto his side, propped up on one arm. "If I had known," he said. "You should have said. Really? No one?"

She shook her head.

He stroked her breasts. "You are so beautiful, so perfect. A girl like you is a gift. Don't you have boyfriends?"

"No."

"You know, the first one you remember forever. And the first time, for the girl, it's not so good. That comes later. Do you know what I'm saying?"

"Not really."

"A man feels pleasure right away. A woman needs to learn."

She turned and faced him. "Teach me," she said.

She kept her eyes closed the whole time. He unwrapped a condom and began slowly. His weight was on his elbows. She was afraid to make a sound, afraid he might realize he was hurting her and stop before it was done. He was muttering in her ear, words she could not understand. At the end it hurt the most: he shoved hard three times and shouted.

Afterward he brought her a fresh glass of

water and turned on the television. They watched music videos and didn't talk.

"I have to go home now," she said. Her shirt was still slightly damp. He gave her a T-shirt with a decal of a cartoon cat across the front.

"Do you need carfare?" he said. She shook her head. He called the front desk and ordered her a cab.

She went into the bathroom and rolled a toothpaste-covered finger around in her mouth. Her underwear felt sticky, but she didn't want to look. She rolled up some tissues and stuck them between her legs. There was blood on her fingertips. She washed her hands and face with water so hot that it hurt. She looked at herself in the mirror. "Just fucked," she said aloud. There were various soaps and lotions and hair products in black-and-white-striped containers. She slipped a bottle of hair conditioner into her pocket.

He wrapped a towel around his waist and walked her to the door. "You will always remember Gunther, and Gunther will always remember you." He kissed her goodbye on the cheek, their first kiss. He didn't say anything about taking her picture, and she didn't remind him.

Neely flipped through the catalog, looking for pictures of Jenn. There she was: in a big red cotton shirt and matching flip-flops, in a blue polka-dot sundress, in an oversize sweater that hung loosely around her hips. Neely couldn't figure out why there was so much baggy clothing in this catalog; the models were all skinny and would have looked wonderful in tight clothes. But apparently that was their specialty, pretty much everything looked as if it had been borrowed from a boyfriend and been through the washer several times already. The models wore almost no makeup. Their hair was uncombed, and in several shots there was sand stuck to their legs and faces.

Neely ripped out the most striking photograph of Jenn, the one where she was looking just above the camera. There was something complicated in her eyes, something like a dare, something knowing and sad. *Sixteen-year-old girls aren't supposed to look that way,* Neely thought.

Girls had to be absolutely perfect for these kinds of pictures, otherwise they'd just look like slobs. Neely remembered Anne's old glamour shots: the foundation, the complicated lip colors, the twenty kinds of powder applied just so, every hair sprayed into place. Jenn was prettier than Anne, and these photographs proved it. Anne had needed so much help, but Jenn could be wearing nothing but lip gloss, they could throw dirt across her face, and she'd still be gorgeous. It gave Neely some satisfaction to think of Anne looking at these photographs of Jenn, realizing how beautiful her daughter was.

Something that gave Neely even more satisfaction: Anne was getting her eyes done! Anne had tried to keep it a secret, but Neely had finagled it out of her. So much for all that talk about aging gracefully! Television wasn't like the movies; the lighting was terrible, and there wasn't much you could get away with on videotape. Neely knew it had just been a matter of time. Look at Nancy Bergen—almost seventy, and her skin pulled so tight that you could bounce a quarter off her neck. Neely was dying to be interviewed by Nancy Bergen. All kinds of people won Oscars, and there were over fifty issues of *People* a year, but only the biggest stars got a full twenty minutes with Nancy Bergen. Maybe it was time to get a new publicist.

It was only seven in the morning, but Lyon had already left for the office. They were both working insane hours, Lyon waking up at the crack of dawn to get in early phone calls to New York, Neely on the set sometimes till eight in the evening. She came home too exhausted to go out and too wired to go to sleep. The cook left meals in the refrigerator that Neely reheated in the microwave and then ate alone in front of the television set. She longed for some wine, one little glass to take the edge off her mood, but she was five pounds over her target weight, so Lyon wouldn't let her have any alcohol. Some nights she stared at the ceiling for hours before falling asleep.

The movie wasn't going well. The director had been replaced after the second week of shooting, and the script was being rewritten as they went. The film was set in the forties, and the producer was a stickler for period detail, so Neely had to wear a girdle in all her shots. It was an actual girdle from the forties: no Lycra, no spandex, just rubbery fabric that was hot as hell and stiff boning that dug into her flesh whenever she crossed her legs.

The car would be coming for her in forty-five minutes. She took a quick shower and got dressed. There was a blister on one of her toes (she had to wear period shoes as well) that looked as though it were about to burst. Where were the Band-Aids? She couldn't find any in her bathroom or the boys' bathroom, either.

She looked through Lyon's medicine chest: nothing. Then she remembered that he kept a first-aid kit in his large brown suitcase for overseas trips. The suitcases were stored along the back wall of his walk-in closet, behind a rack of dress shirts. Neely realized that Lyon's closet was about the same size as her first apartment in New York.

She sat on the floor and opened the suitcase. There were Band-Aids in three sizes; Neely picked medium and gently pressed it around her toe. There were all kinds of other stuff in the kit as well—three kinds of antacid, two full vials of antibiotics, various tubes of lotion, for bug bites, for itching, for burns, for cuts . . . Geez, Lyon was such a hypochondriac! But then most men were. There were not one but three Ace bandages! Something was wrapped inside one of them. Neely undid the little metal hooks and rolled it across the floor: a vial of large white pills. It was Vicodin, prescribed by his dentist. The bottle was almost full, and the prescription was over a year old. "For pain," the label read.

Neely couldn't remember what she had heard about Vicodin. It was some souped-up form of aspirin, she guessed. Well, that girdle was going to hurt plenty. She worked up some spit and swallowed a pill. It probably wouldn't last very long. She tucked the bottle into her jeans pocket and put back everything exactly as she had found it. Lyon wouldn't miss the pills; he had probably forgotten all about them.

Just before she turned out the lights, she noticed the outline of the suitcase in the deep plush of the closet carpet. *Just in case,* she thought. She got the portable handheld vacuum from the linen closet and ran it over the carpet, walking backward, erasing her footprints as she went. She didn't think any pill could work in five minutes, but she already felt better: happier, lighter, ready to face the day ahead. She heard the car arrive, and she skipped downstairs to meet it, singing all the way.

1995.

It was Anne's favorite time of year: late spring, just a hint of hot weather on the noon breeze, the lilacs in full bloom, her favorite flower. She was in Connecticut for a long weekend of gardening and parties. Curtis and Jerry were visiting, their first official house visit. The two couples had had a few dinners in the city. It turned out that Jerry and Bill shared several enthusiasms: the architecture of Venice, the history of the spice trade, and an almost encyclopedic knowledge of the various recordings of Mozart.

"Jerry makes Bill feel smarter," Curtis told

Anne over the telephone, "and Bill makes Jerry feel straighter. The best friendships have been built on less."

"Who would have guessed," said Anne.

"And with them busy talking about *The Magic Flute,* you and I can gossip as much as we want. Oh Annie, we miss you out here. Are you really going to get married?"

"I really am. Eventually."

"I want to be your bridesmaid."

On Saturday morning Curtis and Jerry borrowed the Jeep to go shopping for antiques, and Bill headed for the golf course. Anne drove into town to pick up dessert.

It was a storybook Main Street, with a pretty steepled church at one end and an old stone library at the other. In between were offices and shops and two small restaurants that had been run by the same family for three generations. Anne went into the bakery and studied the selection.

She asked the clerk for a large chocolate cheesecake.

"Oh, we just sold the last one, just two seconds ago." The clerk nodded toward the far end of the counter.

There was Nancy Bergen, watching the last chocolate cheesecake being slipped into a green-and-white-striped cardboard box.

"Be careful with the edges," Nancy Bergen was saying. "Don't crush it now." She looked up. "Hello, Anne!" she cried, wiggling her fingers. "I saw you looking at this, and I knew I just had to have one!" They had been introduced, and then reintroduced, at several parties in the city. Each time Nancy said she would call Anne to schedule a lunch, but she never did. Anne knew she was too low in the pecking order. And everyone knew that Nancy didn't really care for the company of women, unless the woman was married to someone extremely famous or accomplished.

"Yes, hello," Anne said. Turning back to the clerk, she pointed to a plain cheesecake, of which there were several left. "Are you visiting for the weekend?" she asked Nancy.

Nancy dropped the name of the famous writer she was staying with. Anne knew he lived around here, but she had never seen him: unless their children were in school together, the artists and the bankers never mixed.

They left the shop together. Nancy was

overdressed for the country, in camel-colored wool trousers and low patent-leather pumps.

"I believe I owe you a lunch," she said in her famous rasp. "Do you have time?"

Bill wouldn't be back from the golf course for another couple of hours. "I'd love to," Anne said. They went to the Italian restaurant and ordered iced teas and Caesar salads. Nancy talked about her grandson, and a recent trip to Washington, and how much she was learning to love the Internet. Anne mostly listened.

"Such a pretty little town. So, tell me about this Bill," Nancy said.

"He's an investment banker. He grew up around here, actually. His family was—"

"A banker, how wonderful. My second husband was a banker." Nancy told a long story about the year that New York City almost went broke. "I picked up my apartment for nothing in 1975. I mean, peanuts. You would die if I told you. Eight rooms on Park Avenue. Every night I go to bed and I tell myself, Nancy, you've come a long way from the Bronx! Where are you from, dear?"

"Lawrenceville, Massachusetts."

"Of course, of course, how could I forget." Nancy was staring at her eyes. "Dr. Barker?" she asked.

"Excuse me?"

"Your eyes. Wonderful work. Dr. Barker, am I right?"

Anne didn't know what to say.

"Oh, my dear, you don't have to pretend with me." She raised her arm like a traffic cop and then flicked her hand down from the wrist. Anne tried to figure out who Nancy reminded her of. *A gay man,* Anne thought. *She talks just like a gay man.* "We all do it. Dr. Barker is great with eyes, but when you're ready to get the rest of it done, you call me and we'll find you someone else. But what am I talking about? You look wonderful. You won't have to worry about *that* for another three years at least."

Nancy picked up the check. "This is a lovely little town, but I'd lose my mind if I came up here every weekend. But of course you must love it. You and Bill." She laid her corporate credit card on the china plate. "You know, we must get together for lunch in the city. I'm going to take you to the Four Seasons. We should be seen together, dear. Otherwise people will gossip. We don't want them thinking we're competitive, do we? Playing one network off against the other? People say such awful things about the women in our business. They pretend everything is one big catfight. And of course it isn't that way at all, is it? You and I, after all, we do such different things. So different."

"So very different," Anne said. But it wasn't true. They went after the same interviews all the time, and almost all the time Nancy won. And it would always be that way, Anne knew, whatever Keith Enright said.

A woman in tennis whites came up and asked for Nancy's autograph. "You are such a dear," Nancy said, taking out her heavy fountain pen. "And of course you'll want Anne's autograph, too."

The woman looked at Anne but didn't seem to recognize her. "Oh, sure," she said. "That would be great."

"Let me get a pen," Anne said. She fished around her bag but couldn't find anything. "May I?" she said to Nancy.

"Of course, dear. But not this one, they take a little bit of know-how, you don't want to get any ink on those pretty fingers of yours." She capped her fountain pen and took a cheap felt-tip out of her purse. "Here you go."

They said goodbye on the sidewalk. "Aren't the lilacs gorgeous?" Nancy said. "They were my favorite when I was growing up."

"Mine too," Anne said.

The sun was bright and hot on their faces. Nancy leaned close and tapped Anne's forehead. "You go get some collagen for that, dear. It makes a world of difference. Even a monkey doctor could do it. You can ask Dr. Barker."

"I love your meat loaf," Curtis was saying. "You have to give me your recipe."

"Never," Mary said. "It's a family secret." There were eight of them altogether: Mary and Jim, Anne and Bill, Curtis and Jerry, and Diana and Dickie, who worked at the firm with Bill. They sat at a round pine table, drinking a good red that Dickie had brought up from the city.

"That's not a family secret," Curtis said. "A family secret is, I don't know. Uncle Harry was an ax murderer. Or an embezzler.

Or boyfriends with J. Edgar Hoover. Meat loaf is not a secret."

"Well, it has a secret ingredient."

"Let me guess." He closed his eyes. "This is too hard. You have to tell me."

"I won't," Mary said. "Oh Anne, he's adorable, how come we haven't met him before?"

"Because there's a quota on homosexuals in Litchfield County. We couldn't come up until someone else left," Jerry said.

"We put them on the list," Bill said. "But it was a long wait."

"Did you know, meat loaf is becoming very fashionable. It's on all the menus now."

"I would never eat meat loaf in a restaurant," said Diana. "My mother always told me there are three rules in life. Never let anyone take your picture naked. Never eat ground meat out. And I forget the third."

"Never forget to send a thank-you note?" offered Mary.

"Never wear white after Labor Day?" said Jim.

"I can't remember. It's going to make me crazy. This is good wine!"

"Never borrow money from a friend?" said Bill.

"Never wear diamonds before five?" said Anne.

"That's it, that's it!" cried Diana. "Though now people wear diamonds to lunch. I see the pictures in the paper."

"Which pictures?"

"You know, in *The New York Times* on Sunday. Right before the wedding pages. Speaking of which. I could do without all these couples pictures they've begun running. Ugh."

"But I love them," Mary said. "It's so interesting, isn't it? How people tend to find other people who are so, you know."

"At the same level," Jim said.

"Exactly. At least most of the time. Sometimes one of them is really much more attractive than the other."

"Those are the most fun to read."

"We play a little game with those," Jim said. "It's called 'find the money.' "

"Mother went crazy when she found out they wouldn't settle the newspaper strike before Jim and I got married," Mary said. "She called Mr. Sulzberger to make a complaint. Time for dessert." The women cleared the plates. Jerry and Curtis began to stand up, but Anne shook her head.

"You know who I saw at the market?" Diana said, scraping plates into the garbage. "Casey Alexander. She was in that marvelous Vermont movie, remember? They bought the old Hilliard place. For about a zillion dollars."

"Well, her husband can afford it," said Mary.

"And they asked the real estate agent about joining the club. Can you imagine? Alexander isn't his real name, you know. It's his first name. His real name has all these C's and Z's and J's in it. It's about eighty letters long."

"And he's about eighty years old," Mary said.

"She seems nice," Anne said. The two women turned to her.

"You've met her?" Mary asked.

"No, but. You know. From her interviews. She seems lovely. They wanted me to interview her for the show, but apparently she doesn't do television interviews, just print."

"Well, I'm glad they're fixing up the Hilliard house, because it was such a wreck. But I hope that's the end of it. Jim says if too many more of these Hollywood types buy property in town, we're moving."

"You wouldn't really," Diana said.

"You know how Jim is. He says they'll run up the prices, and then it will be silly not to sell. And he says whenever these kinds of people move in, the whole town changes, and not for the better."

"Changes how?" Anne asked.

"Oh, you know. Restaurants and all kinds of people who . . . well, don't make me say it. They have plenty of places to live already. They don't have to come here."

"Who is 'they'?"

"Anne, you know exactly what I mean. Just look what's happened to Southampton! Anyway. I saw her at the market, she was wearing these big dark sunglasses and this broad-brimmed hat, as if no one would notice. She looked ridiculous. And speaking of diamonds before five."

They got out the dessert plates and forks.

"Chocolate cheesecake!" said Diana. "My favorite. You are too naughty. I haven't had this in ages. They always run out on the weekends."

Anne had switched boxes when Nancy had gone to the bathroom to reapply her lipstick. "It was the last one," she said.

"So," Diana said. "I'm thinking of redoing

the library. Do you think Jerry could give me some advice?"

"He's an architect, not a decorator."

"But they always have such good taste," Diana said.

"Maybe next time."

Dickie had brought out the brandy. They talked for another hour—about a new sports car that had just come on the market, about whether e-mail would ever replace the telephone—and then it was time to go home.

"That really was fabulous meat loaf," Curtis said in the car. "I loved the touch of cinnamon."

"There was cinnamon?" Bill said.

"Tons of it. The so-called secret ingredient. Isn't that just so waspy? Thinking cinnamon is exotic. You two have such nice friends."

"They're not really so nice," Anne said.

"They're not?"

"They're just nice to us," Anne said. "Because they know us."

"Isn't that how everyone is?" Jerry asked.

"You're nice to everyone," Anne said to Jerry.

"You're nice to everyone, too," Bill said to Anne.

"I'm not always so nice," Anne said.

"Please! You're the Queen of Nice!" Curtis said.

"You should see me at work."

"Oh, I doubt it."

"I have another side." She told them about the switched cakes.

"But that just proves it," Bill said as they pulled into the driveway. "You had to confess. You felt guilty. That just proves how nice you are. Nancy Bergen wouldn't have felt guilty for a second."

Later, when they were undressing upstairs, she turned to him. "I wish I could have seen her face."

"Ah, revenge," Bill said, turning back the covers. "A dish best served sweet."

The next day Anne decided to prove how nice she really was: she telephoned Casey Alexander and invited her to lunch the following weekend.

"I understand if you're busy," Anne said, "on such short notice. I just wanted to welcome you to the neighborhood."

"Are you joking?" Casey said. "We've been here three weeks and our next-door neighbors haven't even come by to say hello. I knew we wouldn't exactly fit in, but I wasn't expecting the cold-shoulder treatment." Her voice was breathy, and higher than Anne expected. From her over-enunciated consonants and too-correct pronunciation, Anne could tell there had been voice lessons. It was a real old-fashioned movie-star accent, a Hollywood imitation of the kind of Park Avenue glamour girl that didn't exist anymore.

They met at a restaurant at the local inn. "This is just like that old Bing Crosby movie," Casey said. "You know, the one where they're singing all the time?"

"That's pretty much all the old Bing Crosby movies," Anne said. "*Holiday Inn*?"

"Yes! I love that movie! I can't wait for Christmas. I hope it snows every day. I've been in California too many years. I miss the snow."

"How many years was that?" Anne asked.

"A bunch," Casey said. Anne noticed that Casey gave vague answers to specific questions: about where she had lived, and for how long. She had been a waitress, serving breakfast to an older man who came in every day with *The Wall Street Journal.* Gregor always ordered the same thing, and he always left a precise 15 percent tip. After two months he asked her out, and two months after that they were married. Casey swore she didn't know who he really was until a week before the wedding, when the pre-nup appeared.

"I thought he was just some nice old Jewish guy," she said. "My mother always told me they took good care of their women. He was such a gentleman, you know, and we always had a lot of laughs together, you know? I didn't have a clue about the money! He lived in this little apartment, there were a lot of paintings, but I didn't really get what they were. When he first told me I thought it was a big joke. Gregor loves to play jokes." She started to giggle. "The movie thing was his idea. I went to the first few classes just to humor him, really. I thought maybe he didn't want me hanging around the house all day. And I could guess what people were saying behind my back, you know, rich older man trying to buy his young wife a career. But it turned out that I really enjoyed it, and then it turned out that I'm pretty good at it." She laughed again. "Gregor says it's the best joke of all."

Casey was wearing a hat and a pair of large tinted glasses. People turned to look at her as they came in.

"You should hear what Gregor says about the people around here." Casey told a story about a party they had gone to at the club. Their real estate agent had taken them before they bought the house. "The way those wives were looking at me," she said. "I guess I danced a little too close. Gregor loves to dance. He can dance all night." She talked about how she wanted children. "A bunch of children," she said. "I guess I better get started quick. Do you have children?"

Anne told her about Jenn.

"Seventeen?" Casey said. "But you don't look it." She asked to see a picture. Anne showed her the photograph she carried in her wallet: a picture of Jenn from last Christmas, rolling a snowball between her palms.

"She's beautiful," Casey said. "Seventeen. Not necessarily such a fun age."

"We had our rough patch," Anne said. "But lately she's been a total sweetheart."

She knocked on the wooden table. "The divorce was so hard on her."

"And she likes Bill?"

"She calls him the Overgrown Preppy. Here," Anne said, passing Casey a tissue.

"Look at me," Casey said. "Wow. The power of hormones. Every month it's like this. Even the commercials make me cry. *Especially* the commercials. But I really do want kids."

The coffee arrived. "You remind me of a friend I used to have," Anne said. "So much. Jennifer North?"

"Oh, yeah, people say that," Casey said. She leaned back and adjusted her sunglasses. "I've seen the pictures. And there's a drag queen in Los Angeles who makes a pretty good living out of imitating Jennifer North."

"No, not how you look, though I can see the resemblance. I mean, wanting kids so much. That's all she ever talked about." Anne took a sip. "Too hot. Anyway. I probably shouldn't say this, we've just met, but I'll say it anyway. Don't wait too long. Don't listen to what people say about your career. If you want a family, have a family."

"But you stopped after one."

"Long story."

"Maybe with Bill. Plenty of women have kids at forty-two now."

Anne shook her head. "One is enough."

"You have to get me more," Neely said. "You promised me there would be more." She was up to her shoulders in ginger-scented bubbles, wearing a small black headset. The bathroom was her favorite room in the Malibu house; after the fire she had rebuilt it at twice its original size, annexing a small guest bedroom. The door opened onto a sitting area with two divans, track lighting, and shelving filled with aromatherapy candles. One step up was a marble sink and a five-foot-square shower stall with eight heads set at various heights. Across from the shower was Neely's vanity; the maid came in every morning to clean her makeup brushes with a special imported soap and to make sure all her cosmetics were arranged by color. Two steps up from that was an enormous bathtub set against a picture window that faced into the canyon. The window was made of chemically coated glass—Neely could see out, but no one could see in—and up above was a skylight of rose-tinted glass. Lyon thought the bathroom was slightly ridiculous and never used it. His own bathroom was spartan by comparison, the only extravagance being a heated towel rack that he rarely turned on.

Six tiny stereo speakers were hung high on the walls, the two-hundred-disk CD changer controlled by a waterproof remote. A mural of vines and flowers was painted across the walls, and the floor was tiled in warm terra-cotta. A feng shui expert had been brought in to make some last-minute additions: a pair of potted palms, a few extra mirrors to circulate the chi, and a painting of two goldfish, for harmony and luck.

"That's all you can give me? You gotta be joking," Neely said. Her voice turned from vinegar to honey. "I know it's hard right now. . . . But sweetie, I don't want to call anyone else, you're the only one I trust. . . . No, not the yellow ones, they make my tummy rumble, just the white ones. . . . You're the best. . . ." She looked up from her bath. There was Jenn, standing in the doorway. "Sweetie, I gotta go," Neely whispered into the headset. "No, don't call me back. I'll call you back."

Jenn just stood there and stared.

"How long have you been there, honey," Neely asked.

"Long enough."

"Did you come for some makeup? You can take whatever you want. You know, you should really knock first. I could have been sitting on the pot."

"I know what you're doing."

"I'm just taking a bath, honey. You know how stiff my back gets. There's nothing like a nice long, hot bath to relax the muscles." Neely pushed a pile of bubbles over her breasts. "I have some great new ginger bath foam, if you want to try some. You look tense."

"I know what I heard."

"What, just now? That was the caterer, I was ordering some stuff for this party I'm giving."

"What party."

"It's a surprise. For your father. A dinner party, won't that be nice?"

"I'm not stupid. I know what's going on. You're high."

"I am so *not* high. This is pain medication, honey. I need it for my back."

"There's nothing wrong with your back."

"You sound just like your father. And my stupid doctors. What do they know? Not everything shows up on those machines."

"I know what I heard."

"Oh all right," Neely said. "So what. It's none of your business. I wouldn't expect a kid to understand. You think it's so easy, what I do? You have no idea how much pressure I'm under. How much everything costs. Who do you think is bringing in all the money around here?"

"My father makes good money."

"Your father makes *good* money, but he doesn't make *real* money. Pass me a towel, will ya? . . . Thanks. I have a right to privacy, you know. It's in the Constitution. Are you going to run to your daddy now? Like a little girl? I bet you can't wait to tell him. You know what you are? You're a user. You just used me, used my connections for your little modeling career. You don't really like me, you never did. I wasn't fooled. Don't think you can fool Neely O'Hara. You're using me to get close to Dylan, too. You think I haven't figured that out? Go on, you go tell

Lyon whatever you want. There's plenty I could tell him, too."

"You wouldn't," Jenn said.

"Probably not," Neely said. She uncapped a jar and began to massage lotion onto her neck. "Who knows. Here, try some of this. It's the most amazing stuff. An astronaut invented it. So, do we have an understanding?"

Neely walked toward the door. Jenn took a step back.

"Because you do not want to fuck with me," Neely said. She took another step. This time Jenn stood her ground.

"I'm not going to say anything," said Jenn, "and it doesn't have anything to do with my father. He knows what you are. I don't have to tell him. You know why I'm not going to say anything? Because I don't give a shit what happens to you. Go ahead and kill yourself. See if I care. See if *anyone* cares." She turned and left.

Neely finished drying herself off. The familiar chills were coming on. She got a fresh towel from the heated rack, but that didn't help. She was supposed to be on the set in three hours, but she felt as though she were coming down with something—there was that flu going around. And now there was that tightening across her forehead, the beginning of another awful headache. She had to pull herself together; she was late twice last week and people were starting to notice. She counted out the remaining pills: just over a dozen, they wouldn't last long.

She snapped a pill in half and took the larger piece. She lit a lavender-scented candle and lay down on the divan. There it was, that lovely feeling . . . it started in her neck and spread up around the back of her head . . . everything was fine again . . . she wasn't even worried about Jenn anymore . . . she wasn't worried about anything at all. . . .

She got to the set only twenty minutes late, but they had already started without her. They were shooting the scene where Neely rode out to visit the owner of a neighboring ranch. Her stunt double was on horseback, trotting across a field of low grass.

"I'll just be a minute!" Neely called out. She raced to her trailer. She barked at the makeup artist. "Make it quick. And can you do something about these?" She patted the puffy skin under her eyes. "I didn't sleep so good last night. I think I'm coming down with something."

The woman sat there and shrugged.

"I said move it!" Neely yelled.

"Whatever," the woman said. She got out a pan of yellow-toned concealer and slowly brushed the cream around Neely's eyes.

One of the producers appeared a few minutes later and sent the woman away. "You can go home, Neely. We're shooting around you."

"What are you talking about? I'll be ready in a sec."

"Look at yourself. You're a mess. You look like hell."

"They can fix that with makeup. I'm just feeling a little under the weather."

"I'm not putting you up on a horse. Not in your condition."

"But I took all those lessons!" Neely said.

"And you're slurring again."

"I just need to get warmed up." She began doing her vocal exercises. "The tip of the tongue, the lips and the teeth. The tip of the tongue, the lips and the teeth." But it sounded more like *lipth*.

"Don't bother. We're already going to have to dub over everything we shot on

Monday. We're three days behind. Do you know how much that's going to cost?"

"Money, schmoney. I'm so sick of everyone talking about money all the time. Fine, I could use a day off. It smells like horse poop around here anyway."

On the way home, she picked up a couple of vodka minis and drove to the beach. When was the last time she'd been to the beach? Or watched a sunset? She didn't have time for anything anymore. They drove her like a farm animal. All the director cared about was making his schedule. He didn't know what he was doing. She was used to working with artists, people who came up through the theater and understood how important it was to take your time and get every scene right. It was her reputation on the line. This guy was a hack. She would call the agency tomorrow. They needed to start treating her better. She was an artist! But it wasn't good to get so tense. She took another pill and did some deep breathing.

By the time she got home it was dark. She poured herself an inch of vodka and kicked off her boots. There was a little bit of light coming from the den.

"Hey," she said. Lyon was sitting in the dark, watching a video with the sound off. "What are you doing home so early?"

"I know what happened today, Neely. They called me from the set."

"Why would they call *you*?"

"Sit down, Neely."

She plopped onto the sofa. He was watching one of her early movies. The clothes they used to wear! She prayed they never brought shoulder pads back.

"You're off the picture," he said. "You're being replaced."

"No way," Neely said. "We're already three weeks into shooting. They can't replace me."

"They can and they have. They warned you what would happen if you were late again. It's over, Neely."

"Ugh, don't be so dramatic." She giggled. "I'm the actor around here."

"You know how long I've been sitting here, waiting for you to come home? Two hours. So I've had plenty of time to think. And I've made some decisions. About you. About us."

Neely stood up. "All right, whatever, let

me get changed and then you can tell me all about it."

"Sit down. We can't go on like this anymore, Neely. I can't watch you do this any longer."

"Do what?"

"I know what's going on. I know about the pills. I think on some level I've known about them from the beginning. You know, in some ways this is as much my fault as it is yours. On some level I knew what was going on, I just chose not to see it. You haven't been yourself for a long time. The mood swings. The out-of-control spending. Calling in sick. All the signs were there, I just didn't want to believe it. I take full responsibility for that. I shouldn't have let you take so much on—the movies, the recording, the insane schedule, it's too much. I should have taken better care of you. But it has to stop." He lit a cigarette. She counted the butts in the ashtray: eight.

"I know, I know," Neely said. "I want to stop. It's just that I've been under so much pressure. You know how it gets, I just needed a little something to take the edge off. I'll stop as soon as this movie is finished, I promise."

"I want to take you somewhere you can get help. Somewhere quiet, where you can rest up for a while."

So that was it. The director had turned everyone against her, even Lyon. Men always stuck together. Hollywood would always be a boys' club. It threatened them, that a woman could be more powerful and talented than they were. It had been this way with Mel, and then with Ted. At the beginning they were supportive, they were proud of her work, and then after a while it was too much for them, they had to cut her down to size to make themselves feel big. What was that word people used to say about successful women? *Emasculating.* No one said it anymore, but that's still how they felt. Men all wanted the same thing. A housewife to meet them at the door when they came home.

"I won't," Neely said. "I don't need to. I can rest right here. I just need a couple of weeks off."

Lyon shook his head. "There's a good place outside of San Francisco."

"I'm not going back into rehab," Neely said. "You can't make me. I know the law."

"You're right, I can't make you." He sat

back and crossed his hands behind his head. "I'm asking you to check yourself in. You need to be around people who know how to handle this kind of thing."

"But I don't need people. I just need you. I need you to take care of me," Neely said. "I need you to take care of me the way you used to. You can be my manager again. Then we could be together all the time. That's what I need, someone to look after me all the time. Someone who really cares about me. These other people, they don't really care about me. It's just business with them."

"Neely. Listen to me. I've thought about this for a long time. You can't do everything. You have to choose. The music. The movies. Me. You can't have it all."

"What are you saying?"

"You can't keep going at this pace. You're going to have to give something up."

"I'll cut back," Neely said. "I'll call Gordon. I'll tell him to cancel the Atlantic City dates."

"You don't get it, do you."

"You want me to give up . . . all of it?"

"Just for a while."

"Are you kidding? You know how long it

took me to get back where I am? You think I'm just going to walk away from it now? You're out of your mind. I thought you were on my side. I thought we were partners. That's what marriage is supposed to be, a partnership."

"This hasn't been a marriage in a long time."

So that was it. All men thought alike, their brains were in their pants. There hadn't been any sex in months, but Neely assumed he understood that it was just temporary. They both had crazy schedules, and most nights when she got home from work she was too tired to do anything except watch television. She knew he was getting a little action on the side, and she had been a good wife, looked the other way, she knew he had needs, and she didn't mind if he occasionally satisfied himself elsewhere. And now he was threatening to leave her! He probably had a little bimbo stashed away somewhere. Someone who made him feel like a big deal. Well, she didn't have time for that! Everyone knew things changed once you were married. If only she weren't so tired all the time . . . She knelt at his feet and put her head in his lap.

"But this is what marriage is," she said. "It's sticking together when things get tough." She wrapped her arms around his knees. "I'll go back to Dr. Mitchell. It always gets better when I have someone to talk to. You'll see. And then we can take a trip. We can go to Italy, we always have a great time in Italy. When was the last time we took a vacation, just the two of us?"

He stroked her hair. "Oh baby," he murmured. "My poor sweet baby."

She kissed his knees and reached up between his legs. She would remind him how good it could be. She knew there were things only she could do for him. Her mouth felt dry and cottony, but once she got started everything would be fine. He'd remember: she was the best. "Baby loves you," she whispered, pulling at his belt buckle.

He pushed her off and stood up. "You almost had me fooled. Get up." He grabbed her arm and pulled her up. "You're pathetic."

"Get out!" she screamed. "Get out of my house! No one tells me what to do. You think I need you? I don't need anyone. Go on, leave. You're the one who's pathetic.

Trying to make me think that everything is my fault. And I almost believed you! Look at me, look at this body! There's nothing wrong with me. But I bet there's something wrong with you. You're twisting everything around. You haven't touched me in months, and it's not because there's anything wrong with me. You can't get it up anymore, that's it, isn't it. I should have figured it out earlier. That's why I've been so unhappy. I don't get enough love! It's your fault! You have nothing to give!"

She turned the sound back on after he left . . . she had forgotten how good this movie was . . . she sang along to the musical numbers, she still knew every word . . . she took another pill . . . Lyon would come around . . . what kind of man turned down a blow-job . . . he was at that age . . . she'd be more sensitive, he was under a lot of pressure, too . . . she would talk to Dr. Mitchell about it . . . Dr. Mitchell would know what to do.

When the movie was over, she made herself a cup of coffee.

"Lyon?" she called out. "Sweetie, where are you?" She would tell him she understood. They would work it out together. She went from room to room, calling his name.

But Lyon was gone . . . he was afraid, he was a quitter . . . he had quit on Anne, too . . . no, that wasn't right, Anne had walked out on him . . . Anne had figured out what a loser he was . . . Neely should have paid more attention . . . she should have known better than to take Anne's leftovers . . . she had married him for the sex, it was just about sex, and now that the sex was over, there was nothing left at all . . . she knew she should feel sad . . . but she didn't feel anything at all.

1996.

Neely left the country two weeks later.

She missed Judd's graduation from Harvard in June. Ted flew out alone, taking Judd to dinner in Boston afterward. "I'm sorry," he told his son.

"But I'm used to it," Judd replied. As a graduation present, Ted bought him a loft in Seattle, where Judd was going to work for an Internet company.

She missed the August premiere of Dylan's first music video on MTV. Dylan had gotten the directing job through a high school friend. The band was a watered-down version of Green Day on a troubled label. After three weeks the video was dropped from rotation.

She missed Jenn's first big magazine job: the September cover of *Gloss.* Jenn wore a fawn-colored suede jacket with nothing but a strand of freshwater pearls underneath. It was the best-selling issue of *Gloss* in the last five years. Jenn moved to a better agency and flew to Europe for runway work.

She missed Anne's interview with Perry Hayes (the one where he broke down in tears and talked about his wife's eating disorder), and she missed Nancy Bergen's interview with the First Lady, one of the highest-rated news shows of all time. She missed George Dunbar's fiftieth birthday party and Dave Feld's funeral (complications following prostate cancer) six weeks later.

Eventually she called Lyon, asking for money. Their lawyers met for three hours, at the end of which various financial arrangements were made. Their money was divided into seven separate accounts, three of which were held in trust for the children. There was an account from which all their shared bills would be paid: the mortgages, the taxes, the insurance, and the salaries

for the household staff. There was an account in Lyon's name only: half a million
dollars free and clear. There was another
account for Neely: a million dollars she
could spend as she pleased. The rest of
their assets, including their stock portfolio,
could not be touched by either of them. The
houses were heavily mortgaged, but the
stocks, mostly high-growth tech invest-
ments, had multiplied in value many times
over. There was no talk of divorce. Lyon
made a down payment on a condo in
Brentwood and lived there with rented furniture. He didn't want to see anything that reminded him of his wife.

No one heard from Neely except the
bankers: any withdrawals of ten thousand
dollars or more (of which there were plenty)
required special approval. Photographs of
her appeared occasionally in the tabloids.
She was in Switzerland, getting injected
with an experimental synthetic hormone
that would reverse the aging process. She
was in Greece, living on a yacht with some
of the least popular members of the English
royal family. She was in the Virgin Islands,
hanging out with an aging rock-and-roll
band who was recording a new album.

As the months wore on, the photographs grew fuzzier and fuzzier. The information became less reliable. And Neely gained weight. Her publicist, kept on a generous monthly retainer, explained that Neely was taking some time to think about her priorities after an exhausting year in which her marriage had run aground. Her fans were sympathetic. Hadn't she fallen apart before, and hadn't she always come back? Every so often there would be a rumor: Neely had rented a sound studio somewhere in Ireland, Neely had reserved a week at Madison Square Garden, Neely had lost eighty pounds on the sleep cure and was planning a surprise appearance at the Academy Awards.

She was away for over a year. She finally surfaced at Heathrow in August, waiting in line for a ticket to Kennedy.

The clerk didn't even blink at her passport.

"Any way you could upgrade me to first class?" Neely asked. "I'd really rather fly in first class."

"First class is sold out," the clerk said without looking up. She punched her keyboard. "There's only one seat left on your flight. Unless you want to wait till tomorrow." She handed Neely her boarding pass: 34D.

Neely went to the bar and bought herself a martini. 34D! That wasn't a seat, that was a bra size. She tried again at the gate, marching right up to the front of the line.

"Excuse me, we're all waiting," someone said to her.

"I can see that," Neely said. She turned to the clerk. "Hi, I'm Neely O'Hara. I was hoping you could find me a seat in first class."

"I'm sorry, I'll be with you in a minute, I'm in the middle of helping this gentleman," she said.

"It'll just take you a second," Neely insisted. "I'm Neely O'Hara. Maybe you didn't recognize me. I always fly first class."

"I'm really sorry, but you'll have to wait like everyone else."

Like everyone else: the three ugliest words in the English language.

"You don't understand," Neely said. "This is really important."

But there was nothing available. She made her way through first class, hoping that if she walked slowly enough, someone might recognize her, someone whom she might be able to talk into switching seats.

No one even looked up from their drinks. She squeezed into her window seat and rang for the flight attendant.

"I'd like a bottle of Stoli with some mineral water on the side," she said.

"We'll be bringing the cart through in about twenty minutes."

"But I always get a drink before takeoff."

"Welcome to coach," someone yelled over from the bank of seats in front of her.

She palmed a couple of pills. Someone behind her reeked of Obsession . . . they sat on the runway for twenty minutes . . . a baby started to cry . . . her legs were cramping up . . . takeoff was bumpy . . . Neely realized she wasn't going to make it. They were going to have to let her off the plane . . . but they were already in the air . . . four more hours . . . she took another pill, and did her deep-breathing exercises.

Finally the beverage cart came through. She ordered four bottles of vodka, just in case. There was an announcement about turbulence and keeping your seat belt fastened. The air reeked of diapers.

Neely got up and wobbled toward the front of the plane.

"Please," she said to the attendant, "I have to be in first class. I'm not feeling well. I was supposed to be in first class. Can't you find someone to switch with me? I'll pay for their ticket. I'll pay double."

The attendant asked whether she needed medical attention.

"I don't need a doctor, I just need a seat in goddamn first class!"

Another attendant came over and they walked her back to her seat. The flight wasn't even half over. The baby wouldn't stop crying. She opened another vodka and turned her headphones to the easy-listening channel. They were playing one of her songs! She began to sing along.

The woman next to her gave her a poke. "Do you mind?" she said. "I'm trying to sleep."

"In Las Vegas it would cost you a hundred bucks to hear me sing," Neely said.

"Another reason never to visit Las Vegas," the woman said.

They hit a bump and then another. It felt as though the plane were coming apart. She was going to die on this plane! The woman next to her began to pray. One more vodka . . . it was funny, when you really thought about it . . . it was the funniest thing in the world.

At last they landed. They sat on the runway for what seemed like forever, waiting for a gate to become available. "We should just open the emergency exits and slide out!" Neely yelled. "Everyone in favor raise their hands." The plane rolled up to a gate, and people began to shove their way into the aisle.

"Hey," Neely said. "You stepped on my foot."

"I didn't feel anything," the man said.

"Oh yeah? Well, maybe you'll feel this," she said, pressing her high heel into his sneaker. On her way out she said goodbye to the pilot. "Thank you for the worst fucking flight of my life." He sent a hand signal to the flight attendant, and she stepped forward.

"Ma'am," she said in a syrupy southern accent, "ma'am, do you need some help? Would you like us to call someone?"

"Don't touch me!" Neely cried. She went looking for her driver, then remembered she didn't have a driver. She wasn't sure where she was planning to go next. California! Of course! She would surprise Lyon. She couldn't wait to see his face. So she was fat; he'd seen worse. He was still her husband, he had to love her. There must be plenty of flights going to Los Angeles. But first she had to find her luggage.

The baggage claim area was filled with families hugging and kissing each other. There were children running around everywhere. *There should be a rule,* Neely thought, *they ought to be on leashes.* The bags came up the ramp and began circling around. All the suitcases looked the same. She grabbed a few that turned out not to be hers.

"It was an honest mistake!" she yelled out. Finally she saw her bag. She went to lift it, but it was too heavy. She toppled over onto the carousel.

"Whee!" she cried. People were staring at her and pointing. A woman in a navy suit and a man in a uniform came and helped her up.

"Is there someone you'd like us to call?" the woman asked. "Someone in New York?"

"I'm going to California."

They asked to see her ticket. She couldn't find her wallet. Another man came over.

"Stop crowding me," she said. She began to feel dizzy. She sat on her suitcase. She felt as if she were about to black out.

"Do you know anyone in New York?" the woman asked again. "You really aren't in any shape to fly."

Neely began to cry. Where were her pills? Where was Lyon? She had to get out of here. All these people were staring at her. . . . Then she remembered; it had been a long time, but she still remembered. She whispered the number to the woman: "212-555-9679." Anne would come get her . . . Anne would take care of her . . . she always had.

Lyon flew out from California to help Anne put Neely into rehab. They drove up to Massachusetts, listening to oldies stations all the way. Neely sat in the backseat and giggled.

"I thought she would put up more of a fight," Anne said to Lyon.

"What choice does she have," he said.

On her first day back, Neely had been arrested for passing forged prescriptions at
three pharmacies in Anne's neighborhood
under various assumed names.

"I'm so fat now, I didn't think anyone
would recognize me," Neely told the lawyer
Anne had hired for her. It was rehab or jail.

They were doling out pills to Neely, every
hour on the hour. At the rest stops Anne ac-
companied her to the bathroom, to make
sure she didn't get into any trouble and also
to keep her away from the newspapers.
Pictures had been taken at the airport. The
shot of Neely lying on the baggage carousel
had made the front page of several
tabloids. Her publicist had issued an un-
convincing statement about a bad reaction
to an over-the-counter flu medication. The
late-night talk-show hosts were having a
field day with Neely O'Hara jokes.

They pulled up to the front steps. Neely
began singing the theme to the old Dick
Van Dyke show. "Dah-dah-dah-dah-dah-
dah Dah-dum, De-dah-dum, De-dah-
dum . . ."

"Shut up, Neely," Lyon said. He signed
the papers quickly, without reading them.

"You shut up," she said. "It's your fault

I'm here. This never would have happened if I'd gotten laid properly." She turned to the nurse and spread her arms wide. "Honey, I'm home!"

It was harder this time around. By the end of the month she was clean. Her liver was shot, not from the alcohol, but from all the acetaminophen in the Vicodin. She had lost twenty pounds from the constant vomiting and diarrhea.

"I feel terrible," she whispered to her doctor. "Last time I didn't feel this terrible."

The doctor explained what was different about recovering from an addiction to painkillers. And Neely had changed, too: she was older, and her body would not bounce back so easily.

The clinic had changed as well. The arts-and-crafts room had been converted into a yoga studio. A nutritionist had overhauled the menu. The library was full of little books filled with bumper-sticker sayings. And worst of all, as far as Neely was concerned, was how much talking everyone was now expected to do. There were individual sessions with a shrink, plus group therapy, plus women's group, plus family meetings. The list of rules had grown much longer. There was no sex allowed between patients, which was no problem for Neely: for the first time in her life, she felt too depressed and too disgusting even for that.

Eventually she was transferred to a halfway house. Then there was a slip, and she was transferred back.

"How long do I have to be here?" she asked Lyon.

"As long as it takes."

"But I don't have any money, it's so expensive."

"We've sold some of the stock."

"Another month?" she asked. "I don't think I can take another month of this. These people are so creepy." She whined for another twenty minutes. Her therapist was a fool. Her roommate was a lesbian. She was more depressed than ever. "I want to come home for Christmas. Promise me I'll be out by Christmas?"

"No promises, Neely," Lyon said. "I told you: as long as it takes."

She was there for a year.

*   *   *

The only one who never flew back east for family therapy was Dylan. He had moved to Portland in early 1996.

"It's the land o' plenty," he told Judd. "Plenty of music, plenty of cheap apartments, plenty of willing women." There were plenty of drugs, too. He was living off the money he had gotten from Lyon and Neely, and from filming occasional videos.

Jenn called him the day before Thanksgiving. "What are you doing?" she asked.

"The usual," he said. "Where are you?"

"Wyoming."

"What's in Wyoming?"

"A shoot for *Gloss.*" She asked if he was free for Thanksgiving; she had met a man who was flying to Portland out of Jackson, and there was room on his plane. "I know it's last-minute. I guess you have plans."

"No plans." He gave her the address.

She arrived on Wednesday afternoon. They drove to a strip mall and got high in the car before heading into the supermarket.

"This is the biggest supermarket I have ever seen," Jenn said. "What kind of stuffing do you want? I never knew there were so many kinds."

"The stuffing is the best part," Dylan said. They picked up a small turkey breast, a few jars of gravy, and six bags of stuffing. By the time they got to the register, their large cart was full. Jenn got out her credit card.

Dylan's apartment was smaller than she expected. There wasn't much furniture: an old sofa, a card table with four mismatched folding chairs, a king-size mattress lying on the bare floor. The bathroom was filled with things that women had left behind: toothbrushes, makeup, tampons, nail polish remover.

"Why don't you throw this stuff out?" Jenn asked.

"You never know who might be coming back," he said.

The first night they ordered in pizza. Dylan didn't remember Jenn being so talkative. After two beers there was no stopping her.

"When I see the pictures, half the time I barely recognize myself. You wouldn't believe how much retouching they do. They fix our skin, and they change the shapes of our bodies, it's amazing, they can do anything with computers: put highlights in your hair, add cleavage, lengthen your legs, anything.

Makes me wonder why they make such a fuss about what we really look like.

"And that's not even what the clothes really look like! If anyone buys clothes based on what they see in a magazine, they're in for a big surprise. The stylist takes this tape and these clamps and pulls it all in from the back till it looks the way they want.

"I thought Jackson would be fun, but it was just boring. There's nothing to do there except shop for ugly silver jewelry. Of course in the photographs they'll make it look really glamorous. But I couldn't wait to get out."

"Well," Dylan said. "I'm glad you came."

"A family Thanksgiving," Jenn said. He gave her a sleeping bag and she curled up on the sofa.

Dylan fell asleep first. She watched him for a while. She wished she hadn't talked so much. She turned out to be more nervous than she expected. He wasn't like the men she usually spent time with; she was used to a world where all she had to do was look pretty and the man did the rest. *Tomorrow, remember to shut up,* she said to herself, *shut up shut up shut up.* On Saturday she was flying back to New York. *Two more*

*nights. Two more chances to make him fall
in love with me.*

She had coffee waiting for him the next
morning. Dylan watched television, Jenn
did the cooking. She found an extra bed-
sheet and draped it over the card table.

"The cornbread stuffing is the best,"
Dylan said. He hadn't put on a shirt. Jenn
could barely bring herself to look at him.
"You know, I don't think my mother ever
cooked a single Thanksgiving dinner the
whole time I was growing up."

"She was so busy," Jenn said.

"Busy fucking up," he said. "You know
she ran through over a million dollars in less
than a year? And if you ask her how, she
says she doesn't remember. And it wasn't
just the drugs. She would go shopping to
cheer herself up, she would drop like
twenty thousand dollars in one afternoon at
Armani, and then a few weeks later she'd
have gained all this weight and nothing fit
anymore, so she'd go out and do it again.
She would buy all this jewelry, and then
when she was high she would give it away.
And the money she spent on pills. That stuff
is more expensive than cocaine. You know
where some of it comes from? People steal

it from their own families. Someone has some horrible disease, or they've been in a car crash, whatever, and their doctor prescribes all this stuff for them, and then someone in their own family, someone who is theoretically taking care of them, steals it for resale. Brutal. The government can say whatever it wants about this," he said, waving at the bag of marijuana, "but the pill business is much worse."

"It's a sickness," Jenn said. "Isn't it?"

"Don't make excuses for her. She's a bitch. You had it easy."

"My mother isn't exactly perfect," Jenn said.

"Isn't she? Lyon thinks so. 'Miss Perfect,' that's what he calls her." He got up to put in a new CD. "What do you want to hear?" he asked.

"Whatever you want." All he ever played was Tom Waits and Leonard Cohen.

"She ever going to marry that guy?" Dylan asked.

"Nope. If you ask me, they're permanently engaged. It's been years, right? I think they only got engaged because everyone knew they were sleeping together."

"How old is he?"

"I don't know."

"Well, your mother is still a fox. I saw her on TV last week, she looks good."

"Stop!" Jenn said. "I don't want to talk about this."

"You have good genes. You'll hold up well."

"I guess." She had read somewhere that men always wanted to meet the mother, to see how their future wives would age. *Consuelo Casablanca,* she thought.

The turkey made them sleepy. They fell asleep on the bed, too tired to turn off the television. When they woke up it was almost dark.

"What do you want to do," Dylan asked.

"I don't know. Go see a movie?"

But that was too complicated for Dylan. "Hey, I have a little bit of X left from last week. We can split it."

"You go ahead," Jenn said. She had never taken Ecstasy.

"You'll love it, it isn't scary or anything," Dylan said. "It just makes you happy."

They washed the pills down with cranberry juice and waited.

"Oh," Jenn said. "This is nice. This is very nice." She put on an old Rolling Stones CD and began to dance. "Come on," she said, pulling him up. She felt as though she could dance all night. Every so often Dylan brought her a glass of water.

"You have to stay hydrated," he said.

She sat on the edge of the bed and drank the water, thinking how lovely he was, to be taking such good care of her. She didn't know why she had felt so nervous the night before. Being with Dylan was the easiest thing in the world. Everything he said was wonderful, and everything she said was wonderful, and everything he did was wonderful, and everything she did was wonderful.

She lay down on the bed and took off her socks. "Look," she said. Her toenails were painted silver.

He lay down next to her. "Cool," he said. He nudged her bare foot with his. They lay there, laughing, kicking each other gently. Their shoulders and hips were touching. Dylan turned onto his side and looked at her.

"You really are beautiful," he said.

"So are you."

A slow song came on. He put his arm around her and held her close. "We're all lined up," he said. They lay there for a long time, just breathing. Jenn wasn't used to being held. She walked her fingers up his spine, counting the bones. The only light in the apartment was the green glow of the stereo equipment.

"If you weren't my sister," he whispered in her ear.

"I'm not your sister. I'm practically not even your stepsister, when you think about it. We were pretty old when our parents got together."

"True," he said, "true." He kissed her on the neck, a slow kiss, and then another. "Your skin is so soft."

He pulled his head back and they stared at each other, listening to the music, not talking. She felt she could look into his eyes forever. At last he kissed her. It felt like the kiss she had been waiting for her whole life.

"We can't do this," he said.

"We already are doing this."

"We haven't really done anything yet," Dylan said.

She kissed him on the ear. "It's okay," she said, "everything is okay."

"We can't," he said. "But we can do other things."

"Like what."

He smiled. "It doesn't count if we keep our clothes on."

He unbuttoned her flannel shirt but left her bra on. "Just hands," he said, pressing his knee between her legs. Eventually their jeans came off, but their underwear stayed on. There was baby oil in the night table. They poured it onto each other's bodies: across their bellies, over their backs, down the lengths of their legs. They took turns massaging each other, and then they found positions where they could massage each other at once. He was hard the whole time. She curled up behind him and worked his neck, hooking a leg over his back so that he could rub her foot. They lay head to toe, toe to head, kneading each other's thighs.

He poured oil into her palm and guided her hand into his shorts.

"Harder," he said. He unhooked the front of her bra and pressed a hand against her breast. She moved her hand in time to the music. She could tell he was about to come, but he wasn't making a sound. Then there was a quick gasp, as if she had just delivered a piece of shocking news, and he

came across her chest. She cleaned herself
off with the edge of a pillowcase.

Then it was her turn. She was quiet, too.
He used both his hands, playing with her
slowly until she was wet. "Come on," he
whispered, "come on, Jenn." She felt warm,
and wonderful, and happy. She squeezed
herself around his fingers.

Afterward they lay on their backs, just
their shoulders touching.

"Did you," he said, "you know."

"Yes."

"I couldn't tell," he said.

She wished she had made some noise. "I
don't," she began, "I don't really . . . not big
ones."

"What does it feel like," he asked.

She described it: how it felt warm, and as
if her insides were rolling over.

"That isn't an orgasm," he said. "But
you've . . . I mean, you're not . . ."

"I've been with other men," she said. "It's
. . . they're just small ones, I think. I don't
know."

"If it was an orgasm, you would know,"
Dylan said. "Close your eyes. Lean back.
Here, here's a pillow. Relax. Relax. There
you go. . . . Here we go. . . ." His tongue

was all soft now. He moved his mouth slowly. It wasn't like the other times, when men had used their mouths just to warm her up. He wasn't going to stop. *It's happening,* she thought, *it's finally happening, it's happening to me.* She came hard around his fingers. He rested his cheek on her thigh. Just as her head started to clear, he made her come again.

"*That* was an orgasm," he said. He went to wash his face and came back with more water.

The Ecstasy was beginning to wear off, but it wasn't crash-y at all, it was like floating down into soft feathers. She microwaved a plate of leftover stuffing and brought it to bed with two forks. The telephone rang.

"What time is it?" Dylan asked.

"Almost ten."

"Shit." He answered the phone. "Hey. . . . Okay. . . . Nothing. . . . Yeah, I know where that is. . . . My stepsister is here. . . . Right . . . sure, okay." He began to get dressed. "I have to go," he told her. "I'm supposed to meet these people, I forgot all about it."

"Can I come?" she asked.

"I wish, but . . . maybe later, I'll call you

later." He sat on the edge of the bed and stroked her shoulder. "You are so beautiful right now."

She sat up and gave him a hug. The stone-y part of the drug was over, but the warm part was left. She felt so close to him, so wonderfully close. He held her a long time. Maybe he wouldn't leave. Maybe he was going to come back to bed.

"I love you," she said.

"I love you too, little sister."

"Don't call me that. I'm not your little stepsister anymore." She pouted.

"Hey," he said. "I was just joking. Don't be mad." He offered his hand. "Friends?"

She shook her head. "I love you, Dylan."

"I love you too. Like a . . . okay, not like a sister. Like a friend."

"More than like a friend," she said.

"No, just like a friend." He tousled her hair. "That's the X talking. You'll see. In the morning it'll be different."

"But it won't be different. I've always loved you. Ever since I was eleven years old. Remember that first summer in East Hampton? I still remember exactly what you were wearing. I remember everything about you." She described his old purple T-shirt, and the music he used to listen to, and she recited slang he hadn't heard in years.

"Hey, come on, you're not serious," he said.

She waved at the bed. "What about this? What about all of this?"

"That was just sex," Dylan said.

"Just sex?"

"Technically, it wasn't even sex. Don't be such a . . . Oh, never mind."

"A what? Don't be such a *girl,* is that what you were going to say?"

"Don't be such a kid," he said, and then he was gone.

Jenn waited up until just before dawn. She slept past noon on Friday, then spent the rest of the day watching soap operas and old movies, waiting for the phone to ring. On Saturday morning she packed up her bag, making sure that she left nothing behind.

She took a taxi to the airport. The radio was turned to a top-forty station. It was a relief to hear hip-hop blasting after Dylan's depressing music. She had figured him out, it was just the way the articles in *Gloss* described it: he couldn't love anybody because he didn't love himself. Dylan had used her. Just like all those other men, using a beautiful girl for their own pleasure. To build themselves up. And then tossing her aside when they were through.

The photographers used her, too, and the designers, and the magazines. She was only someone who helped them make money. No one really cared about her. There was no point in being angry about it, that was simply how the world worked. Everybody was always using everybody else. She wasn't going to give herself away so easily again. She deserved to get what she wanted. How many years did she have left? Fifteen, twenty at most. She wasn't going to end like her mother, all alone, looking for a man to live up to her romantic daydreams, eternally disappointed. She was smarter than that.

The flight attendant brought her a glass of champagne before takeoff. They were always so nice in first class, and why shouldn't they be, it cost a fortune. The more you paid, the more you got.

Life could be just like this: you figured out what you wanted, and you decided what you needed to do to get it, how high a price you were willing to pay. Jenn remembered something Neely had once told her: No one ever looks back and says, "I wish I'd been nicer." What women regretted was this: that they hadn't tried for more, that they hadn't put their whole hearts into following their dreams. Being nice is what held a woman back. Dylan never worried about being nice, and neither did her father.

It was Jenn's turn now. The plane lifted off the runway, and she watched the city grow small below. She signaled for another glass of champagne, and this time she didn't say please.

1997.

Neely was staying at the Stanhope, in a two-room suite that overlooked Central Park. She had been asked to present an award at a charity fund-raiser for Project Serenity, an organization that funded research on substance abuse. It was her first public appearance since leaving rehab.

She called Anne in the early afternoon. "You gotta come over," she said. "I'm a wreck, I can't decide what to wear."

"I'm at work, Neely, I can't just up and leave. I've got piles of things to do."

"But I need you," said Neely. "Lyon won't be here until seven, and anyway, men are never any help, they always say you look wonderful even if you're wearing the worst dress in the world. Can't you sneak away early? Or you could go home and change and then swing by here on your way over. Remember when we used to get ready for parties together? It'll be just like old times, only without the hooch, of course."

Anne arrived just after four. The suite was filled with flowers. Neely was lying on the bed, watching television. She was wearing a hotel bathrobe, and her hair was tucked up in a plastic clip.

"I changed my mind, I'm not going," Neely said. "Look at me. I can't go out like this. Everyone is just going to talk about how fat I am."

"People are counting on you," Anne said. "You have to go."

"No I don't."

"I thought someone was coming up to do your hair," Anne said.

"I canceled that, too," Neely said.

"Neely, you have to do this." Anne read some of the cards that had come with the flowers. It was a who's who of Manhattan. Nancy Bergen had sent the costliest arrangement: a dozen peach roses from the most expensive florist in the neighborhood.

"But I'm scared," Neely said. "You should see the list of who's gonna be there. I didn't know Sandy Dunbar was on the board! I thought it was just going to be a bunch of rich doctors and businessmen, but she's invited all these Hollywood people, and of course they all have to come, just because Sandy wiggled her skinny little finger. She never liked me anyway. She's probably expecting me to cancel, just so she can tell her friends 'I told you so.' "

"Then why give her the satisfaction. The columns will be all over this, Neely."

"Well, it's too late now, I canceled the hair guy."

"The concierge can find us someone."

Anne called downstairs. Neely still hadn't decided what she was going to wear. Three designers had sent over clothing, hoping for some free publicity. Neely tried the outfits on one by one, turning slowly in front of the mirror.

"Size twelve, can you believe it?" she said. "You could land a plane on my ass." She chose a navy-blue sleeveless dress with a long matching jacket. An hour later a

hairdresser and manicurist from a neighborhood salon arrived and went to work. Anne
helped her with her makeup, blending a
large dollop of bronzer into her foundation
so Neely wouldn't look so pale.

"There. You look fabulous," Anne said.

At six o'clock Neely's little travel clock
began to beep. She got a vial of Zoloft out
of her bag and opened a bottle of water.
"They raised me to a hundred and fifty milligrams a day," she said. "I'll never lose this
weight. I know, I know, don't make a face,
I'm being a good girl." She shook a small
blue tablet into her palm. "Neely loves her
baby dolls."

"Just one more thing," she said. She took
out a container of glittery gold eyeshadow
and scraped some out into the bottom of a
coffee cup. Then she added a scoop of
moisturizer and mixed them together with
the rounded bottom of a makeup brush
handle.

"Cleavage juice," she said. "Trade secret." She rubbed it onto her chest. "Wait till
you see this under the lights. Who's gonna
look at my face!"

"You really shouldn't be nervous," said

Anne. "You don't have to talk for more than a minute."

"It's the reporters," Neely said. She hadn't talked to the press since going into rehab. "They're like animals. And the photographers, they're the worst. They'll do anything. I try to avoid them, but they're everywhere. I can't even go shopping anymore. I'm a prisoner in my own home!"

"You know how it works. The more you avoid the press, the more they come after you."

"You sound just like my publicist. She says if I give them a little of what they want, they'll ease off."

"Why don't you listen to her, then."

Neely shrugged. "I don't know, I don't feel like it, that's all." Her face lit up. "Hey, I could go on your show. You could come out to Malibu and interview me there." She knew she would be safe with Anne.

Keith had been pressuring Anne to get an interview with Neely, but Anne had kept putting him off, saying Neely was still too fragile.

"It's up to you," Anne told Neely. "I'd love to, but I don't want you to feel like you owe me anything."

"Are you kidding? I owe you everything! You practically saved my life. I just need to lose another twenty pounds," Neely said. "And I want a good slot. I don't want to be the opening act for one of those boring tearjerker stories they're always doing about some kid who has some horrible incurable disease."

Which was exactly the kind of story Anne specialized in. "Are you sure," Anne asked.

"What do you want, a note signed in blood?" Neely said. "Of course I'm sure. And you tell the guys at IBC that I want the big buildup, teasers in prime time and the whole bit."

Anne couldn't wait to tell Keith. There were rumors that IBC was about to be taken over by a cable consortium, the same one that had bought Anne's old station. The news division rarely showed a profit—as the jewel in the IBC crown it wasn't expected to—but who knew what might happen if the network were bought and new management brought in. Keith was under a great deal of stress, and it was starting to show. He had already made veiled comments about what people could expect in the next round of contract negotiations.

Even Charles Brady, who had survived several management regimes, was feeling the heat. He had been threatening to retire for years, but each time his contract was up IBC sweetened the pot. "This time I'm not sure how much longer I'll stay," he had told Anne. "I love this network, it's been my whole life, but I don't want to stick around just to watch some guy from Wyoming tear it to pieces. It would break my heart."

But Anne knew Keith would stay and fight, even if it meant making the lives of everyone who worked under him pure hell. For the last few months he had been on her case constantly, about ratings and the kinds of stories she was bringing in.

"You should have gotten that interview," he would yell at her, after reading about another of Nancy Bergen's coups.

She was sick of it: Nancy this, Nancy that. Last week Anne had snapped. "If you want another Nancy Bergen, why don't you just go out and hire the original."

"Don't think we haven't tried," Keith said. No one's job was secure. Bill told her she should feel free to quit, he made more than enough money to support the both of them. But Trip kept telling her to hold on: she had a rich contract, and they would have to offer her an enormous package if the show were canceled.

It was time to go. Lyon would be picking Neely up in fifteen minutes. Anne was meeting Bill in the bar downstairs for a quick drink.

"You look amazing," Bill said. Her martini was waiting.

"Oh, this tastes so good," Anne said. Maybe it was hard for Neely to be sober, but right now it felt just as hard for Anne to be sober around Neely.

Over the next several weeks, Neely telephoned Anne every few days to talk about the interview.

"I've lost another two pounds!" Neely would shriek into the phone. "But the skin around my neck is all loose. We're going to have to tape it up in back behind my hair. With the right lighting it won't show. Are you gonna hire a special lighting guy? I've noticed sometimes the lighting is a little off, there isn't enough fill. I know it's probably a union thing, but I thought you'd want to know."

And she wanted to talk about potential questions. "So you can ask me what it was like to lose custody of the twins to Ted, and then I'll look kinda hurt and surprised, maybe I'll tear up a little, and then I'll talk about what a great guy Ted is, and how sometimes a mother has to sacrifice to do what's best for her children. They'll eat that up. I think if I work it right, I can come off pretty sympathetic, don't you?"

"Neely, this is journalism, not filmmaking. We can't script everything beforehand," said Anne.

"Why not? No one has to know. I'm only trying to make things better. Don't you want the best interview possible?"

She loved talking about what she was going to wear. "I'm thinking a nice yellow sweater and white slacks. You know, the 'lady of the house' look, Malibu style. And I'll get yellow flowers for the coffee table. We have to be sure we're color coordinated. You can wear a gray suit. Yellow and gray look terrific together, don't you think?"

Anne had always looked washed out in gray. "Neely," she said, "maybe you want your publicist to handle some of these details. Isn't that what she gets paid for?"

"She gets paid to do whatever I want. Isn't it more fun this way?" Neely knew she could count on Anne to make her seem as sympathetic as possible. It was a great plan. She hadn't talked to anyone about work in a long time, but she knew that the morning after the interview aired, her phone would start ringing off the hook. And the ratings would be tremendous. Anne didn't sound nearly appreciative enough. Neely was getting a little tired of Anne pushing her around. Neely didn't need to be baby-sat anymore. Her confidence was back. Whoever invented those little blue baby dolls ought to win a Nobel Prize, or whatever prize they gave out at the pharmaceutical companies.

Anne showed Keith Enright some of Neely's faxes.

"A sketch," Anne said. "Of how she thinks the furniture should be arranged, and where the cameras should be. Apparently certain camera angles are off limits."

"Quite the prima donna," Keith said.

"You have no idea."

"Just keep giving her the star treatment."

"Wait till you see the florist bills."

"Will she be ready in time for sweeps week?" he asked.

"I can't nail her down," said Anne. "She says she needs to lose three more pounds before she can commit to a date."

This went on for another six weeks. The rumors of the IBC takeover were an open secret now. Bill told Anne her stock options might double in value.

In early April, Keith dropped by Anne's office just before five.

"Did we have a nice day?" he asked sarcastically.

"I suppose. What's going on?" she asked.

"You haven't heard."

"Heard what?" she asked. She had rarely seen him so angry. Bill had told her to be prepared for anything. She wondered how long it would take her to pack up her things. There wasn't much that was personal in her office—a few photographs of Jenn and Bill, a watercolor of the house in Southampton, an Hermès scarf that Bill had bought her in Paris, stretched and framed behind her desk.

"You know, I thought maybe I would let you read it in tomorrow's columns like everyone else. But that would be too cruel. And I wanted to see your face when you found out. Nancy Bergen's office has issued a press release about her upcoming interview with Neely O'Hara."

"But that's impossible. I talked to Neely two days ago."

Keith handed her the fax. "Some friend," he said.

"I don't understand," said Anne.

"I understand. I understand perfectly. She suckered you. She's probably been talking to Nancy for months. She just strung you along for leverage, to get what she wanted out of another network. Wake up, Anne." He gave her an ultimatum. Neely's interview was scheduled to run on Wednesday during sweeps. Anne had to find another celebrity to draw viewers to the Tuesday night show. "Or," Keith said.

"You don't have to spell it out. I get it."

"This is do-or-die, Anne. We're a publicly held company in the midst of a hostile takeover. If senior management isn't happy with the ratings, I'll be asked to make some tough decisions."

"It sounds to me like you've already made them."

"You have connections. I'm sure people owe you favors. Now is the time to call them in."

"I can't think of anyone."

"Can't you?"

"To compete with Neely? Perry Hayes is old news. Serena Kyle would have been perfect, but her album is tanking. What about Tommy Sutherland? George Dunbar says he's the next Robert Redford. Or what about George?"

"George Dunbar is a lousy interview. Maybe his movies are great, but his life is boring. You know who I want."

"I have no idea."

"Get Casey Alexander."

"That's impossible and you know it. Casey doesn't do television. She barely does any print. Even Nancy Bergen can't get anywhere with Casey Alexander."

"Exactly. Casey's a pal of yours, I'm sure she'll want to help you out."

"I can't ask her. It's too awkward. She wouldn't agree to it, and the friendship would be over."

"Anne, let me explain something to you. There are no friendships in this business. There are just relationships. You think

Nancy Bergen has friends? Maybe she still hangs out with her high school buddies from the Bronx, but I doubt it. All these people she calls friends, it's all just business relationships. They can do something for her, or she can do something for them. You say Casey is your friend. What does that mean? When you have a cold, does she show up with chicken soup? When you have a bad day at the office, do you call her up and unload? If you had a fight with Bill, would she invite you over to make popcorn and watch old Cary Grant movies? I didn't think so. Think you can come through on this one?"

"I'll try. I'll try my best."

He folded the fax into an airplane and sailed it over her head. "You have one more chance. Don't blow it."

Anne took Casey to lunch at a small French restaurant in the East Fifties.

"Wow, this is really the hard sell," Casey said. "You know, all these rumors about why I avoid the press, they aren't true. I'm just shy. It's one thing when I've got a script, when I'm in character and I'm reading someone else's words. And with print interviews, the publicity people help me, they go over everything and fix it, add the big words in. Otherwise I'd just sound like a dumb blonde. I know what people say about me."

"People don't say anything of the sort," Anne said.

Casey smiled. "You're too nice. But let's face it. I barely graduated from high school. You have to promise you won't make me look stupid." She passed Anne a list of approved topics prepared by her publicist. "I'm supposed to give you this."

"It's a news show," said Anne. "I can't make any guarantees." She passed the memo back to Casey.

"I had to try," Casey said. She could see how much pressure Anne was under. Everyone was talking about how they were about to send her back to a morning slot. She hadn't forgotten how Anne had once reached out to her. "Oh, what the hell. Okay, I'll do it. But you have to promise me I'll come out smelling like a rose."

"Of course you will," said Anne. It was the kind of promise Charlie Brady had taught her never to make, but right now she'd say anything to land the interview.

"Promise?" Casey said.

"Promise," said Anne.

They taped the interview at Casey's house two weeks later. A camera crew followed the two women as Casey gave a tour of the property. Anne walked Casey through the easy questions: about her childhood in a Los Angeles suburb, about meeting her husband at the restaurant, about her screen test with Perry Hayes. Casey had been carefully coached and peppered her answers with references to books that Anne was fairly sure Casey had never read. When Anne asked her about children, Casey got tears in her eyes and gave an emotional answer about how growing up in a broken family might be holding her back. They took a lunch break while the crew set up in Casey's living room.

Keith pulled Anne aside. "You're doing great," he said. "She's nice and relaxed. The stuff about her husband's heart condition is fantastic."

"Of course, Gregor will probably outlive us all," Anne said. "I'm dying for a cigarette."

Keith took out a pack. "Let's go for a walk, I have something I want to show you."

It was a three-page report from one of the researchers. Sections were highlighted in yellow. "Great stuff, hunh?" Keith said.

"This can't be true," Anne said.

"Anne, her story just doesn't play out. Don't tell me you haven't sensed it."

"It's just the usual stuff," Anne said. Everyone in Hollywood embroidered their biographies. "I never imagined there was anything . . ."

"Scandalous?" Keith said. "This is hot stuff. Spend the first hour warming her up with softballs, and then I want you to go for it."

Anne read the report again. Someone had found a fragment of a pornographic videotape, and the woman in it was clearly Casey. There were no records of her ever having lived in California before she met Gregor: no voter registration, no driver's licenses, no passports. And there was a rumor about an earlier marriage, though no one could find hard proof. "Look, this isn't fair," Anne said. "There may be explanations for everything. We don't have enough backup. We'll look ridiculous if we go out there with guns blazing. I'll get creamed, and you know it."

"I'm not asking you to accuse her of any-thing. Just lead the conversation in the right direction. She isn't that smart, she won't know what to say. She's been coached up to her eyeballs, but I'd bet the farm her publicist doesn't have a clue about this stuff. You don't have to say anything, just hint at it, that will be enough. Just show her the rope, she'll hang herself. You'll come out smelling like a rose."

"I won't do it," Anne said.

"You have to do it. Otherwise this is just a puff piece."

"You asked me to get Casey and I did. You should have told me about this earlier. We had a deal."

"I didn't know about this earlier. I swear to you, Anne, the information just came in last night. This is a great story, it's the kind of story that can make a career. Come on, how well do you really know Casey Alexan-der?"

Anne thought about it. "Not so well after all, that's obvious."

"Then what's the problem? It's not like she has you wrapped around her little fin-ger. Remember, you're in charge, it's your interview, you're in control."

Through the French doors Anne could see Casey having her hair fluffed. Maybe Keith was right. Casey was just another movie star, using the press to get what she wanted. The Greta Garbo bit had probably been dreamed up by her publicist, and Anne had fallen for it. Charlie had always called Anne a soft touch, a sucker for a good sob story. She had felt bad about using Casey, but maybe Casey had been using her all along.

"I'm in," Anne said.

They spent the first half hour talking about what it was like to be married to a much older man.

"And this is his second marriage?" asked Anne.

"Yes," she said. She talked about his first wife, who had died of cancer.

"And your first," said Anne.

"Yes," Casey said.

"There's a rumor that you were married before," Anne began. "I know it isn't true, but maybe you want to say something to help clear up the misunderstanding."

Casey blinked and signaled for a time-out. "Could you please turn off the camera," she said.

She leaned over toward Anne. "What's going on?" she whispered. "You know I wasn't married before."

"It's no big deal," said Anne. "We have to ask. Just tell the truth, everything will be fine."

"You must think I'm stupid," Casey said. "What else do you have."

"What do you mean."

"You promised me, no surprises. You promised."

Anne took Casey's hand. "Don't be nervous. Trust me, everything will be fine." She nodded to the crew, and the cameras were turned back on.

"Okay," Anne said, "we'll go back to the marriage stuff later, if we have time. Let's talk about before you met Gregor."

Casey told a few waitressing stories, most of which Anne had already heard.

"And before you were a waitress," said Anne. She read from an index card. "In 1991 . . . No, I must have written it down wrong. In 1992 . . . let's see . . . this doesn't make sense. Forgive me, I'll find it in a minute. . . ."

When she looked up, Casey's face was pale, her mouth set in a nervous line. Casey began to play with her left ear, twisting her earlobe back and forth. Her hand looked so familiar . . . the long, tapering fingers, the delicate bones of her wrist. There had always been something familiar about Casey . . . everyone said she looked so much like Jennifer North. Jennifer had pretty hands, too. But there was something else about her . . . the way Casey was staring at her, like a sad little puppy . . . the way she played with her ear. Her ears were lovely . . . Jennifer had such big ears, that's why she always wore her hair long and loose . . . Anne felt the realization rising up in her like a wave. But it couldn't be . . . it wasn't possible . . .

"Turn off the camera," Anne said. "We're through."

Keith waited with the crew for another two hours before finally packing up.

"Don't bother threatening me," Anne said. "It's over." Casey had locked herself in an upstairs bathroom.

"You bet it's over," Keith said. "You can kiss IBC goodbye."

After they left, Anne poured two glasses of Scotch and went upstairs.

"You can come out now," she said. "It's just us."

Casey's eyes were puffy and her makeup was streaked. "Did you tell them?" she said, sniffling.

"Of course I didn't tell them. What kind of person do you think I am?"

"I was starting to wonder," Casey said. "God, I never should have agreed to this interview. I knew it was a big mistake." She pressed the skin under her eyes. "I must look terrible."

"Not so bad," Anne said. "I've seen worse." She handed Casey the drink.

"Don't you have anything stronger?" Casey said. They split a BuSpar. "You want to hear something funny? I'm kind of relieved. It's so hard, day after day, to be living with all these secrets, to have to lie all the time. You have no idea how many times I almost told you. But I promised Gregor I wouldn't, and a promise is a promise, right?"

"A promise is a promise," said Anne.

"God, Anne, you really scared me there for a few minutes."

"I was just doing my job. Or should I say, my former job."

"Come on! They wouldn't."

Anne shrugged. "It's just a job. But you . . . I don't understand."

"I'll tell you everything," she said. "But you have to swear to me . . ."

"I swear. But first, you better give me a big hug." They wrapped their arms around each other. "It's okay, it's okay," Anne whispered as the other woman began to cry. "Let it all out."

"I'm so sorry," she sobbed. "I didn't want . . . I had to . . . I missed you so much."

"Oh Gretchen," said Anne. "I missed you, too."

Gretchen began her story at the airport in Los Angeles. "I had my return ticket, so I figured I'd fly back to New York and wait for everything to settle down." She glossed over the argument with Jenn, telling Anne it was just one of those ridiculous adolescent tantrums, that she couldn't even remember how it started.

"But I couldn't get a flight till the next day.

I was going to have to spend a whole day and a whole night at the airport."

She went to a bar in the late afternoon and ordered herself a margarita. Men kept coming over, asking if they could join her. She nursed her first drink for a long time, then ordered another. An older woman approached her.

"Excuse me," she said. "My husband and I, we're sitting in the corner and we can't help noticing. A girl like you alone in a bar like this, it must be difficult. Would you like to come join us?"

The woman looked exactly like someone from Southampton. Gretchen could tell—from her hair, from her clothing, from her upper-class accent with just a tinge of Europe in it—that she was from a nice family. Her husband had been in the oil business. They had just returned from three weeks at a spa in Mexico.

"They're painting the house. We weren't supposed to come home until tomorrow," the woman said. "So we thought we would just kill a few hours at the airport, pretend we are still on vacation." Sonia and Harry Chase both had deep tans and looked to be in their late fifties. They sat with Gretchen for two hours, telling her one fascinating story after the other: about Hollywood in the sixties, about their trips all over the world. They were glamorous, and funny, and clearly still madly in love after thirty years of marriage. Gretchen told them her life story.

"Such bad luck," Sonia said. "Life can be so unfair."

"We have been exceptionally lucky," Harry said.

"Exceptionally," said Sonia. Their personal assistant had just quit to work for a studio. They offered Gretchen the job. "Just answering phones, keeping track of appointments, that sort of thing. And Harry has to organize his papers, we need someone to help him organize his papers."

"Thanks, but I really have to go back to New York," Gretchen said.

"But why such a rush?" asked Sonia. "You haven't even seen California. You can stay for a couple of months, no strings attached." They would pay her three hundred dollars a week in cash, with room and board thrown in. "The house is so big, you'll have plenty of privacy," Harry said.

Gretchen had applied for jobs like this in the Hamptons but had always been turned down. She figured it was the way she looked, or maybe her accent. But the Chases didn't seem snobby like the women Gretchen knew in Southampton.

The house was in Beverly Hills, behind tall iron gates. Her room looked over a garden and a small pond. In the mornings she worked for Harry Chase; he was only semi-retired, and there was still plenty to do. Her afternoons were free.

"But I almost never went out," Gretchen said. "I didn't want to see anyone. I kept thinking, No one knows where I am. It was like I was safe for the first time, you know?" Her husband would never be able to find her.

"And they treated me like family," Gretchen told Anne. "Harry picked out all these books for me to read. And Sonia, she was always shopping, and she would buy me clothing, all this amazing stuff. They didn't have any children." After two months Gretchen asked whether she could stay.

"But of course," Sonia said. "We love having you here. It was all so disorganized before you came. You can stay as long as you like." Every Thursday night, when she went to bed, there was an envelope with fifteen twenty-dollar bills tucked under her pillow.

The Chases were charming but eccentric. They rarely went out at night, preferring to have their friends visit them for the long, elaborate dinner parties they threw every Tuesday evening. Gretchen was not invited to these. It was a big, old-fashioned house, with a long formal dining room and a small ballroom and a billiards room in the back. Gretchen would watch the staff set the table, and then, just before the guests arrived, she would retreat to her bedroom at the far end of the house.

"I kept waiting for them to include me, but they never did," Gretchen said. "It was so silly. I knew I was basically just a glorified servant, but they were so nice, after a while I sort of resented not being included. One time, I guess I had had a little too much wine with dinner, I asked if I could come to one of their parties. You should have seen the look on Harry's face. I thought he would die."

Two weeks later an envelope arrived in the mail. Inside was the longed-for invitation.

"And we have to get you a dress," Sonia

said. "You can't go like that." Gretchen was hoping Sonia would take her shopping, to one of the stores on Rodeo Drive that she had always heard about. Instead a shiny black box was delivered. Inside was a white silk dress.

"I spent that whole dinner terrified that I would spill something on the dress," Gretchen told Anne. The other guests were two married couples the same age as the Chases and a few actors Gretchen hadn't heard of. "I felt like it was the greatest night of my life. They talked about music, and paintings, and opera, and a lot about books, and when they talked about a book I had read, when I joined in the conversation, they didn't make me feel stupid at all. Just the opposite. I was so happy. I felt like I'd been waiting my whole life for a night like that."

After dinner, the men shot billiards and the women moved into the living room. One of the actresses tapped Gretchen on the knee. "You must love it here," she said. "The Chases are such wonderful people."

"They are," Gretchen said.

"And so generous," the woman said.

Sonia stood up. "Gretchen, you look

tired. You don't have to stay up with us if you don't want."

"Oh, but I'm not tired. I'm having a great time."

"You are too polite," Sonia said. "I can see how tired you are." Gretchen felt she was being dismissed. Reluctantly, she went back to her room.

That Thursday, there was an extra twenty in her envelope. She thought perhaps it was a mistake, and she brought it up at breakfast the next day.

"No, it wasn't a mistake," Harry said. "You are doing a marvelous job."

The next week, Sonia asked her about her teeth. "You should have them fixed. It's so easy now, with the caps."

"I know, I know. But it's so expensive."

"We will send you to someone." After the dentist there was the hairdresser, who gave her a new cut and toned down her brassy highlights. After the hairdresser came the dermatologist and a series of painful peels and injections that smoothed out all the scars.

Then came another dinner invitation, and another white dress. The men went to play billiards, and the women once again re-treated to the living room.

Sonia pulled Gretchen aside. "You look tired, darling, you should go to bed."

"But I'm not tired at all. I want to stay."

"You should go to bed, really."

Gretchen left for her room, but she didn't go to sleep. She read for an hour and then snuck back downstairs.

The living room was empty. So was the billiards room. The dining room had been cleared. She heard music coming from the ballroom. She tiptoed to the door. Someone was laughing, but she couldn't tell who. She pushed the door open a few inches.

It was unbelievable. The ballroom had been decorated like a harem. There were pillows everywhere, and thick black candles in tall wrought-iron holders. And the cou-ples . . . Sonia and Harry . . . but Harry was with another woman . . . Sonia was loung-ing in the corner, laughing and watching . . . It was an orgy!

Sonia called to her. "Gretchen, you naughty girl, you know it is past your bed-time."

"Let her come in," one of the men said.

"No," Sonia insisted. "Gretchen, be a good girl, go back to bed."

Gretchen ran back to her room. Images of what she had seen raced through her head—Harry with the young actress . . . a woman sandwiched between two men . . . Sonia, naked from the waist up, her long breasts falling against the pillow . . . All this time, and she had never guessed.

The next day, Sonia and Harry behaved as usual, neither one mentioning the night before. That Thursday there was an extra sixty dollars in her envelope. This time she knew it was not a mistake.

Sonia came to visit her late the following Monday. "Gretchen," she said, "tomorrow is Tuesday. I don't want you to be upset with us. Harry and I, we love you, we love having you here. What happens downstairs, you don't have to think about it."

But Gretchen couldn't stop thinking about it.

"I can't explain it, really," Sonia said. "It's just that, you get to a certain point in your life, and you realize life is so short, and you discover what you want, and then you begin thinking it's not so bad to have it. What we do, no one gets hurt. Everyone knows the rules. Harry and I, we used to watch these movies. You know the kind of movies I mean. And then one day we realized, it doesn't just have to be a movie. We were in Mexico, Harry had just gone for a nice long massage, and when he got back to the room I told him I had a birthday present for him. I had hired a girl. Someone from the hotel. At first I thought maybe Harry would just watch, I knew he always wanted to watch me with another woman, but eventually all three of us were together. And . . . and we just kept going from there."

"How do you find them," Gretchen asked. "The other people."

"Some are old friends. Others . . . well, it's Los Angeles. No one is shy. You know, when we first saw you in the airport, we thought . . . well, you can guess what we thought. But then you turned out to be a nice old-fashioned girl."

Gretchen wanted to ask another question, but Sonia shook her head. "It's best not to be too curious."

The next Tuesday, Gretchen poured herself a big glass of wine and went to bed early, hoping to sleep through everything. She woke up at midnight, wide awake. She wondered whether it was time to go back to New York. She had been saving her money, she had enough to live on for a few months. She could go back to being a waitress or maybe get a secretarial job. But she didn't want to go back . . . to live in some awful little apartment in Brooklyn . . . to give up all of this . . . the beautiful house, where she never had to make a bed or fold a towel. Sonia and Harry always took care of everything . . . Sonia and Harry loved her, they would never hurt her. She wanted to stay here forever, but Harry was almost entirely retired now; there was less work to do than at the beginning.

She put on one of the white dresses. No, that was all wrong. She went to Sonia's closet and found a red dress . . . perfect . . . it was loose in the waist, but she could fix that with a belt. She went downstairs and opened the door. Sonia came over and placed her hands on Gretchen's shoulders.

"Are you sure?" Sonia asked.

Gretchen shook her head.

"Don't be afraid. Everyone knows the rules."

And so it began. The first time it was simple; a handsome young man made love to her on the floor. If she closed her eyes, she could pretend it was almost normal, that no one was watching. The next time she was with a woman . . . and then with a couple. People were teaching her things, and her body was responding. No one would be hurt, everyone knew the rules. And then it wasn't just Tuesday nights . . . sometimes she would sleep with Harry and Sonia. Harry liked to be tied up . . . he liked to watch Gretchen and Sonia. But Tuesday nights were the best . . . so much pleasure, how could it be wrong? And she was good at it, she had always been good at it. And every week there was two thousand dollars in her envelope. And they were always so generous . . . there were presents, too . . . and trips to the plastic surgeon—first her nose, then the cheek and chin implants. At the doctor's office, there were photographs of models and actresses. There was even a photograph of Anne. Gretchen went through Harry's photography books until she found a picture of Jennifer North. Gretchen didn't just want to be beautiful, she wanted to be achingly, heartstoppingly beautiful . . . the way Anne had described Jennifer . . . just a few more procedures. . . .

Gretchen told Anne about the plastic surgery but left out most of the rest of it. She told Anne just enough to leave her thinking that perhaps she'd occasionally slept with Harry.

"And one night," she told Anne, "the most remarkable man came to dinner. He was so elegant, and he had this sexy Hungarian accent, and we ended up spending almost the entire night talking about books. Me, talking about books! I talked about all the books Sonia and Harry had given me to read, and I knew I wasn't pronouncing all the names right, but he never made me feel stupid." They had done other things, too, but Gretchen figured Anne could connect the dots if she wanted. "And that's how I met Gregor."

"So there was never any restaurant," Anne said.

"Sure there was a restaurant." Gretchen giggled. "But I never worked there. Harry owned a couple of places in Westwood. There was all this cash around, who knows from what, they never told and I never asked, and the restaurants made it easier. They put me on the payroll at one of them, so I wouldn't get into trouble with my taxes. The IRS must have thought I made the best tips in Los Angeles!

"It's really love, with Gregor," Gretchen continued. "I think I fell in love the first night we met." Gregor had gone to Harry, asked for Gretchen's hand as if she were Harry's daughter. What it felt like, to have a man know your worst secret and love you anyway. They flew to the Virgin Islands, where Gregor's lawyers had arranged for some kind of divorce for her. When she got back to Los Angeles she changed her name to Casey Alexander, and the lawyers took care of the rest. She had a new husband, and a new name, and a new face. She could start all over, and no one would ever know.

"I have to ask you," Gretchen said. "How did you figure it out?"

Anne twisted her ear. "In poker, it's called a 'tell.' You always twisted your ear when you were nervous."

Gretchen smiled. "I guess I'm not such a good actress after all."

Anne went into the city a few days later to pack up her office. Trip had begged her to wait and see what happened—she had a contract and if they fired her there would be a handsome settlement—but Anne was done with all of it.

Everything she cared about fit into a

briefcase and two shoeboxes. Keith Enright tapped on her open door.

"Don't say a word," Anne told him, "don't you dare say a word."

"Oh Annie, it's just business."

She asked him what he was planning to do with the information about Casey's past.

"It'll hold," he said. "It's a good story."

"You bury it," Anne said. "You bury it so deep no one can ever find it."

"I don't think so. It's too good."

"Sit down," Anne said. "You listen to me. If anyone at IBC ever does anything to hurt her, and I mean *anything,* I'm going to . . ."

"You're going to what?" Keith said. "You're out of here. Don't get all dramatic on me. Once you walk out of that door, you're nobody."

"I'll file a sexual harassment suit," she said. "All these little visits of yours, I've kept my old appointment books, it won't look good for you. I moved up awfully fast, didn't I? A little too fast, that's what a lot of people think. And you were the one who did the moving. It won't look good for you at all."

"That's rich. I almost believed you there for a minute."

"I'll do it."

"Come on, Anne. I never laid a finger on you."

"Unlike plenty of other women I can name. People will believe what they want to believe. With your reputation, it will be a piece of cake."

"You'll never make it stick."

"I don't have to, Keith. I just have to make a little fuss, and the press will take it from there."

"You wouldn't dare. You're bluffing. You don't have the *cojones,*" he said.

"You're right, I don't. But my attorney does." She named a law firm that had successfully sued a large petrochemical company, and she watched him wince. "You know what I've learned? It's not what you're born with. Balls are like everything else: cars, houses, people."

He frowned, she laughed.

"Like everything else in this town," Anne said. "They can be rented."

"Ten more minutes!" Neely cried. "Hurry up, you'll miss the opening."

"I'm on my way," Lyon called down from the bedroom. At the last minute, Neely had decided she wanted to tape her interview on two VCRs, just in case.

They had ordered in sushi. Lyon used chopsticks; Neely ate with her fingers.

"You should have seen the teasers," Neely said. "I got more buildup than the First Lady! Did you put in a fresh tape?"

"Yes, darling, I put in a fresh tape."

"On slow?"

"Yes, darling, on slow."

Neely was in high spirits. The night before, she had watched Anne's interview with Casey Alexander. It was nothing but a puff piece. Nancy Bergen had told her that Casey walked out halfway through, and the producers had been left holding the bag. The overnight ratings were disastrous. Well, what did they expect, Neely thought. Casey Alexander was just a boring Valley girl, who would be interested in her story?

Lyon didn't know that Anne wasn't talking to her. Maybe he would never find out; it would probably all blow over in a few weeks. Neely was confident Anne would come crawling back like always. Anne had blown everything out of proportion. It was just show business. Who in her right mind would turn down a chance to be interviewed by Nancy Bergen? Nancy was a legend, a real journalist. Anne was in over her head. She should have stuck to something she could be good at, Neely thought, like that old morning show. Or the weather.

Neely could hardly breathe during the interview.

"That was fantastic," Lyon said afterward. "You're a pro."

"Really?" Neely asked. "You're not just saying that."

"You really have no idea?" he said.

"I dunno. I think I looked kind of fat."

"You looked beautiful," he said.

The next day the papers confirmed it: the ratings were tremendous, and even the nastiest television critics thought Neely had handled herself exceptionally well. There were a few comments about her appearance, but Neely shrugged them off. She had lost a lot of weight quickly, and everyone knew that after a certain age your skin didn't bounce back the way it used to. She was forty-three years old, what did they expect! Exercise could do only so much, not that she exercised very much anymore. It was hard to find the energy.

The doctors had told her that might be

one of the side effects. They had warned her about the other side effects, too. Loss of libido. She just wasn't that interested anymore. Sometimes Lyon rented a dirty movie, and they watched it together, Lyon waiting to see if it put her in the mood. About half the time it did. But it didn't feel the same. It was harder to come, and then when she finally did, sometimes it was as small as a sneeze. She tried to make a lot of noise so Lyon wouldn't miss it.

Anyway, soon she'd be as good as new. If she kept her weight stable for another eight weeks, she'd be ready for another face lift. And this time she needed a tummy tuck, too. She had been to the doctor, and he'd marked her up with a big purple pen, drawing arrows on all the places that could stand a procedure. She needed to replace her implants and do something about her legs. There were all kinds of new stuff now. They could even hypnotize you so you didn't need painkillers afterward. Why be depressed about what was wrong? With the right doctors, anything could be fixed.

1999.

They would be married the third week of August. Anne and Bill had decided on a small civil ceremony: just a few friends and family in the backyard, with dinner and dancing afterward at the club. In May Anne went to Southampton by herself for a few weeks. "I want you to miss me a little before the wedding," she told Bill. And she wanted to see her lilacs bloom one last time. She planned to put the house on the market when the season was over.

She met Terry Abernathy at a party the Dunbars gave on Memorial Day weekend. He didn't look at all like his pictures.

"He's handsomer, isn't he," Sandy whispered to her in the kitchen. Abernathy had started the cable company that had swallowed up IBC and was now making a run at one of the Hollywood studios. Anne supposed that in some sense he was now Keith Enright's boss. She rarely watched television anymore, except for the occasional special that Charles Brady hosted. Charlie still took her to lunch every few months, telling her she was too young to retire, she'd go crazy if she didn't start working again. But she didn't miss it. In the fall she would take the train down to the city twice a week, to teach a class in broadcast journalism at Columbia.

She ran into Terry Abernathy a few weeks later, in a bookstore on Main Street.

"Anne Welles," he said. "What have you got." He took the book from her hand. "Haven't heard of it."

"It isn't out yet," she said. "It's an advance copy, they're just letting me borrow it."

He read the copy on the back. "Sounds depressing. You aren't depressed, are you?"

"Definitely not," she said. "Are you?"

"I was until I ran into you. Walk with me. I need to pick up a house present for these people I'm staying with. I could use your help."

She had no place to be. They went down the street and settled on an antique tea set. He asked her to dinner.

She wiggled her finger. "You know I'm getting married in about two minutes."

"It's just dinner. I'll have you home by nine."

Anne knew she shouldn't go, but how often did one get invited to dinner by someone like Terry Abernathy? He was so different from the men she knew in the Hamptons. He carried himself with a confidence that didn't come from money, or power that derived from his job. His confidence was different: she imagined he had always had it, even as a child. He seemed to say whatever was on his mind, without caring what anyone thought. She had spent the last year almost entirely in Connecticut, living with Bill, going out with his friends. A year of dinners with Mary and Jim, Diana and Dickie. A year of parties at the club. A year of salads at lunch, girl talk with

Gretchen and Stella. That would be her whole world soon enough.

They met at a restaurant in Bridgehampton. He was wearing jeans, boots, and a tan suede jacket. He carried a cowboy hat but didn't wear it. He ordered a bottle of wine but didn't drink any. He told stories about growing up in Wyoming, and the early days of cable. She couldn't remember the last time she had laughed so hard.

"Everyone said I was crazy," he said. "And they're right, I am crazy. But I knew right away what cable would turn into. I always know right away."

"I'm just the opposite," Anne said. "I never know until it's too late."

"Give me an example."

She told him a story about a piece she had done on the Everglades and a source who had gotten away. "Now you. What else did you know right away."

"I knew about you right away."

"Stop," she said.

"The minute I met you. At that terrible party. I was just about to leave, and then George introduced us."

"I told you," she said. "No flirting allowed."

"You have to let me flirt. How can I get you to marry me if I don't flirt a little?" He said it in a way that made her laugh.

"You keep laughing," he said. "But I'm always right. I've been right five times! And I've got five ex-wives to prove it."

She laughed some more. He walked her to her car. "Now you're going to let me kiss you," he said.

"I am not," she said. But he leaned in and kissed her right on the mouth. "Hey," she said. "No fair. Thanks for dinner. Don't call." She found herself laughing as she said it. She felt giddy, but she knew it wasn't the wine; when she saw he wasn't drinking she had stopped after one glass.

"I'm not like these eastern gentlemen you're used to. I know how to get what I want." He kissed her again, and this time she kissed him back. It was too nice to stop. She felt something leap up inside her, something that she thought had been long gone.

He took the car keys out of her hand. "I'll drive," he told her. "I said I'd have you home by nine."

"You're crazy," she said. "We can't."

"Honey, you have no idea just how crazy I am. Now get in."

At the first red light, he leaned over and kissed her again. She couldn't get enough of it. Every couple of minutes he pulled over—into a gas station, into a parking lot—and they kissed some more.

"I can't believe I'm doing this," she said. "This isn't like me at all."

"I cast a spell on you," he said. He carried her upstairs. It was the easiest thing in the world. She felt as if she were melting.

"I'll want pancakes in the morning," he said afterward.

She laughed. "You're out of your mind. I want you out of here by sunup. I'll call you a cab. I'm getting married in nine weeks. This was just . . . I don't know what this was. It wasn't even a fling. It must be some kind of pre-wedding jitters."

"Next you're going to tell me how much you love your fiancé."

"But I do." She felt utterly ridiculous, protesting her devotion to Bill as she lay naked in bed with another man's cowboy hat on her head.

"Darlin'," he said, her stomach leaping at

the sound of the dropped G, "you haven't been laid right in quite a while."

In the morning she made him pancakes.

"These are quite fine," Abernathy said. "I won't be expecting you to do this every day, just on special occasions. I already have a cook."

"What on earth are you talking about?" Anne asked.

"After we get married, of course." He winked and held out his cup for more coffee. "After I make you my bride."

Lyon was spending a week in East Hampton visiting clients and came over for lunch a few days later. She made ham sandwiches, and they sat in the garden.

"You look . . . different," he said.

"I had a facial," she said. She tried desperately hard not to smile.

"Look at me," Lyon said. But she wouldn't. "Come on, look at me." He broke into a wide grin. "Well, well, well. I haven't seen that expression in years."

"I don't know what you're talking about."

"I hope you can fool Bill more easily than you fool me," Lyon said. "You sly vixen."

"Don't make jokes," Anne said. "I've done something awful. What should I do?"

"What do you want to do?"

"I want everything to be exactly the way it was a week ago. Before."

"Simple: then don't tell Bill."

"God, this is awful. Let's change the subject," she said.

"Easy enough," said Lyon. "I have some big news." He was writing a book. He was more than halfway through, and it had just been accepted by a publisher in New York.

Anne brought out a bottle of champagne. "I can't believe you didn't tell me," she said as she poured.

"Just an inch, I've got tennis this afternoon." He had started writing again when Neely went into rehab. "I didn't feel like seeing anyone," he told her. "I went home every night to that wretched condo in Brentwood. Neely has the television on all the time, but when she's not around I never turn it on. The first few weeks I read like a fiend. And then one night it just came to me." Anne remembered his first two novels. The first one had gotten wonderful reviews but hadn't even sold enough to earn back his advance. The second just disappeared without a trace.

"That was always your first love," she said. "I'm so proud of you." She had bought him a typewriter years ago: her first gift.

"I'm leaving the agency," Lyon said. "We can afford it now, with the way the market is going."

"What does Neely say?"

"She loves that I'll be around all day." Lyon lifted his glass to the light. "I haven't told the agency yet, just you and Neely. Do you miss it—the action?" he asked.

"Never," she said.

"I don't think I will, either. I never meant to stay in it so long. Twenty-two years is an awfully long detour."

"Sometimes I think life is nothing but the detours," Anne said.

"In four years I'll be sixty," said Lyon. "I'm too old to be doing anything other than exactly what I want."

"You're in a rare philosophical mood. How is Neely," she asked.

"Her usual spectacular self. Can you believe we've been together almost eight years? And they said it wouldn't last," he joked. "I really do love her, you know. My precious monster."

"I believe you. I don't quite understand it, but I believe you."

"It's simple," he said. "She's the only woman who doesn't want more of me than I can give. Everyone else was always so . . . disappointed." He leaned back. "I suppose that isn't a very nice thing to say to the ex-wife."

"No, you're right. I expected too much of you."

"You expected me to be someone else. In every relationship, there's the lover. And then there's the person who is loved. I was always the latter. You would think that's the better position to play. But it turns out the greater reward is in doing the loving."

They sat for a while, gossiping about people they both knew in the Hamptons, talking about Jenn.

"Twenty-one years old," Lyon said. "Un-believable."

"If she'd gone to college, she'd be going into her senior year."

"You never give up. I don't know what Jenn is going to do after this, but I can't picture her at college."

"She says she wants to act," Anne said.

"Lord help us, anything but that." Jenn looked like her mother, but lately when she spoke Lyon was reminded of someone else: Neely. Neely with a Park Avenue accent. He looked at his watch and stood up. "Well, I've got one last thing to do before I quit this lousy business." He picked up his tennis racket. "For all the agents and actors and writers everywhere in the world, I've got to drive up to East Hampton and kick George Dunbar's saggy ass." He tossed an imaginary ball into the air and swung at it with his racket. "Beware the spike of a free man."

"Free at last," Anne said.

"Utterly, thoroughly, delightfully free," he said.

He drove up to East Hampton, humming along to Beethoven. The day had grown hot. George could not stop talking about Terry Abernathy.

"The studio's in a panic," George said. He laid it out for Lyon, who was positioning for what. Lyon did his best to act interested, but it felt like reading a news article about something terrible that was happening in a small country far away. By the time the deal went through, he and Neely would have already moved to London.

"Time to play," Lyon said. He won the first set in straight games. He hadn't played this well in years.

"I want to know what you had for breakfast," George said, dripping with sweat. "Man, is it ever hot."

"Excuses, excuses," said Lyon. He was on fire now. The ball came at him, and he hit it with all the saved-up anger he had. Anger at the years he had wasted, doing things that didn't matter, for people he didn't like. He could picture his victory: he would slaughter George Dunbar, and then they would shake hands at the net, and then Lyon would give him the news.

Halfway through the second set he felt it: a ping, as if a bolt had loosened in his chest, and then the pain, as if his heart had caught on fire. He fell hard to the ground. George came racing around the net. It was impossible to breathe.

Not now, not here, not now, not yet. There was so much left to do. There was so much left to say. He thought of Neely, how she had called him last night and sung him good night, an old standard, changing the words around because she couldn't quite remember them anymore. *My funny valentine. Sweet, handsome valentine. You make a smile in your heart.*

It was the kind of funeral Lyon had always hated: too many flowers, too many people, too much fuss. Anne and Bill went back to their hotel to pack quickly before catching the red-eye back to New York. Jenn was staying on with Neely in Malibu.

There had been a reception immediately before the service, in a large, sunny room just to the left of the chapel. Neely and Jenn stood in a corner, greeting the long line of mourners. It was Jenn's first funeral. She wasn't sure how to act, but very little seemed to be expected of her. People came up, taking her hands in theirs, offering sympathy. She did not know most of them—they were movie people, California people, from the part of her father's life that she had been left out of after the divorce.

She watched Dylan and Judd across the room, in dark gray suits that nearly matched. A studio head pulled them both in for a group hug. An actress kissed them on both cheeks, then wiped away her lipstick stains with a pale pink handkerchief. These were the people who ran Hollywood, and they had watched Judd and Dylan grow up.

And who was she? Lyon's first wife's daughter, the one he had left behind in New York. The one who came to California twice a year. They knew her as a model, not as extended family. Jenn wondered what would have happened if she'd moved in with Lyon instead of staying with Anne, not that there had ever been a whisper of a choice. She would have had everything the twins had now: a roomful of powerful people leaning in to murmur, *If there is anything I can do.* It was so unfair! They were only stepsons, and barely that.

On a table by the door was a leather-bound guestbook that people signed as they came in. The man from the chapel said they would send it to Neely right after the service. Jenn would have to figure out a way to get the book for herself. She would write a nice long note to everyone who had signed it. They would remember, and they would help her later on.

"That's better, you were looking way too gloomy," Neely said.

"What?" said Jenn. "Sorry, I spaced for a minute."

"You don't want to look depressed. You want to act as classy as your father." Neely brushed back a loose strand of Jenn's hair.

They were taken to the cemetery in separate cars: Neely and the twins, Anne and Jenn. Anne didn't recognize most of the mourners. They dressed for death differently here: the men in fashionably tailored black suits, and many of the women in hats. She spoke to Neely for only a few moments, just before the burial service began. Neely had dressed with the help of a stylist. She did not lift her heavy black veil to say hello. Anne took Neely's hand, gave it a soft squeeze, and felt Neely's arm stiffen: she did not want to be held.

"They're all gone now," Neely said. "Except you. Everyone who remembers."

"He was so happy," Anne said. "The happiest I've ever seen him."

"Geez, Anne. You can cut the bereaved widow act. He was my husband, okay? I know what he was feeling, you don't have to tell me." She would never forgive Anne for being the one to see him last.

Casey came for lunch a few days later.

"Give me the long version," she said. Anne was surprised to discover how much better it made her feel to talk about the funeral as if it were just another party: who was there and who wasn't, what they wore, what music had been played. The best of Hollywood had turned out to say goodbye. Lyon's cousins had flown in from England. Anne had finally gotten a look at the famous Dr. Mitchell. Stella had pointed out various old girlfriends. Three retired studio heads had stood together in one of the front rows. When the minister announced a silent moment of prayer, they bent their heads together and murmured kaddish. Judd's fiancée was easily in her late thirties, and pregnant. Dylan's head was shaved. Many people got up to speak. There was music: "Amazing Grace" on the bagpipe, and one of Lyon's favorite pieces of Puccini. At the end a mezzo-soprano sang a soft, slow version of "My Funny Valentine."

"Not a dry eye," said Anne.

They talked about a new movie Casey was thinking of doing and how everyone in town was grumbling about the stock market.

"You seem distracted," Casey said.

"I have to tell you something," said Anne. "A secret."

Casey listened without interrupting. "Wow," she said when Anne was through. "Good for you."

"But what do I do now?"

"You don't do anything now. And you can never tell Bill, no matter how much you're tempted to. It was just sex, Anne. Great sex, but just sex."

"That's what I keep telling myself. But I can't stop thinking about it."

"You're getting married in less than two months."

"I know, I know, you don't have to remind me."

"But don't you want to?" Casey asked.

"I don't know anymore." She felt awful saying it. "With Bill it hasn't been . . . you know . . . in a long time."

"Well, of course not. Look how long you waited. Nothing ever stays that hot."

"But even in the beginning," Anne confessed, "it was never really . . ."

Casey lifted an eyebrow. "Not even in the beginning?" Anne shook her head. "But the way you guys dance together," Casey said. "I just assumed."

"I suppose we put on a good show."

"But you love him, right?" Casey asked.

"I don't know anymore. I'm not sure I ever really did. He's just, he's just so exactly who I'm supposed to marry."

"But he loves you, you know that, right?"

"Yes. I know that." Anne thought of what Lyon had told her on that final afternoon: You could love or be loved, it was always uneven. Anne had loved Lyon. Now Bill loved her. And it was a wonderful feeling: to be loved, to be safe, to know someone would always take care of you no matter what, that Bill loved her at her best and at her worst.

"Don't blow it," Casey said. "Promise me you won't blow it. Remember what it was like? To be alone? God, Anne, remember *dating*? And, don't kill me for bringing this up, but how old are you now?"

"Forty-six."

"You know what kind of women forty-six-year-old men go out with? I'm thirty, and I'm already too old for most of them. That's if you go out at all. Trust me, there isn't anything out there that's better than Bill."

"I know, I know," said Anne.

"I mean, Terry Abernathy, everyone

knows about Terry Abernathy. He's totally crazy. If he weren't so rich, no one would put up with him. He's only been married about a million times. He makes Keith Enright look like a choirboy. I'm sure he's incredibly charming, but you know what it would be like. You'd lose your mind. It would be like Lyon all over again."

That night they went to the club to celebrate Diana's birthday. There was coconut cake and dancing. Bill waltzed her out onto the patio.

"Remember," he said, "our first kiss?" He kissed her again. She kissed him back with everything she had, hoping, waiting, praying that she would feel something, anything, feel just the littlest bit. But it was like always. Nothing.

"Wow," he said. "I can't wait to get you home."

In the bathroom, the women were reapplying their lipstick.

"Did you see what the Alexanders have done to their garden?" Cynthia said.

"Ridiculous," said Mary. "So *de trop.*"

Diana pushed at the skin around her mouth. "It's time to take care of this, don't you think? There's that place in West Virginia where they coddle you afterward."

"It costs a fortune," said Cynthia.

"Dickie said for my birthday I can have whatever I want." She cupped her breasts and lifted them a few inches, squeezing to create a deep cleavage. "Of course, this is what *he* wants. And I might just. Wouldn't that be a surprise!" She turned to Anne. "Dickie said I should go to your guy. What's his name again?"

Anne wrote down the name and number on the back of a napkin. Diana folded it into her purse.

"Expensive?" she asked.

Anne nodded.

"Good, Dickie won't be happy unless I tell him I'm going to the most expensive guy there is." She repeated the name. "Not Jewish, right?"

"I'm not sure, I don't think so," said Anne.

"Can you find out?" Diana asked. "My podiatrist is Jewish, but Dickie doesn't want them touching my face."

"I love watching you and Bill dance," Cynthia said. "You're the perfect couple. Everyone can see how much you're in love."

"He's so sexy," Mary said. She sighed. "Oh, to be a newlywed again. Of course, all that will change once you're married. You can kiss the sex goodbye!"

"Mary, stop," Cynthia said. "Not around Anne."

"Oh, pooh," Mary said. "I can say whatever I like." She turned to Anne. "I'm so glad you quit that awful job. It's so much fun to have you around all the time. At long last. You're one of us now. Welcome to the club!"

Diana blotted her lipstick. "This is too brown. Isn't this too brown? I don't know why I always let them talk me into brown lipstick. It washes me out. I should stick to coral."

"They say it's coming back," said Cynthia. "Anne, you have such pretty lipstick. Is it new?"

"Oh, this," Anne said. "I've been wearing the same color for years. They sell me something new, and I try it for a while, but I always go back."

"Let me see," Cynthia said. She held the tube far from her face. "I can't read this without my glasses. What is it?"

"Same old same old," Anne said. "Barely Pink."

The next day Anne took the train into the city. When the taxi pulled up to her apartment, a doorman rushed up to her.

"Miss Welles, I hope it's okay, we weren't sure what to do, it was such a big delivery," he said. "There was so much, we had to put it in your apartment."

"Don't worry, I'm sure whatever you did was fine," said Anne. She slipped him a ten-dollar bill. "Thank you," she said.

He waved off the bill. "It was taken care of," he said. From his expression Anne could tell he had been tipped far more than ten dollars.

Her apartment was filled with flowers, hundreds and hundreds of flowers. Roses, on every surface. In the hallway, on the dining room table, on her dresser, red roses in blue glass vases. There was a separate card with each one, with numbers written on the envelopes.

Anne collected all the cards and read them in order. Each one was signed simply "T."

"Let's drive each other crazy," the first one went. "We were made for each other" was next. Anne flipped through the cards once, twice, and then again. "You'll love Wyoming." "I'm a terrible husband!" "But I promise you, it will never be boring." "Sixth time's a charm." The final card was simply a cell phone number. She went to the kitchen and tossed them all into the trash.

She called Bill at his office. "Change of plans, I'll just meet you at the restaurant," she said. They went to an Italian restaurant down a side street. It was summer, and the place was practically empty. Anne had steeled herself with five milligrams of Valium.

She waited until the coffee arrived. There was no easy way to say it.

"I can't marry you," she said.

He didn't believe her at first. "My God, you can't be serious. The invitations have already gone out."

"I've been thinking about it for weeks."

"Look, Anne, everyone gets all worked up after funerals, questions what they're doing with their lives. It will pass."

"It's not just pre-wedding jitters. This is different." She watched his face fall as he realized she wasn't going to change her mind.

"All right, then," he began. "You understand, there's no going back."

She took off the ring and laid it in the palm of his hand, watching him shrink a little at her touch.

"Dickie was right about you," Bill said. "They were all right."

"Oh Bill, don't. Let's end this as friends."

"Friends? You must be joking. You're about to humiliate me in front of the entire world, and you want to be friends. I don't think so. Tell me," he said. "What has changed?"

"Nothing has changed. Do you remember when you proposed? And you said the kind of love I'm looking for doesn't exist? That this was as good as it gets?"

"I remember."

"Maybe you're right. Maybe this is as good as it gets. But it's not for me. I can't walk down the aisle and say those vows feeling the way I do."

"And all those times you said you loved me."

"I do love you. But not the way you want. And it does exist, I know it does. I've felt that way before. I want to feel that way again. I just have to believe I can feel that way again."

"My God. You've met someone."

"Not really."

"Don't lie to me. You owe me that much."

"I had . . . there was something. Just one night. Someone I'll probably never see again. But it . . . I don't know, it woke me up somehow. What we have, it isn't enough for me. And it can't be enough for you. We both deserve more."

"What a pretty speech," he said. "From such a pretty mouth. But so ugly on the inside."

"You hate me."

"I don't hate you. What I feel is something else. You disgust me. To go from one man's bed to another like a common whore, as if it all washes off in the bath." He picked up the ring. "Did you take this off when you were with him?"

"Yes," she lied.

He slipped the ring into his pocket. "You're making a mistake," he said. "Women like you end up alone, unhappy and alone. I know where I went wrong. I treated you too well. Women like you are all the same. You can't feel love unless some bastard is mistreating you. That's what you're all about, isn't it. You only want what you can't have. The more unavailable a man is, the more you love him. That isn't love. That's just sickness." He threw some money on the table and left.

What had she done. She went home and washed a Valium down with two inches of a good Pinot Grigio. She sat by the kitchen window. It was a clear night. Airplanes circled in from the west. Beyond the East River, the city spread out like a twinkling carpet. Every light was a story, and every story was a woman, someone who was perhaps just like her: waiting for happiness, waiting for the dream of the city to come true. A million women, having a drink or taking a doll, looking out of their windows, thinking about the man who had left or maybe the man who was just around the corner. The airplanes looked so tiny in the distance. She realized she had no idea what kept them aloft. You just got on, and decided not to be afraid.

She remembered a piece she had done years ago, about the euphoria people felt doing dangerous things. Someone who ran a skydiving business had explained to her that it was an addiction just like anything else: you learned to love the chemicals that your body produced when you conquered the fear. Every day hundreds of people jumped out of airplanes just for the fun of it, just to feel alive. Some said the moments before you pulled the ripcord were the best.

She fished the cards out of the trash. The one with his number was on top. She picked up the telephone and dialed.

Epilogue, 2001.

Whatever happened to Anne Welles? It was a game people played at the very end of parties, when they had stayed too late and all the good booze was gone.

No one had to ask what had happened to Neely O'Hara. Her airbrushed story ran every few months on one of the cable stations. She was living alone in Malibu, almost a recluse. She went into Los Angeles every so often, for a fund-raiser or to present an award. She hadn't released an album in years. The program had included clips from a carefully scripted interview. Neely still looked good. It wasn't just the soft lighting. She seemed happy and calm, her expression rarely changing. Or perhaps that was just the surgery. Everyone said she had had so much work, some of her muscles didn't move right anymore. She could smile a little, but she could not frown.

The tabloids still published the rumors, running grainy photographs shot from behind hedges with special long-range lenses. Neely in gay marriage pact with English rock star! Neely wills fortune to household pets! But the fortune was mostly gone. The genius from Wharton had played the wrong cards the year before.

Twice a year she flew to Las Vegas for a five-night engagement. She didn't dance, didn't tell jokes, she just sat on a stool and sang her heart out. Her voice was as glorious as ever. It was the same show every time, but her fans didn't care.

Jenn was in the tabloids now, too. She was engaged to an actor, a Hollywood bad boy with too many cars and a famous tattoo. She was taking acting lessons in the Village. She had a knack for accents, and the camera had always been her friend.

But where was Anne Welles? There were so many television channels now. No one retired anymore, they just moved up the dial. If you flipped around long enough, surely you would find her.

Anne Welles Abernathy was forty-eight years old, but she didn't look it. Every morning she covered herself with sunscreen, tied back her hair with a red velvet ribbon, and took her horse for a ride across her husband's ranch. In the winters, when it was too cold to ride, she went down to her narrow lap pool and swam for precisely forty-five minutes. The pool was a wedding present from Terry. Back and forth, back and forth, it was boring, but that was exercise. She would always miss the ocean.

In the summer evenings she would wrap herself in an old plaid blanket and take a light beer out onto the porch. The sun set so late in Wyoming. She watched it fall behind the mountains, breathing in the piney air. And she said to herself: *Ours, all ours, as far as the eye can see.* She was going to be the last Mrs. Abernathy. She was far too expensive to divorce.

Sometimes, those rare weeks when he wasn't away on business, Terry joined her on the porch. He would smoke an unfiltered cigarette and tell her about a deal he was working on. The deals were endless, and the deals were all the same. The chase was the part he liked. Anne knew there were women on the road, but she was no longer bothered.

Nothing bothered her anymore. She felt as calm as a sleeping animal. She had gotten what she wanted: peace of mind. Two baby dolls a day was all it took. Terry was a big man, he needed three.

They took them together, just before bed.

"What did people do before?" Terry asked her.

She pulled back the covers. "Who can remember," she said.

About the Author

RAE LAWRENCE is the author of the *New York Times* bestselling novel *Satisfaction*. She lives in New York City.